Three Science Fiction Novellas

Three
Science Fiction
Novellas

FROM PREHISTORY TO THE
END OF MANKIND

J.-H. Rosny aîné

Translated and annotated by
Danièle Chatelain and George Slusser

WESLEYAN UNIVERSITY PRESS
Middletown, Connecticut

Wesleyan University Press

Middletown CT 06459

www.wesleyan.edu/wespress

© 2012 Danièle Chatelain and George Slusser

Manufactured in the United States of America

Designed by Katherine B. Kimball

Typeset in Arno Pro by A. W. Bennett, Inc.

Wesleyan University Press is a member of the Green
Press Initiative. The paper used in this book meets
their minimum requirement for recycled paper.

Library of Congress Cataloging-in-Publication Data

Rosny, J.-H., 1856–1940.

[Novellas. English. Selections]

Three science fiction novellas : from prehistory to the end
of mankind / J.-H. Rosny aîné ; translated and annotated by
George Slusser and Danièle Chatelain.

p.   cm. — (The Wesleyan early classics of science fiction series)

Includes bibliographical references.

ISBN 978-0-8195-6945-5 (cloth : alk. paper) —

ISBN 978-0-8195-7230-1 (e-book)

1. Rosny, J.-H., 1856–1940—Translations into English. 2. Science fiction,
French—Translations into English. I. Slusser, George Edgar.
II. Chatelain, Danièle. III. Rosny, J.-H., 1856–1940. Xipéhuz.
English. IV. Rosny, J.-H., 1856–1940. Autre monde. English. V. Rosny,
J.-H., 1856–1940. Mort de la terre. English. VI. Title.

PQ2635.O56A2 2011

843'.912—dc22   2009047219

5 4 3 2 1

We gratefully acknowledge the assistance of the
French Community of the Belgian Ministry of Culture.

Contents

Translators' Note

The translators used, for their translation, the text reproduced in *J.-H. Rosny aîné: Récits de science-fiction*, edited and with a preface by Jean-Baptiste Baronian (Verviers, Belgium: Bibliothèque Marabout), 1975. This omnibus edition is (sadly) the most recent serious publication of Rosny's SF works by a major publishing house. The title page implies that the editors consulted Robert Borel-Rosny, executor of Rosny's literary estate.

As a working method, the translators compared the aforementioned texts with those of the first editions of each Rosny work, using the holdings of the J. Lloyd Eaton Collection, University of California, Riverside:

Les Xipéhuz. Paris: A[ndré] Savine, 1888.
Un autre monde. Paris: E. Plon, Nourrit et Cie, 1898.
La Mort de la Terre. Paris: E. Plon, Nourrit et Cie, 1910.

For each novella, the text of the Baronian anthology is essentially the same as the text of these first editions (there are minor typographical differences). Footnotes to the translation are those of Rosny himself or his characters. Superscript numbers in the text refer to notes supplied by the translators, which are located in the Notes section at the back of the book. All references in the text and notes to works of Rosny, Jules Verne, and H. G. Wells are, respectively, to the following editions:

J.-H. Rosny aîné: Récits de science-fiction. Verviers, Belgium:
   Bibliothèque Marabout, 1975 (French quotations).
Jules Verne. *Les Intégrales Jules Verne*. Paris: Hachette Grands Oeuvres,
   1976–81.
H. G. Wells. *28 Science Fiction Stories*. New York: Dover, 1952.
H. G. Wells. *The Time Machine*. Edited by Harry Geduld.
   Bloomington: Indiana University Press, 1987.

Introduction

Rosny's Evolutionary Ecology

Science fiction has a problem of paternity. French critics routinely refer to Jules Verne as "le père de la science-fiction." Ads for the recent Penguin Classics edition of H. G. Wells proudly trumpet their author as "the father of science fiction." We speak here for another party in this custody battle: the Belgian writer J.-H. Rosny aîné. We would, however, change the designation somewhat: Rosny is the father of hard science fiction. If we ask, with Mark Rose, "in what sense is science fiction about science," the proponents of hard SF answer: it is all about science.[1] Physicist-writer Robert L. Forward goes further. He claims that in order for a narrative to be science fiction, science must write the fiction. Forward means this literally: "I just write a scientific paper about some strange place—and by the time I have the science correct—the science has written the fiction."[2] For Forward, conventional fiction bends the laws of nature to its wishes and desires, whereas science fiction cannot. This in itself is a purist's dream of SF. In light of it, however, our contention is that Rosny, not Verne nor Wells, was the first writer to allow science to write his narratives in the neutral, ahumanistic manner Forward proclaims.

The implications of our claim are great, and some questions are in order. First, what exactly is Rosny's scientific vision, and how does it differ from that of Verne and Wells? We define Rosny's unique perspective as one of "evolutionary ecology," and it sets him apart from both writers. Rosny's scientific education took place in England at the time of the Darwinian controversy, and led him away from the Comtean positivism that dominated Verne's vision and the francophone world. For unlike Comte's laws of phenomena, evolutionary theory emphasizes causality, and takes into account space-time transformation as nonteleological process. Likewise, although Rosny shares evolutionary theory with Wells, the rigors of his pluralist sense of the evolutionary process take him far beyond Wells's humanocentric focus and toward a scientific view of humankind's relation to its environment that we would today call "ecological" in the broad sense.

Second, how does Rosny, in comparison with Verne and Wells, develop his pluralist vision of evolution in fictional form? Rosny's pluralism, as it opens out toward the relativistic sciences of the twentieth century, sees evolution in terms of an ecosystem, the complex and neutral interaction of independent biotic and abiotic factors in a particular location, that of Earth itself. In fictional works that span evolutionary time from human prehistory to the passage of all carbon-based life forms to new sentient life, Rosny strives to remove humankind and human reason, except as localized phenomena, from the center of the evolutionary process. Unlike Verne and Wells, he aspires in his fiction to the most rigorous neutrality and scientific objectivity, and thus is the first writer to set a gold standard for the future hard SF extrapolations of Forward and others.

Rosny strives as hard as any writer can who uses words and addresses a human audience to decenter humankind, to make it part of a larger system of life in evolution. The third question, then, is how and in what ways does the science actually write the fiction in Rosny's work? Forward's program might appear to be inimical to fiction in general, which is traditionally centered on the activity of human beings, and the mind-matter duality that generally defines such activity. Rosny's scientific vision, however, allows him not only to inscribe a fictional arc from prehistory to the end of humankind's world, but to look beyond this trajectory, in the final pages of *La Mort de la Terre*, to the possibility of a transhuman experience. Here humanity, seen as the apogee of carbon-based life passes some aspect of its biological and perhaps cultural heritage to another life form, and thus continues to evolve beyond its extinction as carbon entity. Thus in the final section of this introduction we will compare Rosny's fictional treatment of his Last Man with the Last Men of the more recent hard SF writers Arthur C. Clarke and Gregory Benford.

The comparison reveals a significant difference. For while these recent hard SF writers seem to retreat from the transhuman moment, Rosny pushes transhumanity to the limit of scientific possibility. With perhaps the exception of Olaf Stapledon, there exists to date no more objective, ecologically sound treatment than Rosny's of the passage from humans to new possible forms of life. Despite sympathies for humanity, Rosny realizes that we will someday have to "let go," that the key element in the ecological balance is not humankind but life in whatever form it may take. In light of Rosny, transhumanity becomes the defining problem for hard SF.

Rosny's English Education

Among French-language writers of his time, Rosny's cultural and linguistic situation was unique. He was born Joseph Henri Honoré Boëx, on February 17, 1856, in Brussels. His formal education was cut short by the death of his father and ensuing financial difficulties. Forced to leave school, he learned to be a telegrapher. To find work, he went to London, where he remained for eleven years (1873–1884), working as a night operator for the British Post Office. This English period appears to have been crucial for his intellectual development. A voracious autodidact, Rosny learned English and apparently spent his days in the British Museum, reading widely in world literature. At the same time, he developed a strong interest in science. Controversy was raging over Darwinian evolution, and judging from evidence in works Rosny conceived (and perhaps wrote) during this time, he followed these arguments closely. He could have attended Huxley's lectures at Imperial College.

Too little is known about these formative years in England. One ambitious biography of Rosny exists in English, Amy Louise Downey's dissertation "The Life and Works of J.-H. Rosny aîné, 1856–1940."[3] For information on this English period, Downey claims to rely on documents and letters in possession of the Borel family, that of Rosny's second wife. According to Downey, Rosny published several stories, in English, in London magazines. She sees Rosny moving in intellectual circles, and even posits an encounter with Wells. The latter is unlikely; Wells, born in 1866, was barely eighteen when Rosny left England in 1884. There are, nonetheless, documented facts. While in London, Rosny married and had a family with a young English woman of the poor working class. He most certainly conceived and wrote his first novel, *Nell Horn* (published in French in 1887), while in England. It is a naturalist novel that details life in the London slums the impoverished Rosny knew firsthand. It is also clear that he drew inspiration from English evolutionary debates for his other 1887 novel, *Les Xipéhuz*. Indeed, no analogues to the prehistoric extrapolation of this novel exist in the francophone world. Prehistoric speculations, in the wake of Lyell and Darwin, appear to be a British preoccupation, and famous examples exist from Wells to Brian Aldiss's *Cryptozoic!* (1970).

Darwinian thought informs Rosny's seminal work at the deepest level. Not only does it offer a viable evolutionary model, but there is no hand of God guiding human destiny. If *Les Xipéhuz* displays the triumph of human reason, this triumph is neither preordained nor permanent. If not for contingencies of environment and heredity, the nonhuman life form could prove the fittest.

We have more documented facts about Rosny's subsequent life. He moved with his family to Paris in 1884. The publication of *Nell Horn* and of *Les Xipéhuz*, in 1887, launched him on a successful literary career along parallel tracks, as a naturalist novelist and a writer of speculative fiction. Young Rosny moved in literary circles of the belle époque, becoming acquainted with the leading artists and intellectuals of the time, from Anatole France to Émile Zola and Alphonse Daudet. The naturalism of *Nell Horn* impressed the high priest of this form, Edmond de Goncourt. Rosny was named in Goncourt's will, and later became president of the Académie Goncourt. At the same time Rosny's scientific fiction made him widely known and respected among scientists. It is clear from his popularizing treatises, such as *Les sciences et le pluralisme* (1922), that he kept abreast of scientific advances. A 1936 entry in *Portraits et souvenirs*, the memoirs of the Nobel Prize–winning physicist Jean Perrin, is testimony to the fact that he was respected by the most advanced members of the French scientific community: Perrin cites Rosny's vast knowledge of all the sciences, commenting that "son travail sur le pluralisme abonde en aperçus originaux sur la physique" (his work on pluralism abounds in original ideas on physics).[4] Downey claims Rosny knew the Curies and Einstein personally, and was conversant with the theories of Freud—all possible but undocumented.

Rosny continued to write both naturalist fiction and SF throughout his long life. He died in 1940, on the eve of Germany's entry into Paris. It is ironic that, for a writer whose work is so marked by English Darwinism, his fiction has been so little translated into English. Except for one mass-market paperback—a semitranslation-rewrite by Philip José Farmer for DAW Books of Rosny's 1922 novel *L'étonnant voyage d'Hareton Ironcastle*—and a Hollywood film vaguely based on his 1911 novel *La Guerre du feu* (The War for Fire), mistranslated as *The Quest for Fire*, Rosny's work remains unknown in the Anglo-American sphere.[5] Rosny's English years are possibly more crucial to understanding his work than his many years as a celebrity on the Parisian literary and cultural scene. For it was in England that this Belgian writer was exposed to a very different scientific tradition, and a vision of evolution that remained, even at the time of the novellas in this volume, highly controversial in francophone circles. Critics, for example, have often been content to contrast Wells and Rosny with reference to their sense of how evolution operates: Wells is seen as the Darwinian, Rosny as being closer to Lamarckian ideas.[6] This division follows a comfortable cultural divide. But Rosny's years in Wells's England are mirrored in the evolutionary vision of Rosny's works, which is uniquely ecological and clearly derived from Darwinian principles.

The usual comparison of Darwin and Lamarck is at the level of Lamarck's idea of "soft inheritance"—the inheritability of traits acquired in one lifetime transferred to the next generation. The comparison, however, is moot, for neither Lamarck nor Darwin offers an adequate mechanism for describing the development of species at this level. That was to be the work of Mendel and modern genetics.[7] Lamarck's sense of evolution, however, is much broader than soft inheritance. Evolution, for Lamarck, comprises two central mechanisms: what he calls "le pouvoir de la vie" (the power of life), and "l'influence des circonstances" (the influence of circumstances). The latter involves Lamarck's theory of use and disuse, whereby species develop specialized organs according to the needs of specific environments. This could apply to Rosny's Targ and the Last Men in *La Mort de la Terre*, whose huge chests have developed because of lack of oxygen in the air on a nearly waterless planet. The former idea of the power of life, however, does not fit Rosny. Lamarck sees the development of life as an ever-complexifying process. This would mean that the ferromagnetics in *La Mort de la Terre* represent a "higher" species, when in fact they are better described as at the beginning of their era of evolutionary development. Nor is it evident that the humans who defeat the Xipéhuz in *Les Xipéhuz* are a higher or more complex form of life. If Rosny may seem to promise a Lamarckian development here, from the beginning he throws his reader a Darwinian curve ball. The process Rosny details, as we pass from *Les Xipéhuz* through *La Mort de la Terre*, is a clear product of natural selection. Rosny gives us the birth and death of all carbon species—including humanity itself—as part of a process without preestablished design, the result of ever-changing relationships between life forms and their physical environment. The stuff of Rosny's novels is the struggle for survival, precisely as Darwin describes it: "As many more individuals of each species are born than can possibly survive; and as, consequently, there is a frequently recurring struggle for existence, it follows that any being, if it vary however slightly in any manner profitable to itself, under the complex and sometimes varying conditions of life, will have a better chance of surviving, and thus be *naturally selected*."[8] Both Lamarck and Darwin may revere a life force; but Rosny follows Darwin in his sense of a single source of life, branching out in endless diversity of forms, all of them "beautiful and wonderful" in their own right, be they the nonhuman Xipéhuz, human beings, or the ferromagnetics that replace humanity.

Rosny, we will argue, is not only a steadfastly Darwinist writer but one who developed a supremely modern ecological view of evolution from his Darwinian education. As a Darwinian, he remained, and in a sense remains to critics today in positivist and Cartesian France, a stranger in his own land. He also remained—oddly, for a writer whose work covered the first half of the twentieth century—a stranger to relativity and quantum theory, theories of which he was aware, as we see from his nonfictional treatises. It was evolutionary theory that held lifelong sway over Rosny's scientific vision.

Rosny and Verne

At first glance, Verne and Rosny appear to be separated by a generational chasm. Rosny's earliest scientific novels—from *Les Xipéhuz* to *La Mort de la Terre*—barely overlap Verne's final period, which extends approximately from *Robur le conquérant* (1886) to the posthumous publication of *Le Secret de Wilhelm Storitz* in 1910. Conventional wisdom would see Rosny's essentially evolutionary view of science as different from Verne's abiding positivism. If English science flirted with Auguste Comte and his positivist method, John Stuart Mill rejected that method in 1865 as unscientific because it refuses to consider causality. Comte has little place in the British tradition of empirical science that Rosny encountered in the form of evolutionism. Nonetheless, Verne's scientist-protagonists seem consistently to operate as representatives of that Age of Science Comte saw as the apex of human achievement. They map, classify, generate taxonomic hierarchies. Working in what appears to be a fixed, spatialized system of human knowledge, they legislate order from the position of authority their logically perfected science confers on them. Nature is an intricate grid to be mapped, not a system in transformation. Seen as such, Verne's science bears little resemblance to Rosny's evolutionism, whose method is experimental in the modern sense.

The conventional view, however, may not be adequate, and the comparison of Rosny and Verne is a matter of greater complexity. On the one hand, Rosny was touched by positivism. In fact, the hold of positivism on French science and culture has been a strong one, enduring long after the method and its premises were challenged and finally rejected by science. Rosny began writing long after the end of the Age of Positivism. But his fiction bears the marks of positivist method on at least one level—that of the description of anomalous intelligent nonhuman species (generally of extraterrestrial origin in SF but in Rosny's stories originating on Earth).[9] Rosny's description of the Xipéhuz, and to a lesser degree the Moedigen in *Un autre monde,* is "factual," in the Comtean sense of classification along the axes of similarity and succession. The describer is unwilling to speculate beyond surface forms. These kinds of descriptions are still present in *La Mort de la Terre.*

On the other hand, Verne was not impervious to new, more experimental forms of science that appeared in his time. A serious challenge to dogmatic positivism was launched in France by Claude Bernard in his *Introduction à l'étude de la médicine expérimentale,* whose publication in 1865 coincided with the beginning of Verne's career as writer. In this treatise, Bernard attacks the systematizing of Comte and the "scholastic" nature of much scientific theory in his age, and pleads for an "experimental" approach to nature, whereby science seeks out and confronts the physical unknown by means of observation, formulation of tentative models, and verification through experiment. Bernard's method, closer to that of the empirical science of the Baconian tradition, and to Darwin's evolutionary science, did not materialize all at once with the publication of Bernard's essay. For years he had been professing "experimental medicine" at the Collège de France. It is interesting to note that the major novels published by Verne around the time that Bernard's treatise was published all promise experiment and exploration in their titles: *Voyage au centre de la terre* (1863), *De la terre à la lune* (1965), *Vingt mille lieues sous les mers* (1869) and *Autour de la lune* (1870). Verne, in these works, appears to respond to the advent of this experimental science. But in what way does this response shape his vision of scientific activity? Bernard's experimental method offers a way to compare Verne's and Rosny's approaches to science. How, for example, do Captain Nemo, whose field of investigation lies beneath the seas, or Professor Lidenbrock, who explores the interior of the Earth, process data? Do they question accepted theory when they discover new patterns of natural behavior that go against its conclusions? Likewise, how does Bakhoun proceed in his examination of the Xipéhuz? What method does Targ bring to his search for water beneath the desiccated surface of the Earth?

Bernard's method involves the perception and processing of *new* data, leading to corrections, to reformulations of existing theories that allow science to make incursions into the unknown. This is precisely the method of Darwin's evolutionary science. At the center of *Les Xipéhuz* is humankind's encounter with a new species. Humanity's first reaction, superstitious fear, proves disastrous. It is only when a new type of man, the rational Bakhoun, begins to observe the Xipéhuz, performing experiments in order to determine their physical characteristics and limits, that humankind begins to understand, and thus control, this hitherto unknown phenomenon. Bakhoun's method may at first appear positivist—he classifies the new beings into categories. But he is soon forced to address questions involving causality. By experimenting with different weapons, he discovers that a pointed object, when it hits the pulsating "star" at their centers, causes these otherwise invulnerable adversaries to die.

As noted, Bakhoun himself represents a paradigm shift in terms of human cultural development, from superstitious nomadism to sedentary rational humanity. But this is a shift familiar to paleohistorians and Rosny's readers alike. The battle with the Xipéhuz is an interesting tale, but in terms of evolutionary history, it is tangential. We have won our battle to the death with this competing species; when we do so, they become merely a *might have been* in the story of our evolution. The protagonist of *Un autre monde*, however, represents an event of a different order. Evolutionary change this time occurs within and evolves out of homo sapiens. The mutant is something new in *our* evolutionary process; as such he bears possibilities for future change.

First of all, because of his enhanced perceptual abilities, he becomes an instrument in the hands of science that gains access to a whole new world of beings living side by side with normal humanity, but in another dimension. His early classifications of these beings are positivist, focusing on similarities between forms and their sequential arrangement. He thus delineates the forms of the earthbound Moedigen, and distinguishes their behavior from that of the aerial Vuren. But positivism is not the only model for these descriptions. They remind us also of the first impressions of the two-dimensional being named A Square in Edwin Abbott's *Flatland: A Romance of Many Dimensions*, published in 1884—a work Rosny may have read in English. A Square's first impressions are only a prelude to further reflection, for he is soon confronted with a new phenomenon: a three-dimensional incursion into his two-dimensional world. Reflecting on this, he posits the possibility of a fourth dimension, which his three-dimensional interlocutor, Sphere, rejects as impossible. In like manner Rosny's narrator, reflecting on this other dimension, posits a causal relationship between it and us, whereby actions there may have an impact on us here, to such an extent that understanding them and this possible causal link becomes an evolutionary and ecological necessity for human science: "Un règne, enfin, se mouvant sur les eaux, dans l'atmosphère, sur le sol, modifiant ses eaux, cette atmosphère et ce sol, tout autrement que nous, mais avec une énergie assurément formidable, et par là agissant indirectement sur nous et nos destinées, comme nous agissons indirectment sur lui et ses destinées!" (A kingdom of beings, finally, moving about on the waters, in the atmosphere, on the ground, transforming these waters, this atmosphere, this ground, in completely different ways than we do, but with a certainly formidable energy, and by that means acting indirectly on us and our destiny, just as we act indirectly on it and its destiny!)

La Mort de la Terre is a work whose every detail, almost, exists in a current of evolutionary transformation. At first we may find what seem to be positivist classifications in the descriptions that introduce the ferromagnetics. In chapter 2, these entities are presented as if they were a closed system: "ils comportent des agglomérations de trois, cinq, sept, et même neuf groupes, la forme des groupes revêtant une grande variété" (there are now agglomerations of three, five, seven, even nine groups, the forms of these groups being greatly varied). As in a tableau of Cuvier, we seem to have their formal limits and nothing more: "A partir de l'agglomération par sept, le ferromagnétal dépérit si l'on supprime un des groupes." (For agglomerations of seven or more, the ferromagnetic entity perishes if one of its groups is suppressed.) At once, however, we realize we are in a world of shifting paradigms and evolving forms. It is no longer possible to make abstract categories of rival species, for these creatures are part of a vast, and unfinished, web of evolutionary transformations: "Actuellement, la présence des ferromagnétaux est à peu près inoffensif. Il en serait sans doute différemment si l'humanité s'étendait." (Today the presence of the ferromagnetics is little more than harmless. It would no doubt be a different story if mankind were to expand its domain.) Targ is a scientific adventurer seeking to adapt to a world of dwindling water supplies. He conducts his "hygrometrical" experiments in various locations, hoping to find the water that will allow humanity to "spread out" once again. In terms of his search, the ferromagnetics remain a secondary issue, if an important one. For though they evolve in their own iron-based sphere, they still share the same Earth as Targ, and their evolution benefits from human activities. As opposed to the static-seeming Xipéhuz or Moedigen, Targ discovers late in the novel that the ferromagnetics are continuing to evolve: a new, more powerful "tertiary" form appears on the scene just as the last carbon-based life forms perish.

Rosny's narratives, then, confine positivist method to increasingly localized situations, as experimental science opens new vistas that prove increasingly complex in their interplay of evolutionary factors. Verne's narratives of experimental promise seem to reverse this movement. All of Verne's aforementioned four novels appear to offer the reader startling adventures of scientific observation. New technologies, such as submarines and rocket ships, give scientists the possibility to go where no human has gone, to places where humans can observe and gather new data, facts that promise (like the discovery of the Moedigen) to alter humans' understanding of nature radically.

However, after mounting these expeditions with elaborate detail—it takes almost the entirety of *De la terre à la lune* to prepare the ship and devise experiments—Verne invariably finds ways to deflect his observers from contact with the unknown. There is more to this than what Marie-Hélène Huet and others have noticed—that Verne's discoveries appear to be rediscoveries, and "unknown" territories turn out to have been previously mapped.[10] For there are moments when Verne's scientists find themselves faced with a real possibility of seeing new phenomena, thus of having to revise or abandon the scientific consensus. Verne revels in taking the reader right up to these moments of discovery, only to swerve away from actual contact with the new. One might say that the most extraordinary thing in his "extraordinary voyages" is his creation of an elaborate art of "scientific suspense" that relies on raising and then dashing the hopes of his experimental scientists. The reader is titillated, then reassured, as science glimpses new, even frightening things but comfortably avoids them.

Verne's most famous scientists—Captain Nemo and Professor Aron-nax, the Barbicane-Nicholl-Ardan trio, and especially Professor Liden-brock and Axel—are all confronted with never-before-seen phenomena. In *20,000 Leagues under the Sea*, for example, Nemo takes Aronnax on a scientific underwater tour, offering glimpses of phenomena that, if studied and experimented on, could easily unsettle physical history as science has written it. Well along in the undersea narrative (chapter 9, part 2), Nemo and Aronnax walk among the ruins of a sunken city the reader later learns is Atlantis. Things appear that suggest that in this undersea environment, altered physical conditions have given rise to evolutionary mutations. And Aronnax, who thinks like Claude Bernard's scientist, is ready to give primacy to evidence of the senses: "Et moi-même ne sentais-je cette dif-férence due à la puissante densité de l'eau, quand, malgré mes lourds vête-ments, ma tête de cuivre, mes semelles de métal, je m'élevais sur les pentes d'une impracticable raideur?" (And didn't I myself physically feel this dif-ference, caused by the powerful density of the water, whenever, despite my heavy garments, my copper helmet, my shoes of metal, I lifted myself up on slopes that were impracticably steep? [323].)

Verne's scientist expends much energy and ingenuity in reaching the threshold of discovery, and Verne lavishes much detail on the description of his approach. But once he arrives at the unknown, we realize Verne has handicapped him mightily. We realize that in order for Aronnax to have any access to this environment, he has to wear his cumbersome diving suit. His becomes the torture of Tantalus. In these deep cavities he dis-covers "gigantic" crustaceans, "giant" lobsters, "titanesque" crabs, "terri-fying squid tangling their tentacles like a nest of snakes" ("des poulpes effroyables entrelaçant leurs tentacules comme une broussaille de ser-pents" [324]). He needs his suit to protect him from these creatures, but it isolates him physically from making the first-hand contact a scientist needs to examine such specimens. Nemo must have scientific knowledge of this lost world; but Aronnax, isolated in his suit, as no way to question Nemo about the *origin* or *nature* of the phenomena Aronnax observes. Unable to communicate, his only recourse is to ask himself endless ques-tions. We have the illusion of a scientist at work; the result, however, is tautology. Indeed, the final product of this scientific adventure is not new knowledge. It is rather a general lament, bemoaning the inability of obser-vational science ever to grasp the richness of the phenomenal world: "Je touchais de la main ces ruines mille fois séculaires et contemporaines des époques géologiques! Je marchais là même où avait marché les contemporains du premier homme! J'écrasais sous mes lourdes semelles ces squelettes d'animaux des temps fabuleux!" (With my own hand I was touching ruins that were hundreds of thousands of years old, as old as the geological epochs! I was walking in the same place where contemporaries of the first human being walked! I was crushing under the heavy soles of my boots skeletons of animals from the times of fable! [327]).

A similar isolation besets Verne's Moon explorers. They want to land on the Moon and explore its surface, but a miscalculation, sets them in orbit around it, such that they can only observe along a fixed path. We learn later that even if they had landed on the Moon and done experiments, no word of this would ever have reached Earth. For they fail not only to calculate for enough fuel but also (despite all their preparations) to think of bringing along a communication device capable of sending information. Rosny gives his astronauts the simple if improbable device of Morse code in *Les Navigateurs de l'infini* (1927), his late, and only, space novel. Can we believe that Verne, otherwise prodigious of technological detail, simply "forgot" this all-important device here? We have a similar example of a "naturally" aborted opportunity to gather new knowledge when the explorers, orbiting the Moon, pass over the Dark Side. This is new territory, but they cannot see it. Theirs too, like Aronnax in his diving suit, is the torture of Tantalus, for all they can do is make wild and fanciful theories, all in the dark. Verne throws in a little "scientific" suspense when a meteor suddenly explodes, and for an all-too-brief moment they have a glimpse of the unknown side. But the light fades at once, and they are no closer to making significant new observations. A final act of blindness is their attempt to land on the Moon by blasting their rocket. Miscalculation, however, propels them back to Earth, with no positive data on a new world seen through a glass darkly. At least Ardan and Barbicane are safe and sound. Not only does adventure trump science, but the nature of the adventure itself appears to be the trumping of science.

Geosphere and Anthrosphere

Despite escapades on the Moon or Mars, Verne and Rosny both confine their scientific explorations to the geosphere. The three Rosny novellas in this volume explore (1) a prehistoric Earth environment; (2) a world alternate to our present world yet sharing the same geosphere; and (3) an Earth undergoing ecodisaster, at least from the human perspective. Likewise, Verne's explorers find nothing more in the depths of the sea or on the Moon than what is known on Earth. Verne's and Rosny's scientists, then, explore the same geosphere. It is their respective *uses* of this geosphere, however, that are radically different. For Rosny, the geosphere is the place of evolutionary possibility, where human life some day will be superseded, but where Earth, as place of struggle between animate and inanimate forces, abides. Verne's Earth, however, despite his scientists' stated desire to explore, even exceed, its limits, remains centered in mankind. The geosphere of Verne's scientists proves to be the conventional anthrosphere of Cartesian rationalism.

In this regard, the Verne text to compare with Rosny is *Voyage to the Center of the Earth*. In this novel, Verne's scientists journey farthest into the territory of evolutionary possibility. Ostensibly, the purpose of Professor Lidenbrock's expedition to the center of the Earth is to verify Humphry Davy's theory of chemical oxidation, which says there is no core of heat at the Earth's center. But since Davy, as Allen A. Debus points out, had already disowned his theory four decades before the publication of the novel, he could hardly be the scientific motivation for this expedition.[11] The explorers' voyage, in fact, is not to the geological center of the Earth but to a space of much interest to the reader of Rosny—the space of evolutionary history, of the life forms that lead to the advent of homo sapiens. On their descent, Lidenbrock and Axel discover a "land that time forgot," fifty years before Edgar Rice Burroughs coined the phrase. Their first find is a welter of previously unclassified fossils. In the midst of these they discover something bound to overturn then accepted theory: a humanoid skull, physical evidence that, if heeded, must change the evolutionary picture for mankind.

Not long before Verne wrote this novel, the so-called Moulin-Quignon man had been "discovered" (1863) and then soon denounced as a hoax perpetrated by workers at the site. This denunciation reinforced the Cuvier school, which argued that no human species could have coexisted with the fauna of the Quaternary Era. The Quaternary, however, is the very period of the fossil specimens Lidenbrock and Axel find. What they discover appears to be another "line" of humanity—such as the Neanderthal-like hominids in Rosny's *La Guerre du feu* (1911). For an age of science fascinated by fossil remains and the possibility of "pre-sapiens" species, Liden-brock and Axel have before them tangible evidence that challenges existing theories of the origin of mankind.

As if the bones were not enough, Verne adds new, now irrefutable evidence by bringing his fossil remains to life. Lidenbrock and Axel discover an island in the center of the underground sea where Quaternary flora and fauna flourish. All at once, they come across a giant being apparently a living specimen of the newly discovered humanoid species, tending its "flocks" of giant prehistoric creatures. But at the sight of this giant, Axel and Lidenbrock can only flee in terror. Real scientific evidence is under their feet, all around them, before their very eyes. Yet Axel categorically denies it all, everything the reader has seen and witnessed: "Nulle créature humaine n'existe dans ce monde subterrestre." (No human creature exists in this subterranean world [299].) Moreover, Lidenbrock's mention of the discredited Moulin-Quignon man reinforces the possibility that everything described was indeed a fabulation, the dream of two scientists become a waking nightmare, from which they awaken empty-handed. If this is another false discovery, it only reinforces the already-known.

In a sense, the mention of Moulin-Quignon is part of a script, one already written by science, that the novel's adventures follow. These scientists are not writing their own exploratory text; they follow the traces of Arne Saknussemm, whose path is marked by ancient runes that they merely decipher. Future voyagers, likewise, will have Axel's account to follow, which, he tells us in the end, he has published as *Voyage au centre de la terre*. Moreover, the names these explorers give to places they "discover," like the Lidenbrock sea, only rename what they think is Arne's itinerary; they are places future voyagers will rename in turn, creating a palimpsest rather than a terrain of new discovery. Even more deeply preinscribed in their journey is the text of anthropological positivism, written by Cuvier and his followers, and elaborated by the scientific establishment of Verne's time. As their raft moves offshore, the two explorers observe giant plants that offer "l'aspect de la Terre aux premiers siècles de sa formation" (what the Earth looked like in the first centuries of its formation [186]). However, as they continue, the very nature of their observations reveals that they are not *discovering* a new evolutionary process but instead *describing*, category by category, a taxonomy already written down by Cuvier. They view plants, then giant fish, then a battle of sea reptiles, moving in sequence up the ladder of forms, from amphibians to large land animals.

Cuvier's way leads "naturally" to something that fills the human niche. So we are not surprised to find a "man" striding through this predetermined landscape.

Even so, the reader sees that Axel and Lidenbrock are physically *there*, in a strange and inexplicable place, among what are admittedly never-before-seen prehistoric specimens. Yet, to avoid the shock of the unknown, they continue to mistake the map for the territory. Instead of taking a fresh look at new life forms before their eyes, they imagine encounters in the flesh with creatures that *fit* contemporary paleontologists' theoretical reconstructions: "Peut-être rencontrerons-nous quelques-uns de ces sauriens que la science a su refaire avec un bout d'ossement ou de cartilage?" (Perhaps we will meet up with some of those saurians that science has been able to reconstruct from a piece of bone or of cartilage? [188]) In terms of evolutionary theory, they turn things upside down: instead of locating the origin of species in a natural process, they relocate it in templates that human reason has constructed out of fossil remains. If their voyage proves anything, it is that mind creates matter, not the other way around.

It does not matter that Lidenbrock does not reach the center of the physical Earth. Verne's explorers carry that center with them, for the center of Verne's Earth is the anthrosphere. This is what unfolds from Axel's famous dream. Bakhoun can write a chapter in the history of humankind because he has led humankind to victory over an evolutionary enemy that, had it prevailed, would have ended humankind's story right there. In Verne, Cuvier's "written" history of Earth appears to block all attempts by observational science to expand the knowledge of physical processes. In like manner, the entire history of human evolution appears to be already "written," physically embedded in Axel's being, to be summoned forth whole, in his waking "dream," at his particular moment in humankind's existence.

We think here of Carl Sagan's "dragons of Eden," which represent the idea that the totality of the evolutionary process from reptile to homo sapiens is wired into the cortices of every human brain, and is accessed in the present by dreaming, which subtends the rational mind.[12] Axel exclaims: "tout ce monde fossile renaît dans mon imagination" (the entirety of this fossil world is reborn in my imagination [189]). In the immediacy of his present-tense account, Axel sees his entire being, mind and body, enfolding all of history, bounded by Earth, with mankind at its apex: "Toute la vie de la Terre se résume en moi" (all life forms of the Earth are summed up in me [190]). His dream is a résumé, one that collapses the evolutionary time scale, making it coterminous with his present human form. By quite literally assuming the prehistoric past, Axel ensures that no subsequent discovery will take our knowledge of evolution in any direction other than what culminates in nineteenth-century rational mankind, the prime example of which is Axel. The idea that any example of contemporary mankind contains its entire evolutionary history is everywhere in Verne's narrative, down to such insignificant details as the description of Hans the Islander: "Son masque effrayant est celui d'un homme antediluvien, contemporain des ichthyosaures et des mégatheriums" (the terrifying mask of his face is that of antediluvian man, contemporary to ichthyosauruses and metatheriums [203]).

Axel's dream in a sense preempts any scientific finds he and Lidenbrock will make. In fact, it sets the model for a pattern whereby seemingly incontrovertible facts are captured and enfolded into the human status quo. Lidenbrock and Axel, for example, discover a huge field of fossil remains. It is immediately converted, however, into an "ossuary," one so vast it must be tended by multiples of an all-too-familiar human scientist: "L'existence de mille Cuvier n'aurait pas suffi à recomposer les squelettes des êtres organisés couchés dans ce magnifique ossuaire" (the existence of a thousand Cuviers would not have sufficed to reconstitute the skeletons of the organic beings lying in this magnificent ossuary [216]). In like manner, the discovery of a human skull among these fossils does not bring Lidenbrock to envision alternate theories, future possibilities. Instead he imagines himself in a university lecture hall, engaging in controversy with fellow scientists. The fact that he has before him tangible proof "que l'espèce humaine eût été contemporaine des animaux de l'époque quaternaire" (that the human species had been contemporary to animals of the Quaternary) leads only to more academic disputations. Even when he comes across an entire human fossil, the professor cannot stop his imaginary, past tense lecture. He taunts his "rivals": "Les Saint-Thomas de la paléontologie, s'ils étaient là, le toucheraient du doigt, et seraient bien forcés de reconnaître..." (the Saint Thomases of paleontology, had they been there, would have touched it with a finger, and would have been forced to admit...). Lidenbrock gets so carried away that this fossil, before his eyes, turns into a cadaver his colleagues are invited to see and touch: "Le cadavre est là... vous pouvez le voir, le toucher" (The cadaver is there... you can see it, touch it [221].) Just as Axel's dream contracts all evolutionary history to his living present, so Lidenbrock converts his amazing find into a specimen from some contemporary autopsy room.

Having witnessed Lidenbrock's fossil resurrection, the reader is less surprised when this "cadaver," before the daydreaming scientists' (and the reader's) eyes, actually comes to life. It might seem that when Axel and Lidenbrock come upon a living version of their "spécimen de l'homme quaternaire" (specimen of Quaternary man), they enter the realm of Rosny's narratives of alternate prehistory. Indeed, at this moment, Verne comes as close as he ever does to confronting science with the unknown. His protagonists immediately swerve, however, away from scientific analysis to mythic perception. Instead of envisioning a new future, they evoke a perpetual past. Axel describes them as entering a physical realm that, paradoxically, is no longer subject to the laws of physics: "Par un phénomène que je ne puis expliquer ... la lumière éclairait uniformément les diverses faces des objets." (Through some phenomenon I cannot explain ... the light illuminated the various facets of objects in a uniform manner [224]). Instead of writing a new text in the history of science, they fall back on another script already written: that of the fantastic and its famous literary proponent E. T. A. Hoffmann.

Verne's scientists, with amazingly new phenomena before their eyes, do little more than pay lip service to the fact that this is a situation "à confondre la raison des classificateurs les plus ingénieux" (worthy of confounding the most ingenious classifiers [225]). Axel's response is to turn to human cultural convention, to invoke mankind's endless longing for a Golden Age. Verne's protagonists, even though in possession of proof that a new past might lead to an alternate human future, seem to take refuge in a literary vision of an unchanging present. There is irony, however, in their evocation of this golden age. For however much the surface glitters, the core itself appears to be fallen. The Latin epithet Axel throws at the giant early man they have found, "Immanis pectoris custos, immanior ipse," rephrases Vergil's Eclogue 5:44: "formois pectoris custos, formosior ipse." Vergil's speaker is Daphnis, who refers to himself as "herdsman of a beautiful flock, himself more beautiful," lines that reveal vanity at the heart of the bucolic world. Axel's corruption of the text, by substituting "savage" for "beautiful," places this being lower on the ladder of cultural evolution. In the face of the unknown, experimental science—in the guise of his archetypal scientist-apprentice Axel—defers in Verne to a "humanistic" response, and by doing so, avoids the questions Rosny might ask, questions that challenge the myth of humankind's central position in the earthly scheme of things. For here, at Verne's prime moment of evolutionary promise, scientific investigation loses itself in a web of intertextuality that only reaffirms the conventional ties between mankind and nature on which Verne's worldview rests.

To describe Verne's difference with Rosny, we need only imagine the various ways Rosny might have presented Verne's moment of underground "contact." Axel's discovery of the underground world could have led to impending struggle between rival evolutionary lines. There could have been an entire "race" of antediluvian giants, poised like the Xipéhuz to reclaim the Earth above. If we take their point of view, the Xipéhuz too lived in Edenic harmony with their world; they too are confronted by Western rationalism. The difference is that while Verne's scientists are never allowed to engage the other "world," entering and leaving it without making any meaningful contact with the beings that inhabit it, Rosny's Bakhoun engages, studies, and ultimately defeats, though not without regret, what is understood as an evolutionary rival. Or Rosny, as in *Un autre monde*, might have presented the giant as member of a mutant species. He might even have told the story from the giant's point of view. Surely, in a hypothetical Rosny text, human scientists would not have given in to anthropocentric fears. At the very least, they would seek ways to understand it, and possibly communicate with it. They would hope to make scientific use of its ways of "seeing things," as, from an evolutionary perspective, its faculties would necessarily have evolved along a different yet parallel track with those of human beings. Or, finally, Rosny could have recast Verne's explorers as figures like Targ, in *La Mort de la Terre*, driven by physical necessity as well as scientific curiosity. Their discovery of the subterranean world out of time could, like Targ's discovery of water, give humanity a reprieve from evolutionary forces like dwindling resources. Or even, if we follow Axel's reasoning, the bucolic island and ample underground sea might provide, this time, a millennialist reprieve to Rosny's apocalyptic vision of the Last Man, a place where a parallel human species is living out a moment of calm before its end. What for Axel was a static golden age for Rosny would be an interlude within evolutionary time, itself later doomed to perish in time's inexorable march.

These comparisons mark the limits of Verne's scientific speculation. In doing so, they make his difference from Rosny clear. Rosny's evolutionary science is able to look beyond humankind and human reason as the culminating life form. Verne's science, despite his celebration of the promise of experiment, does not move beyond the limits of its essentially anthropocentric Cartesian worldview. In fact, Verne's literary genius proves a curious one: he makes brilliant and exciting use of science's promise to engage the unknown, but he does so, ultimately, to celebrate the failure of science to engage that unknown. He takes his adventurers to the threshold of new discovery. They glimpse new natural phenomena, even new forms of human life. Then, invariably, acts of "fatality" intervene to cancel science's hope of discovery, thus preserving Mankind's centrality in the order of things. Verne's positivist science remains in thrall to an anthropocentric vision, whose "evolutionary" ladder is Comte's ascending stages of man, and at whose apex sits Scientific Man as Verne depicts him. How different is Rosny's "man": the new, ecological human, aware of himself as an interactive part of a vaster, interconnected whole of physical forces, organic and inorganic. Rosny's world is the much vaster one of life in all its possible forms. It is a world where moments of equilibrium are invariably caught up in tides of transformation, where all things, including our sacred concept of humanity, are subject to change and entropy.

Rosny and Wells

The Wells-Rosny connection might appear to be easier to define. They are of the same generation. They both show a keen interest in experimental science; both were exposed to the theories of Darwin. But Rosny is not simply a "French Wells." Though they share common ground, their fictional approaches to the material of evolution differ greatly. Yet because of this shared background, close comparison is possible between the novellas presented in this book and stories Wells wrote during his "scientific romance" period. We will discover that Rosny's use of science is more uncompromising than that of Wells, his extrapolations bolder. Verne's famous remark about Wells—"mais il invente!" (but he invents)—seems to denote Wells's more speculative use of science. In comparison with Rosny, however, the "inventions" of Wells, as well as those of Verne, reveal their anthropocentric limitations.

Wells wrote at least one prehistoric tale. He envisioned possible human mutations, and wrote short stories in which human beings acquire new senses that allow them to perceive other dimensions or even worlds. His novel *The Time Machine* envisions the end of the same Earth Rosny presents in *La Mort de la Terre*. Yet Wells's treatment of these bold topics, compared with Rosny's, appears surprisingly conservative. Rosny's Targ is limited to small areas of the Earth because resources elsewhere will not sustain life. Wells's Traveler is limited only by his own consciousness: by a theory of time that sees movement only in terms of his mental activity. He goes to 802,701 CE, but remains in terms of space confined to Richmond, and his own laboratory. His scientific investigations in 802,701 display no interest in venturing beyond this narrow area, no curiosity about the unknown wider world. Brought back to his own time and location in the end, the Traveler is oddly out of place in any world but his own. He apparently wore a Victorian day coat and socks (on his return "tattered, bloodstained") on his travels to the death of the Earth. Later, on the journey to the past from which he never returns, he takes a knapsack and vintage camera, like any tourist of his era. Overriding all else in Wells's novels and stories are the dimensions of irony and satire, as contemporary mankind faces, in inadequate manner, its past, future, or the possibility of an altered present. In contrast, there is neither satire nor irony in Rosny's austere extrapolations, whose protagonists *are always different* from the reader. They are beings of a recreated past, an altered present, or a constructed future. The very nature of their fictional worlds is change, evolution in the broadest sense. Rosny takes a sober look at the irreversible workings of the physical world, seeking to envision how humans and other species might evolve within their dynamic limits. To explore the Wells-Rosny comparison, we will examine analogous works by each writer in each of the three areas represented by the stories in this volume: mutations; prehistory; finality.

Victorian Mutants: Wellsian Analogues to *Un autre monde*

In several stories, all written around the time Rosny was writing *Un autre monde*, Wells examines the question of mutated or transformed perception. Before we compare these stories with Rosny's work, however, we must contextualize them. What was Wells's audience, and how might that audience have influenced the way he depicted science and its workings? Wells published his stories, and serialized his scientific romances, in London magazines during the last decade of Queen Victoria's reign. Their readers were, in large part, the same smug, Anglocentric middle-class citizens Wells satirized, indeed detested. Yet it is their world of polite manners and bourgeois order that provides the context for his tales of strange mutations and astounding events.

The Parisian milieu in which Rosny's novellas and novels appeared was not any less bourgeois. But he had several audiences. The audience for his naturalist novels was well defined. The audience for his tales of scientific extrapolation was much vaguer; in fact, as we see reflected in the bafflement of readers like Edmond de Goncourt and others, Rosny was obliged to create his audience. This was the case for "prehistoric" fiction, where an audience soon became familiar with its formulas. But during the first two decades of his literary career, it does not appear that Rosny wanted to write for a particular audience, or to cater to any contemporary frame of values in order to contextualize his scientific tales. On the contrary, estrangement appears to be the effect he sought, an estrangement wherein a phenomenon such as mutated senses could be studied with dispassionate objectivity, outside the barriers of lower-middle-class incomprehension. We see this in *Un autre monde*. It is a tale of contemporary life, but rather than giving it a Parisian setting, Rosny situates his story in the backwater of Dutch-speaking Flanders, a place so isolated that the protagonist has to specify its location in his first spoken sentence: "I am a native of Gelderland. Our patrimony amounts to a few acres of briar and yellow water." Spontaneous genetic mutations are certainly less credible in a London drawing room than in this out-of-the-way place, among a forgotten part of civilized humanity. In contrast, Wells's mutations occur in a milieu of small shopkeepers, middle-class teachers, urban homeowners, amateur scientists. Wells's narrators belong to this milieu. And, in conformity with their milieu, all of them display a similar skeptical attitude toward these strange or uncanny occurrences, even in cases where science has "plausible" explanations for them. When something unusual happens in Wells's stories, it begins and ends in this well-mannered world.[13]

Let us look briefly at a couple of Wells's stories that deal with the same theme as *Un autre monde*: "spontaneous" physical mutations that lead to new perceptual capacities, capacities that attract scientific speculation, even manipulation by science. The opening sentence of "The Remarkable Case of Davidson's Eyes" (1895) prejudges the events to follow from a "common sense" point of view: "The transitory mental aberration of Sidney Davidson, remarkable enough in itself, is still more remarkable if Wade's explanation is to be credited" (430). It is Dr. Wade who will pronounce science's final judgment on the "case" of Davidson, a scientist who, while working with electromagnetic equipment in his laboratory during a lightning storm, believes his eyes, his organs of sight, have been altered. Unable to see what is physically in front of him, Davidson claims instead to see a strange seascape, a barren island with penguins, animals that exist only on the other side of the world. As Davidson slowly recovers normal sight in the familiar world of his friends, the narrator ponders the possibility that Davidson's is "perhaps the best authenticated case in existence of real vision at a distance." This appears to be confirmed when a dinner guest, Atkins, shows the recovered Davidson a photo of the ship H.M.S. *Fulmar*. Although this ship has never been out of the South Seas, Davidson recognizes it as the ship he saw: "And then, bit by bit, it came out that on the very day Davidson was seized, H.M.S. *Fulmar* had actually been off a little rock to the south of Antipodes Island" (439). As explanation, Dr. Wade posits the Fourth Dimension much discussed in *The Time Machine*. Now, however, it is question of a *spatial dimension*, as in Heinlein's story "And He Built a Crooked House"—a "fold" in space, whereby Davidson, "stooping between the poles of the big electro-magnet, had some extraordinary twist given to his retinal elements" (439). Wade's conclusion, that it might be possible to "live visually in one part of the world, while one lives bodily in another" is dismissed by the narrator as "fantastic," as another dubious claim for déjà vu. He permits himself to make fun of Wade, who has "even made some experiments in support of his views, but so far . . . has simply succeeded in blinding a few dogs" (440).

Unlike Rosny's mutant, Davidson's change is temporary, and he recovers normal sight. Yet there is a much more troubling aspect to Davidson's description that goes unnoticed by the narrator. One incident in particular suggests there is more involved in Davidson's "mutation" than just seeing in one world and physically being in another. He describes a sightless ride around London in a bath chair, during which he experiences the tactile experience of entering water: "Very slowly, for I rode slanting into it, the water crept up to my eyes. Then I went under and the skin seemed to break and heal again about my eyes." He is "seeing" here with his entire physical being, and what he "sees" is not of the world of contemporary London: "A horror came upon me. Ugh! I should have driven right into those half-eaten . . . things" (437). It is hard to dismiss this, as the narrator does with Davidson's sight at a distance, as a "mental aberration." For what Davidson describes is not simply a mutation; it is a devolutionary process.

For now new eyes appear to be developing in a new body, while this body, at the same time, appears to sink back into primal ooze. The Traveler in *The Time Machine*, published the same year, witnesses a similar horrific scene of devolving life forms. But whereas the Traveler observes, Davidson appears to participate, as mutating flesh, in a process of reversion to a primordial state.

Wells engages in a clever subterfuge here. The narrator can dismiss Dr. Wade's four-dimensional explanation of Davidson's new visual powers, both because they prove temporary (an "aberration") and because they appear to be just another example of discredited paranormal occurrences. Science can dress up phenomena like vision at a distance with fancy theories, but this only renders science more suspicious. What Davidson describes in his London trip, however, is not an "out-of-body" experience. It is more like a slippage in evolutionary space-time, as if a modern man were asked to relive in the flesh an early stage in his development. The changes Rosny's mutant undergoes are complex, but generally progressive, as his sense of sight undergoes further specialization. Davidson's eyes, however, reverse the process of sensory differentiation. The reader shares Davidson's horror as he slides bodily down the evolutionary scale into those half-eaten things. Nothing however is irreversible. He is, like the Traveler returning to comfortable Richmond, happy to regain his sight, and to share in the narrator's mockery of Dr. Wade's experiments. Better blind dogs than Davidson's lost eyes.

"The Plattner Story" (1896) again begins with a skeptical narrator prejudging the facts in another strange case: "Never were there seven more honest seeming witnesses; never was there a more undeniable fact than the inversion of Gottfried Plattner's anatomical structure, and—never was there a more preposterous story than the one they have to tell" (441). Plattner, a language teacher at a small school in the south of England, appears to be a mutant, whose "entire body has had its left and right sides transposed." Indeed, unless a mutation has occurred, "there is no way of taking a man and moving him about in *space*, that will result in our changing sides" (443). This could only occur if we accept the fourth-dimension idea rejected by Davidson's narrator. Plattner's body would have been taken "clean out of ordinary existence ... [and turned] somewhere outside space" (444). Davidson feels himself sliding into a new body and world; Plattner physically enters another world and returns. Because this other world appears to be the mirror inversion of ours, his return leaves its mark on his physical body, inverting his organs. It is as if Davidson's plunge into primal ooze returned him to this world an amphibian.

Plattner comes and goes somewhat like the Time Traveler. He disappears for about a week, then suddenly reappears, in a strawberry patch: "collarless and hatless, his linen was dirty, and there was blood on his hands" (448). His account of how he enters the "other world" seems as fantastic as his altered anatomy is verifiable. He describes being given a "greenish powder" by one of his students. When he mixes this with other substances in his chemistry classroom, there is an explosion, and he vanishes. This may seem farcical, but surrounding events prove uncanny. During his absence, members of the community experience dreams: "In almost all of them, Plattner was seen, sometimes singly, sometimes in company, walking around through a coruscating iridescence" (447). Plattner's story confirms this. He describes a world where shades watch humans as if from the other side of a mirror. Theirs is a world of black buildings, lit by a green sun, inhabited by drifting "things": "They were not walking, they were indeed limbless, and they had the appearance of human heads beneath which a tadpole-like body swung" (454). Plattner physically inhabits this world, but at the price of inverting his organs.

How does Plattner's other world compare with that of Rosny's Moedigen? Plattner's figures, suggesting the degenerate Eloi, or even the Martians of *The War of the Worlds,* remain distortions of the human form. There is no such mirror relation between the Moedigen and humans. The Moedigen are beings of very different form, who evolve to their own rhythm. Plattner's creatures, in their dark streets and sunken church, cling to the form of living humans. Plattner's listeners open their minds to the existence of his other world only if it is seen in terms of conventional myths: these shapes are souls of the dead, ghosts of human regrets, shades of opportunities not taken, "Watchers of the Living." On the other hand, Rosny's figures are interesting because they have no ties whatsoever with their human observers. Natural creatures, evolving in a space never before perceived by humans, the Moedigen are of concern to Rosny's observers precisely because they are new, unmythified beings. The humans have no precedents that help them predict what the Moedigen will do or can do. Mirror images always depend on the beings that project them. Plattner's creatures seem to be less-than-human inhabitants of a lesser world on the other side of the mirror of life. Plattner returns to the normal world, but unlike Davidson, he is permanently altered, his inner organs forever inverted. But what is the consequence of this? No one, short of an X-ray machine, can see it. Nor does what happened have any evolutionary consequence. It simply contains the warning that we may be, instead, secretly devolving. What science sees as breakthrough to another dimension may offer evidence that we are, beneath the uneventful surfaces of our lives, to the contrary losing our central place in the scheme of things. For Rosny, mutation provides the means of accessing new worlds, of advancing science. Wells uses it to warn his Victorian readers that the cracks in their teacups may indeed be lanes to the land of devolutionary death.

"The Crystal Egg" (1897) is not a story of physical alteration of senses or body, but it puts its protagonist in a situation very similar to that of Rosny's narrator in *Un autre monde*. Mr. Cave, the proprietor of a curiosity shop, discovers he can see into another world by means of a crystal egg that mysteriously appears on his shelves one day. Cave hopes to investigate this world, but his greedy wife and sottish in-laws keep him from doing so. He takes his egg and finds sanctuary in the laboratory of Mr. Wace, a "young scientific investigator" with a "particularly lucid and consecutive habit of mind." Like Rosny's Dr. Van den Heuvel in *Un autre monde,* Wace proceeds to deal scientifically with a phenomenon that appears fantastic to the average person: "Directly the crystal and its story came to him, and he had satisfied himself, by seeing the phosphorescence with his own eyes, that there really was a certain evidence for Mr. Cave's statements, he proceeded to develop the matter systematically." Drawing Mr. Cave into the light of reason, he takes notes ("as a science student [he] had learned the trick of writing in the dark") and makes careful descriptions of the "other world" (674).

Like the Time Traveler, Wace proceeds by gathering data, formulating hypotheses, and then correcting these as new data are observed. His first description reminds us in fact of the Traveler's first, mistaken, view of the Eloi: "Incredible as it seemed to Mr. Wace, the persuasion at last became irresistible, that it was these [butterfly-winged] creatures who owned the great quasi-human buildings and the magnificent garden that made the broad valley so splendid" (674). Further investigation leads, however, here as in *The Time Machine*, to discovery of sinister doings beneath the placid surface. For both watchers become convinced that "the crystal into which they peered . . . stood at the summit of the end-most mast on the terrace, and that on one occasion at least one of these inhabitants of this other world had looked into Mr. Cave's face while he was making these observations" (674–75). The egg is a two-way glass, which allows the others to scrutinize our world as well. Where, then, is this other world located? And why do they need to see us?

Rosny's narrator remarks that the Moedigen go about their strange business totally oblivious to us. Their doings in their world may impact what we do in ours, but there is no clear line of cause and effect. There is clearly no invasive intent. In Wells's story, however, written a year before *The War of the Worlds,* the beings observed show themselves hostile to humanoid forms. Wace detects "two small moons" in the otherworldly sky, and surmises that the scene witnessed is on the planet Mars. Along with "winged Martians" they observe "certain clumsy bipeds, dimly suggestive of apes, white and partially translucent . . . and once some of these fled before one of the hopping, round-headed Martians. The latter caught one in its tentacles, and then the picture faded suddenly." Then an ominous "vast thing" appears: "As this drew nearer, Mr. Cave perceived that it was a mechanism of shining metals and extraordinary complexity" (676). This is a preview of *The War of the Worlds,* with its large-headed Martians and their machinery of destruction.

In Rosny, observation of the other world is the main goal; it will continue to be maintained, by other generations of mutants, beyond the life of the narrator. But in Wells, the window suddenly closes; Mr. Cave dies, and Wace learns too late that the egg has been sold to a "tall, dark man in grey" who subsequently disappears. Wells's tales of evolutionary alterations in sense organs culminate with the crystal egg. Indeed, none of Wells's mutations have any lasting physical significance. The reversal of Plattner's organs serves no real purpose. Seen from the exterior he remains, for the narrator, a normal human, neither an "advanced being" nor an oddity: "He is quiet, practical, unobtrusive, and thoroughly sane from the Nordau standpoint" (443). The reference is to Max Nordau's *Degeneracy,* a popular manual for identifying physical and mental "deviants." Davidson's altered eyes are a temporary anomaly. The crystal egg, finally, is an external device of suspicious origin. It disappears, leaving doubts as to its existence, and the record of a series of observations that just as well could be figments of the human imagination.

Wells's idea of evolution, it seems, did not encompass the possibility of such spontaneous mutations ever happening in the span of human time. In a late work on evolutionary theory, *The Science of Life* (1932), written with the biologist Julian Huxley, Wells asserts: "The crises of Evolution, when they occur, are not crises of variation but of selection and elimination; not strange births but selective massacres."[14] As an evolutionist, Wells's idea of humanity is conventionally pessimistic. Mankind's sole hope for development comes not from nature but from acts of conscious mind, from education rather than mutation. His stories and novels, however, reveal just how feeble those acts of mind generally are. In contrast, Rosny's vision remains positive, in the sense that despite cases of "selective massacre" like that of the Xipéhuz and, at the other end of the scale, of carbon-based life forms in *La Mort de la Terre*, the force of life itself endures, capable of vital transformations that continue the adventure of sentience.

Rosny offers a positive view of the birth of the mutant in *Un autre monde*. Here, what is essentially a variant human species, born of man and woman, makes use of human intelligence to adapt and survive. *Un autre monde* can be seen, in fact, as a Lamarckian response to Wells's Huxleyan belief that on the human time scale, meaningful mutations do not occur. Rosny's protagonist may at first call himself a "monster," because of his violet skin and opaque eyes. Yet he quickly qualifies this statement. He realizes he is not the conventional "freak," born with gills, fins, or animal ears. His differences (which he clearly understands) are in fact alterations of normal human senses that, when placed in a positive context, become assets. If he cannot see colors in the normal spectrum, he sees a whole range of colors in the ultraviolet that are black to the normal human eye. He cannot see through ordinary glass or crystal, but he does see through other materials that humans see as solid. He speaks so fast that normal human ears cannot distinguish his thoughts. Writing also proves too slow to capture them. Yet this can be an asset, for if speed of speech indicates speed of thought, he thinks much faster than the normal human. Once science understands that these altered faculties can be used for research purposes, the problems that remain become purely technical. A phonograph is devised to record his speech and play it back at normal speed. He is taught shorthand. In the manner of Asimov, physical obstacles are overcome by means of human ingenuity. Evolution in this story is a matter of increments. And if the potential of these "small" changes is misunderstood, or rejected out of fear, humankind will stagnate. Wells is pessimistic about evolutionary "leaps." He is ultimately pessimistic about mankind's ability to change the course of things at all. Rosny, on the other hand, is optimistic about science's acceptance of small, often overlooked changes, and about its ability to adapt to new challenges.

Prehistory and Alternate Evolutions

Rosny is the clear inventor of "prehistoric fiction." After his early publication of the strikingly original *Les Xipéhuz* in 1887, he continued to produce novels of this sort, and they sustained his reputation in France long after the vogue of naturalism had subsided. Notable among these works are *Vamireh*, 1892), *La Contrée prodigieuse des cavernes* (The Prodigious Land of Caverns, 1896), *La Guerre du feu* (The War for Fire, 1911), *Le Félin géant* (The Giant Cat, 1920), and *Les Conquérants du feu* (The Conquerors of Fire, 1929). In all these tales, Rosny explores the possibility of alternate evolutionary lines for life on Earth. These range from unknown species like the Xipéhuz to various known forms of fauna (the cave lion) and even flora. In his story "Le Voyage" (1897) contemporary explorers discover a region "lost to time" where a race of elephants has evolved a civilization that parallels human development. In the late novel *L'étonnant voyage d'Hareton Ironcastle* (The Astounding Voyage of Hareton Ironcastle, 1919) explorers discover what proves to be an alternately evolved race of intelligent trees.

Wells, in contrast, though writing in the wake of Lyell and the evolutionists, never seriously considered prehistoric reconstructions. His Time Traveler is believed to visit the past but, significantly, there is no record of it. Wells did, however, touch on the possibility of alternate evolutions. Stories like "In the Avu Observatory" (1894) and "Aepyornis Island" (1894), in what appears to be a parody of the "lost race" narrative, often humorously describe modern explorers' or scientists' brushes with prehistoric relics come to life. Nonetheless, a couple of Wells's stories do merit comparison with Rosny's stories of alternate evolution—most notably with the paradigm he creates in *Les Xipéhuz*. In Wells's one specifically prehistoric tale, "A Story of the Stone Age" (1897), he does attempt, after a fashion, to reconstruct a prehistoric landscape of competing species, among which mankind wins the day. In his stories "In the Abyss" (1896) and the later "Empire of the Ants" (1906), mankind comes upon rival species that, like the Xipéhuz, could be alien but are more likely products of Earth evolution.

"A Story of the Stone Age" shows Wells to be well aware of the incongruity of such narratives, and in fact making fun of the artifice. On the surface, the story recounts a very Rosnyan subject: the evolutionary rise of mankind out of a pool of competing species. The story suggests that during the formative time depicted, species other than homo sapiens evolved skills that, like those of the Xipéhuz, might have made them masters of the Earth. This possibility is treated whimsically, however. Wells's talking cave bears (unlike Rosny's talking birds in *La Mort de la Terre*) are not creatures of a well-extrapolated evolutionary scenario. They are fairy-tale entities, beings from animal fables. And there are deeper ironies yet in the way the story is told. The first lines read like a Walter Scott narrative calling attention to its own artifices: "This story is of a time beyond the memory of man, before the beginning of history, a time when one might have walked dryshod from France (as we now call it) to England." The narrator identifies himself as contemporary, thus unable to know time before the memory of man. Nor does the smattering of science he admits to justify the smug tone of his "reconstruction": "Fifty thousand years ago it was, fifty thousand years—if the reckoning of geologists is correct" (360). The reader soon sees that this narrative, which has begun so portentously, is in fact another Victorian "educational" tale for young women, if a rather odd one: "She was stiff, but not as stiff as you would have been, dear young lady (by virtue of your upbringing), and as she had not been trained to eat at least once in every three hours . . . she did not feel uncomfortably hungry" (366).

The content of this story, however, does not fit the stated moralizing framework. Its theme is neither the triumph of rational method and human courage, as in *Les Xipéhuz*, nor the rise of homo sapiens as a tool-using animal. The tools humans use in this story are not fire or some other "good" for mankind; as in the first tableau of Kubrick's *2001: A Space Odyssey*, mankind's advancement in this tale is due to its discovery, and savage use, of superior weapons. The irony goes deeper yet: when the nasty, brutish protagonist Ugh-lomi kills bear and lion and a rival chieftain, his actions do not advance humanity in any way. Instead, he merely takes the place of the leader he slays: "Thereafter for many moons Ugh-lomi was master. . . . And in the fullness of time he was killed and eaten even as Uya had been slain" (417). In contrast with Rosny's work, this tale presents the "evolutionary" process the way Kubrick presents the human odyssey in *2001*: as a biological cycle in which nature is always red in tooth and claw and mankind the worst predator of all. It is classic Wells.

In the tale "In the Abyss" (1896), Wells has his skeptical narrator describe what appears to be the discovery of an alternate evolutionary species. Then again, this story could simply be the delusion of a man trapped for long hours in a bathyscape. The deep-sea explorer Elstead tells of falling on top of an undersea city inhabited by intelligent hominid-like creatures: "It was a strange vertebrated animal. Its dark purple head was dimly suggestive of a chameleon, but it had such a high forehead and such a braincase as no reptile ever displayed before; the vertical pitch of its face gave it a most extraordinary resemblance to a human being" (503). This species breathes water, and has a "dark purple head" that resembles, however dimly, that of a reptile. Elstead's description focuses, however, on the species' high forehead and large braincase, "the vertical pitch of the face," as marks of its affinity with homo sapiens. Its affinity may even be with posthuman creatures, as we are close here, in terms of Wells's fiction, to the invasion of large-headed, humanoid Martians in *The War of the Worlds*.

Though the narrator remains skeptical, he notes that science has strong arguments supporting the validity of Elstead's tale: "Startling as is his story, it is yet more startling to find that scientific men find nothing incredible in it. They tell me they see no reason why intelligent, water-breathing, vertebrated creatures, inured to a low temperature and enormous pressure . . . might not live on the bottom of the deep sea" (507). The narrator seems to lean, however, toward another interpretation of Elstead's experience. Elstead describes being towed in his machine into a building at the center of this undersea "city" that appears to be a place of worship. As with cargo cultists, these undersea beings seem to worship the wreckage that falls on them from human shipwrecks. The walls of their "temple" are made of "water-logged wood, and twisted wire rope, and iron spars and copper, and the bones and skulls of dead men" (506). Whatever degree of civilization these beings have achieved, the narrator finds a way to cast them as superstitious inferiors, and by the same token to reinforce his unthinking sense of man's superiority. For he is flattered to think that these undersea creatures worship human relics, and may in fact see men as gods: "We should be known to them . . . as strange meteoric creatures, wont to fall catastrophically dead out of the mysterious blackness of their watery sky" (508). These misbegotten beings bear resemblance to the creatures under Moreau's "law" in *The Island of Dr. Moreau* (1896). Indeed, the narrator's comments hint at the same human vanity that drove Moreau to experiment cruelly with "lesser" forms of life. In Wells's tales, his narrators generally hold to the norm; as representatives of what for his time was seen as normative humanity, these narrators occupy the middle ground between the devolved monsters below us in the abyss and the evolved Martians of *The War of the Worlds* who observe us with their "cool intelligences" from on high.

In Wells's tales of discovery of what seem to be alternately evolved sentient species, the scientific picture remains clouded. The focus shifts instead to the fragility of the human condition, the mediocrity of normative humanity. Rosny's treatment of the same sort of discovery stands out in contrast. The Xipéhuz can be called "strange meteoric creatures" only if we see them through the eyes of the superstitious nomads, who sacrifice themselves to them in suicidal manner. The true approach to this phenomenon—as validated by human history—is Bakhoun's objectivity, the observation and analysis of the facts before him. The same is true for the protagonist of *Un autre monde*, and of Targ as he faces the question of the ferromagnetics in *La Mort de la Terre*. Rosny's figures exist to observe, and thrive or perish by their observations. They possess neither ulterior motives nor emotional flaws that might deflect them from this primary task.[15]

In situations where humans encounter alternately evolved beings, Wells invariably refers to them as "aliens." This dichotomizing of "aliens" and humans implies that there is something called human nature, and that it is a constant fact, unchanging in its endless opposition to the "other"—whether it be the alternately evolved beings, animals, or inferior humans. All of Rosny's works feature encounters between humans and alternately evolved species, yet neither is ever treated as a static entity. Rosny may offer an example of human "advancement" in *Les Xipéhuz*. But he immediately puts this idea, like every other abstraction, in evolutionary brackets. Bakhoun displays the quality—the inquiring rational mind—that ultimately leads homo sapiens to master its environment; but Rosny also invokes the dynamics of evolution in order to imagine new life forms that will challenge humankind's sense of its unique destiny. Humans do triumph in this narrative. Bakhoun represents an evolutionary "leap" from superstitious nomad to sedentary, rational man. But Rosny will show in *La Mort de la Terre* that he understands this "evolved" humankind to be one that in turn will pass: for Targ, cleverness and practical reason are no longer enough to overcome the forces of evolutionary transformation. Rosny does not allow serendipitous events to save humankind. He refuses to invoke a deus ex machina, like the Earth microbes that save humans from annihilation in *War of the Worlds.*

Bakhoun, then, is not "representative man." He is simply one of many possible stages in human development. His qualities are still recognizable in Heinlein's "special" man, who, when his peers succumb to terror, calmly studies the nature and habits of the enemy, and then acts effectively. Bakhoun, in a sense, is the ancestor of a figure like Sam in Heinlein's novel *The Puppet Masters* (1951). But whereas Heinlein makes his special being *the* human archetype, ready to act in any day and age, Rosny places Bakhoun in a broader, pluralistic context. First of all, the Xipéhuz are not the parasitic "slugs" of Heinlein's novel. Their forms have beauty to the human eye. In addition, they appear to observe a chivalrous code of conduct, sparing women and children in otherwise ferocious attacks. Finally, in good evolutionary terms, it is Bakhoun's altruism in recognizing their beauty and nobility that leads to his defeating them. For the secret to human victory here is, as much as anything, Bakhoun's respect for the adversary, his realization that there are higher evolutionary processes at work than simply human survival. The Xipéhuz teach Bakhoun many things. Most of all, they reveal that they (and no doubt many other species) are worthy to displace us, thus that such displacement is not a "bad" thing in itself, merely a viable option in the evolutionary course of things, which says that there can be neither communication nor compromise between two competing species, only territorial struggle to the death.

In a scenario repeated in many later SF novels, Bakhoun makes use of human cunning and courage—"low technology" and high mobility—to defeat the enemy's superior "firepower." Bakhoun annihilates the Xipéhuz, but at the cost of tremendous human loss. As in Heinlein, mankind has defeated a monolithic force through the fragile agility of the individual human mind and spirit. Quite unlike Heinlein, however, is Bakhoun's final lament at the condition of life itself, where an element of design seems to enter the picture: "For now that the Xipéhuz have perished, my soul misses them, and I ask of the Unique One what Fatality has wished it that the splendor of life be soiled by the blackness of Murder?" Bakhoun's experience has taught him to think not in terms of tribes or species, but in terms of life in the broadest sense. The Xipéhuz do not appear to be carbon-based life forms. Yet they share with humans the common goal of the advancement of life as opposed to death. It is this primary struggle of life against death that seems to define Rosny's ecosphere in general. Even so, Rosny's idea of evolutionary struggle evolves significantly from *Les Xipéhuz* to *La Mort de la Terre*. For in this work, perhaps his greatest, Rosny redefines equality of species not in terms of battlefield victory but as a matter of subtle balance and *imbalance* of resources. What is more, we now see, in Targ's final gesture, the possibility that there might be communication between competing species. There might, in fact, be the possibility of transhuman progression, some sort of bridge from the human species to the life form that succeeds it. Rosny implies that the human faculty of mind Descartes sees as unique in the universe not only might have come to us from elsewhere but also might evolve, via the human bridge, beyond carbon life into new and unknown regions.

Tales of the End of Human Time

It seems obvious to compare *La Mort de la Terre* and Wells's *Time Machine*. Indeed, at first glance, Rosny's title seems to fit Wells's story better than his own. For in the eyes of Wells's Traveler, the death of all the life forms that have culminated in mankind *is* the death of the Earth. Rosny's Targ, however, comes to a very different realization. The Earth that sustains life as he knows it passes. But the same Earth abides to sustain a new species, the ferromagnetics. This difference is fundamental.

Both works are alike, however, in that they take their protagonist, and the reader, *physically* to the end of human time. For Wells's Traveler, time travel is no longer the purview of armchair dreamers or Merlin's spells, for he builds a machine that lets him travel a material time line. The evolutionary journey becomes, for him, a physical voyage that takes him to the entropy beach, where he witnesses firsthand the waning of vital energy, the recession of life forms. He becomes, in a sense, a Last Man in the flesh. Yet his voyage remains, in terms of his travels, a classic one because he returns to where he started. Once back in his time and place, the Traveler is no longer the Last Man; he is now instead an actor who plays the part of Last Man, a role he has incarnated in the flesh for a biological week and no more. The evolutionary voyage has left physical marks on his clothes, but there is no change in his material body. In contrast, the evolutionary voyage of Rosny's Targ is that of all carbon-based life forms, and it is without return. Last Man Targ bears, along with all of his species, the physical marks of a long agony—large chests to process rarified air, narrow abdomens from lack of food. These changes are irreversible; Targ cannot simply change his clothes.

A point of comparison and contrast between these two works is their recreation, in the context of evolutionary theory, of the story of humankind's mythical beginning—that of Adam and Eve. Since it invented this story, Western humanity has dreamt of an arcadia or golden age, a new Garden of Eden, where somehow time is stopped, perhaps even the inevitable end of things is reversed. For Wells, this end of things is entropy; for Rosny, it is ecodisaster. These different designations are essential if we are to understand each author's sense of beginnings and endings. For both writers, some form of millennial pause is possible. But the end remains inexorable; there is no cycle of time, no regeneration of humankind and nature. Both pauses must, by the logic of evolution, come to the same conclusion. The nature of the Edenic moment, however, differs greatly between Wells and Rosny. For Wells's Traveler, finding a future Eden appears to be a psychological necessity. This proves, in the end, a delusion, swept away by the iron logic of evolution. For Rosny's Targ, however, Eden is a physical possibility, born of a resurgent genetic line and a fortuitous discovery of water that allows it to exist, and made conceivable through human ingenuity and technology. Eden for Rosny is the reawakened potential of experimental science, a potential that is soon dashed by physical forces beyond human control.

The Traveler's time machine opens the entire future to scientific investigation. A curious traveler would hop around, studying the development of certain phenomena, much as Bakhoun studied the Xipéhuz. Wells's Traveler, however, roars off impetuously into the future and comes to what appears to be a random stop in 802,701CE. Moreover, he stays with the Eloi and Morlocks for most of his narrative. Why does he do so? If we remember that time is a dimension of *his* consciousness, it is possible that he wished to land in this future, his hand guided by some deep prelapsarian desire. Indeed, his first thought on arriving is that he has found a postindustrial Eden in this lush Thames valley of the future. The verdigris-covered Sphinx he first encounters ought to have warned him that physical time is also present in arcadia. On an unconscious level, however, he seems to dismiss his training as an observer, to deny the evolutionary vision that has brought him to the future in the first place. Through a series of painful corrections, he reluctantly comes to see the hidden horror behind the Edenic vision he obviously prefers to see.

Evolution posits irreversible, nonpurposive change through time. The future is, by nature, neither predetermined nor predictable; it must always be different, new. In spite of this (or perhaps because of it), many in Wells's England feared that if mankind, then considered to be at its apogee, poked too far into the future, it would find degeneracy, devolution. Thus the initial reaction of the Traveler on entering his brave new world: "What might not have happened to men? What if cruelty had grown into a common passion? What if in this interval the race . . . had developed into something inhuman, unsympathetic, and overwhelmingly powerful?" (25). When he spies the Eloi, however, he is almost too glad to confirm the opposite. He finds attractive, carefree beings, who live in communal dwellings. They cavort and play. He sees the dream of a "communist" commune of his time come true.

The Traveler is too keen an observer, however, to give in totally to wishful thinking. He notes that Eloi buildings show signs of disrepair. But if these people do not work, where do they get their food and clothes? There is not simply peaceful cohabitation of species here, for plants and weeds grow untended, chaotically. He chooses however to ignore these details for another one that points, this time, toward utopia in evolutionary terms. The Eloi are oddly alike physically. Might this not be the result of man's mastery of nature, where variations and "accidents" have been eliminated, and no contagious diseases remain? There are no more pests, no more need to toil, to "struggle" in the Darwinian sense. Again, to whatever extent he is seduced by this arcadian vision, the Traveler remains enough of a scientist to sense a darker truth behind the Eloi facade. In conquering nature, mankind may have conquered itself: "I thought of the physical slightness of these people, their lack of intelligence . . . and it strengthened my belief in a perfect conquest of Nature. For after the battle comes Quiet. Humanity had been strong . . . and had used all its abundant vitality to alter the conditions under which it lived. And now came the reaction of the altered conditions" (39). He begins to realize he is in the future, and it is a time of winding down, not of genesis. Yet even in the act of admitting so, the Traveler's vision remains clouded by elegiac regret. He retains his Eden in a lament for Eden lost.

To recreate Eden, we need a man and a woman. The Traveler is given his Edenic chance when he returns and finds his machine missing. Thinking he can never return home, he now becomes free to make this new world his own, to make himself Adam within it. Thus the meeting with Weena is significant, for she is his potential Eve. In fact, a certain "back to the Garden" symbolism surrounds their meeting. When he spies Weena drowning in a stream, and no Eloi attempting to rescue her, he "slips off" his clothes and wades in to save her. Having seen by now the lack of vigor of the Eloi, he thinks he has found in Weena something different, an atavism among a weakened gene pool: "I had got such a low estimate of their kind that I did not expect any gratitude from her. In that, however, I was wrong" ([58]). If gratitude is still present among these degenerates, there must be nobler sentiments yet. The dream is rekindled.

Interestingly, in the minds of modern readers, this barest of hints about Weena still inspires full-blown Edenic scenarios. Two such "readings" are found in George Pal's 1960 film based on Wells's novel and the Simon Wells remake (2002). In Pal's film, the Adam and Eve motif is highlighted by the visual fact that Weena is a beautiful woman. She is, as in Wells's story, initially an empty vessel. The difference, however, is that Pal's Traveler reenergizes the beautiful body, and in doing so fashions his own Eve. Ultimately he restores to Weena and her people the capacity to resist, and evil and sin (the deformed Morlocks) are expelled from the land. The Traveler goes back to the present, gathers a set of encyclopedias, and returns to the virgin land (*pace* Henry Nash Smith), a fresh start, a new Eden. The Simon Wells remake uses a dizzying manipulation of time lines to give the Traveler two possible endings, one humdrum (a staid career with a blond Edwardian wife and a family), the other a new start with a dusky Weena in a future world of lush beauty, over which they rule as Adam and Eve.

Both films end here, giving proof of some deep cultural desire for an Edenic second chance. Both avoid sending the Traveler on to an encounter with a dying Earth. For Wells's Traveler, however, Eden is ultimately a nostalgic interlude. Once the Traveler is forced to open his eyes to the scientific reality of the situation, his awakening is all the more horrific. Weena is seen as she really is, "a poor mite," more a domestic animal than a child with promise. After he explores the underground lair of the Morlocks, he can no longer entertain his delusion that he has discovered arcadian innocence. But his thinking remains wishful, and he briefly imagines a sort of capitalist utopia, a world order based on a fragile equilibrium between Carolingian aristocrats and brutish workers. This is the tainted dream of Victorian apologists, the playful gardens and underground workers' city depicted by Fritz Lang in *Metropolis*. The Traveler seeks to hold on to this vision, even in the face of evidence that the Morlocks are cannibals. It takes, finally, a Morlock attack to make him see the truth. What he discovers in the ruins of the Green Palace, in the night forest as he flees with club and matches, is raw physical devolution. The Morlocks raise the Eloi for food, Weena is lost, the Traveler recuperates his machine as white hands clutch at him in the dark. Fleeing this world, further flight only takes him to a more horrific future, where mankind has perished, and its Earth dying apace.

Rosny's Edenic moment resembles that of Wells in that it comes at the end of human history, and seems to offer a final chance to renew humanity. Nonetheless, the difference from Wells, though simple, is fundamental. Because of his time machine, the Traveler is in violation of the process of physical evolution that has shaped the world of Eloi and Morlock. His story of time travel, therefore, is at best an evolutionary romance. He has seen the terrible future; he could have been trapped there. But luck and his fears bring him back to tell his tale. The narrator, on hearing this tale, says that to remain sane, he must assert the Edenic dream at every moment, knowing the end but living every day "as though it were not so." Another lesson comes clear from the story itself: no time traveler will ever recover Eden lost, for no time traveler can change any part of the time continuum. A time traveler is merely an observer in the stream of time. All glide ghostlike through time; they are Emerson's bird that never alights. Rosny's Moedigen may resemble ghosts, but they appear to share a common space-time continuum with humans, thus may be an active element in the ecology of our Earth. The Traveler, however, is in violation of the laws of time everywhere except in his own biological existence, moving inexorably from Eden to end.

In contrast, Rosny's Targ, by virtue of his evolutionary development, belongs biologically to a far future world. *La Mort de la Terre* is not a romance but an evolutionary epic. As such, it offers a sweep of time that is neither observed nor remembered but *lived*, biologically and ecologically, over a vast time line, at the end of which we find Targ and his peers, evolved humans who rightfully call themselves, in a strictly evolutionary sense, Last Men. Long historical analepses in this novella recount the collective wisdom of generations. They tell that life once thrived on sea and land, that humankind ultimately became the master of things. They also detail the logic of evolutionary forces whereby humankind's rise has created the necessary conditions for its demise: "L'homme capta jusqu'à la force mystérieuse qui a assemblée les atomes. Cette frénésie annonçait la Mort de la Terre." (Mankind harnessed everything right down to the mysterious force that bound together the atom. This frenzy heralded the Death of the Earth.) For Targ, a man living in this final time, the discovery of a new Eve is neither dream nor desire. It is an atavistic accident to seize on, one that offers the biological possibility of species regeneration.

Targ's people preside over an empty wasteland without water. They are the final survivors of an "agony" of the human species that has lasted for a span of a hundred thousand years. Over this period humans have adapted, physically and culturally, to severe environmental changes. Human society is now rigidly legislated, and population control has been codified into iron law. These Last Men, said in the opening pages to possess "resigned grace" ("son être exhalait une grâce résignée, un charme craintif"), at first may suggest Wells's Eloi, an effete and decadent race. But unlike the Eloi, Rosny's Last Men have technology, developed in humankind's past, that continues to sustain them, even in their decline. Wells thinks in terms of rupture, of radical rise and fall. Here instead the trajectory is a continuous curve, sloping up and then gradually downward to zero. These people have not lost the marvelous machines in Wells's Palace of Green Porcelain, their books have not turned to dust. But the fact that Rosny's humanity has retained them reveals just how insignificant mankind and its machines are when measured against the irreversible changes in the natural environment that are destroying all carbon life on Earth.

There is no need here, as in *The Time Machine*, to see through a green illusion. Targ's evolved future world is an antiarcadia by virtue of its sheer physical nature: a harsh desert world where surviving humans are resigned to a slow, inevitable drying up of all sources of water. If one is tempted to see the small number of oases dotted around the desert Earth as utopian colonies, one should look again. True, their inhabitants have mastered agronomy; they have inherited sophisticated communication devices, "planetaries" and "gliders" invented in the past, that allow these islands in the net to interrelate across vast arid wastes. Yet a utopian stasis, set against the larger play of forces, is unsustainable. Targ must literally heed the slightest shaking of the ground. More and more frequent small tremors—"butterflies" in relation to the vaster cataclysms of the past—gradually send the existing water supply deeper and deeper into the ground: "Ainsi, le malheur qui ruinait la suprême espérance n'était pas une grande convulsion de la nature, mais un accident infinitésimal, à la taille des faibles créatures englouties." (Thus the disaster that destroyed the last hope of mankind was no great convulsion of nature, but an infinitesimally small accident, of the same magnitude as the feeble creatures it engulfed.) Another difference: the iron-based ferromagnetics that stir outside the walls are, unlike the Morlocks, only indirectly born of humankind. Our industry prepared the terrain, and perhaps gave the spark, for their creation. Yet in the large view, they are merely another part of the general transformation of Earth. All the adversarial dualities of human thought simply dissolve into a complex web of cause and effect over which humankind ultimately has no control. The farthest thing from the sparse lives of these Last Men is desire for a golden age. Nor does Rosny need to place a sphinx at the portals of his future to remind us of the ravages of time.

Evolutionary atavisms do occur in Rosny's terminal world. In Targ and his sister Arva, for example, old human traits of initiative and adventurousness are physically resurgent. Targ is a doer rather than a dreamer, a Bakhoun at the end of human time, a new incarnation of an earlier, now long-forgotten humankind that was willing to struggle against overwhelming odds. Despite this, Targ's adventure is doomed because the conditions that sustain heroic human activity on the most basic, physical level are no longer present. Given this physical reality, it is all the more poignant that Targ does find, in Érê, a woman in the flesh who is capable of replenishing the Earth with a new race of vigorous humans. She is a new Eve in a world that has long lost the luxury of eschatology, of pondering such things as the "Fall." Her blond hair merely signals atavistic genes from a heroic past. In her the blond heroine of legend is recast as a genetic gift. And Targ wins her hand with a deed that, if it might long before have been seen as heroic chivalry, is now the product of sheerest physical necessity. In the end, this couple and their family gain their Eden. But it in turn is nothing more than a material enclave, a place temporarily sheltered from change by humankind's perfect machines. Targ's colony, technically, could perpetuate itself forever in terms of energy and food; but it is doomed by forces beyond its control. Evolutionary time is an arrow, and what occurred in the beginning of humankind's history cannot be repeated. Targ and Érê must face their inevitable End.

Is Rosny cruel to suggest the myth of Eden at the end of time, when everything points to the futility of such myths when faced with the iron laws of physical nature? Or is he simply presenting the terminal world in a neutral manner, as a world where all things, even our most sacred stories, are in the end reduced to a common denominator of genetic and biological survival? Either way, or both, Wells's narrative, however grim, is comforting in comparison, because its subtext remains anthropocentric. It speaks for mankind, not for processes. The Traveler misunderstands the future, not because the physical conditions he faces are so complex as to be ultimately beyond his control,, but because the models he applies are human models: Edenic utopia, the labor-capital equation. A Rosny protagonist would study the Eloi and Morlocks as new facts, as objective phenomena. The Traveler reacts, and his reactions prove all too human. Because he is seeking a human future, he would neither see nor understand a species like Rosny's ferromagnetics, beings that are chemically variant but still a form of life. When asked to look beyond human time, to a landscape that is empty of human life yet still has living forms in it, his response is to look back in horror, uttering a recessional that traces the process of life back from himself, the Last Man sitting on his machine, through mammalian life, to amphibians, and finally to the primal sea from which these "ancestors" of man first emerged. Just as his physical travel is regulated by the exactly equal stretching forward and backward of Mrs. Watchett, so his journey in evolutionary time comes full circle in himself, and his time—a humanity that, perhaps, never moved from 1895 at all.

How different is the vast evolutionary processional that accompanies Targ's final moments! Wells's Traveler, in his vision, moves back along his chain of evolution. In opposite fashion, Axel's famous dream brings the entire process of evolving life forward to culminate in himself, nineteenth-century mankind at its evolutionary apogee. In contrast, Targ's vision is unique, because it is not centered in humankind but tells of the rise and fall of all carbon-based life forms: "Il refaisait, une fois encore, le grand voyage vers l'amont des temps. . . . Et d'abord, il revit la mer primitive, tiède encore, où la vie foisonnait, inconsciente, insensible." (He made, one more time, the grand voyage back toward the beginning of time. . . . And first, he saw again the primeval sea, still warm, swarming with life, unconscious and unfeeling.) Notice that the emphasis is not on ancestral forms of life that lead to humankind but rather on the physical conditions ("la mer primitive, tiède encore" [the *primeval* sea, still *warm*]) that result in the creation of carbon-based life in general. In this huge flow and ebb of flora and fauna, of names and learned designations, humankind is dwarfed, its "triumph" merely a brief instant in the history of life on Earth. Rosny gives us instead a vitalist dream of the awakening and proliferation of a plurality of evolutionary forms—iguanodons, cave bears, aurochs. Rosny's only distinction, in this mighty paean to organic life, is between animate and inanimate things; he sees that all forms of life have emerged from the mineral and must someday return to the mineral. Thus, because the ferromagnetics will abide, humankind's passing is not the end of life, but only of life as we know it. The single, raw fact is that another form of life inherits our world.

For his time, Rosny's pluralistic vision is unique in its attempt to create a balanced ecosystem, in which humankind is neither all-powerful nor all-destructive but merely a significant element in a larger equation. True, in Targ's dream, mankind is called "le destructeur prodigieux de la vie" (the prodigious destroyer of life). But though it ruled and ravaged, in this larger picture mankind is, if anything, only partly responsible for its end. For Rosny, the process of evolution is beyond human power or desire, and humans are neither to be praised nor blamed. Wells, in contrast, seems to place the blame on mankind. In his arrogance as new "scientific" man, the Traveler is the embodiment of the process that leads to the Palace of Green Porcelain. He and his kind write the theories and make the machines that, as we discover, have robbed mankind, and by analogy the Earth, of its vital energy. Man's society will create the degenerate ecology of Morlocks feeding on Eloi, a cannibalistic machine of diminishing energy that mirrors the final entropy of all life forms. Seen through the eyes of mankind, the future panorama of *The Time Machine* inscribes a closed circle, where back to the future is now forward to the past. The Traveler's narrative remains an elegy for mankind trapped between its mythic Sphinx and its modern myth of the culminating ape.

Targ's vision, on the other hand, has clearly evolved. For example, most of his peers still see the ferromagnetics as vampires, beings who "drink" humans' blood. For Targ, however, this is like calling humans vampires for breathing air; Targ is able to describe this process as a simple transfer of needed chemical elements. He and his circle have learned the lesson of mankind's evolutionary adventure: the ferromagnetics are not our enemy but our successor. If we aided in their development, this was unavoidable, as they are a by-product of the same transformation of iron that fueled human industry. Rosny's humans are presented as like any other population that grows, swells, and ultimately wanes and dies as the elements that sustain it are depleted. The rise of the ferromagnetics is simply another such evolutionary cycle. Despite obvious pangs of sympathy for humanity, Rosny's narrator strives to present the geological upheavals that destroy carbon-based life as the doings of an indifferent nature.

Rosny's evolutionary vision was unique for its time. It is still unique today, even in our age of "ecology." It strives to present human beings engaged in a complex interplay of physical forces, and to do so in as neutral a manner as a human being can. Its approach is systemic, always seeing mankind as part of a larger system in transformation, and steadfastly refusing any theological or teleological subtext. Rosny notes the classic human hubris, and says mankind must bear some responsibility for changing the environment. But mankind is never wholly responsible, and in the end *natural* selection, seen in the most neutral manner possible, wins out. Nor does Rosny, in the opposite sense, exonerate mankind, making us the victim of hostile forces from without. The superstitious nomads first see the Xipéhuz as hostile invaders. But essentially the Xipéhuz are minding their own business, and merely react to defend their territory. The problem is that their territory, through natural population pressures, is growing, and begins to overlap with human expansion. Mutually impacting populations is the core problem in all three Rosny narratives. And though Rosny must, because he is human, tell these stories from the human point of view, he strives by all means possible to keep to the ecological middle ground, to present the workings of the system without taking sides. This is a very difficult stance to take when the story, as in *La Mort de la Terre*, is about the demise of humanity along with all accompanying forms of life. Yet the narrator of this novella openly states that the ferromagnetics alone are not the cause, or even the main reason, for humankind's annihilation: "On ne peut pas dire que les ferromagnétaux aient participé à notre destruction" (One cannot say that the ferromagnetics actively participated in our destruction). Theirs is a life form that, in the classic Darwinian sense, has adapted and survived in a changing environment. Very few writers have wanted to carry the "inconvenient truths" of ecology this far.

Hard SF has been defined by Gregory Benford as writing "with the net up," playing according to the rules of nature rather than to the sentimental desires of human beings. This defines a mode of storytelling that, in an age of modern science in which rational humankind is suspended between material infinities large and small, will not give in to the usual contrivances of conventional suspension-of-disbelief. In theory at least, hard SF does not allow its readers to avail themselves of the various retrieval strategies that might permit them to salvage their sense of humanity as they confront the edge of the abyss, the prospect of humanity's extinction. If in Thomas Mann's *Doktor Faustus* we are told that the final note of Adrian Leverkühn's cantata, humankind's last hope for a presence in the material void, resonates endlessly in dark silence, hard SF tells us sound does not carry in the vacuum of outer space.[16]

But hard SF also comprises a worldview, a vision of the human condition and human evolution that does not violate material process but coincides with it, as far as we understand its workings. Essential to this vision, as it develops over the twentieth century, is the question of a posthuman or, more accurately, transhuman possibility: how and in what ways can we go beyond our spatiotemporal limits? Long before J. D. Bernal, Olaf Stapledon, and other evolutionary visionaries, Rosny posed the transhuman question in his writing. He did so in a strikingly speculative way in *La Mort de la Terre*, a work that predates Bernal by twenty years.

Bernal's treatise *The World, the Flesh, and the Devil: An Enquiry into the Future of the Three Enemies of the Rational Soul* (1929) could serve as a metanarrative for the development of hard SF. It takes scientific humankind to the threshold of a dimorphic split. Seeking to envision what a posthuman condition might be, Bernal restates the major questions that have accompanied the development of Western science since the seventeenth century: What is special about humankind—now seen as material entity? If that specifically human quality is thought, intelligence, is it possible for this quality to evolve beyond its human source without losing its specificity? The recent physicist-writer Robert L. Forward sounds like an evolutionist when he states that "there is a human world, and the real world out there; from the viewpoint of the scientist there are plenty more species to take your place. . . . Humans are not important, intelligence is."[17] In saying this, however, Forward does little more than restate the mind-matter duality that continues to shape hard SF speculation on transhumanity to this day. For the Cartesians, thought is the defining human quality; the rest of the universe is nonthinking. Therefore, either thought dies with humanity or whatever faculty evolves as posthuman must a priori resemble human thought. For Baconian skeptics, the human limit remains as well. For their part, Baconians challenge the centrality of reason, as a faculty severely limited by the imperfection of human sense organs. As they do so, they arrive, like the Cartesians, at a like rupture between mind and world. Their impasse, too, is similar: either we deny that we can ever know our posthuman self; or we find ourselves doomed to depict that self as the mirror of what we are—imperfect thought.

Forward's statement that "intelligence," as something larger than human reason, is the motor of interspecies evolution may seem to be an important step in defining transhuman possibility. Seventy years earlier, however, Rosny's speculative masterpiece *La Mort de la Terre* offers a probing examination of a similar pluralist vision. In previous works, Rosny focused on the struggle of intelligent species. Now the focus is squarely on humankind, on its demise (how the human is no longer a factor in the changing ecology of Earth), and on the possibility that, in the broader ecology of evolving life forms, humanity may contribute to and ultimately communicate with the species that replaces it. By the logic of his narrative, Rosny leads readers to speculate on the possibility that some kind of message, informing future life forms of what we were, could be sent across the gulf that separates expiring and emerging life. He asks readers to imagine *how* this transfer might occur, and to ponder whether this message might have contributed to the creation of an intelligence a million years in the future. Furthermore, he asks if such a message might provoke this future intelligence's interest in hearing our story, a story that is part of their evolution as well? Rosny's narrative may be the first to suggest a genuine transhuman experience. As such, it is an essential element in the history of hard SF.

La Mort de la Terre is, in its own right, a masterpiece, whose speculative reach is unparalleled. For in terms of future life and intelligence, Rosny looks not only beyond humankind but far beyond carbon-based life itself. On a scale from fast life forms to infinitely slow ones, he is willing to see beyond his ferromagnetics and to include in his vast evolutionary picture the inert mineral reign as well. His vision, in the largest evolutionary sense, is that of Norman O. Brown: life against death. Therefore, his challenge to the mind-matter duality is sweeping. In giving this challenge fictional form, he sets the benchmark for further hard SF speculations on humankind's place in the universe.

The fact that Rosny's work is so significant yet remains unknown to most SF writers and readers today, even in the Francophone world, suggests the synchronicity of SF's development across national cultural lines. In the three representative works presented here, Rosny develops a vision and methods of constructing fiction that parallels the development of scientific or hard SF in the Anglo-American sphere. Rosny's fiction calls for scientific responses to questions suggested by the imagining of figures such as aliens, intelligent nonhuman beings, and mutants. In doing so ultimately, it raises Bernal's question of transhuman possibility. It is Rosny, more than either Verne or Wells, who follows the road map that Bernal laid down in 1929 and that has proven to be the masterplot at least for SF at the harder extreme of its spectrum.

Let us discuss Rosny's SF legacy point by point. First of all, he appears to be the first writer systematically to use neologisms, even invented words, in the construction of other and future worlds. As early as the late 1880s, Edmond de Goncourt described Rosny's speculative novels as "fantastico-scientifico-*phono*-littéraires" (fantastico-scientifico-*phono*-literary),[18] attesting to the power of word sounds alone to create worlds. For example, when one searches Google for historical antecedents to the tribal names in *Les Xipéhuz*—Zahelals, Dzoums, Xisoastres, Pjarvanns— one finds Rosny as the sole source. These are in effect phonetic constructions that *suggest* pre-Assyrian times, words whose sole function is to create resonant bridges between our world and imagined little-known or unknown worlds. The designation "Xipéhuz," beginning with *x* and ending with *z*, phonetically suggests that the species it conjures is near the omega of its evolutionary cycle. In *Un autre monde*, the name Moedigen, which pops unbidden into the mind of the protagonist, suggests there might be, in its Germanic echoes, some obscure link between the kobolds of Nordic fairy tale and the other-dimensional species that is observed here for the first time. These overtones are mere suggestions, but they work to close the gap between known and unknown.

In *La Mort de la Terre*, Rosny not only conjures new devices and machines by means of neologisms, but actually builds a coherent future world around these terms, exactly as Robert A. Heinlein will later do with his rolling roads and waldoes. The process is the opposite of that of Verne. Verne describes Nemo's fabulous underwater vessel in great technical detail. In the end, however, he gives it a name that falls short of designating a future class or type of machine. On the contrary, Robert Fulton's earlier submarine (1800) was named *Nautilus* (in fact a banal derivation from the Greek *nautilos*, sailor). In contrast Rosny, like Heinlein, throws out designations—*Grand Planétaire, radiatrix, resonateurs, motrices*—that indicate something we can imagine, but something with no ties to anything concrete we know. These are devices that already exist in this future world, and the reader is left the task of explaining their function by witnessing them in action. Rosny also presents future phenomena without analyzing or explaining them. An example is his offhand mention of "un repas de gluten concentré et d'hydrocarbures essentiels" (a meal of concentrated gluten and essential hydrocarbons)— all its components are known, but their combination and use remain for the reader to fathom. Likewise, Rosny mixes invented terms like *ferromagnétaux* with already existing specialized terms such as *hygroscope*, a neologism coined in 1790 to refer to a real machine that measures humidity in the air. Finally, it appears that Rosny, like Heinlein with his waldoes, may have coined words that subsequently, in the real world, have given rise to actual things or classes of things. For example, Rosny's use of the word *aviateur* (which we translate as "aviator")—from the neologism *avion* (a thing with wings), coined by Clément Ader in 1875—may be the first such use in the French language of a name that has become commonplace today.

Second, Rosny develops, in *Les Xipéhuz* and other similar works, a syncretic and synchronic style that allows him to extrapolate narratives into improbably far-distant worlds yet retain an oblique link with the reader's known world. Later SF writers will use a similar style. With *Les Xipéhuz*, Rosny is said to have invented prehistoric fiction. If so, he would appear to have invented a paradox; for prehistory is, by definition, prewriting. Without writing, there is no bridge, no communication, from there to here. So how can anyone pretend to tell the prehistoric story? Unlike writers who unabashedly invent a lost past as fairy tale, Rosny builds the bridge physically into his story by having Bakhoun invent writing, and by creating a fictitious modern linguist, M. Dessault, who transcribes his tablets. The discovery of prehistory through the scientifically authorized narrative of the very man who invents the means of conveying it is a neat science-fictional trick, born of the need to make literal what otherwise remains conventional.

There remains, however, another question the literal or scientific mind must ask. Rosny's Bakhoun speaks of things he knows; his words vouch for their existence. But the words themselves are merely objects, things an archeologist or linguist has found. From them alone, how can we ever know their context? Moreover, they are a modern discovery. Can we know in what manner Bakhoun actually spoke them? Rosny's "scientific" "attempt" to mediate these words raises these questions, asking the reader, in literal manner, to question what otherwise might pass for convention. Historical novelists like Walter Scott were aware of this problem of "speaking the past"—having a narrator supposedly of the time in question speak in the voice of that time, which the novelist could not know firsthand. Scott tries to "fake it" by giving his novels' narrators (and characters) an "archaic," medievalizing mode of speech, which even in its time was recognized as a nineteenth-century imitation, but accepted as a necessary convention. The opening pages of *Ivanhoe* offer a good example. Later, more scientifically inclined writers like Flaubert scoffed at such artifice. At the same time, Flaubert (along with some of his contemporaries) was genuinely troubled by the fact that we cannot physically know the past. Making the past "speak" then becomes a problem that does not exist for more conventional writers.[19]

Rosny clearly knows he cannot make prehistory "speak"; yet he must find a way to tell the story that does not insult his scientifically inclined reader. Rosny's situation in *Les Xipéhuz* is that of numerous later SF writers who purport to narrate far-distant worlds. These are worlds the reader visits for the first time, in the company of a narrator who is presumed to have been there before, but of course because of the realities of space-time cannot have been. But if that reader does not demand the impossible literal tour, on what level does he or she accept taking the journey? Rosny confronts this problem by moving his narrative to a *synthetic* level, generating out of recognizable *styles* of historical discourse that have been restructured, a narrative that reaches beyond the limits of known history by imitating the *process* itself of evolutionary time, at least as science understands it. Rosny does not use anachronisms so much as cultivate them in syncretic fashion. The result is a minisimulacrum, in terms of narrative style, of humankind's evolutionary history—past, present, and future.

The first narrator in *Les Xipéhuz* does not pretend to historical omniscience. Its opening remarks seem to echo the precise, methodical descriptions of nineteenth-century science, detailing the new beings in a manner we identify as "objective." The tone suddenly modulates, however, as the focus shifts from the soon-to-be-called Xipéhuz to the superstitious nomads. Describing the frenzied actions of the astrologer Yushik, the narrator begins to speak a language of emotional excess that invites the reader to experience this world through irrational eyes. Again, when Bakhoun takes up the narrative, his voice brings another shift of tone and manner of speech. He is presented as transitional man, representing humanity's movement from nomadic to sedentary, agricultural existence. And true to his role, Bakhoun is the first human to invent a means of writing. Indeed, the rest of the narration is his account of events as preserved in what is called the Book of Bakhoun. But when Bakhoun speaks and reasons, his voice is that of Comte's Scientific Man. Rosny's contemporary reader would see Bakhoun's method of apprehending phenomena as reflecting this Scientific Man, seen as the culmination of humankind's development. Rosny allows style and language to convey these two different worldviews, or methods of perceiving material reality, contrasting the nomads' superstition with Bakhoun's capacity for cold analysis. In terms of how prehistoric humankind might have *really* spoken or reasoned, both voices are nineteenth-century transpositions, anachronisms. The purpose of their contrast, however, is to overlay what is not known in the past with a plausible historical schema. There is, however, another modulation of tone and vision, this time within Bakhoun's own discourse. This occurs in his final invocation, as his voice suddenly speaks to the future of a human species that has barely emerged from obscure silence, suggesting a possibility that was new to the average nineteenth-century reader, that of evolutionary transformation. The Comtean voice reflects the apogee of human development. But the new, final voice offers a broader vision, one that transcends species boundaries, that speaks of a general "splendor of Life": "Car, maintenant que les Xipéhuz ont succombé, mon âme les regrette, et je demande à l'Unique quelle Fatalité a voulu que la splendeur de la Vie soit souillée par les Ténèbres du Meurtre!" (For now that the Xipéhuz have perished, my soul misses them, and I ask of the Unique One what Fatality has wished it that the splendor of Life be soiled by the Blackness of Murder?) For Bakhoun, any hint of "survival of the fittest" is at once swept away by a broader sense of evolutionary dynamics.

Though the storyteller is obviously anchored in one historical time and place, Rosny uses a controlled spectrum of language—from superstitious effusion to Bakhoun's sober analysis of fact to his evolutionary mysticism—to carry the reader from the present back to the past, and then to suggest an unknown future. When Rosny's narrator tells us "ce fut l'an mil des peuples enfants, le glas de la fin du monde, ou, peut-être, la résignation de l'homme rouge des savanes indiennes" (this was the year 1000 for these infant peoples, the bell that tolled the end of the world, or perhaps, the resignation of the red man of the Indian jungle), we know the voice of the "civilized" nineteenth-century Westerner is speaking. But when we read "un matin d'automne, le Mâle perça les nues, inonda le Tabernacle, atteignit l'autel où fumait un coeur saignant de taureau" (one autumn morning, the Male God burst through the clouds, flooded the tabernacle, reached the altar where the bloody heart of a bull lay steaming), we experience an otherwise unknowable past through words and rhythms, only to be wrenched back to our familiar culture by Bakhoun's language of fact and reason. Bakhoun's final words, however, combining emotion and reason, take us forward, to a possible future of multiple evolutionary possibilities.

In a sense, Rosny's narrative offers the stylistic blueprint for later hard SF extrapolations, for example Benford's Great *Sky River* and *Tides of Light*, or more recent intergalactic playing fields, for example those of Stephen Baxter, where vast distances of never-experienced space-time make "playing with the net up" little more than an exercise in scientific theorizing. Even more than with Rosny, the worlds portrayed in these deep space-time novels lie absurdly far off the reader's historical-linguistic map. To narrate these worlds, the writer must construct a new dynamic from synthetic combinations of known tones and styles that do not simply evoke an unknown world, but render it coherent. For example, Benford cultivates, in a manner quite similar to that of Rosny, an anachronistic alternation between Conan-like primitive speech (a nod to sword and sorcery) and precise and informed scientific discourse. These are the twentieth-century equivalents of Rosny's nomads and positivist Bakhoun. As in Rosny, these opposing forms of discourse come together in outbursts of scientifico-evolutionary mysticism. In analogous manner, Benford's synthesis suggests the possibility that today's humanity could someday find itself in an intergalactic otherness so strange that, in terms solely of reason or of emotion, it must remain inconceivable, let alone uninhabitable. A new SF narrative device, by which we tell by analogy a world otherwise untellable, appears to be born with Rosny. Benford and his contemporaries have simply spread Rosny's technique across seas of suns.

Les Xipéhuz poses another problem that sheds light on the future development of SF. The issue here is the Xipéhuz themselves—where did they come from, and what does their physical presence in early human times signify? Most readers call them "aliens," despite the fact that neither Rosny's narrator nor Bakhoun uses such a designation, nor anywhere suggests that they come from any other location but right here on Earth.[20] Rosny, it seems, does not present them as "alien" because he does not want to swerve away from the scientific task of trying to describe and understand phenomena we encounter, no matter how bizarre they may seem. The use of this designation "alien" in fact, in subsequent SF, marks a dividing line between hard and soft SF. However "other" the Xipéhuz appear, Bakhoun takes them as facts. They are physically present, so it is assumed that they too have evolved as humans did, sharing the same environment. Prehistory is an unmapped territory, so it is quite plausible that they have evolved in some area of Earth that humankind has not yet visited, as when Greek explorers discovered all kinds of "Indian wonders" outside their familiar world, wonders they asked their audiences to believe existed, because those audiences *had not yet seen them.* It is out of fear of such unknowns that we give phenomena like this an extraterrestrial origin, or see them as invaders, beings brought to Earth by some deus ex machina, the chariots-of-the-gods scenario. Moreover, behind our choice of the word "alien" lies a deeper fear: that of the fragility of humankind's domination of its earthly environment. At first, the Xipéhuz appear to be so unlike humans that it is hard to imagine any common origin for both species. Yet, as Bakhoun's persistent observation soon discovers, they do appear to share certain customs and mores with their human adversaries. Because of this possible common ground, they now begin to seem more menacing, because they somehow belong to our world yet prove eminently hostile to our being part of it. What is more, Rosny does not give his readers an extraterrestrial "out." They are invited to speculate on *how* these beings may have existed in our darkest past, to ask scientific questions instead of succumbing to primal fears. For example, what traces might the Xipéhuz have left in humankind's collective unconscious? Might perhaps humankind's common preoccupation with geometry, for instance—a shared language and symbolism of triangles and cones across diverse cultures—be due to some psychic scar left as a result of this far-distant combat with beings like the Xipéhuz? Prehistory has now become virgin territory for scientific, hence science-fictional, speculations.

The struggle with the alien question has had a long life in SF. The phenomenon of déjà vu was much discussed in Rosny's time. Maupassant's protagonist in the second version of "Le Horla," for example, considers the possibility that the demons and monsters of popular lore were in fact sightings of aliens, misunderstood at the time by the superstitious mind.[21] Some eighty years later, Arthur C. Clarke, in *Childhood's End* (1953), created a story line in which, in hard SF fashion, a significant figure of legend is revealed in fact to be a physical reality, and "supernatural" terror is explained away by rational observation. A race of aliens, the Overlords, appears in humankind's near future. They have wings, horns, and tails, and part of the plot centers around their being mistaken for devils. In the end the Overlords themselves explain the mystery: long ago they visited Earth; they were spotted by early humans, who in their fear associated horns and a tail with their most terrible superstitions. In the Xipéhuz, Rosny offers his reader the same problem but, unlike Clarke, does not actually work out a concrete solution in narrative terms. But he does seem to offer his reader, in Bakhoun's efforts to devise a winning military strategy, a concrete example of how humankind, at an early stage of development, might have acquired its geometrical mode of thinking, in this case from physical observation of beings whose essence itself was geometry. Indeed, might not the tight phalanxes Bakhoun employs be the natural response to his observations of the bodily shapes and movements of the enemy facing him?

Seen in the light of Rosny's pluralist vision, the idea of alien invasion marks a persistent refusal to accept an objectively ecological sense of humankind's place in the universe. For it is alongside the alien that the Cartesian ghost slips into SF's back door. In fact, the act of naming another species "alien" is just another way of preserving the Cartesian sanctity of the human mind, now seen to be under threat from hordes of so-called aliens who are automatically presented as physical monstrosities, beings by definition devoid of reason.

In Rosny's work another problem arises, one that is most significant for the future development of SF. This problem is one that threatens, we could say, from within: it is the spontaneous mutation that evolves out of the normative human species, and appears to menace it. *Un autre monde* addresses this question in a very strange manner, given the climate of 1890s fiction; this period saw numerous alien invasion tales, but there were also many tales in which invisible forces take over human victims. These forces' purpose of course is to create a hidden mutation, such that the outward form remains human but the being inside is transformed into an unhuman monster. Bram Stoker's Dracula is the most famous of these "body snatchers." But even earlier in France, the protagonist of Maupassant's "Le Horla" sees himself locked in mortal combat with an invisible being bent on invading his life and mind. Emerging from the research of Pasteur and the theory of germs as microbiological vectors for disease, there appears to arise a fear of unseen alien forces taking hold of our bodies and minds. In light of this fear, it appears to have been more comforting to invent a visible agent, such as Dracula, in order to locate this fear. Once a visible enemy is named, we can perhaps contain or defeat it. Dracula is ultimately tracked down; Maupassant's protagonists are judged to be insane, and put away in an asylum. In contrast, the mutant in *Un autre monde*, much like the Xipéhuz in their story, appears as a natural, neutral phenomenon. He is not the product of "evil" forces or of any human agency. One might imagine that for Rosny, given the phobias of the late nineteenth century, the spontaneous appearance of a mutated being, the potentially dangerous product of a natural process like evolution, might seem all the more frightening. But this is not so. Rosny treats the mutant as a clinical problem, one that human science assimilates, rather than rejects.

Un autre monde in fact has both aspects; there are invisible beings (the Moedigen), and there is a human who has undergone a significant mutation. But they are presented separately, in two very different configurations. First, Rosny's Moedigen are the very opposite of invaders. Even if, as is postulated, they may share with humans the same ecosystem, they exist in a different *dimension* of that system, going about their business indifferent to, and till now unknown by, human beings. Second, the way Rosny introduces his mutant differs surprisingly from the treatment of mutants in other tales of this kind: the mutant himself serves as the intermediary between the visible and invisible worlds. Instead of being a menace to humanity, his mutant powers prove a boon to human science, for they enable humans to observe and study the invisible beings. Not only are they no direct menace to humanity, but we make no attempt to "contact" them either. The humans in this story treat the strange invisible beings as nothing more than another phenomenon to observe, beings apparently as neutral toward us as subatomic particles. They are facts; we may, through observation and study, discover that they could be problematic to us; but this is not a question of intention or malicious agency. They are not "against" us; they are simply with us.

There is another striking difference as well, this time in Rosny's attitude toward science. In the scene in Maupassant's "Horla" in which Dr. Parent hypnotizes and manipulates the narrator's cousin we have the impression that science itself may have some unholy alliance with the invisible forces of the "other." Rosny's Dr. Van den Heuvel, on the other hand, is a "pure" scientist. His bias, if anything, is ecological in nature. For he is able—unusual for a scientist in the last half of the nineteenth century—to entertain the postulate that all phenomena, those we see and those we do not see, may somehow share a common physical world, and perhaps because of this may impact each other in ways yet to be discovered. This hypothesis in itself is radical for a work written at the same time as Wells's *War of the Worlds*. Indeed, the very idea that Moedigen are among us, and that they might be invisibly at work destroying our world, might seem likely to strike more terror in readers' hearts than Wells's overt Martian invasion. Instead, Rosny's scientists propose to study them, much as we study "invisible" particles today, in order to learn about the broader foundations of nature. If in Maupassant and Stoker, as in many of the myriad SF mutation tales that followed, the invisible remains a place of terror, in Rosny, the invisible realm is simply another observational landscape. In this story, Rosny goes against the logic of his time by touting scientific objectivity over fear of the unseen.

There is an even stranger aspect to *Un autre monde*. Rosny's protagonist, though obviously a mutant, is never once referred to as such. Nor do the scientists who deal with him, and thus know his powers, seem to fear him as such, despite the fact that such a spontaneous transformation of human senses would have been deeply troubling to Rosny's contemporaries. For if evolution itself appears to be a safely long-term affair, here radical change suddenly emerges from a normal human situation, implying some terrible breakdown in the processes of nature themselves. No Dracula is responsible for creating Rosny's protagonist; he simply comes to be. What is more astonishing yet is the scientists' lack of reaction when the mutant reveals something infinitely more troubling in the final paragraphs: that he is not a one-time sport of nature but in fact the founder of a lineage of mutants. He calmly informs us that he has found a mate, in an asylum of all places, married her, and produced an offspring who has the same mutated sense of sight, who is "l'exact réédition de mon organisme (the exact replica of my organism)." No reader of the time could miss this blatant dismissal of Mary Shelley's Frankenstein. Even more astonishing is the serene absence, in Dr. Van den Heuvel, of Frankenstein's horrified response to the same prospect—that a "race" of mutants might ensue.

Rosny's mutant, like Frankenstein's creature, is presented as a mixture of monstrous and superior traits. Shelley's creature addresses its creator and requests he give him a mate. Frankenstein refuses, fearing the consequences for humankind of this new race of beings. Denying his crea-ture its future, Frankenstein forces it, in the role of avenger, to turn on and destroy its creator's present existence. This is the Frankenstein impasse: to deny the bride is to obliterate all possibility of an evolutionary future for the new species; to give the bride is to breed fear of the future, of the creation of a more powerful and intelligent race that, although somehow born of man, threatens the destruction of mankind. This impasse stands in the way of an evolutionary vision of humankind going beyond itself. Most subsequent SF has come up against this barrier.[22] Classic works such as Van Vogt's *Slan*, Sturgeon's *More Than Human*, and Heinlein's *Methuselah's Children* feature groups of mutated humans whom society, out of fear of their difference and potential power, persecutes. If such stories suggest any evolutionary message, it is generally a twisted one. In Heinlein especially, the mutants fight back, developing their new genetic material in secret in order to create the superior "race" that Frankenstein (as these cases rightfully prove) so feared.

Rosny's story simply ignores the Frankenstein impasse. Without resistance or fear, Rosny's world seems to accept the advent of this new race of mutants, in the name of the advancement of science. Moreover, the mutant protagonist himself has no real fear of being persecuted. He has no intention of using his mutational advantage for any other purpose than aiding human science. "J'eus le frisson de la Terre promise" (I trembled as if I saw the Promised Land), he exclaims, when he enters the presence of Dr. Van den Heuvel, the scientist he will work with. To be sure, Rosny's mutant is aware that he is different. He prudently (given the cultural climate in which he appears) conceals his differences on the road to Amsterdam and modern science. Even so, even though he looks and acts odd, and his speech seems incomprehensible, the crowd is not hostile, merely bemused, taking him for a savage from Borneo (a Dutch colony at the time).

He has a brief fear of his otherness when taken in the hospital to a room filled with aborted monstrosities of nature in jars: "Je me trouvai assis parmi des monstres conservés dans l'alcool: foetus, enfants à forme bestiale, batraciens colosses, sauriens vaguement anthropomorphes. C'est bien là, pensai-je, ma salle d'attente. . . . Ne suis-je pas candidat à l'un de ses sépulcres à l'eau-de-vie?" (I found myself seated amidst monsters preserved in alcohol: fetuses, children with bestial shapes, colossal batrachians, saurians that were vaguely anthropomorphic. . . . Am I not a candidate for one of these sepulchers, to be preserved in alcohol?) This fear, however, is not the paranoia of Maupassant's protagonists. It is placed on an evolutionary level—the fear that he might be a one-time "sport," an evolutionary dead end. But the scientists do not quarantine him, either in a jar or in an asylum. They simply accept him and his mutated sense as an object of study. And he in turn accepts existing for the good of science. He knows he has further powers of use to science, and will reveal them when the time is right.

There remains the problematic fact that his new optical sense can perceive invisible beings in another dimension. Society would surely brand this as "paranormal," and "rational" science of the time would reject his claim without seeking to verify it. Rosny's mutant, however, not only knows he has this ability but also knows he has a moral duty to use it solely to obtain scientific knowledge of the physical world. The mutant in fact has a plan to circumvent social obstacles. He cleverly maximizes the impact of a full revelation of his powers: "Avant d'appeler l'attention sur mes connaissances extra-humaines, ne pouvais-je exciter le désir de faire étudier ma personne? Les seuls aspects physiques de mon être n'étaient-ils pas dignes d'analyse?" (Before calling attention to my knowledge of extra-human phenomena, might I not stimulate the desire in people to study my person? Were not my physical attributes alone worthy of being studied?) The mutant makes odd assumptions for his time. He assumes all future scientists will be Van den Heuvel. He also assumes that they will, like Van den Heuvel, accept this gift in his descendants, and will continue to use this new sense of sight as a scientific instrument to study the Moedigen. In the opposite sense, he is serenely certain that his descendants will continue to serve human science the way he has, that they will not seek personal advantage, or launch a vendetta against humankind: "Pourquoi ne naîtrait-il pas, de lui-aussi, des voyants du monde invisible?" (Why would there not be born, from [my son] himself as well, more seers of the invisible world?) and so on down the line.

Rosny's scientists, unlike Victor Frankenstein and his progeny, prove capable of looking beyond their fears of a mutant future. Instead of a struggle, they seek partnership with the mutants, such that both can focus on a common goal, in this case the avoidance of a possible ecological crisis brought on by the Moedigen. Rosny's mutant embodies the spirit of science in its purest form. In his final moment, he says "une béatitude infinie me pénètre " (an infinite bliss passes into me, an expression of his disinterested love of learning). In this sense, *Un autre monde* is the ancestor of later SF tales that favor cooperation with other species over paranoia and conflict, for example Murray Leinster's "First Contact" (1946). More to the point, as a story of cooperative scientific research between potentially rival human evolutionary variants, *Un autre monde* moves toward a transhuman vision.

It can be argued that most hard SF confronts the same questions Rosny raises—aliens, intelligent nonhuman beings, mutants, the Frankenstein impasse—in the same rigorous way his work does, opposing objective reason to sentimental anthropocentrism. The implacable evolutionary logic of Rosny's depiction of the death of humankind and humankind's Earth, however, offers a situation that even the hardest SF has great difficulty in resolving. In *La Mort de la Terre* Rosny presents carbon life at the end of its tether, with humankind literally its last form, in a world ecology terminally hostile to its existence. Humanity's end, however, as seen here in the broader ecology of evolving life forms, raises the possibility of a transhuman event. Can, in strictly evolutionary terms, some aspect of humanity not only pass to its successor life form, but have a significant effect on that life form's future development? Can some kind of human legacy survive the death of humans' carbon environment? How might this legacy be encoded—as species memory, genetic codes, or some other form of biophysical information—so as to be read by a posthuman entity?

Hard SF has speculated much on the posthuman, from Bernal to the significant symposium in *Foundation* 78 (2000).[23] In all of this, humankind's successor tends to remain a Bernalian construct: either some form of hybridized "enhancement" or a being composed of mental energy, like Bernal's dimorph. In neither aspect do we see beyond the mind-matter duality that continues to ensure humankind a central role in future evolution, in a sense making evolution *humankind's* evolution. In contrast, Rosny's pluralistic sense of multiple life forms' continuity-in-transformation opens a field of speculation where process is more important than product, where the *trans*human rather than the *post*human is the focus. Even after a century of speculation—scientific and fictional—on humanity's future, Rosny's rigorously evolutionary Last Man scenario remains unique, and should make us rethink our approach to this problem. Such rethinking is especially needed today, in light of recent scientific theories of the possibility of "extremophile" forms of life on Mars and, most telling, of the NASA discovery, right here on Earth at Mono Lake, California, of a form of life that has arsenic as an essential element of its DNA. The idea of an iron-based life form reclaiming the Earth seems less preposterous in light of these discoveries.

Rosny's title *La Mort de la Terre* is significant. Its focus on the death of *humankind's* Earth cements the evolutionary link between human beings and their changing physical environment. Targ is both Last Man and last example of carbon-based life. Where he stands, there can only be two possibilities: life as we embody it perishes entirely, leaving no trace, or some aspect of that life is transmuted, passed on through the ferromagnetics to some future life form. Increasingly, as we follow Targ's heroic but futile efforts to find water, to restore the lost environmental conditions that support his life form, death appears to be the only possible outcome. If science sees life going on, that is small consolation, for *our* life form will not. Even so, a close look at Targ's final moment suggests that a transhuman event might be possible within the parameters of a thoroughly scientific view of things. Indeed, if we respect the logic of the narrative, it may *already* have occurred.

The account of Targ's struggle is moving. He is clearly the conventional hero, the special man who struggles valiantly against impossible odds, and loses. On the level of human myth, he at first appears to be a recurrent figure: the chivalric knight who by means of his deeds claims the hand of the woman he most desires. Rosny's Last Man is, in this traditional sense, the finest example of human tenacity, ingenuity, and virtue. But no hero in previous fiction has faced such an extreme collective tragedy. The idea itself of a hero assumes there will always be heroes, Beowulf will always arise to fight against darkness and brutish nature. Now, however, Targ's sole "enemy" is a radical and irreversible transformation of life conditions, for which humans are only partly responsible. As hero, he is beyond good and evil. And he knows—as all forms of carbon life perish with him, despite moments of hope and wishful thinking—that there is no possibility, mythical or physical, of survival.

Targ knows his condition and its finality. Yet his final act is a free one: he gives himself consciously and of his free will to the ferromagnetics, in a quasi-existential manner. Targ knows that because he consciously accepts annihilation, he is free to exercise a final act of will, the sole freedom left to humankind at this extreme juncture. He could take the euthanasia drug, like his sister Arva and the other Last Humans, and simply drift into oblivion. Instead, Targ chooses to affirm his terminal humanity, by a willed act, in the face of the ferromagnetic successor: "Il eut un dernier sanglot; la mort entra dans son coeur et, refusant l'euthanasie, il sortit des ruines, il alla s'étendre dans l'oasis, parmi les ferromagnétaux." (He uttered a final sob; death entered into his heart and, refusing euthanasia, he left the ruins, he went to lie down in the oasis, among the ferromagnetics.)[24]

These views of Targ's final heroic act can, however, be subsumed in Rosny's broader sense of a transhuman act. For in a sense, Targ does not face his end alone after all. In the paragraph immediately preceding his act of giving himself to the ferromagnetics, he offers a short meditation on his personal relationship with Earth's environment, where humankind's Earth becomes, one last time, *his personal Earth*. Indeed, Targ's final sense of his human condition is an ecological one, in the basic sense of the word as referring to *home*. His final musings concern neither his personal act nor the terrifying certainty that his species must die with him. The full impact of his situation only comes when he understands that as Last Man, he is also the last living carbon-based life specimen on the planet, and with his passing an entire kingdom of life must pass.

Let us trace the steps whereby Targ comes to his acceptance of this sweeping vision, and to personalizing it as an ecological one, which contextualizes his final act of giving self. Targ has, in a sense, already personalized the entire history of carbon life, in a vast retrospective meditation in which he has reviewed the total evolutionary sweep, beginning with the primal sea and ending with mankind as master of the atom: "Le vainqueur capta jusqu'à la force mystérieuse qui a assemblé les atomes. 'Cette frénésie même annonçait la mort de la terre . . . la mort de la terre pour notre Règne,' murmura doucement Targ." (The conqueror harnessed everything right down to the mysterious force that bound together the atoms. "This frenzy itself announced the death of the Earth . . . the death of the Earth for our Kingdom!" Targ murmured softly.)

If Targ now has his moment of despair, it is despair on an evolutionary scale: "Un frisson secoua sa douleur. Il songea que ce qui subsistait encore de sa chair s'était transmis, sans arrêt, depuis les origines. Quelque chose qui avait vécu dans la mer primitive, sur les limons naissants, dans les marécages, dans les forêts, au sien des savanes, et parmi les cités innombrables de l'homme, ne s'était jamais interrompu jusqu'à lui. . . . Et voilà! Il était le seul homme qui palpait sur la face, redevenue immense, de la terre!" (He shivered in his suffering. He thought that whatever remained now of his flesh had been transmitted, *in an unbroken line*, since the origin of things. Some thing that had once lived in the primeval sea, on emerging alluvia, in the swamps, in the forests, in the midst of savannas, and among the multitude of man's cities, had continued unbroken down to him. . . . And here it was, the end! He was the only man whose heart beat on the face of the Earth, once again vast and empty!) With Targ, the culminating species has literally become the last piece of the life form that nurtured that species' own rise. As such, however, Targ now feels the very opposite of Pascalian alienation. For one last time, Targ finds himself at home among familiar stars, the same stars that have comforted the gaze of the trillions of humans who have preceded him: "La nuit venait. Le firmament montra ces feux charmants qu'avaient connus les yeux de trillions d'hommes. Il ne restait que deux yeux pour les contempler!" (Night fell. The firmament displayed the lovely stars that had shone for the eyes of trillions of men. There remained only two eyes to contemplate them!) Moreover, Targ, in this situation, does more than simply contemplate. He now counts the stars he knows best, *his stars*. ("Targ dénombra ceux qu'il avait préférés aux autres" [Targ counted out those stars he had preferred to all others].) Finally, at the end of human time, he looks on as the most familiar of mankind's heavenly bodies rises, "l'astre ruineux . . . l'astre troué, argentin et légendaire" (the star of disasters . . . the star riddled with holes, silvery, the stuff of legend). The Moon has accompanied humankind on its rise and fall, has been its most constant companion. It is at this moment, when Targ is fully in harmony with his ecology—physical and mythical—that he chooses to join the ferromagnetics. It is an act that makes him a willing part of the larger evolutionary process as it unfolds.

But the novella does not end here. Its simple, one-sentence final paragraph clearly suggests that something more has occurred than a terminal, statistically meaningless offering of the last carbon molecules that exist on Earth: "Ensuite, humblement, quelques parcelles de la dernière vie humaine entrèrent dans la Vie Nouvelle." (Then, humbly, a few small pieces of the last human life entered into the New Life.) This final sentence suggests the possibility of a startling shift of focus from the human to the transhuman. It offers the outline for three important steps in tracing this process.

First, the narrator indicates *what* has happened; second, the narrator suggests *why* this might have happened; third, the narrator offers a possible speculation on *how* Targ's act may have effected the transhuman passage. First, following the temporal adverb *ensuite* (then), marking movement beyond the human, comes the narrator's use of the preterite, the tense that designates completed action in the past: *entrèrent*. The narrator who has followed Targ's final moments so closely is now, by the logic of the tenses, speaking *after the death* of the last human. The use of this past tense certainly suggests that what, logically, must now be a posthuman entity, is at this point speaking to an audience that, because all human life is gone, has to be posthuman as well. Mankind's story, at least, has passed to a successor life form. Second, the word *parcelle* points to an interconnected, ecological system of life, a system in which whatever Targ has passed on must continue, in the larger scheme of things, to have a function. In such a system, if individual forms of life perish, life itself continues to change and evolve. Third, the adverb *humblement* appears to be a sign of empathy on the part of the narrator, this time for what Targ has given, and for his decision to become the vector for now-dead carbon life. This expression of sympathy, responding across the void to Targ's selfless act, may explain the mechanism that has allowed a special form of information not only to pass into the new life but also to significantly influence its further evolution, indeed the creation of a future intelligence, which in turn is interested in telling and hearing Targ's story. This mechanism is altruism.

The temporal logic of the narrator's final sentence is striking. The adverb *ensuite* (then) indicates a narrative instance that follows Targ's death. Then, as noted, the preterite *entrèrent* (entered into) indicates the absolute pastness of human life. The narrator's use of the preterite is highly significant in this context. Had the narrator chosen the imperfect tense *entraient* (were entering into), we could perhaps still place the narration before Targ's death. Targ having lain down among the ferromagnetics, the imperfect verb would depict him not as dead but in the act of dying; and these final words could then be said to represent his dying thoughts, presented in *style indirect libre*, with the narrator showing such intimate knowledge of Targ's thoughts that the two voices become almost indistinguishable. The use of the *passé simple* preterite, however, places narrator and audience beyond Targ, locates them somewhere in a distant evolutionary future. The narrative logic of this verb tense affirms that some significant part of Targ's "matter" *has already* passed on to future life forms. At this specific moment, the logic of tenses is clear. If Targ the Last Man is dead, who or what is narrating this final moment? To whom is it being told? A narrator and listener are out there, beyond Targ; and they are clearly capable of understanding and sympathizing with his, and humankind's, final moments.

In both *Les Xipéhuz* and *Un autre monde,* a sudden shift of evolutionary perspective takes place in the final paragraph. These final shifts bring about a broader vision, a promise of evolutionary development. The same is true for the last statement of *La Mort de la Terre,* but the vision here is infinitely more challenging. For humankind is not ascending but perishing, hence forced to imagine what, if any, role human achievements might have in the evolutionary future of life. The contrast with *Les Xipéhuz* is clear. In that work, Bakhoun meets and defeats a rival species with whom he has no direct communication. The passing of the Xipéhuz is as final as is the total extinction of carbon life here. But to the human reader, Bakhoun's culminating act, his empathy for the lost species, looks forward to a new vision of life, one capable of condemning the law of survival of the fittest as a cosmic crime against life. The final paragraph of *Un autre monde* offers a similar leap across evolutionary boundaries. This time the voice is that of the mutant whose "race," now a physical reality, might in some future time conflict with mankind. Instead, however, the mutant chooses willingly to cooperate with human science, working toward the common exploration of a larger ecological system, one that now widens to include the alternately evolved Moedigen and the possibility that their activities may in fact impact what has now become a common or shared world.

In *La Mort de la Terre,* the question of evolutionary continuity is more problematic, for here humankind is the dying species that sees its evolutionary progress ruptured forever. In the final sentence, however, after that rupture has occurred, the narrator's use of the strange word *parcelle* for the part of Targ that passes into the new life form suggests the presence of an evolving system of life, with which Targ's seemingly terminal act is interconnected, its past given a future. In contrast, in the earlier passage where Targ's situation is presented in terms that echo Pascal's reed, the narrator's word is *particule,* which simply means "small part" (*petite partie*). *Particule* implies no concern about *what* the particle is a part of. It is a word, as in *la physique des particules* (particle physics), that belongs to what Pascal calls the *esprit de géometrie,* to the world as defined by the mind-matter duality. The word *parcelle,* in contrast, implies the larger context of what we call today an ecological system. The *Dictionnaire de l'Académie française* defines it as a "petite partie de quelque chose" (a small part of something). Its use, at this juncture, more than suggests that we are dealing with an ecological vision; it asserts that even in the seeming finality of Targ's death as *particule*, he remains, as *parcelle*, part of a whole. The word signifies both an assemblage of diverse parts and something that, potentially at least, remains a constituent portion of some larger, future whole.[25] It is stated that what Targ gives is an element in a dynamic system of events, a system in continuous transformation and evolution.

In order for there to be interconnection, there must be some form of communication between species and life forms in evolution. But what is the agent of such communication? What element makes *particules* into *parcelles*? In every case of interspecies conflict or rivalry in these three novellas, an act of what Rosny calls "sympathy" (*sympathie*) appears to enable some factor—call it a meme, a gene, or something not yet known—to pass from species to species, creating a chain of communication that permits life forms to continue to evolve. Seen in this light, Targ's situation is different only in degree, with passage now from one *kingdom* of life to another. Targ's kingdom finds itself, however, in the situation of the Xipéhuz: another life form is displacing us. Despite this, several times during the narrative, Targ has expressed sympathy with the ferromagnetics, overcoming his bitterness toward his situation: "Parfois, Targ l'exécrait; parfois, une sympathie craintive s'éveillait dans son âme. N'y avait-il pas une analogie mystérieuse, et même une obscure fraternité, entre ces êtres et les hommes? Certes, les deux règnes étaient moins loin l'un de l'autre que chacun ne l'était du minéral inerte. Qui sait si leur consciences, à la longue, ne se seraient pas comprises!" (At times Targ reviled it; at times a fearful sympathy awakened in his soul. Was there not some mysterious analogy, an obscure fraternity even, between these beings and mankind? Certainly, the two kingdoms were closer to each other than either was to the inert mineral world. Who knew whether their forms of consciousness, in time, might not come to understand each other!) Targ's evolutionary empathy in fact, at one point, stretches beyond even the ferromagnetic rival to embrace what he sees as the endlessly patient, ultimately triumphant, mineral kingdom of life: "A chaque mouvement de la lampe, des éclairs rebondissaient, mystérieux et féeriques. Les innombrables âmes des cristaux s'éveillaient à la lumière. . . . Targ y voyait un reflet de la vie minérale, de cette vie vaste et minuscule, menaçante et profonde, qui avait le dernier mot avec les hommes, que aurait, un jour, le dernier mot avec le règne ferromagnétique." (At each movement of the lamp, rays bounced around the walls, mysterious and enchanting. The souls of myriad crystals awoke to his light. . . . Targ saw there a reflection of mineral life, of that life form both vast and minuscule, menacing and deep, that had the last word on mankind, that, one day, would have the last word on the ferromagnetic kingdom as well.)

Beyond Targ's death, however, if there is to be communication, the act of sympathy must come from the other side of the evolutionary divide, in this case from the ferromagnetics. But they, at the time of Targ's demise, are clearly at a precognitive stage. The question of course arises: Being as we know them to be at present, are they ultimately capable of developing the faculties needed for such an act of "sympathy"? And yet the statement of Rosny's narrator in the final sentence suggests that some such development has had to take place, otherwise there would be no post-Targ narration. The preterite tense tells us that transfer has occurred, and we may infer that it was brought about by means of some kind of sympathy. We are left, however to speculate on how this might have happened. Rosny's story, at this point, is an early example of the SF mystery, asking us to take a seemingly impossible event as literal truth and then inviting us to speculate on ways it might have come about. Did Targ's *parcelles* contain a code, gene, or other means of transferring information? Did this in turn affect the course of ferromagnetic evolution? Did it provide a factor that determined the creation of a form of consciousness ultimately allowing communication across the gulf of evolutionary time?

Rosny gives us a clue to how the transhuman transfer of evolutionary traits occurred. To follow it, however, the reader must abandon anthropocentric thinking. Anthropocentrism has let other Last Man stories execute a last-minute swerve that saves some part of the human from total annihilation. Narratives from Granville's *Le dernier homme* (1803) to recent works including Maurice Blanchot's *Le dernier homme* (1957) and Margaret Atwood's *Oryx and Crake* (which the French again translate as *Le dernier homme;* 2004) have deployed the same anthropocentric gambit: at the final moment they allow the last human to escape humankind's material destiny by moving from history to allegory. The form of fiction that by its very premise abolishes humankind ends by preserving a single human voice, speaking endlessly into the void, as if human consciousness will always exist, and the human voice will always have an audience.[26]

In contrast, Rosny builds anthropocentrism into his text only to pass beyond it. At one point Targ and Arva, as they contemplate the ferromagnetics, see themselves in the mirror of the future: "C'étaient les vainqueurs. Le temps était devant eux et pour eux, les choses coïncidaient avec leur volonté obscure; un jour, leurs descendants produiraient des pensées admirables et manieraient des énergies merveilleuses." (They were the conquerors. Time lay before them, was on their side, the way of things coincided with their obscure will; one day, their descendants would produce admirable thoughts, and wield marvelous sources of energy.) In light of Targ's ultimate sense of physical finality, this vision of a ferromagnetic golden age might appear to be wishful thinking. Yet what if Targ's *parcelles*, as freely given, in fact have transmitted this same message, this same desire for development, across the evolutionary void—might it not have become physical reality in some far-distant future?

Rosny's narrator has from the outset suggested sympathy with humanity by closely focusing on the thoughts and actions of Targ and the Last Men throughout the telling. There is nothing unusual in this for a narrator this side of Targ's death. But for the posthuman narrator of the final paragraph, any such expression of sympathy is not only surprising but revealing. Targ, as we know, has given the last elements of his carbon life freely, as a willed gift, in contradistinction to the unwillingness of his fellow humans to give this life at all. Now the narrator makes a comment on the quality of the gift itself, describing the nature of the *parcelles* as themselves entering "humbly" (*humblement*) into the New Life. The narrator's choice of this word, which implies sympathetic judgment of Targ's act, offers an evolutionary clue that the mechanism that has enabled the transfer of information between life forms is *altruism*.

At this point, some might object that Rosny's narrator is simply the conventional omniscient narrator, and that all this discussion of past tense narration and narrative audience after the death of the Last Man is specious. A clear case can be made, however, that Rosny may have seen his narrator as an "evolutionary narrator," that is, a narrator that speaks for the evolutionary process itself. Such a narrator, by definition, can never be omniscient, because evolution is an always-ongoing, open-ended process. Evidence that Rosny intends to create an evolutionary narrator comes from the carefully controlled change he makes in narrative focus as the story of the Last Men proceeds. The narrator of chapter 1 appears to be the conventional third person narrator—the detached, objective eye recording an important scene (the beginning of the fatal earthquakes) in the drama of the Last Men. Recorded dialogue and general commentary dominate. This is the *mise en scène* of Targ as principal actor. A sudden rupture occurs in chapter 2, however. All at once, the focus shifts from outside Targ's mind to the workings of his memory, which contains "the history of the great catastrophes," the retrospective story that now unfolds: "Depuis cinq siècles, les hommes n'occupaient plus, sur la planète, que des îlots dérisoires." (For five hundred centuries, men have occupied, on the entire surface of the planet, ridiculously small enclaves.) The narrative focus, now inside Targ's memory, sweeps back to encompass the story of the gradual fall of humankind and its environment from its industrial apogee to Targ's own situation. Mirroring this, the narrative tenses undergo their own radical change of focus. For without warning, the narrator seems to abandon history for an act of empathy, modulating its voice from third person, first to the first person plural "nous," then to a totally unexplained "je," a first person singular now capable of speaking in the future tense: "Lorsqu'une conscience supérieure se décèlera dans le nouveau règne, je pense qu'elle reflétera surtout cet étrange phenomène." (Whenever a superior consciousness will be discovered in the new species, I think it will especially reflect this strange phenomenon.) With this shift, the narrator places itself within the community of Last Man ("nous") and at the same time speaks in a personal voice that says that it both "thinks" and thinks within the broader framework of the future evolution of new species. This narrator will revert to third-person discourse. But its focus, from this moment until Targ's final act, becomes an increasingly intimate one, a third-person narration that, at the moments Targ meditates on humanity's past or dreams of things to come, becomes almost indistinguishable from the protagonist's own speaking voice, in a sort of *style indirect libre*. The two voices join in an empathy that culminates in Targ's great visionary dream that itself spans all of carbon life. If we admit on the basis of the past tense of the final sentence that the voice of the narrator now speaks from a time beyond Targ's death, then the empathy this narrator displays for Targ as he approaches his terminal moment may be an indication that some aspect of the Last Man not only has survived, but may have acted as a force of transformation for the narrating species' subsequent evolution. Rosny asks us to consider here, on the vaster scale of posthuman destiny, an act of evolutionary altruism expressing the same motivation as Bakhoun's final invocation. Targ, however, has grown beyond Bakhoun. For Targ is acting for the good not of another competing species but of a new kingdom of life, whose species have not yet been defined by evolutionary process. Targ looks beyond the survival of species to the survival of the principle of Life, even if that means mineral life. Still today, Darwinians ponder the possibility that such acts of selflessness may do more to advance the evolutionary process than adversarial struggle or heroic defiance.[27] It is Targ's final act that sets him apart from the other last humans. This could mean that his genetic, or memetic, material is special among all of surviving carbon life. His altruism may provide the vector whereby this material, given selflessly, is able to pass, effectively, across the evolutionary gulf. If we take the narrator's posthuman situation as material truth, then it appears that Targ's gift may have succeeded, where the same material, given reluctantly, or defiantly, might have failed.

Certainly Rosny, as rigorous evolutionist, does not minimize the immensity of the transhuman gulf. Altruism remains an improbable bottle in the evolutionary sea, and Rosny understands this. Yet he uses the possibility of a posthuman narrator to startle us into thinking that a purely material transfer may be feasible in strictly evolutionary terms. Altruism, in fact, plays a similar role in many endgames in later SF. An altruistic act, for example, is at the center of Heinlein's much later novel *Have Space Suit, Will Travel* (1958). Here young Kip stands before a cosmic bar of justice. The judges rule to wipe out humanity as a dangerous species, condemning the entire human race to "rotation," to total annihilation. Kip's first act is to blurt out his defiance of this judgment. In doing so, he does little more than affirm the judges' conviction that humanity is dangerous because it is unpredictable by nature. Nonetheless, they offer Kip the individual the option of staying with them, in a sense of becoming the Last Man. He refuses and insists on being sent back to share the fate of the rest of humanity This altruistic act stops the inflexible judges cold in their tracks. Their "logic" is so confounded by Kip, his response is so inconceivable, that they suspend their judgment. Kip finds himself in Targ's position, if for different reasons. By refusing to save his own life, he becomes, in the eyes of the alien judges, the redeemer of a species whose collective acts have proven powerless to prevent their annihilation. It is Kip's sole act, as much a statistical improbability as the passage of Targ's genetic material, that gives all human beings a reprieve, more time to evolve and possibly to avoid their future fate by acquiring, in this interim, the power to challenge and defeat their judges. The fact that Kip's single altruistic act results in such sweeping consequences can be dismissed as a juvenile fantasy. Read in the light of Rosny's Last Man, however, the foundation of Heinlein's narrative can be understood to be a very real, if highly speculative, evolutionary concept.

Rosny and the Logic of Hard SF

Rosny is important in the history of SF because of his rigorous adherence to the scientific vision of evolution, and his ability to construct complex narratives that reject humanist for pluralist visions of evolutionary history. He is perhaps the first writer to launch the master narrative of SF, which traces the evolution of humankind through its technological and environmental transformations, up to the ultimate challenge of transhuman possibility. It is the same master narrative, elaborated (and in the end possibly betrayed) by writers from Bernal and Clarke to the cyberpunks, that could be said to define SF in the twentieth century. Of all his achievements, however, Rosny is finally important as the inventor of a science-fictional manner of thinking. It was Rosny who first created, in *Un autre monde*, *La Mort de la Terre*, and other works, a genuine logic of hard SF. Rosny was first to adhere to what became, for later SF, a material imperative. His narratives ground all possibility of figurative interpretation in the literal, material fact of what is stated. Thus, in the final paragraph of Targ's story, the reader cannot dismiss the past tense, and its denoting of a posthuman narrator, as "convention." We cannot simply reject the logic of space and time (and grammatical tense) in favor of conventional "suspension of disbelief." Rather we are asked to take the situation as literal fact, and then to work, in extrapolative fashion, within the parameters of material logic to find some physical means of explaining the existence of this narrator, and from there to identify the vector that has permitted vital communication between two profoundly different chemical kingdoms and histories. Rosny's bequest to later hard SF writers may be the transhuman problem; more than that, however, his legacy is a particular way of reading narrative, in a purely literal manner. Rosny offers future writers a new way of thinking; he asks them to look beyond metaphors and conventions to the physical facts of the narrative. Let us look briefly at how Rosny's logic works in two narratives that rewrite the Last Man story in very different scientific climates: Arthur C. Clarke's *Childhood's End* (1953) and Gregory Benford's *Timescape* (1980).

As noted, Rosny's use of tense makes us define as posthuman the narrator who speaks in the last lines of *La Mort de la Terre*. And by the same token, Rosny asks us to conceive an audience for this narrator, hence to find a motive for posthumans wanting to listen to this terminal story. By the time of his *Childhood's End*, Clarke is clearly aware of the problem Rosny raised: that the conventional Last Man narrative is illogical, and that he must devise a new narrative strategy to tell it. He is also aware that readers will ask why anyone would want to hear that story, if humanity has already transcended itself and become something totally other. In the novel, human children suddenly opt out of the adult world and become the catalysts that convert all earthly matter, animate or inanimate, into the "Overmind." The novel could end here, for the Overmind is so radically other that, logically, it neither hears nor cares about any story humankind could tell. At the very most, the Overmind might be interested in humankind's creation myth. But that is not the story told. Instead we have the story of humankind's demise, a story that logically no longer has a human audience. Clarke understands the paradox, but he persists in wanting a Last Man and his story. He also understands that this Last Man must have a listener within the text. And he creates one—the Overlords.

If we follow Clarke's logic, humankind is simply the match that starts the fire, the spark that transforms everything on Earth into transcendent energy. Nothing we call "human" passes into the Overmind. At the same time, however, Clarke keeps open the possibility that some aspect of the human might survive, might be passed on to someone somewhere. Clarke thus creates an alternate narrative to that of the Overmind, one in which such a transhuman transfer might be possible. His protagonist, Jan, successfully schemes to be taken to the Overlords' planet in the belly of a whale they transport to their museum of cosmic species. He does so knowing that when he returns from this near-the-speed-of-light adventure, all that he knows and loves will be gone. But he does not imagine that he will find even the Earth dying, and himself the sole witness to its destruction. Jan tells his story. But now he has a declared listener, for the Overlords are there, located between his dying words and the cosmic void, taking in his words, recording them for some obscure posterity.

Rosny's Last Man narrative retells the myths of human destiny, exhausting them, until Targ stands as purely material entity before his evolutionary future. Clarke seems to follow a similar logic. Step by step, the story of Jan both evokes and demythologizes the Christian narrative. Jan has a role like that of Jonah, and perhaps his avatar, Christ. If so, Jan's death may offer hope of "salvation" to someone or something; indeed, if his words then become the "gospel," they too must be saved. The Overlords (their name suggests the pride that goeth before a fall) are an advanced yet inexplicably reprobate intergalactic race. If the Overmind is a God entity, then they, like Lucifer's fallen horde, are its emissaries, must do its bidding. As a race they have been passed over by a process that reminds us of election, a process that has chosen humankind instead of them as its vehicle for transcendence. The Overlords remain curators of a Cuvier-like inventory of extinct or dead-end species. What they collect from Earth, however, may offer them a way out of eternal damnation. Transporting the whale, they catch Jan, and literally place him, the Christ-Jonah figure, at the center of their world. He thus becomes their potential savior, his words the Logos that might allow them to escape from evolutionary stagnation.

All of this, however, we learn, like the Overlords' horns and tails, is preevolutionary apprehension, earlier humankind's superstitious vision of what is now revealed as secular scientific reality. In fact, humankind's relation to the Overlords is more like that of Pascal's rational man to the overbearing universe. They are powerful, and have vast technological superiority over humankind. Yet it is because of its rational (here pararational) faculties that humanity, however physically weak, finds the way to Overmind. Once the Overmind forms, Jan's final words, his Logos, are meaningless to it. Yet for the Overlords, might not these words, like Targ's *parcelles*, contain a code or some information that would open up, to Overlord cryptographers, a path to evolutionary destiny? Might not these words, as with Targ's legacy, someday become flesh, giving the Overlords the means to *become human*, or at least let them incorporate some aspect of our otherwise lost species, putting them on an evolutionary path toward eventual access to Overmind?

Gregory Benford, in his novel *Timescape* (1980), again takes up the Last Man challenge.[28] It would seem at first that the science Benford deploys—communication faster than the speed of light and the physical possibility it raises of an infinite number of worlds—abolishes any need for a transhuman experience. In such a universe, the iron laws of causality seem to be circumvented, election and evolution are reduced to localized phenomena within a larger "timescape." Even so, in this highly flexible space-time net, with its infinity of apparent doors and escape hatches, the fact remains that if there are many worlds, each of these worlds must end, each must have its Last Man. Localizing the Last Man problem has not made it go away. If there is a myriad of Last Men, each must face the same problem Targ and Jan face: they all hope somehow to transmit something of humanity across the barrier of finality, to create the continuity that defines the transhuman moment. In Benford's novel, Targ's final moment has been multiplied by x. Each space-time world out of infinitely many has been localized. The question has become: as each world ends, how can the words of *its* Last Man breach the gulf of *its* causality? In such a universe, is it meaningful to speak of a trans-anything? Is the timescape nothing more than a bundle of disconnected *particules?*

In *Timescape*, the not-too-distant Earth of 1998 is dying from ecocatastrophe, one caused this time wholly by humankind. Two Cambridge scientists, Gregory Markham and John Renfrew, seek to avert disaster by using tachyons, particles that move faster than light, to send messages to the scientists of the past, warning them of the impending danger, hoping to get earlier humankind to alter the course of things before it is too late. They succeed in communicating this information to a scientist in 1963, Gordon Bernstein, and in the nick of time the process is halted, Earth is saved. But the question is: whose Earth is saved? Apparently, at the instant the message from the future is received, the time line splits. Bernstein's Earth of 1963 will trace its own path, in which there will be no diatom bloom, and no assassination of John F. Kennedy. The world of 1998, however, the sender of the message, remains the world of ecodisaster and Kennedy's assassination; it must go to its doom.

It seems at first that possibilities for new worlds are infinite. In the dazzling flux of tachyons, each instant divides into its own universe, new worlds without end. There is no longer a need either for apocalypse or for the protracted agonies of evolution. The long view of things is the very opposite of Rosny's. Yet, just as Rosny's readers must focus on Targ's fate, Benford's readers, still bound by the laws of narrative, must follow the individual destiny of Markham and his world. The infinity of possibilities remains a theoretical construct; as concrete reality, Markham's world perishes as inexorably as the world of Targ. And in its demise, it snares the reader in Rosny's ecological play of forces within which and only within which the transhuman possibility can occur.

Rosny's story is poignant because it holds to a linear vision of time. Edens can be dreamt, but time, like Heraclitus's river, is physically anchored in the vast flow of living things for which Targ's humankind speaks. Benford's physics localizes linear time to individual human units. In Rosny's space-time, each individual action interconnects to, resonates with, the whole of evolutionary history. In Benford's world, on the contrary, it appears that each action, even those that alter the past, concerns only its local time line and no other. We realize this when Gordon, in his present, meets the physicist Markham. The reader has already seen Markham die in a plane crash in 1999. But now we have a different "Markham" time line, with no plane crash in its future, and probably no tachyons either. Here we have two world lines, out of a vast possible number, bifurcating, each moving inexorably forward. Most likely it is the particles that move faster than the speed of light, shooting through our universe, invisible like Moedigen, that bring about such moments of double vision, improbably connecting two of an infinite number of possible time tracks.

As if in answer to Rosny's monolithic evolutionary endgame, Benford's tachyons seem to promise recapture of a human constant in a vast universe of otherwise indifferent and incomprehensible forces. For if each of us, theoretically, can at any instant generate another world, then causality fails. The river metaphor for time gives way to a Spinozan vision of space-time as a great tableau, where nature itself appears to be modeled on the paradigm of rational order: "Time and space were themselves players, vast lands engulfing the figures, a weave of future and past. There was no river-run of years. The abiding loops of causality ran both forward and back. The timescape rippled with waves, roiled and flexed, a great beast in the dark sea" (238).

Even so, Benford's very description seems to tell us there is no escape from Rosny's linear evolution. For even in the act of discarding individual human importance in the great canvas of time, his narrator seems to reassert the human element by using the all-too-human device of metaphor. Because this "timescape" remains the product of a "painter," there abides, even in this neutral field of forces, the *necessity* of a human consciousness, a sentient entity capable of deciding to "collapse" wave functions, or not to collapse them. And so, despite the fearful symmetry of the mind-universe it posits, Benford's text remains haunted by Rosny's classic sense of time as a one-way stream of life and death. As its loops and waves morph into some great beast in the sea, Benford's timescape resounds with echoes of Rosny's paean to life in the cosmic sense. A plane crash in 1999 plunges Markham to his physical end. As the plane plunges, the hard fact of linear time, of his single time line, emerges within his interior monologue, to coincide with, then overwhelm, his unified theory to space, time, and the universe, a theory he will never utter: "They [the trees] rushed by faster and faster and Markham thought of a universe with one wave function, scattering into the new states of being as a paradox formed inside it like the kernel of an idea—If the wave function did not collapse. . . . Worlds lay ahead of him, and worlds behind. There was a sharp crack and he suddenly saw what should have been" (309).

Beyond all the paradoxes of time displacement, there is always a single, irreducible fact—that of biological time. Time displacements may challenge the universality of time. But there is no denying, and the quantified universe of tachyons is no exception, that for any localized time line there is always an end. In Benford's novel, that locality remains Markham's 1999, set on its inexorable path, experiencing its own unique form of ecodisaster, thus called on to make its own challenge to the transhuman barrier. Even in this relativized timescape, the passing of any world remains poignant, if not tragic in Rosny's sense of the total end of a vast plurality of living species. Thus Benford's novel ends on a muted tone, with Markham's partner John Renfrew 1999's Last Man. As with Targ's final, futile search for water, Renfrew attempts one last time to break out of his time frame, to make tachyon contact with some other space-time location. The message he receives, however, is not from Bernstein's world but from what Renfrew believes to be the year 2349, a location ever so close yet separated by an unfathomable gulf of "noise." He realizes that he stands, in his dying world, at some tachyon junction, a cosmic way station with messages coming from all space-time directions: "He shook his head. All form and structure was eroded by the overlapping of many voices, a chorus. Everyone was talking at once, and no one could hear" (392). We are far from the serene vision of Benford's cosmic artist. From Renfrew's point of view, his world is an impossibly insignificant speck, lost in a vast canvas of worlds. Once again, Renfrew's situation is that of Pascal's human condition. For as the babble of voices changes into terrifying cosmic silence, he remains suspended between infinities. All the generators shut down in Renfrew's laboratory, all the buildings and streets fall suddenly empty. Suddenly he, too, like Targ, knows in his physical body that however complex this "stream" of worlds he envisions, time's river still flows for him: "Causality's leaden hand would win out."

Even so, as is not the case for Rosny's death of the Earth, Renfrew still takes comfort in knowing his world is one among an infinite number of time lines. He senses a vast multidimensional array of worlds that, unlike

Rosny's "other world," have absolutely no contact with each other. This is comforting in a sense, for if there is no single interpenetrating ecology that gathers all these individual time lines, then each world is, as Renfrew puts it, at least "safe" from the others: "The soothing human world of flowing time would go on, a sphinx yielding none of her secrets. An infinite series of grandfathers would live out their lives safe from Renfrew" (393). Once again, the final possibility for Renfrew is Pascal's wager. If he sees himself forever lost in the world of tachyons and its infinite timescape, at the same time, it is by openly accepting that he is lost that he paradoxically feels "elated, free" (393). In his limited world, Renfrew, like Targ, must go to his end. But while Targ and Érê are doomed to live out the terrible collapse of their hopeless Edenic dream, Renfrew finds his arcadia just down the road in his tangible temporal present. His family still awaits him, as well as the famous preserves on the shelf, which can keep all of them alive for a long time. With Rosny we move in a straight line, living through increasingly painful failures to survive, until the family circle itself is decimated. Benford's tour de force, in contrast, ends with a whimper. In this novel all about messages and communication, the final human voice is that of domesticity. But it is still a message; as such, it defies the messageless void of *res extensa*. Benford's Last Man can console himself in his misery. For Renfrew, hearing a myriad of possible messages in the swirl of tachyon data, knows he is not alone. Stories are being told, even though he cannot understand them. What is more, he can retire to his survivalist bunker where, as in Heinlein's Farnham's Freehold, things may keep going on after all. Some serendipitous twist in space-time may save his family yet.

To paraphrase Robert Forward, humans don't count, intelligence does. For Rosny, however, humans do count, but the interconnectedness and continuity of life counts even more. We see, then, why the logic of Rosny's narratives is transhuman rather than simply posthuman. At Targ's transhuman moment, the logic of verb tense and syntax connects to the larger logic of a broad ecology of matter—living and inert—in transformation. Life and world form a vast system that must evolve. In the evolution of hard SF, however, Forward's vision appears today to overshadow Rosny's. Increasingly, the scientist-writer seems to lean toward a vision that favors the conversion of matter into mind. For example, in the lead story of his 1994 anthology *Matter's End*, "Mozart on Morphine," Benford's scientist-protagonist, a string theorist, not only makes the classic case for mind-matter duality but moves in the direction of Spinoza's vision of matter *as mind*.[29] This is a story about accidents and illness, the frailty of thinking reeds: "We seem so small. Yet we have a common, perhaps arrogant impression that we matter, somehow" (21). There is still an echo of Rosny's evolutionism in the pun of the title. For is not the end of matter the end of mind and life as well? But Benford's protagonist reverses this proposition: might not the end of matter instead mark the beginning of mind? With string theory we have the possibility, only suggested by the tachyon universe, that matter and mind are in fact one and the same, with mind becoming an entity like Spinoza's rationalist God, *deus sive natura.* Benford's protagonist goes on to speculate that humans indeed might matter, if the physical universe were revealed by science to be mind: "Still, there emerges now evidence of mental processes at work on many levels of physical reality. We may be part of some larger act. For example, perhaps we contribute remotely to the universe's thinking about itself" (220). The turn is elegant. But the result is the sort of imagined recapture that Rosny ultimately refused, where mind seeks impossible parity between itself and the extended world.

The quotation from Goethe (Mephisto tempting Faust) that Benford offers as an epigraph to "Mozart on Morphine" can serve as an apt description of the difference between the vision of his fictional physicist and that of Rosny: "All theory, my friend, is gray / But the golden tree of life springs green." Rosny chronicles the growth of the tree of life from green to ferromagnetic rust and hopefully beyond. His work remains essential today, for it not only articulates a key crux of SF extrapolation—the transhuman possibility—but offers, in working out Targ's evolutionary destiny, a viable speculative alternative to the resurgent Cartesianism of much hard SF. Rosny's ecological pluralism strives to reach beyond the anthropocentric barrier of human culture. It reaches beyond that faith in reason that serves Bakhoun so well yet confounds Targ. Rosny's broad sense of the evolution of life is a powerful antidote to the humanocentric sentimentality of many SF works, even those that claim to be most "scientific." It offers as well a sobering alternative to much of the "ecological" rhetoric we endure today.

One final comment. Some might conclude from our comparisons of Rosny's work to that of both Verne and Wells that Verne and Wells ultimately set story above science, while Rosny stuck to the text of science, perhaps to the detriment of the art of storytelling. It is true that both Verne and Wells were master storytellers who found novel ways of integrating new or at least novel scientific concepts into conventional narrative forms, especially the historical and travel narrative. Rosny, however, with his sparse prose and plausible analytical descriptions of places, times, and beings that are otherwise products of extrapolative imagination, has created a mode of storytelling that remains unique in its objectivity and honesty. Rosny proves that when science does write the fiction, the writing does not have to be bad. It is true that Rosny's style is often crabbed, lacking in articulation. We have tried to render this faithfully in translation, sometimes to the detriment of the English prose. But there are moments of high poetry. And there are powerful narrative moments. Who can forget Bakhoun's lament at the Darwinian annihilation of the Xipéhuz? Who is not moved when Dr. Van den Heuvel, faced with a being his world would invariably reject as mutant or madman, decides to use his new form of vision to advance knowledge of the unknown? Who does not thrill at the thought that some modest parcel of dying humanity might shoot the gulf, become a creative element in the evolution of the "next" form of life? These moments are proof of the unique literary power of Rosny's blend of fact and vision.

The Xipéhuz[1]

To Léon Hennique, his friend and admirer[2]
—J.-H. Rosny aîné[3]

FIRST BOOK

I. The Forms

The time was a thousand years before that great gathering of peoples that later gave rise to the civilizations of Nineveh, Babylon, Ecbatane.[4] The nomad tribe of Pjehou, with its donkeys, its horses and cattle, was crossing the hostile forest of Kzour,[5] toward sunset, into the sheet of slanting rays. The song of waning day swelled, hovered in the air, wafted down from harmonious flocks. All were extremely tired, they refrained from speaking, seeking a lovely clearing where the tribe could light the sacred fire, prepare the evening meal, sleep protected from marauding beasts, behind a double row of burning coals.

The clouds turned iridescent, illusory landscapes flickered on the four horizons, the night gods exhaled the song that rocks to sleep, and the tribe continued to walk on. A scout reappeared, came galloping up, heralding the clearing and water, a pure spring.

The tribesmen uttered three long cries; all went faster. Childish laughter broke out; the horses and donkeys themselves, accustomed to recognizing the halt was near, seeing the return of the messengers and hearing the cheers of the nomads, tossed their manes proudly.

The clearing appeared. The charming spring forced its way between the moss and bushes. The nomads were confronted with a phantasmagorical sight.

There was first of all a large circle of bluish, translucent cones, with their pointed ends upright, each one with a volume of about half a man. A few clear stripes, a few dark circumvolutions, were scattered over their surface; each had near its base a dazzling star.

Farther away, something just as strange, "strata," strata-like forms, positioned themselves vertically, looking somewhat like birch bark and whorled with versicolored, elliptical markings.[6] There were also, here and there, Forms that were nearly cylindrical, varied in fact, some slender and tall, others short and squat, all of bronze color, dotted with green, all having, like the strata, the same characteristic point of light.

The tribe looked on, awestruck. A superstitious fear paralyzed the bravest among them. It grew even more as the Forms began to undulate in the grayish shadows of the clearing. And suddenly, their stars pulsating and vibrating, the cones became elongated, the cylinders and the strata made a rustling noise like water thrown on flame, all coming toward the nomads with accelerating speed.

The tribe, spellbound by this spectacle, moved not at all, continued to look on. The Forms hit them. The shock was tremendous. Whole clusters of warriors, women, children collapsed to the floor of the forest, mysteriously struck down as if by the sword of lightning. Then, to the survivors, this dark terror gave back their strength, the wings of agile flight. And the Forms, at first massed in formation, organized in ranks, spread out around the tribe, pitilessly clinging to those in flight. The dreadful attack, however, was not totally effective: it killed some, stunned others, but never wounded. A few reddish drops issued from the nose, the eyes, the ears of the dying, but the others, intact, soon got up, resumed their fantastic rout, into the paling dusk.

Whatever was the nature of these Forms, they acted in the manner of sentient beings,[7] not like elemental things, having like living beings inconstancy, and diversity of appearances, clearly choosing their victims, never mistaking the nomads for plants or even for animals.

Soon the fastest tribesmen realized they were no longer being pursued. Exhausted, torn asunder, they did not dare to turn back toward this wondrous thing. Far away, among the tree trunks steeped in shadow, the radiant pursuit went on. And the Forms, by preference, were hunting down, massacring, the warriors, but often turning in disdain from the weak, the women, the children.[8]

Thus at a distance, in the night now fallen, the spectacle seemed more supernatural, more overwhelming to the barbarian mind. The warriors were about to resume their flight. One crucial observation stopped them: this was that, no matter who the fugitives were, *the Forms abandoned their pursuit beyond fixed limits.* And, no matter how tired, how weak the victim might be, even if the victim had fainted, as soon as this ideal boundary was breached, all danger immediately ceased.

This very reassuring observation, soon confirmed by fifty examples, calmed the frayed nerves of those in flight. They dared to wait for their companions, their wives, and their poor little children who escaped the slaughter. One of them even, their Hero, at first stunned, terrified by the superhuman nature of the happening, recovered the strength of his noble soul, lit the communal hearth, sounded the buffalo horn to guide his scattered people.

Then, one by one, the miserable survivors arrived. Many, crippled, dragged themselves along with their hands. Mothers, with the indomitable strength of maternity, had kept, gathered, carried the issue of their womb through the wild fray. And many donkeys, horses, cattle reappeared, less terrified than the humans.[9]

It was a dismal night, spent in silence and sleeplessness, during which the warriors felt themselves continuously shaken to the bone. But dawn came, its paleness passing stealthily through the dense foliage, then the fanfare of dawn, with colors, resounding with the sound of birds, called upon them to live, to cast off the terrors of Darkness.

The Hero, their natural leader, gathering the tribe into groups, began to call roll. Half the warriors—two hundred—were missing. The losses were much less among the women, and almost no children had been killed.

Once roll call ended, and they had gathered the beasts of burden (few were missing, thanks to the superiority of instinct over reason during such a rout), the Hero organized the tribe according to the habitual manner, then, ordering all to wait for him, went alone, pale, toward the fatal clearing. None, even at a distance, dared follow him.

He went toward the spot where the trees were sparsely placed, adventured a little way beyond the invisible barrier that was noticed the night before. He observed.

In the distance, in the clear transparency of morning, the pretty stream was flowing; on its banks, all together, the fantastic troop of Forms stood gleaming. Their color had changed. The Cones were more compact, their turquoise color having shaded toward the green; the Cylinders vaporized toward the violet, the Strata looked like copper ore.[10] In all of them, however, the star shot forth rays of light that, even in broad daylight, dazzled the eye.

The metamorphosis spread out to the contours of these phantasmagorical entities: cones tended to stretch into cylinders; cylinders were expanding their sides, while the strata changed partially into curves.

But, like the night before, all at once the Forms began to undulate, their stars to pulsate; the Hero, slowly, crossed back over the boundary of Salvation.

II. The Priestly Expedition

The Pjehou tribe halted at the door of the great nomad tabernacle, where alone the chiefs entered. At the far end of the room, against a backdrop of stars, beneath the male image of the Sun, the three High Priests were standing. Below them, on rows of golden steps, were the twelve lesser Sacrificers.

The Hero came forward, recounted in great detail the terrible crossing of the forest of Kzour, to which the priests listened in grave astonishment, feeling their power weaken in the face of this inconceivable adventure.

The Supreme High Priest ordered the tribe to sacrifice twelve bulls, seven onagers, three stallions to the Sun. He attributed to these Forms divine powers, and resolved that, after the sacrifice, a priestly mission would be undertaken.

All the priests, all the leaders of the Zahelal nation, were to be present. And messengers scoured the mountains and plains, for hundreds of miles around the place where later Ecbatane of the Wise Ones was erected. Everywhere this somber tale caused men's hair to stand on end, everywhere the chiefs rushed to obey the sacerdotal call.

One autumn morning, the Male God burst through the clouds, flooded the tabernacle, reached the altar where the bloody heart of a bull lay steaming. The High Priests, the Sacrificers, fifty tribal chiefs raised the cry of triumph. A hundred thousand nomads, outside, treading on the wet grass, echoed the clamor, turning their sun-weathered faces toward the prodigious forest of Kzour, scarcely trembling. The augury was favorable.

So, with the priests at their head, an entire people marched off through the woods. In the afternoon, about three o'clock, the Hero of the Pjehou called the multitude to a halt. The great clearing, rusty with colors of autumn, a sea of dead leaves hiding its mosses, stretched before them majestically; on the banks of the stream, the priests saw the things they had come to worship and propitiate—the Forms. These were gentle to the eye, in the shade of the trees, with their shimmering play of colors, the pure flame of their stars, their peaceful activity along the banks of the stream.

"Here," said the High Priest, "we must offer up the sacrifice: let them know that we submit to their power."

All the ancient ones bowed. One voice spoke out, however. It was Yushik, of the tribe of Nim, a young reckoner of stars, a pale Watcher of prophesies, of growing fame, who audaciously demanded to approach closer to the Forms.

But the ancient ones, grown old in the art of wise words, overruled him: the altar was built, the victim brought forward—a dazzling stallion, superb servant of mankind. Then, amid the silence, the prostration of a whole people, the bronze blade found the noble heart of the animal. A great wailing arose. And the High Priest spoke:

"Are you appeased, O Gods?"

In the distance, among the silent tree trunks, the Forms continued to move about, making themselves shine, preferring those places where the sunlight flowed in more dense waves.

"Yes, Yes," the ecstatic Yushik exclaimed, "they are appeased!" And snatching up the warm heart of the stallion, before the curious High Priest could say a word, Yushik rushed across the clearing.

Some fanatics, uttering cries, followed after him. Slowly, the Forms were undulating, massing together, keeping close to the ground; then suddenly, as they hurled themselves at the rash intruders, a pitiful massacre horrified the fifty tribes.

Six or seven fugitives, with great effort, relentlessly pursued, were able to reach the limit. The rest perished and Yushik with them.

"These Gods know no mercy," the High Priest said solemnly.

Then a Council assembled, the venerable council of priests, elders and chiefs.

They decided to trace, beyond the limit of Safety, a wall of stakes, and to force slaves, in order to determine the boundaries of this wall, to expose themselves to attack by the Forms in successive manner all around its perimeter.[11]

And it was done. Under threat of death, slaves entered the perimeter. Few lives were lost there, however, because excellent precautions were taken. The boundary was firmly established, made visible to all by means of its circle of stakes.[12]

Thus happily ended the sacred mission, and the Zahelals believed themselves protected from this subtle enemy.

But the preventive system devised by the Council soon proved inadequate. The following spring, the tribes of Hertoth and Nazzum, as they were passing near the boundary of stakes, unsuspecting, in somewhat disorderly manner, were savagely attacked by the Forms and decimated.

The chiefs who escaped this slaughter told the Grand Council of Zahelals that now there were many more Forms than last autumn. Still, as before, their range of pursuit seemed limited, only the limits had grown larger.

This news caused consternation among the peoples: there was great mourning and great sacrifices. Then, the Council decided to destroy the forest of Kzour by putting it to the torch.

Despite all their efforts, they were only able to burn the edge of the forest. Then, the priests, in despair, declared the forest sacred ground, forbade all men to enter it. And several summers passed.

One October night the sleeping Zulf tribe, camped at a distance of ten bowshots from the fateful forest, was overrun by the Forms. Once again three hundred warriors lost their lives.

From that day on a sinister tale, corrosive, mysterious, spread from tribe to tribe, whispered from ear to ear, at night, beneath the vast star-filled Mesopotamian sky. Mankind was *going to perish!* The *Other*, ever growing larger, in the forest, on the plains, indestructible, day by day would devour the fallen race! And this secret, fearful and black, haunted these poor minds, robbed them all of the will to fight, the brilliant optimism of youthful races. Wandering mankind, dreaming on these things, no longer dared to love its sumptuous native pastures, but searched on high, with its burdened eye, the verdict of the stars. This was the year 1000 for these infant peoples, the bell that tolled the end of the world, or perhaps, the resignation of the red man in the Indian jungle.[13]

And, from deep within this anguish, the thinkers among them fashioned a bitter cult, a cult of death preached by pale prophets, a cult of Darkness more powerful than the Stars, Darkness that was to submerge, devour the holy Light, the resplendent fire.

Everywhere, on the edge of these solitudes, one encountered the shades of fanatics, immobile, emaciated, men of silence, who, from time to time, passing among the tribes, recounted their frightening dreams, of the Twilight before impending Great Night, of the Sun in throes of agony.[14]

IV. Bakhoun

And so, at that time, there lived an extraordinary man named Bakhoun, descended from the tribe of Ptuh, and brother to the first High Priest of the Zahelals. Early in life he abandoned the nomadic way, chose to dwell in pleasant solitude, flanked by four hills, in a narrow and sprightly valley, where sang the flow of a limpid stream. Quarters of great stones made for him a tent that did not move, a cyclopean dwelling.[15] Patience, and the help of domesticated cattle or horses, had given him riches, regular crops. His four wives, his thirty children, lived there the life of Eden.

Bakhoun professed strange ideas, which would have gotten him stoned to death, were it not for the respect the Zahelals had for his elder brother, the Supreme High Priest.

First, he espoused the idea that sedentary existence was preferable to nomadic life, allowing man to channel vital forces toward the development of the mind.

Second, he thought that the Sun, the Moon and the Stars were not gods but luminous bodies.

Third, he taught that man should only believe in things that can be proven by Measurement.[16]

The Zahelals attributed magical powers to him, and on occasion the boldest among them risked consulting him. They never regretted having done so. They admitted that he had often helped unfortunate tribes by giving them foodstuffs.

And thus, during this dark hour, when faced with the sad choice either of leaving their fertile plains or being destroyed by these inexorable divinities, the tribes thought of Bakhoun, and the priests themselves, after struggling with their pride, delegated three of the highest ranking of their order to go to him.

Bakhoun listened to their tales with the most anxious attentiveness, making them repeat the accounts, asking many and precise questions. He asked for two days to meditate. At the end of that time, he announced simply that he was ready to devote himself to the study of the Forms.

The tribes were somewhat disappointed, for they had hoped Bakhoun might be able to deliver the land by means of sorcery. Nonetheless the chiefs showed themselves happy with his decision and hoped great things would come of it.

Thus Bakhoun took up camp at the edge of the forest of Kzour, withdrawing at the hour of rest, and all day long he watched, mounted upon the swiftest Chaldean stallion. Soon, convinced of the superiority of his splendid animal over even the most agile Form, he was able to begin his bold and scrupulous study of the enemies of mankind, the study to which we owe the great, precuneiform book in sixty tablets, the most splendid stone book that the nomadic ages have bequeathed to the modern races.[17]

It is in this book, an admirable example of patient observation and austerity, that one finds the description of a life system totally dissimilar to our animal and vegetable kingdoms, a system Bakhoun humbly admits he was able to analyze only in its crudest and most external aspect. It is impossible for Mankind not to shudder in reading this monograph concerning the creatures Bakhoun calls the Xipéhuz, where, set down by the ancient scribe, are objective details, never carried to extremes of the marvelous, that reveal their actions, their means of locomotion, of combat, of procreation, and that demonstrate how close the human race came to the brink of nothingness, how close the Earth came to becoming the patrimony of a *Kingdom* the very conception of which is lost to us.

One must read the marvelous translation of Monsieur Dessault, his surprising discoveries in the area of pre-Assyrian linguistics, discoveries sadly more admired abroad—in England and Germany—than in his own land.[18] This illustrious scholar has agreed to put at our disposition the most salient passages of this precious work, and these passages, which we offer hereafter to the general public, will perhaps incite the desire to read more widely in the superb translations of the Master.*

V. Excerpts from the Book of Bakhoun

The Xipéhuz are obviously Living Creatures. Everything about them shows they possess will, capriciousness, the ability to make associations, that partial capacity for independence of mind that allows us to distinguish animal Beings from plants or inert things.[19] Although their manner of locomotion cannot be defined by comparing it to anything we know— they simply slide along the ground—it is easy to see they have full control of their movements. We see them stop suddenly, turn around, rush in

---

The Precursors of Ninevah, by B. Dessault, edition in-octavo, Calmann-Lévy, Paris. In the interest of the reader, I have converted the extract from the Book of Bakhoun that follows into modern scientific language. [Rosny's note]

pursuit of each other, move about in twos or threes, show preferences that lead them to leave one companion and go far away to rejoin another. They have no ability whatever to climb trees, but are able to kill birds *by attracting them* through some unknown means. One often sees them surrounding forest animals, or lying in wait for them behind a bush; they never fail to kill them, and incinerate them afterward. One can state as general rule that they kill *all animals indiscriminately,* if they can get to them, and do so without apparent motive, for they never eat them, but merely reduce them to ashes.

Their manner of burning things does not oblige them to build a fire: the incandescent spot situated at their base is sufficient for this operation. Ten or twenty of them gather to form a circle around any large animal they kill, and focus their rays on the carcass. For small animals—birds, for example—the rays from a single Xipéhuz suffice to incinerate one. It is necessary to note that the heat they are able to produce is in no way immediately harmful. On many occasions I have received on my hand the ray of a Xipéhuz, and the skin did not begin to heat up until after a certain amount of time. I do not know whether one should say that the Xipéhuz have different forms, for each one of them has the power to change successively into cones, cylinders, and planes, and all in the same day. Their color varies continually, which I believe I can attribute, in general, to changes in light from morning to evening, and from evening to morning. Nevertheless, some of these variations, in their nuances, appear to be due to the capriciousness of individuals, and especially to their *passions,* if I can speak thus, and hence constitute veritable expressions of individual features, of which I have been completely powerless, despite arduous study, to delineate even the simplest, except as hypothesis. Thus, I have never been able to distinguish between a *nuance* that indicates anger and a *nuance* that expresses gentleness, which would have surely been the first discovery in this area.

I spoke of their *passions.* Earlier I already mentioned their preferences, what I will call their *friendships.* They have their *hatreds* as well. A certain Xipéhuz will constantly avoid another and vice versa. Their fits of anger appear to be violent. They run into each other with movements identical to those observed when they attack large animals or humans, and it is these same combats that have taught me that they were in no way immortal, as I first felt disposed to believe, for two or three times I have seen Xipéhuz succumb in these combats, that is to say, *fall, condense, and become petrified*. I have carefully preserved several of these strange cadavers,* and perhaps they will be able to serve later to discover the nature of the Xipéhuz. They are yellowish crystals, irregularly distributed, and streaked with blue lines.[20]

From the fact that the Xipéhuz were in no way immortal, I was able to deduce that it would be possible to fight and defeat them, and since then I have begun a series of experiments in combat techniques about which I will say more later.

Because the Xipéhuz always radiate a quantity of light sufficient to allow them to be seen through bushes and even behind large tree trunks—a strong aureole emanates from them in all directions and warns of their approach—I was able to risk making frequent incursions into the forest, relying on the swiftness of my stallion.

There, I tried to discover whether or not they build shelters, but must admit that I failed at this research. They move neither stones nor plants, and appear to be strangers to any kind of *tangible* or *visible* industry, the only sort of industry visible to a human observer.[21] Consequently, they have no weapons of any sort, in the sense we give that word. It is certain that they cannot kill at a distance: any animal that has been able to flee without having *direct* contact with a Xipéhuz has invariably escaped, and I was many times witness to this fact.

As the unfortunate Pjehou tribe has already attested, they are unable to cross certain absolute boundaries; their actions are thus limited.[22] But these limits have grown ever larger from year to year, from month to month. I was obliged to seek out the cause.

The cause appears to be nothing more than a phenomenon of *collective growth*, and like most things about the Xipéhuz, it is incomprehensible to human intelligence. Briefly, here is the law: the limits of Xipéhuzian action expand in direct proportion to the number of individuals present; therefore, as soon as new beings are born, there is proportionate expansion of their boundaries. But where their number remains invariable, each individual being is totally incapable of crossing the boundary of the habitat allocated—by the force of things?—to the entirety of the race. This rule

---

*The Kensington Museum in London, and M. Dessault himself, possess some mineral debris, similar in all respects to those described by Bakhoun, which modern chemical analysis has been unable to *break down* and *combine* with other substances, and which, consequently, cannot be subsumed under any nomenclature of known bodies. [Rosny's note]

allows us to see a more intimate correlation between the mass and the individual than the similar correlation noticed between men and animals. The obverse of this rule was later witnessed, for once the Xipéhuz began to diminish in number, their boundaries shrank in direct proportion.[23]

On the phenomenon of procreation itself, I have little to say; but this little is true in a general sense. First of all, reproduction takes place four times a year, shortly before the equinoxes and the solstices, and only on nights that are extremely clear. The Xipéhuz gather in groups of three, and these groups, little by little, eventually come to form one single group, tightly amalgamated and shaped into a long ellipse. They remain thus through the entire night, and into the morning, until the Sun reaches its zenith. When they separate, one witnesses the rise of forms that are vague, vaporous and *huge*.

These forms condense slowly, shrink, transform themselves after ten days into cones of amber hue, still considerably larger than the adult Xipéhuz. Two months and several days are needed for these forms to achieve their maximum development, that is, to reach their maximum shrinkage. After this time, they become like the other beings in their species, with colors and forms that vary according to the hour of the day, the weather, or the whims of the individual.[24] A few days after their complete development (or shrinkage), the radius of their actions gets larger. It was of course just before this fearsome moment occurred that I beat the flanks of my noble Kouath, in order to move my camp farther out of reach.

Whether or not the Xipéhuz possess senses is something that is not possible to affirm. They certainly have apparatuses that serve a like purpose.

The ease with which they are able to perceive the presence of animals, and especially men, at great distances, tells us that their organs of investigation are at least the equivalent of our eyes. I have never seen them mistake a plant for an animal, even in circumstances where I could have easily made that error, misled by light filtered through branches, the color of the object, its position. The fact that they deploy twenty of their kind in order to consume a large animal, while a single one of them takes on the task of incinerating a bird, demonstrates an exact agreement of proportions, and this agreement seems all the more perfect when one watches them form groups of ten, twelve, fifteen, always in conformity with the relative size of the carcass. An even better argument in favor of either the existence of organs analogous to our sense organs or to our form of intelligence is how they act when they attack our tribes, for they pay little or no attention to the women or children, but pursue the warriors implacably.

Now—a more important question—do they have a language? To this I can reply without the least hesitation: "Yes, they have a language." And this language is comprised of signs, of which I was even able to decipher a few.

Suppose, for example, that a Xipéhuz might wish to speak to another. To do so, it need only direct the rays of its star toward its companion, and this is always instantly perceived. The one thus summoned, if it is walking, stops, waits. The speaker, then, rapidly traces, on the surface itself of its interlocutor—and from whatever side—a series of short luminous characters, by means of a play of beams continuously emanating from its base, and these characters remain for a moment imprinted, then fade away.

The interlocutor, after a short interval, answers.

Preceding any action involving combat or an ambush, I have always seen the Xipéhuz use the following signs:[25]

⊕ℜ⌐

Whenever it was question of me—and it was often question of me, as they did all they could to exterminate us, my brave Kouath and me—they always exchanged the following signs:

≤∧

—among other signs, as with the word, or sentence

א ⌐∧

given above.

The common sign for a state of alert was

Ɜ

and this brought the individual running who received it. Whenever the Xipéhuz were called to a general gathering, I never failed to see a sign that had the following form:

◊◊◊

representing the triune nature of these beings.

The Xipéhuz in fact have more complex signs, which refer not only to actions similar to ours, but to an order of things that is totally extraordinary, and which I have been completely unable to decipher. One cannot have the least doubt about their faculty that allows them to exchange ideas of an abstract nature, ideas most likely similar to those of humans, for they are able to remain immobile for a long time doing nothing but conversing among themselves, which indicates a genuine accumulation of thought.[26]

My prolonged sojourn among them led me, despite their metamorphoses (the laws governing which vary for each individual, to a minor degree perhaps, but with characteristics sufficiently different to be noticed by a determined observer), to get to know several Xipéhuz with a certain intimacy, and to reveal to me particularities that indicate differences about their persons . . . or should I say about their "characters"? I knew some who were taciturn, who barely ever traced a sign; there were others who were outgoing, who wrote veritable discourses; there were attentive ones; there were gossips who spoke in groups, where each interrupted the other. There were some who liked to retire, to be solitary; others clearly sought social contacts; there were ferocious ones who endlessly hunted wild beasts, birds; and there were merciful ones who often spared animals, let them live in peace. Does not all this open to the imagination a vast realm of speculation? Does it not bring one to imagine the great diversity of abilities, of intelligences, of forces in the universe that are analogous to those of the human race?[27]

They educate their young. How many times have I observed an elder Xipéhuz sitting amidst a large group of young, flashing signs to them, which they repeated back to him in turn, and which he made them do all over again whenever their form seemed imperfect.[28]

To me these lessons were marvelous, and of everything the Xipéhuz did, there is nothing that held my attention more, nothing that occupied more my sleepless nights. It seemed to me that it was here, in this dawning of the race, that the veil of mystery might part, here that some simple, primitive idea would perhaps issue forth, would illuminate for me a small corner of this deep dark abyss. No, nothing held me back; for years, I was witness to this education, I hazarded innumerable hypotheses. How many times did I feel myself at that moment on the verge of grasping some fleeting glimpse of the Xipéhuz's essential nature, an extrasensory glimpse, a pure abstraction, and which, alas, my poor senses buried in flesh were never able to pursue.

I said previously that I had long believed the Xipéhuz to be immortal.[29] This belief having been shattered once I had witnessed the violent deaths that resulted from several encounters between Xipéhuz, I was naturally led to look for their point of vulnerability, seeking each day, from then on, to find ways to destroy them, as the Xipéhuz were growing in number, so much so that after they had overrun the forest of Kzour to the south, north and west, they were beginning to invade the plains to the east. Just a few more birth cycles, and they would have dispossessed mankind of his earthly domain.

Thus I armed myself with a slingshot, and whenever a Xipéhuz came out of the forest within reach, I aimed and hurled my missile at him. This was to no avail, even though I hit all the individuals I had aimed at on every part of their surface, even on their luminous spot. They seemed perfectly insensitive to my attacks, and none of them ever turned aside to avoid my projectiles. After trying this for a month, I finally had to admit to myself that the slingshot was powerless against them, and I abandoned this weapon.

I turned to the bow and arrow. I discovered, with the first arrows I fired, that the Xipéhuz were highly fearful of them, for they turned around and moved out of range, avoiding me as much as they could. For a week I sought in vain to hit one of them. The eighth day a party of Xipéhuz, spurred on apparently by the ardor of the hunt, passed close enough to me in pursuit of a beautiful gazelle. I fired several arrows in haste, *without any apparent effect on them,* and the party fled, with myself in pursuit firing my weapon. As soon as I had spent my last arrow, they all turned around and converged on me from all sides at top speed. I was three-quarters encircled, and had it not been for the prodigious speed of my valiant Kouath, I would have perished.

This adventure left me full of uncertainties and hopes; I spent the entire week that followed in a state of inertia, lost in a deep and vague meditation, wrestling with a problem that was excessively passionate, subtle, one apt to chase away sleep, and one that filled me, at one and the same time, with suffering and pleasure. Why did the Xipéhuz fear my arrows? Why, on the other hand, given the great number of projectiles I fired that hit members of the hunting party, did none have any effect? What I knew about the intelligence of my enemies did not allow me to posit a terror without precise cause. To the contrary, everything I knew led me to suppose that the *arrow,* shot in particular circumstances, must be an effective weapon against them. But what were these circumstances? What was the vulnerable spot of the Xipéhuz? Suddenly it struck me that it was the *star* that one had to hit. In a instant I was certain, a blinding and ecstatic certitude! Then I was struck with doubt.

With the slingshot, had I not, a number of times, aimed at and hit that spot? Why was the arrow more effective than the stone?

And then it was night, the incommensurable abyss, its marvelous canopy of lamps spread above the earth. And I, my head buried in my hands, dreamt on, my heart blacker than the night.

A lion began to roar, jackals passed on the plain, and once again a glimmer of hope lit up my darkness. I had just reasoned that the stone in the sling had been relatively large, and the star of the Xipéhuz so minuscule! Perhaps, to have an effect on it, one had to penetrate deep, pierce it with a sharp point, and thus their terror of the arrow became clear.[30]

All the while, Vega turned slowly at the pole, dawn was near, and for several hours fatigue, in my skull, blotted out the world of the mind.

The days following, armed with my bow, I was in constant pursuit of the Xipéhuz, penetrating as far into their perimeter as wisdom allowed. But they all avoided my attack, keeping distant, beyond the range of my weapon. There was no question of their letting themselves be drawn into an ambush, as their mode of perception allowed them to be aware of my presence even through solid obstacles.

Toward the end of the fifth day an event occurred that, in itself, proved that the Xipéhuz were beings who, like men, were at one and the same time fallible and perfectible. That day, at dusk, a Xipéhuz deliberately approached me, with that constantly accelerating speed they prefer to use when they attack. Surprised, my heart beating, I flexed my bow. He, ever coming toward me, like a column of turquoise in the early night sky, almost reached me. But as I was about to fire my arrow, I saw him, with stupefaction, turn around and hide his star, as he continued to advance toward me. I barely had time to spur Kouath to a gallop, and put myself out of reach of this formidable adversary.

Thus, this simple maneuver, which no Xipéhuz had apparently thought to use before, on top of the fact that it revealed once more that the enemy was capable of personal initiative and individual inventiveness, suggested two things: one, that I was fortunate to have reasoned correctly concerning the vulnerability of the Xipéhuz's star; two, less encouraging, that the same tactic, were it to be adopted by all of them, would make my task extraordinarily difficult, if not impossible.

And yet, having gone through so much to arrive at this truth, I felt my courage grow in the face of the obstacle, and dared to hope that my mind would possess the necessary subtlety to overcome it.*

*In the following chapters, where the mode is generally narrative, I condense the literal translation of M. Dessault, without however forcing myself to make the tiresome division by verses, nor to make useless repetitions. [Rosny's note]

I returned to my solitude.[31] Anakhre, the third son by my wife Tepai, was a skilled maker of arms. I ordered him to make me a bow with an extraordinary reach. He took a branch of the Waham tree, whose wood is hard as iron, and the bow he fashioned from it was four times stronger than the bow of Zankann the priest, the best archer in the thousand tribes. No man living would have been able to draw such a bow. But I had devised a way to do so, and Anakhre having worked under my direction, the result was that the huge bow could be strung and unstrung by a woman.

Thus, I had always been expert with both spear and bow, and in several days I came to know the weapon made by my son Anakhre so well that I never missed a target, be it small as a fly or swift as a falcon.

This accomplished, I returned to Kzour, mounted on Kouath of the flaming eyes, and once again I began to prowl around the enemies of mankind.

To gain their confidence, I fired a large number of arrows from my old bow each time one of their parties came near the boundary, and my arrows fell well short of them. They thus came to know the exact range of the weapon, hence to believe they were absolutely out of danger at such fixed distances. Nevertheless, they remained distrustful, which kept them moving in capricious ways, whenever they were not under cover of the forest, and made them conceal their stars from my sight.

By being patient, I finally wore down their fears, and on the sixth morning a troop took up positions facing me, beneath a great chestnut tree, at a distance three times the range of my conventional bow.

At once I fired a volley of useless arrows. Their vigilance relaxed more and more, and their demeanor became as free as it had been during the early times of my presence.[32]

This was the crucial moment. My heart was pounding so fast that at first, I felt myself without force. I waited, for the glorious future rested on a single arrow. If the arrow failed to hit its mark, the Xipéhuz would never again let themselves be part of my experiment, and then, how could one know whether or not they were vulnerable to man's attacks?

Nonetheless, little by little, my will triumphed, caused my breathing to be calm, made my limbs supple and strong, my eye steady. Slowly then I raised Anakhre's bow. Over there, far away, a large emerald-colored cone stood still in the shadow of a tree; its brilliant star was turned toward me.

The huge bow strained; through the air, whistling, the arrow flew . . . and the Xipéhuz, struck, *fell, shrank, became a petrified heap.*

A loud cry of triumph poured forth from my chest. Opening my arms to the heavens, in ecstasy, I thanked the Unique One.

And so, after all, the dreadful Xipéhuz were vulnerable to man's weapons! We could hope to destroy them!

Now, without fear, I roared with all my lungs, I let sound the music of joy, I who had so despaired for the future of my race, I who, beneath the boundless heavens, beneath the deep blue of the abyss, had so often estimated that in two centuries the vast world would have seen its limits collapse in the face of the Xipéhuz invasion.

And yet, when it did come, beloved Night, pensive Night, a pall also fell over my joy, the sorrowful realization that mankind and Xipéhuz could not coexist, that the total destruction of one must be the terrible condition of life for the other.[33]

SECOND BOOK

VII. Third Period of the Book of Bakhoun

1

The priests, elders, and chiefs listened in amazement to my tale. Runners sped off to the most isolated regions to repeat the good news. The Grand Council ordered the warriors to gather on the plain of Mehour-Asar at the sixth moon in the year 22,649, and prophets preached the holy war. More than a hundred thousand Zahelal warriors answered the call; a great number of combatants from foreign races—Dzoums, Sahrs, Khaldes—drawn by the promise of fame, came to offer their services to the great nation.

Kzour was surrounded by ten rings of archers, but their arrows had failed in the face of the Xipéhuz tactic, and the imprudent warriors perished in great numbers.

And thus, for several weeks, a great terror reigned among the men.

The third day of the eighth moon, armed with a sharp-pointed knife, I announced to the multitudes that I was going alone to fight the Xipéhuz in the hope of dispelling the doubts beginning to grow as to the truth of my tale.

My sons Loum, Demja, and Anakhre violently opposed my project and wanted to take my place. And Loum said: "You cannot go there, for once you were dead, all would believe the Xipéhuz invulnerable, and the human race would perish."

Demja, Anakhre, and many other chiefs having said the same thing, I found their arguments to be true, and I withdrew.

And so Loum, taking up my long bone-handled knife, crossed the deadly boundary, and the Xipéhuz rushed toward him. One of them, more rapid than the others, was almost on him, but Loum, more agile than a leopard, dodged aside, went around the Xipéhuz, then with a giant leap, closed with him, and plunged in the sharp point.

The people, standing immobile, saw the adversary *fall, contract, and turn to stone.* A hundred thousand voices rose in the blue morning, and already Loum was returning, crossing the boundary. His glorious name spread among the armies.

2. The First Battle

The seventh day of the eighth moon in the year 22,649.[34] At dawn the horns sounded; the heavy hammers struck the great bells of brass to announce the great battle. A hundred black buffalo, two hundred stallions were sacrificed by the priests, and my fifty sons and I offered prayers to the Unique One.

The rising planet of the Sun was engulfed in the red dawn, the chiefs galloped before their armies, the tumult of the attack spread forth with the impetuous surge of a hundred thousand combatants.

The tribe of Nazzum was the first to engage the enemy, and the combat was tremendous. Helpless at first, struck down by mysterious blows, soon the warriors learned the art of striking the Xipéhuz and destroying them. Then all the nations—Zahelals, Dzoums, Sahrs, Khaldes, Xisoastres and Pjarvanns—roaring like the oceans, swept over the plain and forest, surrounded the silent adversaries on all sides.[35]

For a long while the battle was chaos; messengers continuously came to inform the priests that men were dying by the hundreds, but that their deaths were avenged.

At the ardent hour, my swift-footed son Sourdar, sent by Loum, came to tell me that for every Xipéhuz slain, twelve of our men perished. My soul was filled with blackness, my heart without strength, but my lips murmured: Thy will be done, O Only Father!

Remembering the slaughter of the warriors, 140,000 of them, and knowing that there were approximately four thousand Xipéhuz, I reasoned that more than a third of the entire army would perish, but that the Earth would remain Man's. It could have been the case that the army would not have sufficed:

"It is therefore a victory," I muttered sadly.

But as I was pondering these things, suddenly the clamor of battle shook the forest more violently, then, in great waves, the warriors reappeared, and all, with cries of distress, were fleeing toward the boundary of Safety.

Then I saw the Xipéhuz appear at the edge of the forest, no longer separated one from the other as in the morning, but united in groups of twenty or so, in circular formation, their fires turned inward. In this formation, invulnerable, they advanced on our helpless warriors, and massacred them in a horrible manner.

It was a debacle.

The bravest fighters thought only of flight. Nevertheless, despite the mourning that grew in my soul, I remained a patient observer of this fatal turn of events, hoping to find some remedy at the very heart of misfortune, for often poison and antidote exist side by side.

Destiny rewarded me for my confidence in reason with two discoveries. I noticed, first of all, that in the locations where our tribes were a great many and the Xipéhuz few, the slaughter, at first tremendous, *slowed* as the enemy's blows had *less and less* force, and many of those stricken rose to their feet after a brief moment of confusion. The more robust finally were able to resist the blows completely, continuing to flee despite repeated strikes. With the same thing happening all over the battlefield, I hazarded a conclusion that the Xipéhuz were becoming tired, that their destructive force could not go beyond a certain limit.

The second insight, which happily complemented the first, was given to me by a group of Khaldes. These poor souls, completely encircled by the enemy, losing confidence in their short knives, tore up bushes and made clubs out of them, with which they attempted to clear a passage. To my great surprise, their attempt succeeded. I saw Xipéhuz, by the dozens, lose their balance under the rain of blows, and about half of the Khaldes were able to escape through the opening thus made, but, oddly enough, those who made use of instruments of bronze instead of bushes (in this case several of the chiefs) were immediately killed as they struck the enemy. It must again be noted that the blows with the clubs did no visible damage to the Xipéhuz, for those who had fallen got up at once and continued their pursuit. I in no way minimize the extreme importance of this double discovery to future battles.

All the while the debacle continued. The earth resounded with the flight of the defeated; before evening, all that remained within the Xipéhuz's boundaries were our dead, and several hundred combatants who had climbed trees. As for the latter, their fate was horrible, for the Xipéhuz burned them alive by converging a thousand beams of fire on the branches that held them. Their terrible cries echoed for hours beneath the vast firmament.

3. Bakhoun Is Elected

The next morning the tribes counted the survivors. It happened that the battle had claimed some nine thousand lives; a cautious estimate numbered the Xipéhuz dead at six hundred. The conclusion was that the death of each enemy cost fifteen human lives.

Despair settled in every heart, many cried out against their chiefs, and spoke of abandoning this dreadful enterprise. Thus, in the midst of these murmurings, I advanced to the center of camp and began openly to reproach the warriors for the weakness of their souls. I asked them whether it was preferable to let all mankind perish or to sacrifice a part of humanity; I demonstrated to them that in ten years the land of the Zahelals would be invaded by the Forms, and in twenty years the country of the Khaldes, the Sahrs, the Pjarvanns and the Xisoastres; then, having thus awakened their conscience, I made them admit that already a sixth of the formidable Xipéhuz territory had been taken back by man, that on three sides the enemy had been pushed back into the forest. Finally, I told them my observations, I made them understand that the Xipéhuz became tired after a while, that wooden clubs could knock them over and force them to expose their vulnerable spot.

A great silence reigned on the plain, hope was returning to the hearts of the countless warriors who were hearing my words. And to build their confidence, I described a series of wooden devices that I had conceived, suited both for the attack and the defense. Enthusiasm was reborn, the tribes applauded my words, and the chiefs laid their mandate at my feet.

4. The Armament Is Transformed

During the next few days I ordered a large number of trees felled, and provided the model for light, portable barriers, which I describe briefly here: an outer frame six cubits long and two cubits wide, linked by crossbeams to an inner frame one cubit wide and five cubits long.[36] Six men (two carriers, two warriors armed with heavy lances of thick wood, two others also armed with wooden lances, but these equipped with very fine metal points, and armed as well with bows and arrows) can easily fit inside, and move through the forest, protected from the initial attack of the Xipéhuz. Once within range of the enemy, the warriors armed with blunt lances would strike, knock down the enemy, force it to expose itself, and the archer-lancers were to aim for the stars, using spear or bow as the occasion demanded. Insofar as the average height of the Xipéhuz reached a little above a cubit and a half, I designed the barriers so that the outer shield, during the march, was no higher than a cubit and a quarter above the ground, and to achieve this all that was needed was to incline a bit the supporting beams that joined it to the inner frame carried by human hands. Moreover, because the Xipéhuz do not know how to surmount unexpected obstacles with any degree of rapidity, or to advance except in an upright position, the barrier as thus conceived was adequate to protect against their initial attacks. Of course, they would make an effort to set fire to these new weapons, and in more than one instance they would surely succeed, but as their fire was barely effective from beyond the range of the arrow, they would have to expose themselves in order to effect this charring. Furthermore, as the charring was not immediate, one could, by means of swift and deft maneuvers, keep mostly out of range.

5. The Second Battle

The year of the world 22,649, the eleventh day of the eighth moon. On this day was waged the second battle against the Xipéhuz, and the chiefs appointed me supreme commander. Thus I divided the tribes into three armies. Shortly before dawn I ordered forty thousand warriors, armed with the system of barriers, to attack Kzour. This attack was less disorderly than that of the seventh day. The tribes slowly entered the forest, in small units disposed in proper order, and the engagement began. During the first hour of combat mankind had the total advantage, the Xipéhuz were completely routed by the new tactic; more than a hundred Forms perished, barely avenged by the deaths of but a dozen warriors. But once the initial surprise was over, the Xipéhuz undertook to burn our mobile frames. They were able, in some instances, to do so. They adopted a more risky maneuver toward the fourth hour of the day: taking advantage of their speed, groups of Xipéhuz, closing ranks with one another, rushed toward the frames, and were able to overturn them. Thus, in this manner, a great many men perished, so many in fact that the enemy regained the upper hand, and part of our army was plunged into despair.

Toward the fifth hour the Zahelal tribes of Khemar, of Djoh, and a part of the Xisoastres and Sahrs started to flee. Wishing to avoid a catastrophe, I dispatched couriers protected by strong barriers to announce that reinforcements were on the way. At the same time I marshaled a second army for the attack. Beforehand, however, I gave new instructions: the barriers were to remain disposed in groups as tight as the forest terrain would permit, and were to deploy in compact squares as soon as a somewhat sizeable group of Xipéhuz came near, without however abandoning the offensive.[37]

That said, I signaled the attack; in a short time I had the joy of seeing victory return to the United Peoples. Finally, toward midday, an approximate casualty count—estimating the number of losses for our army at two thousand men and those of the Xipéhuz at three hundred—proved beyond doubt we were making inroads, and filled all our souls with confidence.

Yet toward the fourteenth hour the balance tipped slightly against us, the Peoples having lost four thousand individuals and the Xipéhuz five hundred.

It was then that I deployed the third corps: the battle reached its greatest intensity, the enthusiasm of the warriors grew minute by minute, until the hour when the sun was ready to fall into the West.

Around this moment, the Xipéhuz resumed the offensive at the north of Kzour; a retreat by the Dzoums and Pjarvanns caused me to become worried. Judging, moreover, that darkness would be more favorable to the enemy than to our troops, I sounded the retreat. The return of the troops took place with calm, triumphantly; much of the night was spent celebrating our success. It was considerable: eight hundred Xipéhuz had perished, their field of activity had been reduced to two-thirds of Kzour forest. It is true that we left seven thousand of our own fallen in the forest, but these losses were far fewer, proportionate to the result, than those of the first battle. Thus, my heart filled with hope, I dared to conceive a bolder and more decisive plan of attack against the twenty-six hundred Xipéhuz still alive.

6. The Extermination

The year of the world 22,649, the fifteenth day of the eighth moon.

As the reddish sun descended upon the eastern hills, the Peoples were ranged in battle formation before Kzour.

My soul swelled with hope, I finished giving my instructions to my chiefs, the horns sounded, the heavy hammers struck the gongs of bronze, and the first army marched toward the forest.

This time the barriers were stronger, a little larger, and held twelve men instead of six, except for about a third of them, which were built according to the old model.

Thus, they were more difficult both to burn and to overturn.

The initial moments of combat were favorable; after the third hour four hundred Xipéhuz had been exterminated, as opposed to only two thousand of our men. Encouraged by this good news, I ordered the second corps to attack. On both sides the fighting was horrendous, our combatants becoming used to victory, their adversaries deploying the stubborn courage of a noble Kingdom. From the fourth to the eighth hour, we sacrificed no less than ten thousand lives; but the Xipéhuz paid for them with a thousand of their own, such that only a thousand remained in the depths of Kzour.

It was then I realized that Mankind would inherit the Earth; my remaining doubts subsided.

Nevertheless, during the ninth hour a great shadow fell on our victory. Now the Xipéhuz never confronted us except in large masses and in forest clearings, concealing their stars, and they became almost impossible to knock over. Inflamed by warlike zeal, many of our troops rushed headlong against these masses. Thus, in rapidly changing fashion, a large group of Xipéhuz detached itself, knocking down and massacring these foolhardy men.

A thousand men thus perished, without appreciable loss for the enemy. When the Pjarvanns saw this, they began to shout that all was lost; a panic prevailed which caused more than ten thousand men to flee, a large number of whom imprudently abandoned their barriers in order to run more rapidly. This cost them dearly. A hundred Xipéhuz, in hot pursuit, cut down more than two thousand Pjarvanns and Zahelals: terror began to spread through all the ranks.

When the runners brought me this dire news, I knew that the day would be lost if I were not able, through some deft maneuver, to retake the lost positions. Immediately I gave the order to their chiefs for the third army to attack, and I announced that I would lead it into battle. Then, I swiftly moved my reserves in the direction from which the troops were fleeing. We soon found ourselves face-to-face with the pursuing Xipéhuz. Made bold by their success in their slaughter, they were unable to regroup fast enough, and, in a few instants, I caused them to be surrounded. Very few escaped; the mighty acclamation of our victory restored courage in our troops.

From that moment on, I had no difficulty regaining the offensive; we limited our tactic to constantly detaching segments from the enemy clusters, then surrounding these segments and annihilating them.

Soon, realizing just how effective this tactic was against them, the Xipéhuz again began to fight us in small units, and the massacre of the two Kingdoms, one of which could exist only by annihilating the other, doubled horribly in intensity. But any doubt as to the final outcome soon vanished from the souls of the most fainthearted. Toward the fourteenth hour, barely five hundred Xipéhuz were facing a hundred thousand men, and these few adversaries were enclosed in increasingly narrow boundaries, more or less a sixth of the forest of Kzour, which made our movements extremely easy.

Nonetheless, the red light of dusk flowed through the trees and, fearing ambushes in the shadows of night, I interrupted the combat.

The immensity of the victory swelled in every soul; the chiefs spoke of making me ruler of all the tribes. I advised them never to place the destinies of so many men in the hands of one poor fallible creature, but to adore the Unique One, and to elect *Wisdom* for their earthly ruler.[38]

VIII. Last Period of the Book of Bakhoun

The Earth belongs to Mankind. Two days of fighting has exterminated the Xipéhuz; the entire domain occupied by the last two hundred of them has been razed, every tree, every plant, every blade of grass has been destroyed. And I have finished, for the edification of future peoples, with the help of Loum, Azah and Simho my sons, inscribing the story of the Xipéhuz on tablets of granite.

Now I am alone, at the edge of Kzour, in the pale night. A half moon of copper color stands fixed above the Setting Sun. Lions roar at the stars.

The river wanders on its peaceful course through the willows; its never-ending voice speaks of times that pass, the melancholy of things that perish. And I bury my face in my hands and a cry of sorrow arises in my heart. For now that the Xipéhuz have perished, my soul misses them, and I ask of the Unique One what Fatality has ordained that the splendor of Life be soiled by the Blackness of Murder?[39]

Another World

I.

I am a native of Gelderland.[1] Our property consists only of a few acres of briar and brackish water. Pines that rustle with a metallic sound grow on its boundaries. Only a few rare inhabitable rooms remain on the farm, which is dying stone by stone in solitude. We issue from an old family of shepherds, formerly large, now reduced to my parents, my sister, and me.

My destiny, rather gloomy at first, has become the most beautiful that I am aware of. I have met The One Being who has understood me; it is he who will teach to others what I alone among men now know. For a long time, however, I suffered, I despaired, prey to doubt, to solitude of the soul, which in the end gnaws away everything right down to the most absolute certainties.

I came into the world with a unique constitution. Right from the beginning, I was an object of wonder. Not that I seemed to be misshapen: I was, I was told, more graceful of body and face than one is usually at birth.[2] But I had the most extraordinary complexion, of a sort of pale violet color—very pale but very clear. In the lamplight, especially that of oil lamps, this nuance became paler yet, took on a strange whiteness, like a lily submerged in water. This is, at least, what other men saw: for I myself see myself differently, just as I see differently all the objects in this world. To this first oddity others were added that came to light later.

Although born with the appearance of health, I grew with difficulty. I was thin, I cried constantly; by the age of eight months, no one had yet seen me smile. Before long, they despaired of ever raising me. The doctor from Zwartendam declared that I was suffering from a physiological malady: he saw no other remedy but a rigorous health regimen. Nonetheless I continued to waste away; from one day to the next, they expected to see me die. My father, I believe, had resigned himself to this, having been vexed in his self-pride—in his Dutch amour propre made up of order and regularity—by the strange aspect of his child. My mother, to the contrary, loved me all the more in proportion to my strangeness, finally coming to find the color of my skin pleasant.

Things had reached this point, when a very simple event came to my rescue: as everything concerning me of course had to be abnormal, this event became a cause of scandal and apprehension.

When one of the servants left, she was replaced by a strong Friesland girl, hardworking and honest, but given to drinking. I was placed in the care of the newcomer. Seeing me so feeble, she fancied that she could give me in secret a little beer and water mixed with Schiedam,[3] the remedies, according to her, best for any illness.

The most curious thing is that I soon began to regain strength, and that from then on I showed an extraordinary predilection for alcoholic drinks. The good-hearted lass secretly rejoiced, not without taking some pleasure in causing puzzlement in my parents and the doctor. But, confronted with the evidence, she finally revealed the mystery. My father became violently angry, the doctor ranted against ignorance and superstition. Strict orders were given to all the servants, I was removed from the care of the Friesland girl.

I began again to lose weight, to waste away, until my mother, harking only to her tenderness, put me back on the beer and Schiedam diet. At once, I regained strength and liveliness. The experiment was conclusive: alcohol proved to be essential to my health. My father was humiliated by this; the doctor saved face by prescribing medicinal wine, and my health has been excellent ever since: everyone hastened to predict that I would have a life of drunkenness and debauchery.

Soon after this incident, a new anomaly struck those around me. My eyes, that had at first seemed normal, became oddly opaque, took on a corneous look, like the elytra of certain coleoptera.[4] The doctor predicted that I would lose my sight; he admitted nonetheless that the illness seemed totally odd to him and that he had never been given the opportunity of studying anything like it before. Soon the pupil became so much like the iris that it was impossible to tell one from the other. In addition, they noticed that I could look into the sun without being troubled by it. To tell the truth, I was in no way blind, in fact one finally had to admit that I saw with my eyes very well indeed.

In this manner I reached the age of three. I was then, in the opinion of our neighbors, a little monster. There had been little change in the violet hue of my skin; my eyes were completely opaque. I spoke incorrectly and with an astounding speed. I was dextrous with my hands, and well endowed to perform movements that demand more agility than physical strength. No one denied that I would have been graceful and even pretty had I had a normal complexion and transparent pupils. I showed some intelligence, but with gaps in knowledge that people around me did not try to understand, all the more because, with the exception of my mother and the Friesland girl, I was hardly liked by anyone. I was in the eyes of strangers an object of curiosity, and for my father a continual source of humiliation.

If in fact the latter had preserved any hope of seeing me become like other human beings, time acted to dissuade him of this. I became stranger and stranger, in my tastes, my habits, and even my good qualities. At the age of six, I nourished myself almost entirely with alcohol. I barely ate a few mouthfuls of vegetables and fruit. I grew incredibly fast, I was astonishingly thin and light. I mean "light" in a literal sense, which is precisely the opposite of being thin: thus, I was able to swim without the least effort, I floated like a plank of poplar wood. My head was no more immersed than the rest of my body.

I was agile in proportion to this lightness. I ran with the speed of a deer, I leapt easily over ditches and obstacles no one would even have tried to jump over. In the twinkling of an eye, I would reach the top of a beech tree; or, even more surprising, I would jump to the roof of our farm. On the other hand, the least burden exceeded my strength.

* * *

All these, in fact, were merely phenomena that indicated a unique nature, phenomena that in themselves could only have served to single me out and make me unwelcome; none placed me outside the realm of Humanity. Without doubt, I was a monster, but certainly not so much as someone born with horns, or ears like a beast, the head of a calf or a horse, or with fins, no eyes, or an extra eye, four arms, four legs, or without arms or legs. My skin, despite its surprising hue, was close to being like skin that was suntanned; my eyes had nothing repugnant about them, despite their opacity. My extreme agility of movement was a positive quality; my need for alcohol could pass as a mere vice, the hereditary trait of a drunkard: the bumpkins, in fact, like our Frieslander, only saw in all of that a confirmation of their sense of the "strength" of Schiedam, a slightly excessive demonstration of how excellent their tastes were. As for the rapidity of my speech, its glibness, which was impossible to follow, this could be confused with speech defects—stammering, lisping, stuttering—commonly found in so many small children. Therefore, strictly speaking, I had no marked signs of monstrosity, although all these things taken together were extraordinary: the fact was that the most unusual aspect of my nature escaped detection by those around me, for nobody realized that my vision differed strangely from the normal way of seeing.[5]

If I saw certain things less clearly than other men, I saw a large number of things that no one else sees. This difference was especially marked in the case of colors. All those colors known as red, orange, yellow, green, blue, indigo appeared to me as a more or less blackish gray, while I did see the color violet, and a series of colors beyond this end of the spectrum, colors that are only night for normal eyes. I later came to understand that I can distinguish fifteen or so colors that are as different from each other as, for example, yellow and green—with, of course, an infinity of gradations.

Second, my eye cannot perceive transparency under normal conditions. I see poorly through a windowpane, and through water: I see glass as a highly colored substance; water is slightly colored, even when there is little thickness.[6] Many crystals said to be diaphanous are more or less opaque for me; then again, a large number of bodies said to be opaque do not stop my seeing through them. Generally, I see through bodies much more frequently than you do; and translucency, cloudy transparency, occurs so often that I can say that, for my eye, it is the rule of nature, while total opacity is an exception. It is thus that I distinguish objects through wood, leaves, flower petals, magnetic iron, coal, and so on. However, when the thickness varies, these bodies become an obstacle: as with a huge tree, or a meter's depth of water, or a thick chunk of coal or quartz.

Gold, platinum, mercury are black and opaque, ice appears blackish. Air and water vapor are transparent, and yet tinted, as well as certain samples of steel, certain very pure clays. Clouds do not prevent me from seeing the sun and the stars. In addition, I clearly distinguish the same clouds hovering in the atmosphere.

The difference between my sight and that of other men was, as I have mentioned, rarely noticed by those close to me; they simply thought that I perceived colors only with difficulty; this is too common an infirmity to attract attention. It had no importance for the everyday activities of my life, as I could see the forms of objects in the same way as—and perhaps more subtly than—the majority of men. The designation of an object by its color, when color was needed to distinguish it from another object of the same shape, did not bother me unless the objects were new to me. If somebody called the color of a vest "blue" and the color of another "red," it made little difference to me what the real colors were in which these vests appeared to me: blue and red became terms of a purely mnemonic nature.

From all of this, you might believe that there was some kind of agreement between my colors and those of others, and that therefore it was the same as if I had seen their colors. But, as I have already written, red, green, yellow, blue, and so on, *when they are pure*, like the colors of the prism—I see them all as a more or less blackish gray; they are not colors for me. In nature, where no color is pure, it is not the same: such and such a substance called green, for example, is made up for me of a certain compound color;* but another substance called green, and which for you is identical in shade to the first one, is not at all the same color for me.[7] Thus you can see that my spectrum of colors does not correspond to yours: when I accept calling both brass and gold yellow, it is somewhat as if you accepted calling both a cornflower and a poppy "red."

II.

If the difference between my way of seeing and that of general humanity had stopped there, it would have indeed seemed extraordinary enough. It is only a small part, however, in comparison with the remainder of what I have to tell you. This differently colored world, differently transparent and opaque—the faculty that enables to see through clouds, to perceive stars on the most cloudy nights, to discern through a wooden wall what is taking place in the neighboring room, or outside a house—what is all of that in comparison with the perception of a living world, a world of Beings that are alive, moving next to and all around man, without man being aware of it, without him being alerted to it by any kind of direct contact? What is all of that, next to the realization that a fauna other than ours exists on

---

*And this compound color, of course, has no green in it, for the color green, for me, is darkness.

Earth, a fauna without the least resemblance to our own, neither in form, nor in organization, nor in habits, nor in patterns of growth, of birth and of death? A fauna that lives next to, and through, our own fauna, influences the elements that surround us, and is influenced, strengthened by those elements, without our having the least suspicion of its presence. A fauna that—as I have demonstrated—ignores us just as we ignore it; and as we evolve without it knowing about us, it evolves without our knowing about it. A living world, as varied as ours, as powerful as ours—and perhaps more so—in its effects on the surface of the planet![8] A kingdom of beings, finally, moving about upon the waters, in the atmosphere, on the ground, transforming these waters, this atmosphere, this ground, in completely different ways than we do, but with a certainly formidable energy, by means of which it acts indirectly upon us and our destiny, just as we act indirectly on it and its destiny! . . . This is, however, what I saw, what I see now, alone among men and beasts alike, here is what I have been passionately *studying* for five years, after having spent childhood and adolescence simply *noticing* its presence.

III.

Noticing it! As far back as I can remember, I have by instinct succumbed to the seduction of this creation alien to our own. At first, I confused it with other living things. Noticing that no one else was bothered by its presence, that everyone else, on the contrary, seemed to ignore it, I hardly felt the need to point out its singularities. At the age of six, I knew perfectly how it differed from the plants in the fields, from animals of the farmyard and the stable, but I confused it somewhat with inert phenomena like the glow of light, the drift of waters and clouds. This was because these beings were intangible: whenever they came to me, I never felt any effect from their contact. Their form, quite varied in fact, had nevertheless the particularity of being so thin, in one of their three dimensions, that one could compare them to drawn figures, to flat surfaces, to geometric lines that would be moving about.[9] They passed through all organic bodies; on the other hand, they appeared to be stopped sometimes, to get tangled up in invisible obstacles . . . But I will describe them later. For the time being, I only wish to indicate their presence, to affirm the variety of their contours and lines, their near absence of thickness, their *impalpability*, all combined with the autonomy of their movements.

* * *

As I approached my eighth year, I realized perfectly well that they were just as distinct from atmospheric phenomena as animals are from our kingdom. In the rapture this discovery brought me, I attempted to express it. I was never able to do so. Beside the fact that my speech was almost entirely incomprehensible, as I have said, the extraordinary nature of my vision made it suspicious. No one attempted to disentangle my gestures and sentences, any more than they were ready to admit that I might be able to see through wooden panels, even though I had given proof of this many times. There was, between me and the others, an almost insurmountable barrier.

I sank into a state of discouragement and reverie; I became a sort of little solitary being; I provoked uneasiness, and felt the same in return, in the company of children of my age. I was not exactly a victim, because my speed of movement kept me out of reach of childish mischief, and gave me the means of avenging myself with ease. At the least sign of menace, I was already at a safe distance, I mocked my pursuers. However great their number might be, no boys were ever able to surround me, let alone constrain me. It was also futile to attempt to take me by ruse. However weak I might have been in shouldering burdens, my forward momentum was unstoppable, immediately extricated me. I could come back by surprise, subdue the adversary, indeed adversaries, with swift and sure blows. Therefore they left me alone. They considered me at one and the same time naive and a bit of a sorcerer, but one whose sorcery was little feared, but despised instead. Little by little I created a life outside society, wild, contemplative, not entirely devoid of gentleness. My mother's tenderness alone rendered me human, even though, too occupied during the day, she rarely found time for caresses.

IV.

I now will attempt to describe, in summary fashion, a few scenes from my tenth year, in order to give concrete form to the preceding explanations.

It is in the morning. A strong glow lights up the kitchen, a glow that is pale yellow to my parents and to the servants, but for me a very diverse light. Breakfast is being served, bread with tea. But I don't drink tea. They have given me a glass of Schiedam with a raw egg. My mother cares for me tenderly; my father asks me questions. I try to answer him, I slow down my speech; he only understands a syllable here and there, he shrugs his shoulders.

"He will never speak."

My mother looks at me compassionately, persuaded that I am a bit simple-minded. The servants and maids are no longer even curious about the little violet monster; the Friesland girl has gone back to her region long ago. As for my sister—she is two years old—she plays next to me, and I have a deep tenderness for her.

Once breakfast is over, my father goes out into the fields with the servants, my mother begins to go about the daily chores. I follow her into the courtyard. The animals come toward her. I look at them with interest, I love them. But all around them, the other Kingdom is moving and captivates my interest to a greater degree: this is the mysterious domain that I am alone in knowing.[10]

Against the dark soil, there are a few forms spread out; they move about, they stop, they pulsate at the level of the ground. They belong to several species, differentiated by their contours, by their movements, and especially by the arrangement, the design, and the nuances of the lines that traverse them. These lines in fact constitute the essence of their being, and, as a young child, I perceived this very clearly. While the mass of their form is dull, grayish, the lines are almost always sparkling. They constitute very complicated networks, they emanate from centers, they radiate out from these, until they become lost, imprecise.[11] Their nuances are countless, their curves infinite. These nuances vary within a single line, as the form also varies within that line, if to a lesser degree.

In general, this being is shaped by rather irregular, but very distinct, contours, by centers that irradiate outward, by multicolored lines that crisscross each other abundantly. When it moves, the lines vibrate, oscillate, the centers contract and dilate, while the outer shape varies little.

All of that, ever since that time, I see very clearly, although I am incapable of defining its nature: a delightful charm invades me when I contemplate the *Moedigen*.* One of them, a colossus ten meters long and almost as wide, passes slowly across the courtyard, and disappears. This one, with several bands as large as cables, with centers as large as the wings of eagles, is of extreme interest to me, and almost frightens me. I hesitate a

---

*This is the name I spontaneously gave to these creatures during my childhood, and which I have kept, even though it does not in the least correspond to any quality or form these beings have.

moment to follow it, but others attract my attention. They are of all sizes: some are no longer than our tiniest insects, while I have seen others reach a length of more than thirty meters. They move along the ground itself, as if attached to solid surfaces. Whenever a material obstacle—a wall or a house—presents itself, they breach it by molding themselves to its surface, always without making any important modifications to their shapes. But wherever the obstacle is composed of matter that is either alive or has lived, they pass directly through it: it is thus that I have seen them a thousand times emerge from a tree or from under the foot of an animal or a man. They also pass through water, but prefer to remain on the surface.

These terrestrial Moedigen are not the only intangible beings. There is an aerial population, of marvelous splendor, incomparable in subtlety, variety, and brightness, next to which the most beautiful of birds are dull, slow and ponderous. Here again, there is a contour and some lines. But the background is no longer grayish; it is strangely luminous; it sparkles like the sun, and the lines stand out against it like vibrating veins, its centers vibrate violently. The *Vuren*, as I thus call them, have a more irregular shape than the terrestrial Moedigen, and generally, they navigate by means of rhythmical arrangements, of crisscrossings and uncrossings that, in my ignorance, I cannot grasp, and that confound my imagination.

Then, I strike out across a field recently mowed: the fight between one Moedig and another attracts my attention. Such combats are frequent; I have a violent passion for them. Sometimes, it is a fight between equals; more often, it is the attack of a strong one on a weak one (the weak one is not necessarily the smaller). This time, the weak one, after a brief defense, starts to flee, closely pursued by its attacker. Despite the speed of their chase, I follow them, I succeed in keeping them in sight, until the moment when the fight begins anew. They rush toward each other, in a hard, even rigid manner, as each one is solid to the other. With each shock, their lines become phosphorescent, converge toward the point of contact, their centers pale and shrink. First, the struggle remains more or less equal, the weak one deploys the most intense energy, and succeeds even in gaining a respite from its attacker. It takes advantage of this to flee again, but it is soon caught up with, attacked with force, and finally captured, that is, held in an opening in the contour of the other. This is exactly what the weak one had tried to avoid, by responding to the shocks from the strong one with less energetic, but more rapid, shocks. Now, I see all its lines vibrate, its centers struggle desperately; and as this continues the lines become paler, thinner, the centers lose their precise form. After a few minutes, it is given back its freedom; it moves away slowly, dull, debilitated. The antagonist, to the contrary, sparkles more, its lines take on more color, its centers become sharper and pulsate more rapidly.

This struggle moved me deeply; I dream of it, I compare it to fights I see sometimes between *our* animals and *our* small creatures; I understand dimly that the Moedigen in fact do not kill each other, or rarely, that the victor contents itself with *drawing energy* at the expense of the vanquished.[12]

The morning advances, it is close to eight o'clock; the school in Zwartendam is about to open: I make a leap up to the farm, I take my books, and here I am among my peers, where no one guesses the deep mysteries that palpitate around me, where no one has even the most confused idea of living beings through which all humanity passes, and which pass through humanity, without any indication of this mutual inter-penetration.

I am a very poor student. My handwriting is no more than a hasty scrawl, formless, unreadable; my speech remains incomprehensible; it is obvious I am distracted. The teacher continuously exclaims:

"Karel Ondereet, when are you going to stop looking at flies in flight!"

Alas! my dear teacher, it is true that I am watching the flies flying around, but how much more does my soul soar along with those mysterious Vuren that are moving about the room! And what strange feelings obsess my childlike soul, when I realize the blindness of all around me, and above all, your own, O solemn shepherd of minds.

V.

The most difficult period of my life was that from twelve to eighteen years.

First of all, my parents tried to send me to high school; there I knew only misery and failures. As a result of exhausting efforts, I succeeded in expressing the most common things in an almost comprehensible manner: making a great effort to slow down my syllables, I blurted them out awkwardly, and with the stresses of a deaf person. But as soon as it was a matter of expressing something complex, my speech regained its fatal rapidity: no one was able to follow me.[13] Thus, I was not able to make people aware of my progress orally. And my handwriting was atrocious, my letters overlapped each other, and in my impatience, I forgot syllables, words: it was monstrous gibberish. Besides, writing for me was a torture perhaps even more intolerable than speaking—it was so ponderous, so stiflingly slow!—If, sometimes, after great effort and the sweat of my brow, I managed to begin my homework, soon I was exhausted and out of patience, I felt myself fainting. I preferred therefore the reprimands of the teacher, my father's bouts of fury, punishments, privations, scorn, to this horrible labor.

Thus, I was almost totally deprived of means of expressing myself: already an object of ridicule because of my thinness and my odd complexion, because of my strange eyes, even more I was seen as being some sort of idiot. It was necessary to take me out of school, to accept the fact that I must become a peasant. The day my father decided to give up all hope, he said to me with an unaccustomed gentleness:

"My poor lad, you see, I have done my duty . . . my entire duty! Never reproach me your fate!"

I was violently moved, I cried all the tears of my heart: never before had I felt with so much bitterness how isolated I was in the midst of mankind. I dared to kiss my father tenderly; I murmured:

"Yet it is not true that I am an imbecile!"

And in fact I felt superior to those who had been my peers. For some time now, my intelligence had been undergoing a remarkable development. I read, I understood, I intuited things, and I had, more than other men have, immense possibilities for meditation, within this universe that was visible to me alone.

My father was unable to untangle my words, but he was moved by my affection.

"Poor lad!" he said.

I looked at him; I felt a terrible despair, knowing all the more that the void that separated us would never be filled. My mother, through her loving intuition, realized at that moment that I was not inferior to other boys of my age: she stared at me tenderly, she spoke sweet words to me that came from the utmost depths of her being. Despite all that, I was condemned to cease my studies.

Because of my weak muscular strength, I was relegated to tending the flocks and livestock. I did the job marvelously well; I needed no dog to tend the herds, for no colt, no stallion had greater agility than I did. Thus I lived, from fourteen to seventeen, the solitary life of a shepherd. It suited me more than any other. Given over to observation and contemplation, and also to some readings, my mind did not stop developing. Endlessly, I made comparisons between the dual creation I had before my eyes. From this I deduced ideas about the nature of the universe, I formulated vague hypotheses and systems. If it is true that my thoughts at that time did not perfectly correlate, did not achieve a clear synthesis—for they were the thoughts of an adolescent, uncoordinated, hasty, enthusiastic—they were nevertheless original and fertile. I will not deny that their value was especially dependent on my unique constitution. But they did not derive their full power from this alone. Without the least vanity, I believe I can assert that they far outstripped, in subtlety as in logic, those of ordinary young men.

They alone brought consolation to my sad life as a semipariah, without companions, without any real communication with those surrounding me, not even with my adorable mother.

* * *

At seventeen, life became undeniably intolerable for me. I was tired of dreaming, tired of vegetating in a wasteland of thought. I languished with boredom. I remained motionless for long hours, disinterested in the entire world, paying no attention to what took place in my family. Of what avail to me was it to know things more marvelous than other men, insofar as this knowledge was destined to perish with me? Of what avail to me this mystery of other living beings, and even the dual nature of two living systems passing though each other without knowing each other? These things could have turned my head, could have filled me with enthusiasm and ardor, if only I could, in some way or other, have taught them or shared them with others. But to what avail! Vain and sterile, absurd and wretched, they contributed instead to my perpetual psychic quarantine.

Several times, I dreamt of writing, in order at least to establish, as the reward of continued efforts, some of my observations. Yet ever since leaving school, I had completely abandoned writing. Already such a wretched scribbler, I was barely able, even if I applied myself to the task, to inscribe the twenty-six letters of the alphabet. Had I had the least glimpse of hope, perhaps I would have persisted! But who would take my miserable ramblings seriously? Where was the reader who would not think me mad? Or the wise man who would not dismiss me with disdain or irony? What was the use, from now on, of devoting myself to that vain task, to that vexing torture, which is almost what it would be like for an ordinary man to have to inscribe his thoughts on a marble tablet, with a large chisel and a cyclopean hammer! My own handwriting was like a shorthand—and even then, a shorthand much faster than normal![14]

Thus I had no courage at all to write, and yet I ardently hoped for I don't know what unknown occurrence, for some fortunate and unique act of fate, to happen. It seemed to me that there must exist, in some corner of the Earth, minds that were impartial, lucid, discerning, suited to studying me, to understanding me, to drawing from me my great secret, and communicating it to others. But where are such men? What hope did I have of ever meeting them?

And I would fall back into a deep melancholy, into a desire to remain immobile, to annihilate myself. During an entire autumn, I despaired of the Universe. I languished in a vegetative state, from which I emerged only to give myself over to long moans, followed by agonizing moments of revolt.

I became thinner yet, to the point of becoming fantastical in appearance. The folks of the village called me, with irony, "den Heyligen Gheest," the Holy Spirit. My silhouette trembled like those of young poplar trees, was as light as a reflected image, and because of this I attained the stature of giants.

Slowly, a project began to form in my mind. Insofar as my life had been sacrificed, because none of my days bore me any pleasure, and all to me was darkness and bitterness, why stagnate in inaction? Supposing that no soul existed capable of responding to mine, at least it seemed worthwhile to make the effort to convince myself of the fact. At least it seemed worthwhile to leave this gloomy land, to go find in the large cities the scientists and philosophers. Was I not myself an object of curiosity? Before calling attention to my knowledge of extrahuman phenomena, might I not stimulate the desire in people to study my person? Were not my physical attributes alone worthy of being studied, and my vision as well, and the extreme rapidity of my movements, and my strange manner of taking nourishment?[15]

The more I dreamt of it, the more it seemed reasonable for me to hope, and the more my resolve grew. The day came when that resolve became unshakeable, when I revealed it to my parents. Neither one of them understood much of this, but both finally gave in to my repeated entreaties: I was allowed to go to Amsterdam, with the possibility of returning home if fate were unkind to me.

I departed one morning.

VI.

From Zwartendam to Amsterdam is a hundred or so kilometers. I easily covered that distance in two hours, without other adventures than the extreme surprise of those coming and going to see me running with such speed, and several gatherings of people at the entrances to the little towns and larger villages, which I avoided. To make sure I was on the right road, I inquired two or three times of elderly people who were alone. My sense of direction, which is excellent, did the rest.

It was around nine o'clock when I reached Amsterdam. Determined, I entered the big city, I passed along the beautiful, dreamy canals, filled with pleasant merchant fleets. I did not attract as much attention as I had feared. I walked quickly, among people busy with their affairs, here and there enduring the taunts of a few young vagabonds. Nevertheless, I did not decide to stop here. I crisscrossed the city somewhat in all directions, after which I finally resolved to enter a pub, on one of the banks of the Heeren Gracht.[16] The place was peaceful; the splendid canal spread before me, full of life, between shady rows of trees; and among the Moedigen I saw moving on its banks, I seemed to see some that belonged to a new species. After some hesitation, I went into the pub, and directing my question to the owner, as slowly as I was able to, I entreated him to be so kind as to direct me to a hospital.

The host gazed at me with astonishment, defiance and curiosity, took his big pipe from his mouth and put it back several times, then finally said:

"You are, no doubt, from the colonies?"

As it was perfectly useless to contradict the man, I answered:

"Yes indeed!"

He appeared delighted with his perspicacity. He asked me a new question:

"Perhaps you come from that region of Borneo which no one has ever been able to enter?"[17]

"Exactly!"

I spoke too rapidly: he opened his eyes wide.

"Exactly!" I repeated more slowly.

The host smiled with satisfaction:

"You speak Dutch with difficulty, true? So, it's a hospital you're looking for . . . probably you're sick?"

"Yes."

The patrons had come closer. The news spread already that I was a cannibal from Borneo; even so, I was looked upon much more with curiosity than with antipathy. People ran in from the street. I became nervous, anxious. Nonetheless, I composed myself, and I repeated, coughing:

"I am very sick!"

"It's just like the monkeys from that country," replied a very fat man with indulgence. . . . "Holland is killing them!"

"What strange skin," another added.

"And how does he see?" asked a third man, pointing to my eyes.

The circle drew close, I was surrounded with a hundred curious stares, and still more people were coming into the room.

"How tall he is!"

It is true that I was a head taller than the tallest among them.

"And skinny!" . . .

"Cannibalism does not appear to give them much nourishment!"

Not all the voices were malicious. A few sympathetic individuals protected me:

"Don't press him like that, he is sick!"

"Come on, friend, courage!" the fat man said, when he noticed my nervousness. "I will take you myself to a hospital."

He took me by the arm; he gave himself the task of plowing through the crowd, and called out:

"Make way for a sick man."

Dutch crowds are not very fierce: they let us pass, but they accompanied us. We went along the canal, followed by a compact crowd; and some people cried out:

"He's a cannibal from Borneo!"

* * *

Finally we reached a hospital. It was during consultation hours. I was taken before an intern, a young man with blue glasses, who greeted me sullenly. My companion said to him:

"He is a savage from the colonies."

"What do you mean, a savage," the other exclaimed.

He took off his glasses to look at me. He stood for a while motionless in astonishment. Abruptly he asked me:

"Are you able to see?"

"I see very well . . ."

I had spoken too rapidly.

"It's his accent," the fat man said proudly. "Repeat yourself, my friend!"

I repeated myself, I made myself understood.

"Those are not the eyes of a human," the medical student muttered. "And the complexion! . . . Is this the complexion of your race?"

Then, I said, struggling terribly to slow down my speech:

"I came here to be seen by a man of science!"

"You are not sick then?"

"No!"

"And are you from Borneo?"

"No!"

"Then where are you from?"

"From Zwartendam, near Duisburg!"

"Then why does your friend claim you are from Borneo?"

"I didn't want to contradict him."

"And you want to see a man of science?"

"Yes."

"Why?"

"To be studied."

"To make money?"

"No, for nothing."

"You are not poor then? A beggar?"

"No!"

"Then what drives you to want to be studied?"

"My constitution . . ."

But again, despite my efforts, I had spoken too rapidly. I had to repeat myself.

"Are you sure you can see me?" he asked, staring fixedly at me. "Your eyes seem like calluses."

"I see very well . . ."

And, moving right and left, I picked up objects rapidly, I set them down, I tossed them in the air in order to catch them.

"This is extraordinary," the young man exclaimed.

His voice, softened, almost friendly, filled me with hope:

"Listen," he said finally, "I think that Dr. Van den Heuvel will be interested in your case . . . I will have someone inform him about it. You wait in the next room . . . and, by the way . . . I forgot to ask, you are not sick, in fact?"

"Not at all."

"Good. Come . . . enter here . . . the doctor will come soon."

I found myself seated amidst monsters preserved in alcohol: fetuses, children with bestial shapes, colossal batrachians, saurians that were vaguely anthropomorphic.

This, I thought, was the waiting room just for me! Am I not a candidate for one of these sepulchers, to be preserved in alcohol?

VII.

When Dr. Van den Heuvel appeared, I was overwhelmed with emotion: I trembled as if I saw the Promised Land, felt the joy of entering it, the fear of being banished from it. The doctor, with his large bald forehead, the penetrating gaze of an analyst, a mouth that was soft and yet displayed resoluteness, examined me in silence, and my excessive thinness, my extreme height, my darkly circled eyes, my violet complexion were causes of astonishment for him, as they were for everyone else.

"You say that you want to be studied?" he finally asked.

I answered forcefully, almost violently:

"Yes!"

He smiled approvingly, and asked me the usual question:

"Can you see well through those eyes?"

"Very well . . . I can even see through wood, through clouds . . ."

But I spoke too fast. He glanced at me with anxiety. I repeated, sweating profusely:

"I even see through wood, through clouds . . ."

"Really! That would be extraordinary . . . Then tell me, what do you see through that door . . . there?"

He showed me a blind door.

"A big glass bookcase . . . a sculpted table . . ."

"Yes, truly!" he repeated, astonished.

My chest relaxed, a deep serenity descended upon my soul.

The scientist remained silent a few seconds, then:

"You speak with great difficulty."

"Otherwise I speak too rapidly! I cannot speak slowly."

"Then, speak in your natural manner."

Then I told him the story of my entry into Amsterdam. He listened with extreme attentiveness, with a sense of intelligence and observation that

I had never before encountered among my fellow men. He understood nothing of what I was saying, but the analysis that followed revealed his sagacity:

"I am not mistaken . . . you utter fifteen to twenty syllables per second, that is, three to four times more than the human ear is capable of perceiving. Your voice, moreover, is much higher pitched than any human voice I have ever heard. Your gestures, excessively rapid, clearly correspond to this manner of speaking. Your metabolism on the whole probably functions much faster than ours."

"I run," I said, "faster than a greyhound . . . I write . . ."

"Ah!" he interrupted. "Let's see the handwriting . . ."

I scribbled a few words on a blotter that he held out to me, the first were readable enough, the others increasingly scrambled, abbreviated:

"Perfect!" he said, and a certain pleasure mingled with his astonishment. "I believe that our meeting is most felicitous. Surely, it would be most interesting to study you . . ."

"It is my most ardent, my sole desire!"

"And mine as well . . . most surely . . . Science . . ."

He seemed preoccupied, lost in dreams; at last he said:

"If only we could find an easy means of communicating . . ."

He paced back and forth, his eyebrows knitted. All at once:

"How stupid of me! You will learn shorthand, by god! . . . Yes, Yes . . ."

A jovial expression appeared on his face:

"And, I forgot, what about the phonograph . . . the faithful confidant![18] One need only play it back more slowly than the speed at which recorded . . . It's all settled: you will live with me during your stay in Amsterdam!"

O joy at wishes fulfilled, what sweetness not to have to spend days in vain and sterile doings! In the presence of the doctor's intelligent personality, in this scientific milieu, I felt a delightful sense of well-being; the melancholy that beset my solitary soul, the regret that my faculties might be lost, my long suffering as pariah that crushed me for so many years, all vanished, evaporated before the sense that a new life was mine, a true life, a destiny preserved!

VIII.

The very next day the doctor made the necessary arrangements. He wrote to my parents; he found me a professor of shorthand, and procured phonographs. As he was a very rich man, and entirely devoted to science, there was no experiment he was not willing to undertake, and my sight, my hearing, my musculature, the color of my skin, were all subjected to rigorous examination, all of which made him increasingly enthusiastic, exclaiming:

"This is of the nature of prodigy!"

I understood perfectly, after the first days, just how important it was that things be done with method, from the simplest to the most complex task, from the simplest to the most astonishing abnormality. Thus I had recourse to a little maneuver, which I did not keep secret from the doctor: to reveal my faculties to him only in a gradual manner.

The speed of my perceptions and movements kept him busy at first. He was able to conclude that the subtle nature of my hearing corresponded to the rapidity of my speech. This point was proven conclusively by gradually more rigorous experiments on increasingly inaudible noises, which I imitated with ease, the voices of ten or fifteen people all talking at once, all of which I detected. The rapidity of my vision was likewise demonstrated; and comparative experiments between my ability to divide a horse's gallop, the flight of an insect, into increments and the same thing done with stop-motion photography only confirmed the superiority of my eye. As for my perception of ordinary things, such as the simultaneous movements of a group of men, of children playing in a playground, of machines in movement, of stones thrown into the air or of little balls cast into an alleyway that were to be counted in flight—these astounded the doctor's family and friends.

My running in the garden, my twenty-meter leaps, my ability to seize objects instantaneously, or to catch up with them, were more admired yet, less by the doctor than by his entourage. And it was an ever-renewed pleasure for the children and wife of my host, during a walk in the country, to see me outrun a horseman going at full gallop, or follow the path of some flitting sparrow: there was no purebred to which I could not give a two-thirds lead, no matter what the distance covered, or any bird I could not easily overtake.

As for the doctor, increasingly satisfied with the results of his experiments, he defined my nature in the following manner:

"A human being gifted, in all its movements, with a speed incomparably superior not only to that of other men, but even to that of all known animals. This speed, detected as much in the most tenuous parts of its organism as in its whole, makes it a being so distinct from the rest of creation that it merits all by itself to have a special designation in the hierarchy of animals. In the case of the very curious makeup of its eye, as well as the violet color of its skin, one must consider these as simple indications of this special nature."

Once my muscular system was examined, no peculiarity was found, except for my excessive thinness. Nor did my ear offer any unusual data, nor did my skin for that matter, aside from its hue. As for my hair, with its dark color of a bluish black nature, it was fine like a spider's web, and the doctor studied it with minute care:

He laughingly said to me on occasion: "One would need to be able to dissect you!"

In this manner time passed pleasantly. I had learned very rapidly to do shorthand, thanks to the ardor of my desire and to the natural aptitude I had for this mode of rapid transcription, to which by the way I introduced a few new abbreviations. I began to take notes, which my stenographer translated; and beyond this, we had phonographs, which were built to specifications specially conceived by the doctor, and turned out to be perfectly adapted to reproducing my speech, in a slowed-down manner.

The confidence my host had in me, over time, became complete. During the first weeks, he could not help but suspect, quite naturally, that the unique nature of my faculties might go hand in hand with some form of madness, some mental derangement. This fear once overcome, our relations became completely cordial and, I believe, as captivating for the one as for the other. We analyzed the nature of my faculty of perception, in relation to a great number of substances considered to be opaque, and in relation to the dark coloration that water, glass, quartz took on for me at a certain thickness or depth. You remember that I see easily through wood, tree leaves, clouds, and many other substances, and that I see poorly the bottom of a pool of water half a meter deep, and that a windowpane, although transparent for me, is less so than for ordinary men, and somewhat dark in color. A large piece of glass appears blackish to me. The doctor took ample time to convince himself of all these unusual phenomena, astonished above all to see me pick out stars on cloudy nights.

It was only during this period that I began to tell him that I also perceive color differently. A number of experiments proved conclusively that the colors red, orange, yellow, green, blue and indigo are as completely invisible to me, as is infrared or ultraviolet light to the normal eye. On the other hand, I was able to demonstrate* that I do perceive the color violet and, beyond violet, a whole scale of nuances, a spectrum of colors at least twice that which lies between red and violet.

This astonished the doctor more than all the rest. The study of this phenomenon was long, detailed and, what is more, conducted with infinite skill. It became, in the hands of this adept experimenter, the source of subtle discoveries in the domain of those scientific disciplines classified by humanity; it gave him the key to ancient phenomena such as magnetism, to elective affinities, to inductive powers, and guided him toward new concepts of physiology.[19] To know that a given metal consists of a series of unknown shadings, variable with changes in pressure, temperature, electric charge; that the most diaphanous gasses have distinct colors, even at the most minute thickness; to make inquiries into the infinite richness of tonalities of objects that appear more or less black, when in fact they yield up a more magnificent scale of hues in the ultraviolet range than that of all the known colors; finally to understand how much variation of unknown nuances are given off by an electric circuit, the bark of a tree, the skin of a human, in a single day, a single hour, a single minute—one easily imagines all the advantages an ingenious scientist can derive from such notions.

In any case, this study plunged the doctor into the delights of scientific discovery, in comparison with which the products of pure imagination are as cold as ashes after fire. He never ceased telling me:

"It is clear to me! Your enhanced perception of light is in fact nothing but the result of your organism having developed with such speed."

We worked patiently an entire year, without my mentioning the Moedigen—I absolutely wanted to convince my host, give him numerous proofs of my visual faculties, before I hazarded my supreme confidence. At last the moment came when I believed I could reveal everything.

*Quartz gives me a spectrum of approximately eight colors: extreme violet and seven following colors in the ultraviolet range. But there remain some eight colors that quartz is unable to distinguish from each other, and which other substances are more or less able to separate.

IX.

It was a mild fall morning full of clouds, which for a week rolled across the dome of the sky, without the least rain falling from them. Van den Heuvel and I were walking in the garden. The doctor was silent, totally absorbed in speculations of which I was the main object. Finally, he said:

"It is nonetheless a beautiful dream to be able to see through those clouds, to penetrate to the very ether, when we, blind as we are . . ."

"If only all that I saw were the sky! . . ." I replied.

"Ah! Yes, the entire world so different . . ."

"Much more different even than what I have told you!"

"What?" he exclaimed with avid curiosity, "could you have hidden something from me?"

"The main thing!"

He stood before me, looked at me fixedly, with true anxiety, mingled with something I know not what of the mystical.

"Yes, the main thing!"

We had come back to the house, I rushed to ask for a phonograph. The instrument that was brought was up to the task, highly perfected by my friend, and capable of recording a long speech; the servant placed it on the stone table where the doctor and his family were accustomed to take their coffee on warm summer evenings. The good machine, timed to the second, was admirably suited to record discussions. Our conversation went forward then more or less as though it were a normal one:

"Yes, I hid the main thing from you, wanting first to gain your complete confidence. And even now, after all the discoveries that my organism allowed you to make, I still fear that you will believe me only with great difficulty, at first at least."

I stopped speaking, in order to let the machine play back the sentence, I saw the doctor become pale with that pallor only great scientists experience before the discovery of some new property of matter. His hands were trembling.

"I shall believe you!" he said with a certain solemnity.

"Even if I assert that our creation, I mean our animal and vegetable kingdoms, is not the only form of life on earth . . . that there is another form, as vast, as numerous, as varied . . . invisible to your eyes?"

He suspected occultism, and could not help saying:

"The world of the fourth state[20] . . . souls, ghosts of spirits."

"No, no, nothing like that! A world of living beings, condemned as we are to a short life, to the needs of an organic body, to birth, growth, struggle . . . a world weak and ephemeral like ours, a world subjected to laws just as rigid, if not to the same laws, a world just as much prisoner of the earth, just as helpless in the face of contingencies . . . But still completely different from our world, without any influence on us, just as we have no influence on it, except through the modifications that it makes on our shared ground, the Earth, or through the parallel modifications that we force that same Earth to endure."[21]

I do not know if Van den Heuvel believed me or not, but it was certain that he was struck by a strong emotion:

"In essence, are they fluid in nature?" he asked.

"That's what I am not able to tell, because their properties are too contradictory to the idea that we have of what matter is. The earth is as resistant to them as to us, and in like manner so are the majority of minerals, although they can penetrate to some degree into a *humus*.[22] They also remain totally impermeable, solid, in relation to one another. Yet they pass, if sometimes with a certain difficulty, through plants, animals, organic tissues; and we, we pass through them as well. If one of them could perceive us, we would perhaps appear to it as something fluid in relation to them, as they appear fluid to me in comparison to us; but they would probably not be able to come to a conclusion any more than I can, they would be confounded by parallel contradictions . . . Their form is strange in the sense that they have very little thickness. Their size varies infinitely. I have known some of them to reach a length of a hundred meters, others are tiny like our smallest insects. Some take their nourishment at the expense of the earth and atmospheric changes; others feed on weather changes and members of their own species, without however this being a cause of death as it is with us, for it suffices for the stronger one to extract energy, and such energy can be taken without exhausting the sources of life."[23]

The doctor abruptly asked me:

"Have you seen these beings since you were a child?" I guessed that he suspected, deep down, some disorder that had taken place more or less recently in my organism:

"Since I was a child!" I replied forcefully. . . . "I will give you all the necessary proofs."

"Do you see them at this moment?"

"I see them . . . there are a great many of them in the garden . . ."

"Where?"

"On the path, on the grass, on the walls, in the air . . . for you need to know that some are earthbound and some airborne . . . and there are also aquatic forms, but they rarely leave the surface of water."

"Are there a lot of them everywhere?"

"Yes . . . and hardly less numerous in town than in the countryside, in dwellings than in the street. Those that like living inside, however, are smaller, no doubt because of the difficulty they have in going inside, although wooden doors are not an obstacle for them!"

"And what about iron . . . windowpanes . . . bricks . . . ?"

"These are impermeable to them."

"Would you like to describe one of them to me . . . preferably one of the large ones?"

"I see one next to that tree. Its form is highly elongated, somewhat irregular. Toward the right, it is convex, toward the left concave, with bulges and indentations: one might therefore imagine that the projection of a gigantic, bulky larva would look this way. But its form is not characteristic of its Kingdom, because form varies greatly from one species (if one can use this word here) to another. Their infinitely small thickness is, on the other hand, a quality common to all: that thickness must not be more than barely a tenth of a millimeter, while their length reaches five feet, and their largest width forty centimeters. What is its supremely defining mark, and that of its entire Kingdom, is the lines that crisscross it, somewhat in every direction, that terminate in networks that become more delicate between two systems of lines. Each system of lines has a center, a sort of spot that bulges slightly above the mass of the body, but is sometimes, on the contrary, hollowed out. These centers have no fixed shape, sometimes they are nearly circular or elliptical, sometimes curved and spiral-like, occasionally divided by several narrowing places. These beings are surprisingly mobile, and their size varies from hour to hour. Their edges palpitate vigorously, by means of a sort of transversal undulation. As a general rule, the lines that stand out are large, although some of them are very thin as well; they diverge, they end in an infinite number of delicate traces, which gradually vanish. Some lines, however, much paler than the others, are not generated by the centers; they remain isolated in the system, and crisscross each other without changing tonality: these lines have the ability to move around in the body, and to vary their curves, while the centers and the connecting lines remain stable in their respective settings . . . As for the colors of my Moedig, I must give up trying to describe them to you: none of them are part of the perceptible spectrum for your eye, for you none of them has a name. They are extremely bright in the networks of lines, less bright in the centers, very faint in the independent lines, which, on the other hand, possess an extreme degree of polish, a metallic ultraviolet, if I can speak in this way . . . I have gathered a few observations about the way the Moedigen live, nourish themselves, and are autonomous, but I do not wish to submit these to you at the present time."

I fell silent; the doctor played back twice my words, recorded by our impeccable translation device, then he remained silent a long while. I had never seen him in such a state: his face was rigid, petrified, his eyes glassy, cataleptic; a profuse sweat ran from his temples and drenched his hair. He tried to speak but was unable to. Trembling, he made a tour of the garden, and, when he reappeared, his eyes and mouth expressed a violent passion, fervent, religious: one would have thought he was the disciple of some new faith, rather than a peaceful hunter of phenomena.

Finally, he muttered:

"You've overwhelmed me! All you have just told me appears desperately lucid. Do I have the right to doubt, after all the marvelous things you have already taught me?"

"Doubt," I ardently told him, "dare to doubt . . . your experiments will be all the more fertile for it!"

"Ah!" he replied with a voice as if in dream, "this is wonder itself, and so magnificently superior to the vain wonders of The Fable![24] . . . My poor human intelligence is so small compared to such knowledge. My enthusiasm is boundless. However, something inside me doubts . . ."

"Let us work to dispel your uncertainties: our efforts will be rewarded one-hundred-fold!"

X.

We went to work. A few weeks were sufficient for the doctor to dissipate all his doubts. Several clever experiments, undeniable connections made between each of my assertions, two or three fortunate discoveries concerning the Moedigen's influence on atmospheric phenomena, left no room for uncertainty. The collaboration of Van den Heuvel's eldest son, a young man possessed of the highest scientific talents, boosted the fruitfulness of our research and even more the certainty of our findings.

Thanks to the methodical minds of my two associates, to the strength of their ability to discover and classify—faculties that increasingly I made my own—what my knowledge of the Moedigen offered as confused and unorganized data was rapidly transformed. Discoveries multiplied, rigorous experiments yielded solid results, in circumstances that, in ancient times and even still in the last century, would have occasioned at the most a few enticing divagations.

Five years have now passed in which we have pursued our research: it is far, very far, from being brought to term. It will be some time before a preliminary paper on our research can be published. We have made it a rule, besides, not to produce anything hastily: our discoveries are of such an intrinsically important nature that they must be set forth in the greatest detail, with the highest degree of patience, and most exacting precision. We have no other researcher to compete with, no patent to take out, nor any ambition to satisfy. We have reached a plane where vanity and pride vanish. How to reconcile the blessed joys of our work with the paltry lure of human fame? Besides, is not the random nature of my physical structure the source of these things? And, henceforth, what pettiness it would be to glorify ourselves because of them![25]

We live passionately, always on the verge of marvelous discoveries, and yet we live in a timeless serenity.

* * *

I have had an adventure that makes my life more interesting, and that, when I am at rest, fills me with infinite joy. You know how ugly I am, and how much odder I am yet, all destined to terrify young women. I have nevertheless found a companion who adapts to my affections to the point of being happy.[26]

It is a poor hysterical girl, neurotic, whom we encountered one day in a poor house in Amsterdam. Others said she looked miserable, pale like plaster, with sunken cheeks and a haggard gaze. For me, the sight of her is pleasant, and her company charming. Far from startling her, as happens with all others, my appearance seemed from the outset to please and comfort her. I was moved by this, I wanted to see her again.

Soon it was apparent that my presence had a beneficial effect on her health and well-being. Under examination, it seemed that I had a magnetic influence on her: my approach, and especially when I placed my hands on her, communicated to her a sense of joy, a serenity, an equanimity of mind that were truly healing. In return, I felt gentleness next to her. Her face seemed pretty to me; her pallor and her thinness were nothing more than refinement; her eyes, capable of seeing the glow of magnets, like those of many sufferers from hyperesthesia, for me did not have that haggard look that people fault them with.[27]

In a word, I felt an attraction to her, which she reciprocated with passion. From that moment on, I resolved to marry her, and I achieved my goal with ease, thanks to the goodwill of my friends.

The union was a happy one. My wife recovered her health, even though she remained extremely nervous and frail; I tasted the joy of being, joy in the essential things of life, like other men. But above all, my fate has become enviable. As of six months ago: A child was born to us, and that child brings together all the characteristics of my constitution. In terms of color, sight, hearing, extreme speed of movement, way of taking nourishment, he promises to be the exact replica of my organism.

The doctor anticipates his growing up with great joy: a delightful hope has come to us—that the study of Moedigen life, of that Kingdom parallel to ours, this labor that demands so much time and patience, will not cease when I am gone.[28] My son will carry it on, no doubt, in his time. Why will he not be able to find collaborators of genius, capable of taking this study to a higher power yet? Why would there not be born, from himself as well, more seers of this invisible world?

I myself, might I not expect to have other children, might I not hope that my dear wife will give birth to other sons of my flesh, similar to their father? Just thinking of it, my heart thrills, an infinite bliss passes into me, and I feel blessed among men.

The Death of the Earth

*Mankind harnessed everything right down to
the mysterious force that bound together the atom.
This frenzy heralded the death of the Earth.*[1]

I. Words across the Vastness

The horrid north wind had fallen silent. For fifteen days its awful voice had filled the oasis with fear and sadness. It had been necessary to erect breaks against the hurricane-force winds, and erect greenhouses of flexible silica. Finally, the oasis began to warm again.

Targ, the watchman of the Great Planetary, felt one of those sudden joys that lit up the lives of men, during the sacred times of the Water.[2] How beautiful the plants still were! They carried Targ back through the ages, to the time when oceans covered three-quarters of the world, when mankind thrived amidst springs, streams, rivers, lakes, swamps. What youthfulness animated these countless generations of plants and animals! The swarm of life reached to the deepest depths of the sea. There were prairies and rain forests of algae just as there were forests of trees and savannahs of grass. A vast future spread out before living creatures; mankind could hardly have imagined its far-distant inheritors who would tremble as they awaited the end of the world. Did it ever imagine that the agony would last more than a hundred thousand years?

Targ looked up at a sky where clouds would never again appear. The morning was still cool, but by noon the oasis would be torrid.

"Harvest time is near," the watchman[3] muttered.

He had a swarthy complexion, eyes and hair as black as coal. Like all the Last Men, his chest was broad, while his waist was narrow. His hands were delicate, his jaws small, his limbs revealed more agility than force. A garment of mineral fibers, as supple and warm as the ancient wools, fit his body exactly; his being exuded a resigned gracefulness,[4] a timid charm underscored by his narrow cheeks and the pensive fire of his eyes.

He paused to contemplate a field of tall grain, some rectangular patches of trees, each one of which bore as much fruit as they had leaves, and he spoke:

"O Sacred times, O prodigious dawns, when plants covered the young planet!"

As the Great Planetary stood at the confines of the oasis and the desert, Targ could see a sinister landscape of granite, silica, and metals, a plain of desolation that stretched to the base of bare mountains, without glaciers, without springs, without a blade of grass or plaque of lichen. In this desert of death, the oasis, with its rectilinear crops and its villages of metal, was nothing more than a miserable spot.

Targ felt the weight of the vast solitude and implacable mountains; he raised his head in melancholy manner toward the conch of the Great Planetary. This conch spread a sulphurous corolla toward the indentation of the mountains. Made of arcum and as sensitive as a retina, it captured only those pulsations from afar that emanated from the oases, and, according to how it was regulated, silenced those to which the watchman was not authorized to respond.[5]

Targ loved this object as an emblem of those rare adventures still possible for human beings; in his fits of sadness, he turned to it, he drew from it courage and hope.

A voice made him start. With a faint smile he watched as a young girl, whose forms were rhythmically proportioned, climbed toward the platform. She wore her sable hair free; her breast undulated with the litheness of a stalk of long grain. The watchman contemplated her lovingly. His sister Arva was the sole creature in whose company he recovered those instants, fleeting, unexpected and charming, when it seemed that at the heart of the mystery, there were forces still that slumbered, ready to rescue mankind.

She exclaimed, with restrained laughter: "What lovely weather, Targ . . . How happy the plants are!"

She filled her nostrils with the consoling odor that issued from the green flesh of the leaves; the dark fire in her eyes sparkled. Three birds came sailing over the treetops, and roosted on the edge of the platform. In size they resembled condors of old, forms as pure as those of beautiful female bodies, huge silvery wings, glazed with amethyst, the tips of which emitted a violet glow. Their heads were large, their beaks very short, very flexible, as red as lips; and the expression in their eyes resembled the expression of humans. One of the birds, raising its head, uttered articulate sounds; Targ anxiously took Arva's hand.

"Did you hear?' he said, "The earth is shaking!"

Though no oasis since a very long time ago had perished from seismic tremors, and though the magnitude of these had significantly diminished since the dark period when they had shattered the power of mankind, Arva shared the concern of her brother.

But a frivolous idea passed through Arva's mind:

"Who knows," she said, "whether or not, after having done so much damage to our brothers, these earthquakes might not begin to work in our favor?"

"And in what way?" Targ asked indulgently.

"By causing some of the water to reappear."

He had often dreamt of this, without ever having spoken of it to anyone, for such a thought would have appeared stupid and almost blasphemous to a fallen humanity, to whom all such terrors evoked the planetary upheavals.

"You also are thinking of this?" he said exaltedly. "Don't tell it to anyone else. You would offend *them* to the depths of their souls!"

"I could only tell it to you."

From all directions bands of white birds surged forth: those that had rejoined Targ and Arva stamped their feet impatiently. The young man addressed them, using a special form of syntax. For these birds, as they had developed their intelligence, had learned to use language—a language that only allowed for concrete terms and image-phrases.

Their notion of the future remained obscure and shortsighted, their foresight instinctive. Ever since men had stopped using them for food, they lived in a state of happiness, unable to imagine their own individual deaths, and even more the end of their species.

The oasis had raised about twelve hundred of them, whose presence was very comforting and most useful. As mankind had not been able to recover its instincts, lost over the ages of its domination, the present nature of its milieu forced it to grapple with phenomena that its machines, inherited from its ancestors, as sensitive as they were, could barely detect, and that the birds could foresee. If these latter, the last vestige of animal life on Earth, had disappeared, an even more bitter desolation would have beset the soul.[6]

"The danger is not immediate!" Targ whispered.

A rumor spread through the oasis. Men emerged from around the villages and sown fields. A stocky man, whose massive skull seemed to be directly placed on his trunk, appeared at the foot of the Great Planetary.

Lidless and dull eyes looked out of a face the color of iodine; his hands, flat and rectangular, swung back and forth at the end of short arms.

"We will witness the end of the world," he growled. "We are the last generation of mankind!"

Behind him was heard a hollow laugh. Dane, the centenarian, stepped forward with his great-great-grandson and a woman with long eyes and hair the color of bronze. She walked as lightly as did the birds.

"No, we will not see it!" she affirmed.... "The death of mankind will be slow ... the water will dry up until there will be only a few families left around a single well. And it will be even more terrible."

"We will witness the end of the world," the stocky man persisted.

"So much the better!" said Dane's great-great-grandson. "Let the Earth, this very day, drink up all the remaining springs."

His sinewy face, very narrow, expressed a sadness beyond limits; he himself was astonished that he had not already put an end to his existence.

"Who knows whether there may not be some hope!" muttered the ancestor.

Targ's heart pounded. He lowered toward the centenarian eyes in which the spark of youth burned.

"Oh! Father ... !" he exclaimed.

Already the old man's face had become immobile. He sank back into that silent dream that made him appear to be a block of basalt; Targ kept his thought to himself.

The crowd was swelling at the confines of the desert and the oasis. Several gliders that came from the Center rose into the air. It was the time of year when men were rarely needed for work; all they had to do was wait for harvest time. For no insect, no microbe, had survived. Enclosed in narrow confines, outside of which all "protoplasmic" life was impossible, the ancestors had carried out a successful struggle against parasites. Even microscopic organisms had been unable to survive, deprived of those random factors that come with dense populations, huge expanses, constant transformations and perpetual movement.

Moreover, as masters of the distribution of water, mankind wielded an irresistible power over those beings it wished to destroy. The disappearance of old strains of domestic and wild animals, constant vectors of epidemics, had further advanced the hour of triumph. Now, mankind, the birds and the plants were forever free of infectious diseases.

They did not live any longer: because many good microbes had disappeared along with the others, maladies proper to the human machine had developed, and new maladies had broken out, maladies that people were able to believe were caused by "mineral microbes." Consequently, men found inside their bodies enemies that were analogous to those that had menaced them from without, and although marriage was a privilege reserved for only the fittest, the human organism rarely reached an advanced age.[7]

Soon several hundred men found themselves gathered around the Great Planetary. There was only a feeble uproar. The tradition of misfortune had run in the veins of these men for too many generations not to have dried up those reserves of fright and suffering that are the price mankind pays for powerful joys and vast hopes. These Last Men had limited sensibilities and little imagination.

Nevertheless, the crowd was anxious: some of the faces were tense; a sigh of relief was heard when a man in his forties jumped from his moto-cruiser,[8] and shouted: "The seismographs[9] haven't registered anything yet . . . the tremor will be weak."

"Why are we so worried then?" shouted the woman with long eyes. "What can we do, what can we foresee? For ages now all possible protective measures have been taken. We are at the mercy of the unknown: it is horrible foolishness to ask questions about peril that is inevitable."

"No, Hele," the forty-year-old man answered, "it's not foolishness, it's simply life. As long as men still have the strength to worry, their days will still bring some comfort. When that is gone, they will be dead the day they are born."

"Let it be so then!" Dane's great-great-grandson snickered. "Our wretched joys and feeble sorrows are worth less than death."

The man in his forties shook his head. Like Targ and his sister, he still held a future in his soul and the force of life in his large chest. His limpid gaze met the shining eyes of Arva, a delicate emotion caused him to breathe more rapidly.

In the meantime other crowds gathered at various places on the periphery. Thanks to the sender-receivers,[10] set up every thousand meters, these groups communicated freely.

Through this network one could hear, *at will*, the sounds of a district, or even of the entire population. This communion fused together the soul of the multitude and acted to stimulate their energy. And there was a sort of exaltation when a message from the oasis of Red-Lands sounded in the conch of the Great Planetary, and echoed from receiver to receiver. The message revealed that there, not only the birds, but the seismographs were warning of subterranean disruptions. This confirmation of peril at hand brought the groups together.

Mano, the forty-year-old man, had climbed to the platform; Targ and Arva were pale. And as the young girl was trembling a bit, the newcomer murmured:

"The very narrowness of the oases, and their small number, should re-assure us. The probability is minimal that they would be located in one of the dangerous zones."

"They are all the less in danger," Targ added, "as it is their location itself that saved them in the past."

Dane's great-great-grandson overheard this. He laughed his sinister laugh:

"As if faults don't shift from period to period. What is more, wouldn't one weak but well-centered quake suffice to cut off the flow of water?"

He moved away, full of gloomy irony. Targ, Arva, and Mano had shuddered. They remained mute for a moment. Then the forty-year-old man continued:

"The faults shift with extreme slowness. For two hundred years, all the heavy tremors have occurred well out in the desert. Their repercussions have not affected the springs. Only three—Red-Lands, Devastation, and Occident—are adjacent to the danger zones."

He contemplated Arva with gentle admiration, in which stirred the bloom of love. A widower for three years, he suffered from loneliness. Despite the fact that his energy and tenderness were in revolt, he had resigned himself to it. The laws rigorously governed the number of marriages and births.

But a few weeks ago, the Council of Fifteen had inscribed Mano on the list of those who could reform a family. The health of his children justified this consideration. Thus the image of Arva underwent a transformation in Mano's soul, the dark legend, once again, emerged into the light.

"Let's mingle hope with our worries," he continued. "Was not the death of each individual man, even during the marvelous epochs of the Water, for him the end of the world? Those who live at this moment on the Earth run many less risks, individually, than did our ancestors from before the radioactive age!"

He spoke with firmness. For he had always rejected the lugubrious resignation that devastated his peers. No doubt, a too deeply rooted atavism allowed him only intermittent freedom from this gloom. Nonetheless, he had known, more than any other, the joy of living the shining moment as it passes.

Arva listened to him approvingly, but Targ could not understand how one could neglect the future of the race. If it happened that, as with Mano, he was suddenly seized by a passing moment of sensual delight, he always mingled with it the grand dream of Time that had driven the ancestors.

"I cannot disinterest myself in the fate of our lineage," he retorted.

And extending his hand toward the solitary vastness:

"How beautiful life would be if *our kingdom* occupied these horrible deserts! Don't you ever dream that once upon a time there were seas there, lakes, rivers . . . plants without number, and before the Radioactive Age, virgin forests? Yes, Mano, virgin forests! . . . And now, an obscure life form devours our ancient heritage . . ."

Mano quietly shrugged his shoulders.

"It's wrong to think of such things, insofar as, outside the oases, the Earth is as uninhabitable for us, perhaps more so, than is Jupiter or Saturn."

A clamor interrupted them; heads looked up, attentively: they saw a new flock of birds appear. They announced that over there, among the boulders, a young girl who had fainted had fallen prey to the ferromagnetics. And while two gliders rose up above the desert, the crowd had thoughts of these strange magnetic creatures that multiplied over the planet as mankind's presence waned. Long moments went by; the gliders returned: one of them carried the lifeless body of a girl everyone recognized as Elma the Nomad. She was a strange girl, an orphan, and little liked, because she had the instincts of a wanderer, whose wild nature frustrated her fellow men. Nothing could stop her, on certain days, from running off into the wastelands . . .

They had laid her out on the platform of the planetary; her face, half-hidden in her long black hair, seemed livid, even though it was dotted with scarlet spots.

"She's dead!" Mano declared, "the *Others* have *drunk* her life."

"Poor little Elma!" Targ exclaimed.

He contemplated her with pity, and, as passive as it was, the crowd grumbled with hatred against the ferromagnetics.

But the resonators,[11] booming out striking sentences, drew attention away:

"The seismographs detect a strong tremor in the sector of the Red-Lands..."

"Oh! Oh!" wailed the plaintive voice of the stocky man.

His cry vanished in the void. The faces were turned toward the Great Planetary. The multitude waited, shivering with impatience.

"Nothing," exclaimed Mano after several minutes of waiting. "If the Red-Lands had been hit, we would know it by now..."

A strident call cut him off. The conch of the Great Planetary blared out:

"A terrible shock... the entire oasis is rising... a catastr..." Then, confused sounds, a dull colliding sound... silence.

All, mesmerized, waited for more than a minute. Then, the crowd uttered a harsh sigh. The least emotional among them stirred.

"It is a massive disaster!" announced old Dane.

Nobody doubted his words. The Red-Lands had ten planetary shells for communication across great distances, which could be pointed in all directions. For all of them to fall silent, they would all have to be uprooted, or the disarray of the inhabitants would have to be extraordinary.

Targ, tuning his transmitter, sent out a prolonged call. No reply. A dark horror weighed on their souls. This was not the acute turmoil earlier humanity experienced, it was a slow distress, wearying, corroding. Strong ties united High Springs and the Red-Lands. For five thousand years the two oases had maintained constant contact with each other, either by means of resonators, or through frequent visits, by gliders or moto-cruisers. Thirty relay stations, equipped with planetary reflectors, dotted the road, seventeen hundred kilometers long, that linked the two peoples.

"We must wait!" Targ exclaimed, leaning over the platform. "If panic is preventing our friends from responding, they will not be long in regaining their composure."

But no one could believe that the men of the Red-Lands were capable of such panic; their race was even less emotive than that of High Springs: capable of sadness, they were hardly capable of fright.

Targ, reading disbelief on all faces, continued:

"If all their transmitters are destroyed, before a quarter of an hour is up messengers can reach the first relay station..."

"Unless," Hele objected, "their gliders were damaged... As for moto-cruisers, it is unlikely, until some time passes, that these can go across a wall reduced to rubble."

Nonetheless, the entire population converged on the southern zone.

Within a few minutes, a thousand men and women arrived by glider or motocruiser near the Great Planetary. Murmurs arose, like long breaths, interspersed with silences. And the members of the Council of Fifteen—interpreters of laws and judges of community actions—gathered on the platform. The angular face, the coarse salt-white hair of old Bamar stood out among them, as did the dented skull of her husband Omal, whose tawny beard had not been whitened by seventy years of life. They were ugly, but venerable, and their authority was great, for theirs had been a lineage without blemish.

Bamar, verifying that the planetary had been well directed, took her turn sending out a few waves. When the receiver remained silent, her face became more somber yet.

"Till now, Devastation is out of danger!" murmured Omal, "and the seismographs announce there are no tremors in the other inhabited zones."

Suddenly, the sound of a call came through shrilly, and, as the crowd rose up, as if hypnotized, the Great Planetary began to rumble:

"Calling from the first relay of the Red-Lands. Two powerful quakes have destroyed the oasis. The number of dead and wounded is huge; the crops have been wiped out; the waters appear to be in danger. Gliders are on the way to High Springs."

It was a stampede. Men, gliders and motocruisers poured forth in torrents. Excitement unknown for centuries stirred these apathetic souls: pity, terror and anxiety rejuvenated this multitude of the Last Age of Man.

The Council of Fifteen was deliberating, while Targ, all atremble, responded to the message from the Red-Lands, and announced the immediate departure of a delegation.

In times of tragedy the three sister oases—Red-Lands, High Springs, and Devastation—had pledged to help each other. Omal, who had a perfect understanding of tradition, declared:

"We have provisions enough for five years. The people of the Red-Lands can request a fourth of these. We are also bound to take in two thousand refugees, if it *cannot be avoided*. But they will only have reduced rations, and will be forbidden to reproduce. We ourselves must limit our families, because we must, *before fifteen years pass*, reduce our population to the traditional number."

The Council approved this reminder to obey the laws, then Bamar shouted to the crowd:

"The Council will now designate those who will leave for the Red-

Lands. There will be no more than nine. Others will be sent when we will know the needs of our brothers."

"I request to go," Targ implored.

"I do also," Arva added immediately.

Mano's eyes sparkled: "If the Council permits, I also wish to be among those sent."

Omal cast a favorable look on them. For long ago, like them, he too had known such impulsive movements, so rare among the Last Men.

Except for Amat, a frail adolescent, the crowd passively awaited the decision of the Council. Subjected to age-old laws, accustomed to a monotonous existence, troubled only by changes in the weather,[12] these peoples had lost all desire to take initiatives. Resigned, patient, endowed with a great passive courage—nothing excited them to adventure. The vast deserts that engulfed them, void of any means of supporting human life, weighed on their acts as on their thoughts.

"Nothing stands in the way of the departure of Targ, Arva and Mano," said the old Bamar, "but the road is long for Amat. Let the Council decide."

While the Council was deliberating, Targ pondered the sinister wasteland. He felt the burden of a bitter sorrow. The disaster of the Red-Lands weighed far more on him than on his brothers. For their hopes were focused only on the slowness of an eventual end, while he persisted in dreaming of fortunate metamorphoses. Yet the circumstances bitterly confirmed the wisdom of The Tradition.

II. Toward the Red-Lands

The nine gliders flew toward the Red-Lands. They barely strayed from the two roads the motocruisers had followed for a hundred centuries. The Ancestors had built large relay stations of unalloyed iron, each with its planetary resonator, and numerous less important relays. The two roads were in good condition. Because motocruisers rarely passed here, and as their wheels were outfitted with very elastic mineral fibers; and as, on the other hand, the men of the two oases still knew how to make partial use of the enormous energy sources their ancestors had tamed, the maintenance of these roads required more surveillance than work. The ferromagnetics were rarely seen there, and caused only negligible damage: a person on foot could have walked there all day without feeling the slightest harmful influence; it would not have been wise, however, to make stops that were too long, and especially to fall asleep; many sick people had, like poor Elna, lost all of their red corpuscles in this manner, and had died of anemia.

The Nine Voyagers ran no such risk. Each flew a light glider that, in fact, could have carried four men. Thus, even if accidents happened to two-thirds of the machines, the expedition would not be compromised.

Endowed with a nearly perfect elasticity, these gliders were built to withstand the most violent shocks, and to defy hurricanes.

Mano had taken the lead; Targ and Arva flew almost in convoy. The young man's agitation only continued to grow. And the story of the great catastrophes, handed down faithfully from generation to generation, haunted his memory.

For five hundred centuries, men have occupied, on the entire surface of the planet, ridiculously small enclaves.[13] The shadow of their decline was cast long before the catastrophes. During these very distant times, during the first centuries of the radioactive era, it was already noticed that the waters were receding; numerous scientists predicted that Mankind would perish by drought. But what effect could such predictions have on people who saw glaciers covering their mountains, rivers without number flowing through their dwellings, immense seas washing up on their continents?[14] And yet, the waters were receding, slowly, inexorably, absorbed into the ground and volatilized into the heavens.* Then came the great catastrophes. One witnessed extraordinary shifts in the Earth's crust; now and then earthquakes, in a single day, destroyed ten or twenty cities, and hundreds of villages; new chains of mountains were created, twice as high as the ancient chains of the Alps, the Andes, or the Himalayas; from century to century the waters dried up. These enormous upheavals grew worse yet. On the surface of the Sun, changes were detected that, obeying laws that were imperfectly understood, redounded on our miserable planet. A terrible series of catastrophes occurred: on the one hand, they caused high mountains to rise to altitudes of twenty-five to thirty thousand meters; on the other, they caused immense quantities of water to disappear.

*In the high regions of the atmosphere water vapor has, since time immemorial, been decomposed by ultraviolet light into oxygen and hydrogen: the hydrogen escaped into interstellar reaches. [Rosny's note]

It is told that on the eve of these sidereal upheavals, the human population had reached twenty-three billion individuals.[15] This horde of people had at its command unlimited energy. They derived it from protoatoms (as we still do ourselves, however imperfectly), and they barely worried about the retreat of the waters, for they had perfected farming techniques and the science of nutrition to such a great degree. They even flattered themselves that they would soon be able to live on organic elements synthesized in the chemist's laboratory. Several times this old dream seemed close to being realized; each time, mysterious maladies or accelerated degeneration decimated the groups subjected to these experiments. Out of necessity they had to content themselves with the foods that had nourished Mankind since its earliest ancestors. In truth, these foods were themselves undergoing subtle changes, due as much to ways of raising livestock and farming as to skillful human manipulations.[16] Reduced rations now sufficed to feed mankind; thus its digestive organs had undergone, in less than a hundred centuries, a notable diminution, while its respiratory system expanded in direct proportion to the increasing rarefaction of the atmosphere.

The last wild animals vanished; animals raised for food, in comparison with their ancestors, became veritable zoophytes,[17] hideous ovoid masses, with members transformed into stumps, and jaws atrophied from force-feeding. Alone, certain species of birds escaped this degradation and experienced a marvelous intellectual development.

Their gentleness, their beauty and their charm grew from age to age. They rendered incalculable services, because of their instinct, more refined than that of their masters, and these services were particularly appreciated in laboratories.

The men of this period of great power lived a troubled existence. The beauties and mysteries of poetry were dead. There was no more life in the wild, its vast, almost untamed spaces no longer existed: the woods, meadows, marshes, steppes, the uncultivated places of the Radioactive Age. In the end, suicide became the most formidable illness the species faced.

In fifteen thousand years the population of the Earth decreased from twenty-three to four billion souls: the seas, having disappeared into the depths, occupied only a quarter of the Earth's surface; the great rivers and large lakes had disappeared; mountains rose everywhere, huge and mournful. Thus the primitive planet returned—but barren of life!

Mankind fought back valiantly however. It prided itself in being able, insofar as it could not live without water, to fabricate the water that it needed for domestic and agricultural uses; but the raw materials used in this process became rare, or were found at such depths that their exploitation became absurdly difficult. It was necessary to fall back on processes of conservation, on ingenious means of husbanding the flow of water, and of making maximum use of this life-giving fluid.

Domestic animals perished, unable to adapt to these new conditions of life; in vain mankind sought to recreate hardier species; two hundred thousand years of degradation had dried up evolutionary energies. Alone, birds and plants resisted. The latter reverted to a few basic ancestral forms, the former adapted to the new environment. Many reverted to the wild state, built their nests on heights where man was even less able to pursue them because rarefaction of the atmosphere, though less significant, occurred along with the receding of the waters. They lived by scavenging and used ruses so refined that it was impossible to prevent them from surviving. As for those species that remained among our ancestors, their fate was at first abominable. Humans sought to debase them to the condition of food animals. But their consciousness had become too lucid; they fought ferociously to escape their fate. There were scenes as hideous as those episodes of primitive times when men devoured fellow men, when entire peoples were reduced to slavery. Horror penetrated the human soul, little by little we ceased brutalizing our companions on the planet, and feasting on them.

Moreover, seismic disturbances continued to reshape the Earth and destroy the cities. After thirty thousand years of struggle, our ancestors understood that the mineral kingdom, conquered for millions of years by the vegetable and animal kingdoms, was taking its ultimate revenge. There was a period of despair that reduced the human population to three hundred million, while the seas shrank to a tenth of the Earth's surface. A respite of three or four thousand years saw the rebirth of modest optimism. Humankind undertook prodigious works of preservation: the war against the birds ceased; humans restricted themselves to placing them in conditions that prevented them from multiplying; they obtained from them in turn invaluable services.

Then the catastrophes returned. The inhabitable lands shrank even more. And finally, about thirty thousand years ago, the culminating modifications took place: humanity found itself reduced to a few scattered enclaves on Earth, which had become as vast and forbidding as at the dawn of things; outside the oases, it became impossible to procure the water necessary to sustain life.

Since that time, a relative calm has reigned. Even though the water drawn from wells carved out of the abyss has again diminished, and the human population has dwindled by a third, and two oases have had to be abandoned, humanity manages to survive: no doubt humanity will continue to survive for fifty or a hundred thousand years more. Mankind's industry has diminished terribly. Of all the energy sources our species commanded in its prime, the men of the oases are no longer able to use any more than a small portion. Communication devices and work machines have become less complex; for many millennia, it has been necessary to abandon the spiraloid flying machines[18] that used to carry our ancestors across vast expanses at a speed ten times greater than that of our gliders.

Mankind now lives in a state of gentle resignation, sad and extremely passive. The creative spark has died out; it rekindles only, in atavistic fashion, in a few individuals. Through natural selection, the race has acquired a spirit of obedience that is automatic, and thus absolute, to laws henceforth immutable.[19] Passion is rare, crime nonexistent. A sort of religion has arisen, without doctrine, without rites: the fear and respect of the mineral kingdom. The Last Men attribute to the planet a slow and inexorable will. At first favorable to those kingdoms born from her womb, the Earth let them achieve great power. The mysterious hour in which she condemned them is also the hour when she came to favor new kingdoms.

At present, nature's obscure energies favor the ferromagnetic kingdom. One cannot say that the ferromagnetics actively participated in our destruction; at the very most, they contributed to the decimation, fatal in the end, of the wild birds.[20] Even though their arrival dates back to a distant time, these new beings have evolved little. Their movements are surprisingly slow; the most agile can only cover ten meters in an hour; and the bismuth-plated walls of native iron that surround the oases are an insurmountable obstacle to them. For them to pose a direct threat to us, they would have to make an evolutionary leap that bears no relation to their earlier development.

One first began to notice the existence of the ferromagnetic kingdom toward the decline of the Radioactive Age. They appeared as strange violet spots on *human* iron, that is, on iron and iron alloys that had been modified by industrial usage. The phenomenon only appeared on products that had been recast many times; these ferromagnetic spots were never dis-covered on *natural iron*. The new kingdom could only have been born, therefore, thanks to a human environment. This crucial fact was a great preoccupation for our ancestors. We had found ourselves perhaps in an analogous situation in relation to some earlier life form that, during its decline, allowed protoplasmic life to flower.

Whatever the case, humanity early on confirmed the existence of the ferromagnetics. Once the scientists had described their basic characteris-tics, there was no doubt that they were organized beings. Their composi-tion is unique. It admits only a single substance: iron.[21] If other bodies, in very small quantities, are sometimes found mixed with theirs, it is in the form of impurities, harmful to ferromagnetic development. Their organ-ism rids itself of these, unless it is too weak to do so, or stricken by some mysterious malady. The structure of iron, in this living state, is quite var-ied: fibrous iron, granulated iron, soft iron, hard iron, and so forth. The whole is malleable and contains no liquids. But what particularly charac-terizes these new organisms is their extreme complexity and a continual instability when in the magnetic state. This instability and complexity are such that even the most tenacious scientists had to renounce all attempts to apply not only laws to them, but even approximate rules of behavior. It is probably in this area that one must seek the dominant characteristic of ferromagnetic life. Whenever a superior consciousness will be discovered in the new species, I think it will especially reflect this strange phenom-enon, or rather, will be the flowering of such. In the meantime, if there does exist a ferromagnetic consciousness, it is still in an elementary stage. They are presently at that stage when the drive to procreate dominates everything. Nonetheless, they have already undergone several important transformations. The writers of the Radioactive Age reveal to us that each individual is composed of three groups, with a marked tendency, in each group, toward a helicoidal form. They were unable, at that period of time, to move more than five or six centimeters in twenty-four hours: when one of their agglomerations was destroyed, they took several weeks to put it together again. Today, as we said, they are able to cover two meters in an hour. What is more, there are now agglomerations of three, five, seven, even nine groups, the forms of these groups being greatly varied. A single group, composed of a considerable number of ferromagnetic corpuscles,[22] cannot subsist alone: it must be completed by two, by four, by six, or by eight other groups. A series of groups consists, obviously, of a number of energy components, although one cannot tell how these function. For agglomerations of seven or more, the ferromagnetic entity perishes if one of its groups is suppressed.

On the other hand, a ternary series can reform itself through the help of a single group, and a series of five with the help of three groups. The reconstitution of a mutilated series, to a great extent, resembles the genesis of the ferromagnetics: this genesis retains for human observers a deeply enigmatic character. It takes place *at a distance*. When a ferromagnetic is born, one invariably notices the presence of several other ferromagnetics. Depending on the species, it takes from six hours to ten days to form an individual; this seems due entirely to the phenomenon of *induction*. The reconstitution of an injured ferromagnetic functions in an analogous manner.

Today the presence of the ferromagnetics is for all purposes harmless. It would no doubt be a different story if mankind were to expand its domain.

At the same time they thought about combating the ferromagnetics, our ancestors sought methods of turning their activity to the advantage of our species. There seemed to be no barrier, for example, to putting the ferromagnetic substance to industrial uses. If this were the case, one would only need to protect the machines (something that, at that time, seems to have been done without too great a cost) in a manner similar to that employed to protect our oases ... This solution, in appearance elegant, was attempted. The ancient annals tell us that it failed. All iron transformed by this new form of life proves refractory to any human usage. Its very different structure and magnetic properties make it a substance that does not lend itself to forming any compounds, or to doing any kind of *directed* work. It is true that this structure seems to change and its magnetic properties disappear when it approaches the temperature of fusion (and, a fortiori, at the moment of fusion itself); but, when the metal is allowed to cool down, the harmful properties reappear.

What is more, a human being cannot stay for any length of time in areas where there is a ferromagnetic presence of any importance. Within a few hours it becomes anemic. After a day and a night, he finds himself in a state of extreme weakness. He soon faints; if he is not rescued, he dies.

The immediate reason for this is clear: the proximity of ferromagnetics tends to draw from us our red corpuscles. These corpuscles, reduced almost to the state of pure hemoglobin, accumulate on the surface of the skin, and are, consequently, drawn toward the ferromagnetics, who decompose them, and appear to assimilate them.

Different causes can counterbalance or retard this phenomenon. If one keeps walking, one has nothing to fear; more effective yet, one need only circulate in a motocruiser. If one dresses in a fabric made of bismuth fibers, one can defy the enemy influence for two days at least; this influence weakens if one sleeps with one's head pointing north; it fades spontaneously when the sun is near the meridian.

Of course, when the number of ferromagnetics decreases, this phenomenon becomes less and less intense: a moment arrives when it cancels itself, for the human organism does not let itself be taken over without resistance. Finally, ferromagnetic action weakens most of all along the curve of distance, and becomes negligible at more than ten meters.

One understands why the destruction of the ferromagnetics seemed necessary to our ancestors. They took up the struggle methodically. During the period that saw the beginning of the great catastrophes, this fight demanded great sacrifices: an evolutionary change had taken place with the ferromagnetics; massive amounts of energy were now needed to stop their proliferation.

The planetary transformations that followed favored the new kingdom: in a compensating manner, its presence became less menacing, for the amount of metal needed by human industry diminished gradually, and seismic disorders brought to the surface massive amounts of iron in its pure state, formerly unattainable to the invaders. Thus, the struggle against them slowed to the point of becoming insignificant. Of what importance was peril on the organic level when one was faced with immense planetary disaster?

At present, the ferromagnetics barely concern us at all. With our walls of red hematite, of limonite and iron spar coated with bismuth, we imagine ourselves impregnable. But if some improbable upheaval brought water back to the surface, the new kingdom would pose incalculable obstacles to human development, at least to development on any large scale.

Targ cast a long look over the plain: everywhere he saw the violet hue and the sinusoidal forms unique to ferromagnetic agglomerations.

"Yes," he murmured, "if humanity would recover some of its former ambition, it would be necessary to begin the work of the ancestors over again. It would have to destroy the enemy or make use of it. I fear that its destruction is impossible: a new kingdom necessarily carries within itself means of success that defy the predictions and the energy of an old kingdom. In opposite manner, why might we not find a means that would permit the two kingdoms to coexist, even to help each other? Yes, why not . . . insofar as the ferromagnetic world has its origin in our industry? Is this not an indication of some deep compatibility?"

Then, lifting his gaze toward the huge peaks in the West:

"Alas, my dreams are foolish. And yet, and yet . . . don't they help me go on living? Don't they give me a bit of that youthful happiness that has forever fled from the souls of men?"

He stood straight, his heart skipped a beat: There before him, in a cleft in the mountain of Shadows, three large white gliders had just appeared.

III. The Homicidal Planet

These gliders appeared to skim the Tooth of Purple, inclining toward the abyss. An orange shadow enshrouded them; then they took on a silvery hue in the sun at its zenith.

"The messengers from the Red-Lands!" cried Mano.

He brought no new news to his traveling companions; in fact his words were nothing more than a signal cry. The two squadrons hastened their course; soon, their pale forms swooped down toward the emerald wing feathers of the High Springs craft. Greetings resounded, followed by a silence; hearts were heavy; the only sound was the soft hum of engines, and the rustle of wings. All felt the cruel force of these deserts that they seemed to crisscross as masters. Finally Targ demanded, in a fearful voice:

"Is the extent of the disaster known?"

"No," answered a swarthy-faced pilot. "It will be many long hours before we will know exactly. All we know is that the number of dead and wounded is considerable. That would be nothing in comparison! But we fear the loss of several springs."

He bowed his head, with bitter calm.

"Not only are the crops lost, but many of our provisions have disappeared. However, provided there are no further tremors, with the help of High Springs and Devastation, we will be able to live for several years. . . . Our race will temporarily cease to reproduce, and perhaps we can get by without sacrificing anyone."

For a moment longer the two squadrons flew side by side, then the pilot with the swarthy face changed direction: those of the Red-Lands moved away.

They passed between formidable peaks, over the abyss, and along a slope that, once upon a time, would have been covered with pastures: now the ferromagnetics were there, multiplying their descendants.

"This proves," Targ mused, "that this slope is rich in human ruins!"

Once again, they were gliding over valleys and hills; with two-thirds of the day gone, they found themselves three hundred kilometers from the Red-Lands.

"Still an hour left," exclaimed Mano.

Targ scanned the space ahead with his telescope; he perceived, still vaguely, the oasis and the scarlet zone from which it had taken its name. The spirit of adventure, numbed by the encounter with the great gliders, awoke once more in the young man's heart; he accelerated the speed of his machine and pulled ahead of Mano.

Flights of birds were circling over the red zone; several advanced toward the squadron. At fifty kilometers from the oasis, they flocked; their monotonous chant confirmed the disaster and predicted immanent tremors. Targ, his heart constricted, listened and watched, unable to speak a word.

The barren earth appeared to have endured the bite of a gigantic plow; as they came nearer, the oasis revealed its collapsed houses, its ruptured wall, its crops nearly engulfed by the earth, miserable human ants swarming among the rubble . . .

Suddenly, an immense clamor tore through the atmosphere; the flight of birds scattered in strange confusion; a terrible quivering shook the vast expanse.

The homicidal planet was finishing its work!

Targ and Arva alone had uttered a cry of pity and horror. The other aviators continued on their flight, with the calm sadness of the Last Men . . . The oasis lay before them. It resounded with sinister moans. One saw pitiful creatures running, crawling, or gasping for breath; others remained motionless, struck down by death; from time to time a bloody head seemed to rise up from the ground. The spectacle became more and more hideous as they gradually were able to make out what had happened.

The Nine hovered, uncertain what to do. But the flight of birds, at first agitated by the terror, regained its harmony; no new tremor was expected, it was safe to land.

Several members of the High Council greeted the delegates from High Springs. Words were few and rapid. The new disaster required all available energies, the Nine joined forces with the rescuers.

The moans seemed intolerable at first. The atrocious wounds overcame the fatalism of the adults; the cries of the children were like the strident and savage soul of Pain.

Finally, the anesthetics worked their salutary effect. The most acute suffering sank into the depths of the unconscious. Only scattered cries were heard, the cries of those trapped deep in the ruins.

One of these cries drew Targ's attention. It was a cry of fear, not of pain; it had a charm that was enigmatic and sweet. For a long time the young man was unable to locate it . . . Finally he discovered a hollow from which the sound emerged more clearly. The watchman was impeded by slabs of rock, which he began to move aside with care. He was constantly obliged to halt his work, in the face of muted menaces from the mineral world: sudden holes formed, stones fell in landslides, or he heard suspicious vibrations.

The moaning stopped; nervous tension and fatigue brought sweat to Targ's temples . . .

Suddenly all seemed lost; a face of the wall was collapsing. The excavator, feeling himself at the mercy of the mineral world, lowered his head and waited. A block brushed by him; he resigned himself to fate; but silence and stability were restored.

Raising his eyes, he saw that a huge cavity, almost a cavern, had opened to his left; in the shadows, a human form lay stretched out. With difficulty the young man lifted this living wreck, and exited the ruins, at the exact instant that a new landslide closed the passage . . .

It was a young woman or an adolescent, dressed in the silver shirt of those of the Red-Lands. Above all other things, her hair stirred the rescuer. It was of that luminous sort that occurred, atavistically, barely once in a century among the daughters of men. Shimmering like precious metals, cool like water welling up from deep springs, it seemed a web of love, a symbol of the grace that had adorned woman throughout the ages.[23]

Targ's heart swelled, a heroic pounding beat through his head; he imagined magnanimous and glorious actions, those which never again came to pass among the Last Men . . . And, as he was admiring the red flower of her lips, the delicate curve of the cheeks and their pearly flesh, two eyes opened, eyes that had the color of mornings, when the sun is vast and nature's soft breath moves across the solitary lands . . .

IV. Into the Depths of the Earth

It was after dusk. The constellations were rekindling their keen flames. The oasis, silent, concealed its distress and its sorrows. And Targ walked near the wall, his soul in the throes of fever.

The hour was horrible for the Last Men. One after another, the planetaries had announced immense disasters. Devastation was destroyed; at the Two-Equatorials, at Grand Combe and Blue Sands, the waters had disappeared; it was receding at High Springs; Clear Oasis and Sulfur Valley reported either destructive tremors or rapid loss of water.

All of humanity was experiencing disaster.

Targ stepped across the ruined wall, he went out into the silent and terrible desert.

The moon, nearly full, rendered the feeblest stars invisible; it lit up the red granite and the violet patches of ferromagnetics; a pale phosphorescence pulsated at intervals, a mysterious sign that these new beings were going about their business.

The young man went forth into the solitude, oblivious of its funereal grandeur.

A brilliant image shone above the distressing aspects of the catastrophe. The star Vega twinkled like the pupil of a blue eye.[24] It seemed to him to be a twin of the vermillion hair. Love was becoming the very essence of his life; and that life was more intense, more profound, prodigious. It opened up to him fully that world of beauty he had intuited, the world for which it was better to die than to live for the dismal ideal of the Last Men. From time to time, like a name become sacred, the name of the one he had pulled from the rubble came to his lips: "Érê."

In the ferocious silence, the silence of the eternal desert, comparable to the silence of the vast ether where the stars flickered, he continued on. The air was as immobile as granite; time seemed dead, the space encountered was other than that of men, a space merciless, glacial, haunted by lugubrious mirages.

And yet, life was there, abominable because it was that which would replace human life, cunning, terrible, unknowable. Twice Targ paused to watch the behavior of the phosphorescent forms. Night never brought them to sleep. They moved here and there, going about some mysterious task; the manner in which they glided across the ground could not be explained as being the product of any organ. But he soon lost interest in them. The image of Érê carried him far away; there was a confused relation between this solitary trek and the heroism reawakened in his soul. In a confused way he was seeking adventure, impossible adventure, chimerical adventure: the discovery of Water!

Water alone could give him Érê. All the laws of mankind separated him from her. Yesterday, he still could have dreamt of taking her as his wife. All that was necessary was that a girl from High Springs be taken, in exchange, by the Red-Lands. After the catastrophe, such an exchange became impossible. High Springs would take in refugees, but would condemn them to celibacy. The law was inexorable; Targ accepted it as a higher necessity...

The moon was bright; it spread its disc of mother of pearl and silver over the western hills. As if hypnotized, Targ made his way toward it. He came to a place where the soil was rocky. Marks of the disaster remained there; several rocks had been overturned, others were split in half. Everywhere, there were cracks in the siliceous earth.

"It would seem," the young man murmured, "that the tremor reached its most violent level here." His dream faded a bit, the surroundings piqued his curiosity. "Why?" he asked himself again. . . . "Yes, why?"

He stopped at each moment to examine the rocks, and out of caution as well; this tortured ground had to be full of traps. A strange sense of elation gripped him. He mused that if there were a path to the Water, there was a good chance it might be found in a place like this that had been so radically reconfigured. Having switched on his "radiatrix," which he always took with him on voyages, he ventured into the cracks and corridors: every one narrowed rapidly, or ended in a cul-de-sac.

Finally, he found himself in front of a narrow crevice, at the base of a tall, very large rock, which the tremors had barely touched. He needed only to look at the rift, which glittered in places like crystals, to tell that it was recent. Targ, judging it unimportant, was about to move away. The glittering attracted him. Why not explore it? If it were not deep, there would only be a couple of steps to take.

The crevice revealed itself to be longer than he would have first thought. Nevertheless, after thirty paces or so, it began to narrow; soon

Targ thought he would not be able to go any farther. He stopped; he scrupulously examined the details of the walls. The passageway was not totally impracticable, but he had to crawl. The watchman hesitated only an instant; he entered a hole, whose diameter was barely larger than that of a man. The passage, sinuous and strewn with sharp rocks, became narrower yet; Targ wondered if it would be possible for him to turn back.

He was as if embedded in the depths of the Earth, captive of the mineral realm, a small thing, infinitely weak, which a single stone could pulverize;[25] but because he had begun the task, a fever pulsed in him. Were he to abandon the task, before it was seen to be totally impossible, he would hate and despise himself ever afterward. He persevered.

His limbs soaked with sweat, he crawled for a long time into the bowels of the rock. Finally, he collapsed. The pounding of his heart, which at first sounded like a beating of giant wings, became weaker. It was no more than a feeble palpitation: courage and hope fell from him like heavy burdens. When his heart regained some strength, Targ judged himself ridiculous to have embarked on such a primitive adventure.

"Am I not a madman?"

And he began to crawl backward. Then he was smitten with a dreadful despair. The image of Érê flashed across his mind so vividly that she seemed to be beside him in this hole.

"My madness is still preferable to the terrible wisdom of my fellow men . . . Forward!"

Again Targ began his adventure; he risked his life with savage determination, resolved only to stop when faced with the insurmountable.

Luck seemed to reward his audacity; the crevice widened, he found himself in a high basalt corridor whose vault seemed supported by columns of anthracite. A violent joy seized him; he began to run, everything seemed possible.

But the world of stone is as full of enigmas as was once upon a time the virgin forest. Suddenly, the corridor ended. Targ found himself facing a dark wall, which absorbed all but a few reflected beams from his radiatrix. Nonetheless, he did not stop exploring the walls. And he discovered, at a spot three meters high, the opening of another crevice.

This was a rather sinuous opening, tilted at a more or less forty-degree angle from the horizontal, large enough to permit the passage of a man. The watchman contemplated it with a mixture of joy and disappointment.

It attracted his idle hopes, because here finally was a passage that was not definitely closed; on the other hand, it showed itself in a discouraging light, because it took an upward direction.

"If it doesn't turn back downward again, chances are it will take me back to the surface instead of into the depths," the explorer grumbled.

He made a gesture that was heedless and defiant, a gesture that was alien to him, as to all men of his time, and that recalled some ancestral gesture. Then, he made preparations to scale the wall.

It was almost vertical and slick. But Targ had brought with him a ladder made of arcum fibers, an item aviators never forgot to carry. He drew it from his tool sack. After having served several successive generations, it was as supple and strong as the day it was made. He unrolled its fine, light texture and, taking it by the middle, gave it the necessary toss. The movement was perfectly executed. The hooks at the end of the ladder took hold effortlessly in the basalt. In a few seconds the explorer reached the opening.

He could not hold back a cry of displeasure. For if the crevice was perfectly accessible, on the other hand it sloped upward quite steeply. So many efforts would then have been in vain!

Nonetheless, after folding the ladder, Targ entered the crevice. The first steps were difficult. Then the terrain leveled off, a corridor opened up, wide enough that several men could have walked down it abreast. Unfortunately, the path still sloped upward. The watchman estimated that he must be some fifteen meters above the level of the external plain; the subterranean voyage was becoming an ascension! . . .

He went on toward the end, whatever it might be, with a bitter calm, all the while reproaching himself about this mad adventure: what had he done to make a discovery that would surpass in importance all the other discoveries men had made for hundreds of centuries? Was it enough merely that he had a fanciful character, a soul more rebellious than others, in order to succeed there where the collective effort, equipped with remarkable tools, had failed? An attempt such as his, did it not call for a resignation and a patience that were absolute?

Distracted, he did not notice that the path was becoming less arduous. It had become horizontal when, with a sudden start, he came to his senses: a few steps in front of him, the gallery was beginning to slope downward! . . .

It descended gradually, for a distance of more than a kilometer. Large, deeper in the middle than on the edges, the path was in general easily practicable, barely impeded by a stone here, a fissure there. Without a doubt, at some distant period in the past, a subterranean stream flowed here.

Even so, debris had piled up, among which was some recent rubble; then the passage seemed blocked again.

"The gallery did not end here," the young man said. "Some upheaval in the Earth's crust caused this rupture, but when? Yesterday . . . a thousand years ago . . . a hundred million years ago?"

He did not stop to examine the mass of fallen rocks, among which he would have recognized signs of recent convulsions. All of his perspicacity was directed toward finding an opening. It was not long before he located a fissure. Narrow and high, hard, rough, repellant, it did not lead him astray: he found *his* gallery again. It continued its descent, becoming more and more spacious as it went: finally, its average width reached more than one hundred meters.

Targ's last doubts vanished: a veritable subterranean river, long ago, had flowed there. A priori, this belief was encouraging. On further reflection, it bothered the Oasis Dweller. Nothing at all proved that because water once flowed here abundantly, that there was water now anywhere close by. On the contrary! All the springs actually being used were located far from the places where the life-giving liquid had once flowed . . . It was almost a law.

Three times more, the gallery seemed to end in a cul-de-sac; each time, Targ found a way through. It finally ended, however. An immense hole, a gulf appeared before the man's eyes.

Sad and tired, he sat down on the stone. This was a moment more terrible than when he crawled, above, through the stifling gallery. Any further effort would be bitter folly. He had to go back! Yet his heart revolted at the thought. The soul of adventure stirred in him, enforced by the astonishing voyage he had just undertaken. The abyss no longer held terror for him.

"And what if one had to die?" he exclaimed.

Already he sought handholds in the granite.

Given over to these sudden inspirations, he had already descended, miraculously, to a depth of thirty meters, when he made a false movement, and slipped.

"It's finished!" he sighed.

He tumbled into the abyss.

A shock broke his fall. Not the brutal shock of falling on granite, but an elastic shock, violent enough however to knock him senseless. When he regained consciousness, he found himself suspended in the semidarkness, and, feeling over himself, he discovered that an outcropping of rock had snagged his tool bag. The straps of the bag, attached to his trunk, supported him; as they were made, like his ladder, of arcum fibers, he knew that they would not break. The bag, however, could slip off the outcropping.

Targ felt strangely calm. He leisurely calculated his chances of being lost, or saved. The sack was caught on the overhang near the place where the straps were attached, which meant the anchor was solid. The explorer felt around the rocky wall. Besides the outcropping, his hand encountered rough surfaces, then the void; his feet found, toward the left, a foothold that he judged, after a few gropings, to be a small platform. By taking hold of the outcropping on one hand, and on the other hand by propping himself up on the platform, he was able to do without any other support.

When he had chosen the position he judged the most convenient, he succeeded in detaching his bag. Much freer to move now, he flashed the beams of his radiatrix in all directions. The platform was large enough for a man to stand erect, and even make slight movements. Above, a ridge of rock allowed at the most for securing the hooks of the ladder; after this, an ascent seemed possible, back to the place from which the Oasis Dweller had fallen. Below, there was nothing but the abyss, sheer vertical walls.

"I can go back up," the young man concluded. . . . "But to go down is impossible."

He no longer pondered the fact that he had just escaped death; vexation at this vain failed effort alone tormented his soul. With a long sigh, he let go of the overhang and, holding on to the rough places, he succeeded in placing himself on the platform. His temples were buzzing, a torpor took hold of his limbs and his brain; his discouragement weighed so heavily that he felt himself little by little succumbing to the dizzying attraction of the void. When he came to his senses, he ran his fingers instinctively over the granite wall, and realized once again that it disappeared, at about halfway his height. He bent down then, he uttered a weak cry: the platform was located at the entrance to a cavity, which the beams of his radiatrix showed to be of considerable magnitude.

He laughed silently. If he went down to defeat, at least he would have lived an adventure that was worth being attempted!

Checking to see that none of his tools were missing, and especially that the arcum ladder was in good working order, he entered into the cavern. It spread before him a vault of rock crystal and gems. At each movement of the lamp, rays bounced around the walls, mysterious and enchanting. The souls of myriad crystals awoke to his light: here was a subterranean twilight, dazzling and fleeting, an infinitesimal hailstorm of colors that were scarlet, orange, jonquil, hyacinth, or red of sinop.[26] Targ saw there a reflection of mineral life, of that life form both vast and minuscule, menacing and deep, that had the last word on mankind, that, one day, would have the last word on the ferromagnetic kingdom as well.

At this moment, Targ had no fear of it. Yet he held this cavern in the same respect that all Last Men vowed to these mute beings that, having presided over the Beginnings, have kept their forms and powers intact.

A vague mysticism stirred within him, not the hopeless mysticism of the decadent Oasis Dwellers, but the mysticism that once, long ago, had inspired reckless hearts. Even though he still distrusted the snares of the Earth, at least he had that faith that derives from successful actions and that carries victories from the past into the future.

Beyond the cavern there was a corridor with irregular slopes. Several times again it was necessary to crawl in order to pass through the channels. Then, the corridor continued; the slope became steep to the point that Targ feared another chasm loomed. This slope became less steep. It became almost as easy to follow as a roadway. And the watchman was descending in all safety, when the traps resumed. The corridor became neither narrower in height or width, it simply closed off. A wall of gneiss was there, which glowed furtively in the lamplight. In vain the Oasis Dweller tested it in every direction: no large fissure was revealed.

"This is the logical end of the adventure!" Targ moaned. "The abyss, which has mocked the efforts, the genius, and the machines of all mankind, could not suddenly give favor to one small, solitary animal!"

He sat down, exhausted by fatigue and sadness. The road would be hard now! Beaten down by defeat, would he even have the strength to go on to the end?

He stayed there a long while, crushed by distress. He could not make himself decide to go on. At intervals, he played his light over the pale wall ... Finally, he got to his feet. But then, overcome by a sort of anger, he thrust his fists into all the small fissures, he pulled desperately at the outcroppings ...

His heart began to pound: something had moved.

Something had moved. A section of the wall was moving. With a dull grunt, and with all his strength, Targ attacked the stone. It fell; it nearly crushed the man; a triangular hole appeared: the adventure was not over yet!

Panting, full of apprehension, Targ entered the opening in the rock, at first bent over, then standing upright, for at every step the opening became larger. And he went on as if in a state of somnambulism, anticipating new obstacles, when all at once he thought he saw an abyss.

He was not wrong. The crack ended with the void; and yet, toward the right, a mass that sloped downward stood out, enormous. In order to reach it, Targ had to lean out over the void and hoist himself by the force of his wrists.

The slope was manageable. When the watchman had gone twenty meters or so, a strange sensation gripped him, and taking the cover from his hygroscope, he held it out over the chasm. Then, he positively felt the paleness and cold settle over his face ...

In the subterranean atmosphere, a vapor was floating, still invisible to the light. There was water there!

Targ shouted in triumph. He had to sit down, paralyzed by the surprise and the joy of victory. Then, uncertainty took hold of him again. Without a doubt, the vital fluid was down there, it would soon be visible; but the deception would be all the more intolerable were it only an insignificant spring or paltry expanse of water. With slow steps, filled with fear, the watchman continued his descent ... There was increasing evidence; at intervals a shimmering was seen ... And suddenly, as Targ rounded an outcropping of vertical rock, the water became visible.

VI. The Ferromagnetics

Two hours before dawn, Targ was back on the plain, at the mouth of the same crevice where he had begun his journey into the world of shadows. Horribly tired, he contemplated, on the far horizon, the scarlet moon, which resembled a round furnace, about to burn out. It disappeared. In the immensity of night, the stars rekindled.

Then, the watchman desired to be under way again. His legs seemed heavy as stone, his shoulders sagged painfully, and throughout his whole body such languidness was felt that he let himself collapse on a rock. He relived, with eyelids half closed, the hours he had just spent in the abyss. The way back had been frightful. Even though he had been careful to multiply the traces of his passage, he had lost his way. Then, already exhausted by his previous efforts, he came close to passing out. The time seemed incommensurably long; Targ was like a miner who had spent long months beneath the cruel earth.

Nevertheless, here he is, back on the surface, where his brothers still dwell, here are the stars that, throughout the ages, exalted the dreams of mankind; soon, the godlike dawn will reappear in the firmament.

"The dawn!" the young man stammered. . . . "The light of day!"

He held out his arms toward the east, in a gesture of ecstasy; then his eyes closed and, without being conscious of it, he stretched out on the ground.

A reddish light awakened him. Raising his eyelids with difficulty, he glimpsed, at the end of the horizon, the immense orb of the sun.

"Let's go . . . get up . . ." he said to himself.

But an invisible torpor pinned him to the ground; his thoughts floated in a numb haze, fatigue exhorted him to renounce his effort. He was about to fall asleep again, when he felt a faint tingling over his entire skin. And he saw, on his hand, next to the scratches he had made climbing over rocks, the characteristic rust-colored dots.

"The ferromagnetics!" he murmured. *"They are drinking my life!"*

In his lassitude, his adventure barely frightened him any more. It seemed like some distant thing, alien, almost symbolic. Not only did he feel no pain whatsoever, but the sensation turned out to be almost pleasant; it was a sort of vertigo, a slight and slow intoxication, which must resemble euthanasia. Suddenly the images of Érê and Arva flashed through his memory, followed by a resurgence of energy.

"I don't want to die!" he moaned. "I don't want to!"

In an obscure manner, he relived his struggle, his sufferings, his victory. Over there, in the Red-Lands, life called to him, fresh and charming. No, he didn't want to die; he wanted to see dawns and dusks for a long time yet. He wanted to fight the mysterious forces.

With a superhuman effort, rousing his sleeping will, he struggled to get to his feet.

In the morning, Arva had not realized at all that Targ was absent. He must have overworked himself the night before; undoubtedly, totally exhausted, he must be sleeping late. Yet, after two hours of waiting, his absence surprised her. Finally she went and knocked on the wall of the room the watchman had chosen. There was no response. Perhaps he had gone out while she was still sleeping. She knocked again, then she pushed the switch for the door; it revealed, as it rolled up, an empty room.[27]

The young girl went inside the room, and saw everything arranged in good order. The arcum bed was raised up against the wall, all the toilet articles were untouched, nothing revealed the recent presence of a man. And a certain apprehension gripped the heart of the visitor.

She went to find Mano; together they questioned birds and men, without receiving a useful response. This was not normal, and perhaps even disquieting. For after the earthquake, the oasis remained full of traps. Targ could have fallen into a crevice, or been caught in a landslide.

"Probably he just went out early in the morning," said Mano the optimist. "Because he is an orderly person, he would first have tidied up his room . . . Let's go look for him!"

Arva remained anxious. Communications had become unreliable and, because many of the sound wave receivers had been knocked down, the searches were going nowhere.

Toward noon, Arva was wandering sadly, among the rubble, at the place where desert and oasis meet, when a flock of birds appeared, with long cries: "Targ has been found."

She only needed to climb up on the wall, she saw him walking toward her, still in the far distance, with weary steps.

His clothing was torn; gashes scarred his neck, his face and hands; his entire body expressed fatigue; his gaze, alone, preserved its cool energy.

"Where have you been?" Arva cried.

He answered: "I come from the depths of the Earth." But he did not want to say anything more.

Word of his return having spread, his traveling companions came to meet him. When one of them reproached him for having delayed their departure, he answered: "Do not reproach me, for I am the bearer of great news."

This answer surprised and shocked his hearers. How could a man bring news that was not already known to all men? Such words had meaning once upon a time, when the Earth was uncharted and full of resources, when chance still lived among human beings, and whole peoples or individuals challenged their destiny. But, now that the planet is depleted, and men are no longer capable of fighting among themselves, when all things are resolved by inflexible law, and when no one predicts perils in advance of the birds or the instruments, such words seemed inept.[28]

"'Great news?" the man who had first reproached him repeated with disdain. "Have you gone crazy, watchman?"

"You will soon see if I've become crazy! Let us go summon the Council of the Red-Lands."

"You have made them wait."

Targ did not respond. He turned to his sister and said: "Go, and bring the girl that I saved yesterday . . . Her presence is necessary."

The High Council of the Red-Lands had gathered, at the center of the oasis. It was not complete, as several of its members had perished in the catastrophe. There was no expression of pain, and barely one of resignation, in the attitude of these survivors. Fatality was bred into them, as deep as life itself.

They greeted the Nine Emissaries with an almost inert calm. And Cimor, who presided, said in a monotonous voice:

"You brought us aid from High Springs, and High Springs has itself been struck by disaster. The end of mankind seems very near. The oases no longer know which ones are capable of helping the others."

"They should no longer even help each other," said Rem, the first master of the Waters. "The law forbids it. Once the waters have disappeared, it is just that solidarity vanishes. Each oasis must tend to its own fate."

Targ stepped before the Nine and spoke: "The waters can return."

Rem considered him with calm disdain: "Anything can return, young man. But they are gone for good."

Then the watchman, having cast a glance toward the back of the hall and perceived the hair of light, went on in a trembling voice:

"The waters will return for the Red-Lands."

A gentle disapproval appeared on some faces; everyone remained silent.

"They will return," Targ exclaimed with force. "And I can say this because I have seen them."

This time a feeble emotion, one born of the sole image capable of moving the Last Men, the image of water springing from the ground, spread from person to person. And Targ's tone of voice, in its vehemence and sincerity, nearly caused hope to be reborn. But doubt soon returned. His overly wild eyes, his wounds and torn clothes, inspired mistrust: although rare, madmen had not yet disappeared from the planet.

Cimor made a slight sign. Slowly several men surrounded the watchman. He saw this move and understood what it meant. Calmly, he opened his tool bag, drew out his thin chromograph, and unrolling one of its sheets, he brought forth the proof that he had gathered in the bowels of the earth.

The images were as precise as reality itself. When the men closest to Targ had set eyes on them, exclamations arose from all quarters. A veritable amazement, a near exaltation, took hold of those present. For all recognized the awesome and sacred fluid.

More excitable than the others, Mano uttered a resounding cry. The cry, magnified by the sound wave receivers, echoed throughout the oasis; a multitude rapidly surrounded the hall. The sole frenzy still capable of arousing the Last Men intoxicated the crowd.

Targ was transfigured; he became almost a god; people's souls, like souls in olden times, offered up to him a mystical enthusiasm; faces opened to the flood of emotion, dull eyes filled with fire, a boundless hope shattered the age-old atavism of resignation. And the members of the High Council themselves, caught up as part of this collective entity, abandoned themselves to the tumult.

Targ alone could command silence. He made a sign to the crowd that he wished to speak; the voices died away, the tumult of heads became calm, a passionate attention blossomed on every face.

The watchman, turning toward Érê's blond glow that stood out from the mass of dark hair, declared:

"People of the Red-Lands, the water I have discovered is on your lands, it belongs to you. But human law gives me rights to it; before giving it up to you, I demand my privilege!"

"You shall be the first among us!" said Cimor. "Such is the rule!"

"That is not what I demand," the watchman replied softly.

He gestured to the crowd to let him pass. Then, he walked toward Érê. When he was near her, he bowed and said in an impassioned voice: "It is in your hands that I place the waters, mistress of my destiny. You alone can give me my reward!"

She listened, surprised and trembling. For such words as these were heard no longer. At some other moment, she would have barely understood what they meant. But in the midst of all these exultant hearts, and in thrall to the magical vision of subterranean springs, her whole being was confounded; the magnificent feelings that stirred the watchman shone in the pearly cheeks of the virgin.

VIII. And Alone the Red-Lands Survive

In the years that followed, the Earth felt only minor tremors.

But the last catastrophe had sufficed to deal the death blow to the oases. Those who had seen all their water disappear had never been able to get it back. At High Springs, it had dried up over eighteen months, then disappeared into the bottomless abyss. The Red-Lands alone had known vast hopes. The water table Targ had found gave water more abundant and less impure than that of the vanished springs. Not only did it suffice to nourish the survivors, but they were able to take in the small group that survived from Devastation, and many refugees from High Springs.

There, all possible aid stopped. As fifty thousand years of heredity have conditioned them to inflexible laws, the Last Men accepted without revolt the verdict of destiny. Therefore, there was no war; a bare few individuals sought to bend the rule and came in supplication to the Red-Lands. There was nothing to do but turn them away: pity would have been a supreme injustice, and an abuse of authority.

As provisions began to dwindle, each oasis designated those of its inhabitants who had to die. First the old were sacrificed, then the children, except for a small number who were kept in reserve, on the hypothesis that there might be a possible change in the planet's evolution, then, there followed all those whose constitutions were depraved or sickly.

Euthanasia was extremely gentle. Once those condemned had taken the wonderful poisons, all fear vanished. Their waking hours were one long ecstasy, their sleep as deep as death. The idea of nothingness delighted them, their joys grew until they reached the final torpor.

Many hastened their end. Little by little, it became a contagion. In the equatorial oases, they did not wait until provisions ran out; water still remained in some of their reservoirs, and already the last inhabitants had disappeared.

Four years were needed to annihilate the inhabitants of High Springs.

Then, these oases were swallowed up by the immense desert, the ferromagnetics occupied the place of humans.

After Targ's discovery, the Red-Lands had prospered. They had rebuilt the oasis to the east, on a site where the paucity of ferromagnetics made their destruction an easy task. The building, the clearing of the land, the harnessing of the waters was done in six months. The first crops were beautiful, the second marvelous.

Despite the successive death of the other communities, the men of the Red Oasis lived with a sort of hope. Were they not the chosen people, those in favor of whom, for the first time in a hundred centuries, the implacable law had bent? Targ maintained this spirit in their souls. His influence was great. He possessed the appeal of those who triumph, and their symbolic prestige.

However, his victory had impressed Targ more than anyone else. In it he saw an obscure reward, and even more, a confirmation of his faith. His spirit of adventure blossomed; he had aspirations almost as great as those of his heroic ancestors. And the love that he felt for Érê and the two children he had by her blended with dreams of which he dared speak to no one, except his wife or his sister, for he knew they would be incomprehensible to all other Last Men.

Mano did not have this fever. His life followed a straight line. He never thought of the past, even less about the future. He tasted the unchanging sweetness of each day; he lived with his wife, Arva, an existence as carefree as that of the silver birds whose flocks, each morning, soared above the oasis. As his first children, because of their sturdy constitutions, had been among the emigrants taken in by the Red-Lands, he barely felt a fleeting pang of melancholy when thinking of the destruction of High Springs.

In contrast, this destruction continued to torment Targ: many times his glider took him back to his native oasis. Doggedly he searched the area for water, he left the safety of the protective roads, he visited the desolate stretches where the ferromagnetics were living the life of young kingdoms. Along with several men from the oasis, he had explored a hundred chasms. Even though his searches were in vain, Targ never became discouraged: he taught that one must merit discoveries through stubborn effort and long patience.

IX. The Receding Waters

One day, as he returned from his solitary explorations, Targ, from the height of his glider, noticed a crowd near the main reservoir. By means of his telescope, he made out the Water Masters and the members of the High Council; several miners were emerging from the wellhead. A flock of birds flew to meet his glider: from them he learned that the spring was causing some concerns. He landed and was immediately surrounded by a jittery crowd, who put their confidence in him. He felt cold to the bone, when he heard Mano say: "'The water level has gone down."

All voices confirmed the sad news. He questioned Rem, the head Water Master, who responded:

"The water level was measured at the wellhead itself. It has fallen six meters."

Among all these faces Rem's was motionless. Joy, sadness, fear, desire never were seen on his cold lips, nor in his eyes, which looked like two pieces of bronze, and whose sclera were barely visible. His professional knowledge was perfect: he knew the entire tradition of the well-masters.

"The water level can vary," Targ remarked.

"That is true! But normal variations are never more than two meters, and such gaps are never sudden . . ."

"Do you know with certitude that they are sudden now?"

"Yes, the instruments have been checked. They're in working order. Still this morning they detected nothing. It was toward midday that the level started to fall. The rate is now more than a meter and a half per hour."

His mineral eye remained fixed; his hand made not a gesture; one saw his lips barely move. Targ's eyes quivered as with the pounding of his heart.

"According to the divers," said Rem, "there are no new fissures in the bed of the lake. The trouble, then, comes from the springs themselves. There are three possible hypotheses: the springs are blocked; they have deviated from their paths; or they have dried up. We are keeping up hope."

Out of his mouth, the word "hope" fell like a block of ice.

Targ asked again, "Are the reservoirs full?"

Rem almost made a gesture: "They are still full. And I've given the order to dig new ones. Within the hour all our machines will be in action."

Things went exactly as Rem had announced. The powerful machines of the Red-Lands dug into the granite. Until the first star appeared, stupor reigned over the oasis.

Targ had gone below ground. By means of galleries outfitted by the miners, there was now rapid access without danger. In the glow of the searchlights, the watchman examined the subterranean site that he, first among all men, had come upon. He studied it feverishly. Two springs fed into the lake. The first came out twenty-six meters deep, the second at a depth of twenty-four meters.

Divers had been able to enter one outlet, but barely. The other one was too narrow.

In order to get additional information, they had attempted to work into the rock; a landslide gave rise to fears. Might not any such rearrangements generate fissures, through which water would be lost?

Agre, the eldest member of the Grand Council, had said: "This water was given to us by the Disaster; without this, it would have remained inaccessible. Perhaps this event also traced its present path. Let us not begin new, uncertain works. It is enough that we have carried to term those that were absolutely necessary."

As these words seemed wise, the men resigned themselves to the mystery.

Toward the end of dusk, the level fell more slowly; a wave of hope passed over the oasis. But neither the Water Masters nor Targ shared their confidence; if the rate of fall was decreasing, it was because the water had receded below the largest fissures into which it was leaking. The water now contained in the lake could fall to a level of four meters, and if the springs remained inaccessible, then this, along with what remained in the reservoir, would be *all the water possessed by the Last Men.*

All night long the machines of the Red-Lands dug new reservoirs; all night as well, water, the mother of life, continued to be lost in the abysmal depths of the planet. By morning the level had fallen to eight meters, but two reservoirs were ready that rapidly took in their provision; they absorbed three thousand cubic meters of liquid.

Filling these lowered the level once again; the mouth of the first spring could be seen to reappear. Targ went inside it ahead of everyone else and saw that the ground had undergone recent changes. Several crevices had formed, masses of porphyry obstructed the passage; it was necessary, provisionally, to give up trying to explain how the disaster occurred.

A second day passed, which was mournful. By five o'clock the underground flow and the filling of another reservoir lowered the water to the level of the second spring, whose mouth had completely disappeared.

From this moment on, the loss stopped; it was no longer necessary to hasten the construction of new reservoirs. Rem nonetheless persisted in finishing his job, and, during six days, the men and machines of the oasis toiled on.

At the end of the sixth day, Targ, harried, his heart in a fever, sat meditating in front of his dwelling. A silvery darkness enveloped the oasis. Jupiter could be seen in the sky; a sharp half moon cleaved the ether: without doubt, this great planet also created kingdoms that, after having known the freshness of youth and the force of adulthood, perished from loss and anguish.

Érê had come. In a beam of moonlight her long hair seemed a soft and warm light. Targ drew her to him; he murmured:

"At your side I had found once again the life of ancient times. You were the dream of a new genesis . . . by simply feeling your presence, I believed in days without number. And now, Érê, if we do not recover the springs, or if we do not find any new water, within ten years the Last Men will have disappeared from the planet."

X. The Earthquake

Six seasons came and went. The masters of the Waters caused great galleries to be dug in order to recover the springs. All failed. Illusory fissures or impenetrable chasms foiled their efforts. From month to month, hope dwindled in their souls. The ancient atavism of resignation weighed on them once more; their passivity seemed even to grow, in the way a chronic illness, after a moment of respite, takes a turn for the worse. All faith, however feeble, abandoned them. Already death gripped these dismal lives.

When the time came for the High Council to order the first deaths by euthanasia, it happened that there were more volunteers ready to die than the law demanded.

Targ, Arva, and Érê alone refused to accept fatality; but Mano became discouraged. Not that he had become provident. No more than before did he think of tomorrow; but for him fatality had become an ever-present reality. Once the euthanasia began, he had acquired such a keen sense of the fading away of things that all energy abandoned him. Light and darkness became, equally, his enemies. He lived on in a lifeless and mournful waiting; his love for Arva had disappeared along with his love for his own person; he lost all interest in his children, knowing that euthanasia would soon take them as well. And the act of speech became unbearable for him, he no longer listened, he remained silent and torpid for days on end. Almost all the inhabitants of the Red-Lands led an existence similar to his.

No effort was capable of stimulating the pitiful amount of energy they had, because there was almost no work to be done. Except for a few clumps of plants, maintained in order to have fresh seeds, all agriculture had disappeared. The water in the reservoirs needed no care: it was kept from evaporating and purified by machines that functioned almost perfectly. As for the reservoirs themselves, they needed, each day, only one inspection, which was made easy by automatic gauges. Thus, nothing occurred to disturb the listlessness of these Last Men. Those best able to escape from these doldrums were the least emotive individuals, who had never loved anyone, and had hardly loved their own persons. These, perfectly adapted to the millennial laws, displayed a plodding perseverance, strangers to all joys as to all sorrows. Inertia dominated them; it bolstered them in the face of excessive depression and against any sudden resolutions; they were the perfect products of a doomed species.

On the other hand, Targ and Arva sustained themselves through a superior capacity for emotion. In revolt against the evidence, they stood against the formidable planet as two small, ardent lives, full of love and hope, pulsing with those vast desires that had kept animal nature alive through a hundred thousand centuries.

The watchman had abandoned none of his explorations; he kept a series of gliders and motocruisers in perfect working order; he even kept the principal planetary reflectors from falling into ruin, and watched over the seismographs.

Thus, one evening, after a voyage in the direction of Devastation, Targ held a solitary vigil in the night. Through the sheet of transparent metal of his windowpane, a constellation appeared that in the time of Legends they called Canis Major. It contained the brightest among the stars, a sun far more vast than our Sun.[29] Targ raised up his inextinguishable yearning toward it. And he thought of what he had seen, toward the middle of the day, as he was gliding close to the earth.

It was on an exceedingly desolate plain, where a few solitary blocks of stone reared their forms. Everywhere the ferromagnetics were tracing out their violet agglomerations. He was barely paying attention to them, when, toward the south, on a clear yellow surface, he perceived a race that he had never before encountered. It produced individuals of large size, each one composed of eighteen groups. Some of these reached a total length of three meters. Targ calculated that the mass of the most powerful could not be less than forty kilograms. They moved about more easily than the most rapid ferromagnetics known up to now; in fact, their speed reached half a kilometer per hour.

"This is terrifying," the watchman murmured. "Were they to get into the oasis, would we not be defeated? The least breach in the wall would put us in mortal danger."

He shuddered; an anxious moment of tenderness took him into the adjoining rooms. In the orange glow of a Radiant, he contemplated Éré's astonishingly luminous hair and the fresh faces of the children. His heart melted. To simply see them living, he could not understand the end of mankind. How could this be! Youth, the mysterious power of generations are in them, so full of sap, and is all of this going to vanish? For some doddering old race, slowly broken down by decadence, to be in this state, that would be logical; but why these, this flesh as lovely and new as that of men from before the Radioactive Era!

As he was returning to himself, still in a dream, a slight jolt shook the ground. He barely had time to perceive it, and already, the immense calm had returned to the oasis. But Targ was full of suspicion. He waited for a while, his ear cocked, listening. All remained peaceful; the gray masses of the landscape, silhouetted in the powdery light of the stars, appeared immutable, and in the sky, implacably pure, Aquila, Pegasus, Perseus, Sagittarius inscribed the minutes as they fleeted upon the dial of the infinite.[30]

"Was I wrong?" the watchman mused, "or could the tremor really have been insignificant?"

He shrugged his shoulders, with a slight shiver. How could he even dare to think that any trembling of the earth could be insignificant? The most infinitely small of such tremors is full of the most menacing mystery!

Worried, he went to look at the seismographs. Device Number 1 registered the small tremor, a slight trace, and barely longer than a millimeter. Device Number 2 showed that the phenomenon had no consequence.

Targ went to the house of the birds; no more than twenty of them had been preserved. When he arrived, all were sleeping; they barely raised their heads when the watchman switched on the light. The quake then must have barely aroused them, for a very brief moment, and they did not anticipate a second one.

Nonetheless, Targ felt he had to alert the chief sentinel. This man, an inert individual with atrophied nerves, had noticed nothing.

"I'm going to make my rounds," he declared. . . . "We will verify the water levels every hour on the hour."

These words reassured Targ.

XI. The Fugitives

Targ was still asleep when someone touched him on the shoulder. When he opened his eyes, he saw his sister, Arva, extremely pale, looking at him. It was a sure sign a disaster had happened. He arose with a start.

"What is happening?"

"Fearsome things," the young woman replied. "You know that, this evening, there was an earthquake, because you yourself were the one who reported it."

"A very slight quake."

"So light that nobody noticed it but you. Yet its consequences are terrible. The water in the main reservoir has disappeared! And there are three huge cracks in the South Reservoir."

Targ turned as pale as Arva. He said, hoarsely:

"But didn't anyone check the water levels?"

"Yes. Until this morning, the levels had not changed. It was only this morning that the large reservoir suddenly collapsed. Within ten minutes the water was gone. In the South Reservoir cracks appeared a half an hour ago. At most a third of the water can be saved."

Targ's head was bent, his shoulders sagged; he was like a man ready to collapse. And he murmured, full of horror:

"Is this, at long last, the death of mankind?"

The catastrophe was complete. As all the granite reservoirs had already been used up for the needs of the oasis, except for those that had just been struck by the accident, the only remaining water was that which was contained in the arcum basins. This would be just enough to slake the thirst of five or six hundred human creatures for a year.

The High Council convened.

It was an icy and nearly silent gathering. The men who comprised it, with the exception of Targ, had attained a perfect state of resignation. There was barely any deliberation: nothing but the reading of the Laws, and a calculation based on unvarying data. Thus, the resolutions were simple, clear, pitiless.

Rem, the grand chief of the Waters, summarized them: "The population of the Red-Lands is still seven thousand people. Six thousand must, this very day, submit to euthanasia. Five hundred will die before the end of the month. The remaining ones will diminish from week to week, in such a way that fifty remaining humans will be able to sustain themselves until the end of the fifth year . . . if by then no new sources of water are discovered, it will be the end of mankind."

The assembly listened impassively. All considerations were in vain: an incommensurable fatality engulfed their souls. And Rem continued:

"Men and women over forty must die. Except for fifty, the rest must accept euthanasia this very day. As for children, nine families out of ten cannot keep them; the others may keep only one. The choice of adults who take euthanasia is determined in advance: we need only consult the established lists."

A faint shock ran through the assembly. Then, heads bowed in an indication of submission, and the crowd outside, who had heard the deliberation over the wave transmitters, fell silent. The youngest seemed barely touched by the slightest cloud of melancholy.

Targ, however, refused to resign himself to this. He rushed back to his dwelling, where Arva and Érê, trembling, were already waiting for him. They clung tightly to their children; emotion aroused them, youthful and tenacious emotion, the source of ancient life and of vast futures.

Nearby, Mano was lost in daydreaming. All their agitation had merely surprised him for a moment. Fatalism weighed like a stone on his shoulders.

At the sight of Targ, Arva exclaimed:

"I don't want to! I don't want to! We will not die like this."

"You are right," Targ responded. "We will brave misfortune."

Mano awoke from his torpor and spoke: "But what will you do? Death is nearer today than if we were a hundred years old."

"No matter," said Targ. "We will leave."

"The Earth is empty for mankind!" Mano said again. "It will kill you in pain and suffering. Here at least the end will be sweet."

Targ was no longer listening to him. The urgent need for action absorbed his attention: it was necessary to flee before midday, the time appointed for the sacrifice.

After having gone with Arva to look at the gliders and motocruisers, he made his choice. Then he distributed among the machines the water and food supply that he kept in reserve, while Arva stored the necessary energy. Their work was speedy. Before nine o'clock, everything was ready.

He found Mano still plunged in his torpor, and Érê, who had gathered the clothes they would need.

"Mano," he said, placing his hand on his brother-in-law's shoulder, "we are going to leave. Come."

Mano slowly shrugged his shoulders:

"I don't want to die in the Desert," he declared.

Arva threw herself on him and hugged him with all her tenderness: a flicker of his old love roused the man. But he was immediately reclaimed by the inevitable:

"I don't want to," he said.

All pleaded with him—for a long time. Targ even attempted to take him by force; Mano resisted with the invincible strength of inertia.

As the hour was advancing, they emptied the fourth glider of its provisions, and, after making a final prayer, Targ gave the signal to leave. The planes rose into the sunlight, Arva cast a long look backward at the dwelling where her mate awaited euthanasia, then sobbing violently, she soared on the boundless emptiness.

XII. Toward the Equatorial Oases

Targ steered toward the equatorial oases: the other oases held only death.

During his explorations, he had visited Desolation, High Springs, Great Combe, Blue Sands, Clear Oasis, and Sulfur Valley: they had some food, but not a drop of water. Alone, the two Equatorial Oases kept small reserves. The nearest, Dune Equatorial, forty-five hundred kilometers distant, could be reached by morning the next day.

The voyage was abominable. Arva could think of nothing but Mano's death. When the sun reached its zenith, she uttered a great funereal cry— it was the hour of euthanasia! Never again would she see the man with whom she had lived the tender adventure!

The Desert spread before them endlessly. In the eyes of humans, Earth had died a horrible death. And yet another form of life was evolving there, for whom now was the time of genesis. It was seen swarming over plains and hills, formidable and incomprehensible. At times Targ reviled it; at times a fearful sympathy awakened in his soul. Was there not some mysterious analogy, an obscure fraternity even, between those beings and mankind? Certainly, the two kingdoms were closer to each other than either was to the inert mineral world. Who knows whether their forms of consciousness, in time, would not have understood each other!

Thinking of this, Targ sighed. And the gliders continued to sail through the blue expanse of oxygen, toward an unknown so terrible that just in thinking of it, the travelers felt their flesh go numb to the bone.

In order to be avoid all surprises, they decided to halt before nightfall. Targ chose a hill dominated by a plateau. Here the ferromagnetics revealed themselves to be rare, and belonging to species that were easy to displace. On the plateau itself stood a rock of green porphyry, which had suitable hollows. The gliders landed; they were attached with the aid of arcum ropes. These vessels, moreover, made of materials selected for their extreme resilience, were more or less invulnerable.

It happened that the rock and its surroundings were home to a very small number of groups of ferromagnetics of the tiniest size. Within fifteen minutes, these were expelled, and they were able to organize the camp.

Having eaten a meal of concentrated gluten and essential hydrocarbons, the fugitives awaited the end of the day. How many other creatures, their kindred, had known, throughout the vast ocean of time, a similar distress? When families prowled in solitude with clubs of wood and fragile tools of stone, there were nights when such handfuls of humans, faced with terrifying emptiness, trembled with hunger, cold, fear at the approach of lions or raging waters. Later, victims of shipwrecks cried out on desert islands, or on the rocks of some deadly shore; voyagers were lost in the midst of carnivorous forests, or in swamps. Innumerable had been such dramas of human distress! . . . Even so, all these unfortunates still stood on the threshold of boundless life; Targ and his companions saw only death!

And yet, the watchman thought as he looked on the children of Érê and of Arva, this fragile group contains all the vital energy needed to rebuild a human race! . . .

He moaned. The pole stars turned in their narrow path. The ferromagnetics were phosphorizing on the plain; for a long time, Targ and Arva dreamed, miserably, beside their sleeping family.

The next day, they arrived at Dune Equatorial. It was located in the midst of a desert formed by sand that over millennia had become petrified. Their arrival made their blood run cold: the bodies of those who, the last, had committed euthanasia lay about unburied. As many Equatorials had preferred to die in the open air, one found them among the ruins, immobile in their terrible sleep. The dry air, infinitely pure, had mummified them. They could have remained thus, for time without end, supreme witnesses to the end of humanity.

But a more menacing sight diverted the fugitives' sadness: the ferromagnetics were everywhere. On all sides, their violet colonies were seen; many were huge in size.

"Keep moving," said Targ, in a lively and worried manner.

He did not need to insist. Arva and Érê, realizing the danger, herded the children away, while Targ studied the site. The oasis had only undergone slight changes. The hurricanes had knocked down only a few dwellings, overturned some of the planetary reflectors, or some sound wave receivers; most of the machines and energy generators seemed to be intact. But the arcum reservoirs especially preoccupied the watchman. There were two, largely used up, whose location he knew. When they came in sight, he did not dare at first to touch them; his heart was beating with fear. When, finally, he decided to do so:

"Intact!' he cried out, with a rush of emotion. "We have water enough for two years. Now we must find shelter."

After long exploration, he decided on a small strip of land, near the protective wall to the west. The ferromagnetics were few here: within a few days a protective barrier could be built. There were two houses, waiting to be occupied, spacious, that the storms had spared.

Targ and Arva took a look through the larger one. The furnishings and instruments turned out to be solid, barely covered with a fine dust; everywhere one felt an indescribably subtle presence. On entering one of the bedrooms, a profound sadness gripped the visitors: on the arcum bed, two humans were visible, stretched out side by side. For a long time, Targ and Arva contemplated these peaceful forms, where once life had dwelt, where joy and pain had pulsed.

Others would have drawn from this a lesson in resignation; but they, full of bitterness and horror, steeled themselves for the struggle.

They removed the bodies, and having put Érê and the children in a safe place, they rid the area of a few groups of ferromagnetics. Then they took their first meal in this new land.

"Courage," said Targ. "There was a moment, back in the night of Eternity, when only one human couple existed; our entire species is evolved from them! We are stronger than this couple. For if it had perished, all humanity would have perished. In our case, several can die, without yet destroying all hope."

"Yes," Érê sighed, "but water covered the Earth!"

Targ contemplated her with infinite tenderness.

"Haven't we already found water once before?" he said in a low voice.

He remained motionless, his eyes as if blinded by an inner dream. Then, coming to his senses:

"While you set up the house, I am going to take stock of our resources."

He explored every corner of the oasis, and evaluated all the provisions left behind by the Equatorials, made sure all the energy generators, machines, gliders, planetary shells and sound wave receivers were in working order. All the industrial treasure house of the Last Men was present, ready to support all possible renaissances. What is more, Targ had brought with him from the Red-Lands his technical manuals and annals, rich in ideas and memories.[31] The presence of the ferromagnetics disturbed him. In certain areas they were found in formidable concentrations: one needed only to pause for a few minutes in order to feel their muffled toilings.

"If we do have a lineage," Targ thought to himself, "their struggle will be tremendous."

He arrived thus at the southern extremity of the Equatorial Oasis.

There he halted, as if hypnotized: in a field where once grain had grown, he came across ferromagnetics of the same large size that he had discovered in the wilderness, near High Springs. His chest constricted. A cold shiver passed along the back of his neck.

XIII. The Resting Place

The seasons flowed into the gulf of eternity. Targ and his family continued to live. The vast world enveloped them in its menace. Earlier, when they lived in the Red-Lands, they had already suffered the melancholy of those deserts, which were harbingers of the end of Mankind. Yet, still, thousands of their kin had occupied along with them that supreme refuge. Now they saw before them a more complete distress; they represented no more than a miniscule trace of the ancient life. From one pole to the other, on all the plains, over all the mountains, every inch of the planet was now their enemy, except for that other oasis, where euthanasia was now in the process of devouring creatures who, unremittingly, had abandoned all hope.

They had surrounded the chosen terrain with a protective wall, once again consolidated the reservoirs, gathered and sheltered their provisions, and Targ often went off, with Érê or Arva, to explore the deserted expanses. All the while searching for the water that creates life, he gathered everywhere he went matter containing hydrogen. This was rare; hydrogen, released in immense quantities during the powerful times of human industry, and again when mankind sought to replace water in its natural state with industrially produced water, had all but disappeared. According to the annals, the largest part of the hydrogen had decomposed into protoatoms and dissipated into interplanetary space. The remaining part had been carried off, through badly understood reactions, into inaccessible depths.

Nonetheless, Targ gathered enough useful substances to augment the supply of water substantially. But this could only be an expedient.

The ferromagnetics, above all, concerned Targ. They were thriving. This was because, beneath the oasis, at a shallow depth, there was a considerable reserve of *human* iron. The ground and surrounding plain covered over a dead city. Thus, the ferromagnetics drew forth this subterranean iron from a distance all the greater because they themselves were larger in size. The latecomers, the "Tertiaries" as Targ nicknamed them, provided they spent the time at it, could extract from depths greater than eight meters. Furthermore, these displacements of metal, in the long run, opened breaches in the ground through which the Tertiaries could pass. The other ferromagnetics produced similar effects, but on a much weaker scale. Besides, they never went deeper than two or three meters. In the case of the Tertiaries, Targ soon realized that their ability to penetrate was limitless: they went down as deep as the breaches permitted.

It was necessary to take special measures to prevent them from undermining the ground on which the two families lived. The machines dug, beneath the protective wall, galleries whose walls were reinforced with arcum, and plated with bismuth. Pillars of cement compounded with granite, set in the rock, assured the solidity of the vaults. This vast labor lasted several months: the powerful energy generators, the agile and clever machines, allowed this work to be done without effort. According to the calculations of Targ and Arva, it should resist for thirty years all the damage caused by the Tertiaries, assuming the hypothesis that their rate of multiplication would be very intense.

And so, after three years, thanks to the supplement furnished by the hydrogenated matter, their supply of water had barely diminished. Solid foodstuffs remained abundant, and more were to be had in the other oases. But no trace of new springs had been detected, even though Arva and Targ had probed the desert, tirelessly and for great distances.

The fate of the Red-Lands troubled the hearts of the refugees. Often, one or the other of them would broadcast a message over the Great Planetary; no one had answered. The brother and sister pushed their travels several times as far as the oasis. Because of the implacable law, they did not dare to land, they glided above it. No inhabitant deigned to notice their presence. And they saw that euthanasia was accomplishing its work. Many more beings than the law required had passed away. Toward the thirtieth month, there remained barely twenty inhabitants.

One fall morning, Arva and Targ left on a trip. They hoped to follow the double road that, since time immemorial, linked Dune Equator to the Red-Lands. En route, Targ was going to turn toward a territory that, on an earlier trip, had caught his attention. Camped on one of the relay stations, Arva would await his return. They could communicate easily, as Targ carried with him a portable sound wave receiver that could transmit and receive a voice over more than a thousand kilometers. As during previous explorations, they would be able to communicate with Érê and the children, because all the oasis planetaries and relay stations had been kept in good condition.

No danger menaced Érê, except for those dangers that surpass human energy to such a degree that they would not cause her to run more risks than they would Targ and Arva. The children had grown; their wisdom, precocious like that of all Last Men, barely differed from that of the adults. The two oldest ones—Mano's son and the watchman's daughter—had a perfect mastery of the power sources and machines. In the struggle against the blind ferromagnetic activity, they were as effective as adults. A reliable atavism guided them. Nevertheless, Targ had spent long hours, the day before leaving, inspecting the family dwelling and its surroundings; everything was normal.

Before the departure, the two families gathered around the gliders. It was, as with all major departures, an impressive moment. In the horizontal light, this little group comprised all human hope, all the will to live, all the old energy of the seas, the forests, the savannas and cities. Over there, in the Red-Lands, those who were still alive were little more than shades. And Targ embraced his race and the race of Arva in a long, loving look. The radiance of the blond races had passed from Érê to her daughter. The two heads, covered with gold, almost touched each other. What freshness emanated from them! What deep and tender legends!

The others as well, despite their swarthy faces and eyes of anthracite, possessed an amazing youthfulness—the burning gaze of Targ, or the propensity to happiness of Mano.

"Ah," he exclaimed, "how difficult it is to leave you! But the danger would be much greater if we all left together!"

They all, even the children, knew well that salvation lay beyond, in some mysterious corner of the deserts. They also knew that the oasis, center of their existence, must always be inhabited. Besides, were they not in contact with each other several times a day, through the voice of the planetaries?

"Let us go," Targ said at last!

The subtle rush of energy spread to the wings of the gliders. They rose into the sky; they faded into the morning light of mother-of-pearl and sapphire. Érê watched them disappear on the horizon. She sighed. When Arva and Targ were no longer there, fate weighed heavier on her. The young woman scanned the oasis with fear in her eyes, and each movement of the children awakened her anxiety. It was odd. Her fears conjured up dangers that no longer existed in this world. She feared neither the mineral kingdom nor the ferromagnetics; rather she feared to see strange men suddenly appear, men who would come from the depths of this uninhabitable vastness. And this strange memory of ancient instincts made her smile at times, yet at other times caused her to shiver, especially when night fell in dark waves over Dune Equator.

Targ and his companion sailed vertiginously on the seas of air. They loved the speed. All these voyages had not been able to dampen the joy of defying space. The dark planet seemed as if vanquished. They watched as its sinister plains, sharp rocks, and mountains appeared to rush forward to annihilate them. But then, with a slight movement, they triumphed over deep chasms and formidable peaks. Terrifying, flexible, harnessed, the energies softly sang their hymn; the mountain was crossed, the light gliders swooped down toward the deserts where, vague, belated, plodding, the ferromagnetics were evolving. How pitiful and pathetic they seemed!

But Targ and Arva knew their secret strength. They were the conquerors. Time lay before them, was on their side, the way of things coincided with their obscure will; one day, their descendants would produce admirable thoughts, and wield marvelous sources of energy.

Targ and Arva resolved first to go as far as the Red-Lands. Their souls hurled themselves toward the ultimate sanctuary of their kindred, with a passionate desire, in which was mixed fear, distress, a deep love, and sorrow. As long as human beings would endure there, some form of subtle and tender promise would remain. When they would finally all be gone, the planet would appear more lugubrious yet, the deserts more hideous and more vast.

After a short night spent on one of the relay stations, the travelers had, by means of the planetary, a conversation with Érê and the children: it was less to reassure themselves than to rejoin their family across a great distance. Then they sailed on toward the oasis. They reached it before midday.

It seemed fixed in time. The way they had left it was the way it stood out in the lenses of their eyeglasses. The houses of arcum shimmered in the sun; they saw the sound wave receivers on their platforms, the hangars housing gliders and motocruisers, the energy transformers, the machines colossal or delicate, the pumps that long ago drew water from the earth, and the fields where once the last plants grew. Everywhere the mark of human power and subtlety remained. At the first command, incalculable forces could be unleashed, then enslaved, vast works accomplished. So many resources that remained as useless as the vibration of a beam of light in infinite ether! Man's powerlessness was itself a function of his structure; born of water, he was vanishing along with it.

For a few minutes, the gliders sailed above the oasis. It seemed deserted. No man, woman, or child could be seen on the thresholds of the dwellings, on the roads, or in the uncultivated fields. And this solitude chilled the souls of the travelers.

"Are they finally all dead?" Arva murmured.

"Perhaps!" Targ answered.

The gliders swooped down until they almost touched the tops of the houses and the platforms of the planetaries. The place had the silence and immobility of a necropolis. The air, somnolent, did not even stir the dust; alone, groups of ferromagnetics moved about slowly.

Targ decided to land on a platform, and caused the transmitter of a sound wave receiver to vibrate: a powerful call echoed from shell to shell.

"Men!" Arva cried suddenly.

Targ took off again. He saw two people at the entrance of a house, and, for a few minutes, hesitated to call to them. Even though the inhabitants of the oasis now comprised but a pitiful handful, in them Targ venerated his Species, and respected the law. This latter was engrained in each fiber of his being; it seemed to him as deep as life itself, formidable and protective, infinitely wise, inviolable. And because that law had exiled him forever from the Red-Lands, he yielded to it.

Thus did his voice tremble when he spoke to those who had just appeared.

"How many are still alive in the oasis?"

The two men raised up their pale faces, which revealed a strange serenity. Then one of them answered:

"There are still five of us . . . Tonight we will be delivered!"

The watchman felt sick at heart. He recognized, in the gazes that met his, the hazy glow of euthanasia.

"Can we land?" he said humbly. "The law has exiled us."

"There is no more law," the second man murmured. "It disappeared the moment that we accepted the Great Cure . . ."

At the noise of the voices, the three other living beings appeared, two men and one young woman. All of them stared at the gliders with a look of ecstasy.

Thus, Targ and Arva landed.

There was a short silence. The watchman examined with intensity the last of his kinsmen. Death was upon them; no remedy could reverse the delightful poisons of euthanasia.

The very young woman was by far the palest of the five. Yesterday still, she carried in her the future, today she was older than a centenarian. And Targ exclaimed:

"Why did you wish to die? Is the water all gone?"

"What use is water to us!" the young woman whispered. "Why would we live? Why did our ancestors live? Some inconceivable madness made them resist, over millennia, the decrees of nature. They wanted to perpetuate themselves in a world that was not their own. They accepted to live an abject existence . . . simply so as not to vanish. How is it possible that we have followed their pitiful example? It is so sweet to die!"

She spoke with a slow, pure voice. Her words caused Targ horrible suffering. Each atom of his flesh revolted against such resignation. And the peaceful joy that burst out on the faces of these dying people remained incomprehensible to him.

Yet he kept silent. What gave him the right to attempt to introduce the least bitterness to their end, as this end was now unavoidable? The young woman half-closed her eyes. Her feeble exaltation was fading, her breath slowed down from moment to moment, and supporting herself against a wall of arcum, she reiterated:

"It is so sweet to die."

And one of the men whispered:

"Deliverance is near."

Then, all waited. The young woman had stretched out on the ground, she was barely breathing. A growing pallor invaded her cheeks. Then, she opened her eyes an instant, she looked at Targ and Arva with tenderness full of pity.

"The folly of suffering abides in you," she stammered.

Her hand lifted, then fell slowly. Her lips trembled. One last spasm shook her body. At last, her members went limp, and she expired as softly as a small star on the low horizon.

Her four companions contemplated her with happy tranquility.

One of them whispered:

"Life has never been desirable . . . Even during the time when the Earth favored the power of mankind . . ."

Struck with horror, Targ and Arva remained silent a long time. Then they solemnly covered the one who, as last woman, had represented the Future for the Red-Lands. But they did not have the courage to remain with the others. The absolute certitude of their death filled them with terror.

"Let us leave, Arva," he said softly.

"Today," the watchman said, as his plane flew alongside that of Arva, "we are truly, we and our offspring, the last and final chance for the human species."

His companion turned to him a face covered with tears.

"Despite everything," she stammered, "it was a great sweetness to know that people were still alive in the Red-Lands. How many times this consoled me . . . And now, now!"

Her gesture swept across the implacable expanse, and the huge mountains to the west. She uttered a cry of abandon:

"All is finished, my brother."

He himself had lowered his head. But he resisted the pain, he exclaimed, his eyes sparkling:

"Death alone will put an end to my hope."

For several hours, the gliders followed the line of the roads. When the country Targ was seeking appeared, they slowed. Arva choose the relay where she was to wait. Then, once the planetary had brought him the voices of Érê and the children, the watchman set off alone toward the solitary lands. He already knew the region, in a rough manner, for an area that extended twelve hundred kilometers away from the roads.

The more he advanced, the more the landscape became chaotic. A series of hills appeared, then, once again, the ragged plain. Now Targ was sailing in fully unknown territory. Several times, he flew down to ground level; a dizziness drove him to push on to new stopping places.

An immense reddish wall blocked the horizon. The aviator flew over it, and soared above the abyss. Huge chasms burrowed into the earth, pits of darkness, whose depth could not even be fathomed. Everywhere marks of immense convulsions were apparent; entire mountains had crumbled, others were twisted, ready to plunge into the measureless void. The glider inscribed long parabolas above this impressive landscape. Most of the chasms were so large that planes could have flown into them by the dozen.

Targ lit his searchlight, and began to explore randomly. First, he entered a crevasse that opened at the bottom of a cliff. The light seemed to dissolve as it reached the depths, which showed themselves to be without issue.

A second chasm seemed at first more favorable for exploration. Several galleries plunged into the earth; Targ explored them without result.

The third voyage was vertiginous. The glider descended more than two thousand meters before touching ground. The bottom of this enormous hole formed a trapezoid, the smallest side of which was two hectometers. Caverns opened out everywhere. It took an hour to explore them. Except for two, all were bounded by straight walls. The others, in contrast, had numerous fissures, but all too narrow to allow a man to pass.

"No matter," Targ murmured, at the moment he decided to abandon the second cavern, "I will come back."

Suddenly, he felt that same strange feeling he had experienced twelve years ago, the night of the great disaster. Quickly drawing out his hygroscope, he looked at the dial, and uttered a cry of triumph: *there was water vapor in the cavern!*

XV. The Enclave Has Disappeared

For a long time Targ walked in the semidarkness. All his thoughts were scattered; a boundless feeling of joy filled his fleshly being. When he came to his senses, he thought:

"Nothing can be done for the time being. In order to reach the mysterious water, I must find a passage somewhere other than at the bottom of the chasm, or make a passage: it is a question of time, or a question of work. In the first case, Arva's presence would be infinitely useful; in the second case, it would be necessary to go back to Dune Equator, and bring back the machines necessary to harness the energy, and cleave the granite rocks."

As he was making these reflections, the young man had taken off again. Soon, the glider had inscribed the helical curves that were to bring him to the surface. Within two minutes, the watchman left the chasm, and immediately, directing his portable sound wave receiver, he sent out a call.

No one answered.

Astonished, he sent stronger signals. The receiver remained silent. A slight anxiety took hold of Targ. He sent out a circular call that, one after another, probed in all directions. And as the silence persisted, he began to fear some disagreeable consequence. Three possibilities came to his mind: an accident had happened; or Arva had left the refuge; or, finally, she had simply fallen asleep.

Before sending out a final call, the explorer marked his present position, with exact precision. Then he boosted his signals to their maximum intensity. These would reverberate against the receptor conches with such force that, even asleep, Arva would have to hear them . . . This time, once again, the vast spaces sent back no reply.

Had the young woman really left the refuge? Certainly, she would not have done so without a serious reason. In any case, he had to rejoin her.

Already, he was in the air and speeding back toward her.

In fewer than three hours, he covered a thousand kilometers; the relay came into view in the lens of his ship's eyeglass. It was empty!

And all around, Targ saw no one. Arva must have left then. But where? But why? She could not have gone far, as her glider was still moored there.

The final minutes were intolerably long; it seemed as if the rapid vessel were no longer moving forward; a mist covered the young man's eyes.

At last, the refuge was there. Targ landed at the middle, secured his glider, and rushed forward. A cry arose in his chest. On the other side of the road, against the vertical embankment—that had made her invisible at first—lay Arva. She was as pale as the woman who, earlier, in the Red-Lands, had succumbed to euthanasia; Targ saw with horror a swarm of ferromagnetics—the Tertiaries of the largest sort—moving around her.

Swiftly, Targ attached his arcum ladder, and then, descending to the level of the young woman, he took her on his shoulder, and climbed back.

She had not moved; her body was inert, and Targ, kneeling down, tried to locate the beat of her heart. In vain! The mysterious energy that imparts rhythm to existence seemed to have vanished.

Trembling, the watchman placed the hygroscope on the young woman's lips. The delicate instrument discovered what the human ear had not been able to discover—Arva was not dead!

But her swoon was so deep, her weakness so great, that she could die from one second to the next.

The cause of her sickness seemed obvious: it was due, if not solely, at least in large part, to the action of the ferromagnetics. Arva's unique pallor indicated an excessive loss of hemoglobin.

Fortunately, Targ never traveled without carrying along medical instruments, stimulants and traditional remedies. He gave her, at intervals of several minutes, two doses of a powerful potion. Her heart began to beat again, though very feebly; Arva's lips murmured:

"The children . . . the Earth . . ."

Then, she fell into a sleep that Targ knew he should and could not resist—a fatal yet salutary sleep, during which, every three hours, he would inject several milligrams of "organic iron." Twenty-two hours at least were necessary before Arva could support a short moment of awakening. No matter! The greatest worry was gone. The watchman, knowing the perfect health of his sister, feared no serious aftereffects. Nevertheless, he remained nervous. The event, in fact, had no explanation. Why was Arva lying at the base of the embankment? Had she, she who was always so vigilant and so agile, taken a fall? It was possible—but not likely.

What was he to do? Stay here until she had recovered all her strength? At least two weeks would be needed for her to recover them completely. It would be better to leave for Dune Equator at once. Nothing was pressing, in any case. The adventure Targ was embarked on was not of the kind whose outcome depends on a few days.

He went to the Great Planetary and unleashed the general call. Just as happened before, when he came from the chasm, he got no answer. Immediately, a terrible emotion shook him. He repeated the signals, he gave them maximum force. It was clear that Érê and the children, for some enigmatic reason, either found it impossible to hear the signal, or were unable to answer. Both alternatives were equally full of menace! There was a clear link between Arva's accident and the silence of the planetary.

An intolerable fear gnawed at the breast of the young man . . . With his legs trembling, forced to lean against the pillar of the planetary, he was incapable of making a decision. Finally, he took a step away, dreary and resolute, inspected with anxious attention all the instruments of his glider, placed Arva on the largest seat, and took off.

It was a miserable voyage. He made only one stop, toward evening, to try another call. As there was no response, he wrapped Arva tightly in a blanket of wool-like silica, and gave her an injection of the potion, stronger than the first. In the depths of her numbness, she was as if barely able to shiver.

All night long, the plane carved through the starry darkness. The cold becoming too great, Targ circumvented Mount Skeleton. Two hours before dawn, the southern constellations appeared. The traveler, his heart pounding, gazed occasionally at the Southern Cross, occasionally at that brilliant star, the closest neighbor to the Sun, whose light[32] takes only three years to reach the Earth. How beautiful this sky must have been, when young humanity gazed at it through the leaves of trees, and more even when silvery clouds blended their fertile promise with the tiny lamps of the infinite. Ah! And to think there will never be clouds again!

A gentle light pearled the East, then the Sun raised up its enormous orb. Dune Equator was near. Through the lens of his aerial telescope, Targ could see, occasionally, in the folds of the dunes, the walls of bismuth and arcum dwellings, ambered by the morning light. Arva still was sleeping, and a new dose of the stimulant did not awaken her. Nevertheless, her pallor was less livid. Her arteries trembled feebly, her skin no longer had that "translucent tautness" that suggested death.

"She is out of danger," Targ reassured himself.

This certainty relieved his pain.

All his attention was fixed on the oasis. He strove to locate the family enclave. Two hillocks still hid it from view. Finally, it appeared, and aghast, Targ twisted the rudder of the glider, which plunged abruptly, like a wounded bird.

The enclave in its entirety, with its houses, its hangars and machines, had disappeared.

XVI. Into the Eternal Night

The glider was no more than twenty meters from the ground. It was heading for a crash at full speed when Targ, instinctively, pulled it out of its nosedive. Then, deftly, and tracing an elegant parabola, he resumed his flight up to the outer limits of the enclave. Having landed, the watchman remained motionless, paralyzed with pain, before an enormous, chaotic pit: there lay buried, beneath the darkness of the earth, the beings he loved more than his very self.

For a long time, thoughts churned in disorder in the poor man's brain. He was not thinking about the causes of this cataclysm, he perceived only its obscure ferocity, he linked it confusedly to all the woes of this last sad seven years. Random images moved through his mind. Constantly, he saw his family, just as he had left them the day before yesterday. Then these tranquil forms were swept away in a nameless horror . . . The ground opened. He saw them disappear. Terror was on their faces. They cried out to him in whom they placed their trust, and who, at the very moment of their death perhaps, believed he had vanquished fate . . .

When he finally came to reason, the Last Man tried to imagine the catastrophe. Was it another planetary quake? No! None of the seismographs had registered the least problem. Besides, outside of a few acres of the oasis and desert, only the enclave had been struck. The event was linked to prior circumstances: the substratum, fractured, had ruptured. Thus, the disaster that destroyed the last hope of mankind was no great convulsion of nature, but an infinitesimally small accident, of the same magnitude as the feeble creatures it engulfed.[33]

And yet, Targ believed he saw manifested there the same cosmic will that had condemned the Oases.

His sorrow did not render him inactive. He studied the ruins. They did not reveal any vestiges of human activity. Machines to store energy, machines to excavate, to drill, to cultivate, to crush, gliders, motocruisers, houses, all had disappeared beneath a formless mass of rocks and stones. Where were Érê and the children buried? The calculations allowed only a rough approximation, which was possibly misleading; he had to act according to chance.

Targ assembled, toward the north, the machines to be used for clearing rubble and excavating, then, having focused the protoatomic energy, he started digging out the huge cavity. For an hour the machines hummed. Jacks lifted the blocks and rejected them automatically. Cobalt paraboloids cleared out the loose rubble, and as they did so, the pile-drivers, with slow, irresistible blows, stabilized the walls. Once the trench reached a length of twenty meters, a glider was revealed, then a large planetary with its granite foundation and accessories, finally an arcum house.

Their location confirmed Targ's calculations. Assuming that the disaster had surprised the family near their home, it was necessary to dig toward the west. If Érê or the children had been able to reach the planetary that Dune Equator used to communicate with the Red-Lands (as Arva's accident led him to believe), then it was toward the southwest that he would have to make his search.

The watchman installed his tools near the two probable locations, and resumed work. "Humanized" by the incalculable effort of generations, the vast machines allied the power of the elements with the dexterity of delicate hands.[34] They lifted rocks, they gathered up dirt and small stones in a steady manner. Only the touch of a finger was necessary to direct them, to make them work faster or slower, or to stop their functioning. They represented, in the hands of this Last Man, more power than a whole tribe, or people, had possessed in primitive times.

An arcum roof was uncovered. It was twisted, dented, and here and there a block of stone had cleaved it. But precise signs made it recognizable. It had sheltered, since the landing at Dune Equator, all the tenderness, the dreams and hopes of this supreme human family. Targ halted the machines that were starting to lift it, he contemplated it with dread and gentleness. What enigma did it conceal? What drama would it reveal to this poor man, already replete with sorrow and fatigue?

During many long minutes, the watchman hesitated to continue his work. Finally, prying open one of the tears in the wall, he let himself slip into the dwelling.

The bedroom he found himself in was empty. A few blocks of stone littered it, and had ripped a bed from the wall and crushed it. A table had been pulverized and several vases of soft aluminum flattened under the stones.

This spectacle revealed the indifferent nature of material destruction. But it suggested more moving scenes. Targ, all trembling, entered the next room; it was empty and in disarray like the first. One by one, he visited all corners of the house. And when he found himself in the first room, a few steps away from the entrance door, his stupor turned to anxiety.

"It is natural enough though," he whispered, "that at the first sign of danger they would have fled outside . . ."

He tried to imagine the manner in which the first shock took place, and also the mental picture Érê might have had in reaction to the peril. All that came to him were sensations and contradictory ideas. One impression alone remained fixed: it was that instinct must have driven the family toward the planetary of the Red-Lands. It was thus logical to proceed in that direction. But how? Did Érê reach the Great Planetary, or did she succumb along the way? The words muttered by Arva came back to the watchman's mind. This event gave those words meaning. Érê, or one of the children, or perhaps all of them, had almost surely reached it. It was thus necessary to resume the work as fast as possible, which would not stop him from beginning to dig a tunnel that might lead there.

His decision made, Targ raised up the front door, and attempted a rapid reconnaissance. But the blocks and rubble before him posed an impenetrable obstacle. He exited through the roof, and restarted the machines in the southwest. Then the positioned his northern machines, and had them begin digging the tunnel. He also looked after Arva, whose lethargy took on, little by little, the appearance of normal sleep.

Then he waited, vigilant, his eyes fixed on the tractable mechanisms. From time to time, he readjusted their workings with a furtive gesture; now and then, he halted a pickaxe, a blade, a propeller, a turbine, in order to examine the terrain. Finally he spied, twisted and dented, the tall shaft of the planetary and the sparkling shell. From then on, he did not cease to marshal their energy. On their own, their subtle organs were functioning; according to the situation, they lifted heavy stones, or scooped up small debris.

Then he uttered a lugubrious wailing, like the cry of a dying man . . . A glow had just become visible, that same supple and vital glow that he had seen, the day of the Disaster, among the ruins of the Red-Lands. His heart froze; his teeth were chattering. His eyes filled with tears, all his movements slowed, he left the work to those metal hands alone, more adroit and gentle than the hands of man.

Then, he halted everything. He lifted up against his chest, with violent sobbing, the body he had so passionately loved.

At first, a ray of hope traversed his state of shock. It seemed to him that Érê was not yet cold. Feverishly, he held the hygroscope to her pale lips . . . She had disappeared into the eternal night.

For a long while, he contemplated her. She had revealed to him the poetry of ancient times; the dreams of an extraordinary youth had transformed the sad planet; Érê was love itself, in all that is vast, pure and nearly eternal. And, whenever he held her in his arms, he seemed to see reborn a race that was new and without number.

"Érê! Érê!" he murmured, "Érê, freshness of the world! Érê, the final dream of mankind!"

Then, his soul steeled itself. He placed on the hair of his companion a bitter and fierce kiss, he returned to work.

One by one, he brought all of them back. The mineral world had shown itself less vicious to them than to the young woman; it had spared them the agony of a slow death, the intolerable dispersion of vital energy. Blocks had crushed their skulls, smashed open their chests, crushed their torsos.

Then, Targ collapsed to the ground, and cried endlessly. Pain filled him, vast as the world itself. He bitterly repented for having struggled against inexorable fatality. And the words of that dying woman, in the Red-Lands, echoed through his pain like the death knell of the immense universe.

A hand touched his shoulder. He started up—it was Arva, leaning over him, livid and unsteady. She was so overcome that no tears came to her eyes; yet all the despair possible in weak human creatures dilated her pupils. She muttered in a toneless voice:

"We have to die! We have to die!"

They stared into each other's eyes. They had loved each other deeply, every day of their lives, throughout all things real and all things dreamed. They had passionately shared the same hopes, and in this infinite misery their suffering was again fraternal.

"We must die!" He repeated it like an echo. Then they embraced, and for the last time, two human hearts beat one against the other.

And thus, in silence, she took to her lips the tube of iridium that she always carried with her . . . As the dose was massive and Arva's weakness so extreme, the euthanasia took only a few minutes.

"Death, death," the dying woman stammered. "Oh, how could we have been so afraid of it!"

Her eyes clouded over, and a blessed torpor relaxed her lips; her thoughts had already completely vanished, when her last breath passed from her bosom.

There was now only one single man on Earth.

Sitting on a block of porphyry, he remained buried in his sadness and his dreams. He made, one more time, the grand voyage back toward the beginning of time, which had so passionately enflamed his soul ... And first, he saw again the primeval sea, still warm, swarming with life, unconscious and unfeeling. Then came the blind and deaf creatures, bursting with extraordinary energy, and limitless fertility. Sight was born, the divine light created her tiny temples; and those beings born of the Sun knew their existence. And solid ground emerged. Thereupon the peoples of the waters, vague, confused, and silent, spread their dominion. For three thousand centuries, they generated complex forms. Insects, batrachians, and reptiles knew the forests of giant ferns, the proliferation of calamites and arrowheads.[35] At the same time trees put forth their magnificent torsos, the giant reptiles also roamed the Earth. The Dinosaurs had the size of cedar trees, the Pterodactyls soared above vast swamps ... During these ages the first mammals, puny, awkward and stupid, are born. They roam about, miserable, and so small that a hundred thousand of them would be needed to equal the weight of an iguanodon. Through endless millennia, their existence remains imperceptible, pathetic almost. And yet they grow. The hour sounds and their turn comes, their many species arise in force from all corners of the savanna, from all the dark places of the mature forests. It is they, now, who are looked on as colossi. The deinotherium, the ancient elephant, the armored rhinoceros with hide like old oak, the hippopotamus with insatiable maw, the urus, the aurochs, the machaerodus, the giant lion and yellow lion, the tiger, the cave bear, and the whale as huge as several diplodoci, and the sperm whale whose mouth is a cavern, all compete to breathe in the scarce energies of life.[36]

Now the planet favored man's ascension. His reign was the most ferocious, the most powerful of all—and the last. He became the prodigious destroyer of life. The forests died alongside their hosts without number, all beasts were exterminated or enslaved. And there was a time when the subtle energies and obscure minerals themselves seemed man's slaves; the conqueror harnessed everything right down to the mysterious power that bound together the atoms.

"This frenzy itself announced the death of the Earth, the death of the Earth for *our* Kingdom!" Targ murmured softly.[37]

He shivered in his suffering. He thought that whatever remained now of his flesh had been transmitted, *in an unbroken line*, since the origin of things. Some thing that had once lived in the primeval sea, on emerging alluvia, in the swamps, in the forests, in the midst of savannas, and among the multitude of man's cities, had continued unbroken down to him. And here, the end! He was the only man whose heart beat on the face of the Earth, once again vast and empty!

Night fell. The firmament displayed the lovely stars that had shone for the eyes of trillions of men. There remained only two eyes to contemplate them! Targ counted out those stars he had preferred to all others, then he saw the star of disasters rise once more in the sky, the star riddled with holes, silvery, the stuff of legend, toward which he raised his hands in sadness . . .

He uttered a final sob; death entered into his heart and, refusing euthanasia, he left the ruins, he went to lie down in the oasis, among the ferromagnetics.

Then, humbly, a few small pieces of the last human life entered into the New Life.

Notes

Introduction: Rosny's Evolutionary Ecology

1. Mark Rose, *Alien Encounters: Anatomy of Science Fiction* (Cambridge, Mass.: Harvard University Press, 1981), 7.

2 Robert L. Forward, "When Science Writes the Fiction," in *Hard Science Fiction*, edited by George E. Slusser and Eric S. Rabkin (Carbondale: Southern Illinois University Press, 1986), 1–21; quotation from epigraph, 1.

3 Amy Louise Downey, "The Life and Works of J.-H. Rosny aîné, 1856–1940" (Ph.D. diss., University of Michigan, 1950), 18–28.

4 Cited in Rosny aîné, *Portraits et souvenirs* (Paris: Cie française des arts graphiques, 1945), 22. Jean Perrin won the Nobel Prize in physics in 1936. The introduction to this posthumous work was written by Robert Borel-Rosny, the son of Rosny's eldest daughter, Irmine Gertrude, who was raised by Rosny and his second wife, Marie Borel. The family of Robert Borel is the executor of Rosny's literary estate.

5. Philip José Farmer and J.-H. Rosny, *Ironcastle* (New York: DAW Books, 1976). Jean-Jacques Annaud's film *La Guerre du feu* was released in 1981. A new English mass-market edition of the Harold Talbott translation: *The Quest for Fire* (New York: Ballantine Books) was released in 1982.

6. See *Europe: Revue littéraire mensuelle* 64, 681–82 (January–February 1986), a special issue partly devoted to the Wells-Rosny comparison. Most interesting are the essays by Roger Bozzetto, "Wells et Rosny devant l'inconnu"; Daniel Compère, "La fin des hommes"; and Daniel Congenas, "Préhistoire et récit préhistorique chez Rosny et Wells."

7. In his *Origin of Species*, however, Darwin did consider what he called "pangenesis" as a hypothesis, that is, the hypothetical existence of "pangenes," some sort of microscopic somatic cells or particles that contain information, respond to environmental stimulus, and—in the form of germ cells in the bloodstream—pass on acquired information from parents to the next generation.

8. "On the Origin of Species by Means of Natural Selection," in *Darwin: A Critical Editon*, edited by Philip Appleman (New York: Norton, 1970), 103.

9. For the sake of clarity, we will use the term "alien" to refer to extraterrestrials only.

10. Marie-Hélène Huet, *L'Histoire des Voyages extraordinaires: Essai sur l'oeuvre de Jules Verne* (Paris: Minard, 1975).

11. Allen A. Debus, "Reframing the Science in Jules Verne's *Journey to the Center of the Earth*," *Science-Fiction Studies* 33, 3 (November 2006), 405–21.

12. Carl Sagan, *The Dragons of Eden: Speculations on the Evolution of Human Intelligence* (New York: Ballantine Books, 1977).

13. An example of how Wells introduces new perspectives of evolutionary science into this middle-class world is the story "The Flowering of the Strange Orchid." At the height of England's colonial empire, adventurers scoured uncharted places like Borneo seeking new species of flora, such as rare orchids. In Wells's tale, however, such rarities are little more than things displayed and sold in London's orchid market. The protagonist, Winter-Wedderburn, is a "shy, lonely, rather ineffectual man, provided with just enough income to keep off the spur of necessity, and not enough nervous energy to make him seek any exacting employment" (343). A bachelor, he lives with his cousin-housekeeper. His sole passion is collecting orchids. He buys an orchid with a particularly violent history: it was found under the crushed body of Batten the explorer: "Every drop of blood, they say, was taken out of him by jungle leeches" (346).

Wedderburn fancies himself a Darwinist as he ponders his plant: "Darwin studied their fertilization. . . . Well it seems there are lots of orchids known the flower of which cannot possibly be used for fertilization" (348). He speculates that *his* orchid may reproduce through its tubers. But if that is so, then what purpose do its flowers serve? This he learns firsthand. Day-to-day contact with his "new darling" in his hothouse culminates in an apparent *liebestod*. When the orchid blooms, it apparently emits a scent that overpowers Wedderburn's senses. Wary (or jealous) of the plant, his cousin finds him in the nick of time, "lying, face upward, at the foot of the strange orchid." What ensues seems a struggle between rival lovers—the cousin tears him from the plant's "embrace" and kills it.

The reader's first reaction is that the plant is a vampire. This reaction of horror, however, is meant to suggest another explanation, a scientific one certainly more shocking to a Victorian audience. Recovering from his encounter, Wedderburn is a new man. Tired and vapid before, he is now "bright and garrulous upstairs in the glory of his strange adventure" (351). Darwin's question may have an answer: the purpose of the orchid's flower is *reproductive*, and in a quite shocking way. What has taken place could be some form of transspecies fertilization. The reenergized Wedderburn could have undergone a possible mutation. The reader knows, however, that in civilized London, such a mutation, if it occurred, could have no consequence. The bourgeois actors, and their readers, may be shaken, but they remain safe in their domestic world.

14. H. G. Wells, Julian S. Huxley, and G. P. Wells, *The Science of Life* (London: Literary Guild, 1934), 63.

15. "The Empire of the Ants" (1906) sheds light on the previous story. We have the same skeptical narrator, who recounts a tale told by the explorer Holroyd of murderous, intelligent ants that threaten human dominion over the Earth, according to Holroyd. The narrator at first dismisses this as the story of a paranoiac. The difference here is that the narrator seems won over in the end by the paranoia: "By 1920, they will be halfway down the Amazon. I fix 1950 or '60 at the latest for the discovery of Europe" (285). Just as Columbus discovered America, now these ants reverse this journey, bringing destruction back to the place from which it formerly came. In contrast with Rosny's observers, "facts" rarely get through to Wells's Everyman narrators. When they do get through, as here, they plunge these narrators into the irrational. This narrator displays the insanity of

Gulliver returned from the Houynhmhms, or Prendick in London after Moreau's island in *The Island of Dr. Moreau* (1897). If Elstead's story has plausibility in scientific terms, this account is "without detailed information," a response to alternate evolution more like that of Maupassant's protagonist in "Le Horla."

16. Thomas Mann, *Doktor Faustus: The Life of the German Composer Adrian Leverkühn as Told by a Friend,* translated by H. T. Lowe-Porter (New York: Knopf, 1948). Leverkühn's cantata offers a terminal vision, a *Götterdämmerung* brought about by the Nazis' attempts to use science to annihilate all that is human on Earth: "Then nothing more: silence and night. But that tone which vibrates in the silence, which is no longer there, to which only the spirit hearkens, and which was the voice of mourning, is no more. It changes its meaning, it abides as a light in the night" (491). Again there are obvious Pascalian overtones. The note, because it alone in the empty universe is heard by the human spirit, somehow abides in the void: silence and night.

17. Robert L. Forward, letter to George Slusser, May 13, 1983.

18. In a journal entry dated February 19, 1888, Edmond de Goncourt comments on the dizzying array of technological inventions in Rosny's scientific novels: "Rosny m'effraie un peu par ses imaginations de livres où il veut faire voir les aveugles au moyen du sens frontal, entendre les sourds par l'éléctricité . . . annonçant une série de livres fantastico-scientifico-phono-littéraires. Au fond, c'est une cervelle très curieuse." (Rosny frightens me a bit with his imaginings of books where he wants to make the blind see by means of senses in their foreheads, the deaf hear by means of electricity . . . all of which announce a series of fanastico-scientifico-phono-literary books. In fact, he has a very curious brain.) Jules and Edmond de Goncourt, *Journal: Mémoires de la vie littéraire* (Paris: Robert Laffont, 1989), 3:247. The term "phono-literary" is prophetic of SF to come (a literature Goncourt dreaded). It announces the proliferation of "scientific" neologisms from Gernsback to the present.

19. In nineteenth-century fiction, the problem of knowing and presenting what went on in a distant historical world was perhaps first raised by Flaubert in his novel *Salammbô* (1862). The question Flaubert asked was, essentially, how could he make the people of his fictional Carthage speak and think as historical Carthaginians did, when nothing remains of that world but fragments, objects, words, all without contexts? He abandoned archeological data as useless. The archeologists' coherent stories were little more than fictional constructs built on the most scattered evidence. Only by dreaming on objects and words left behind, things without referents, could one conjure Carthage, but this time as a construct that was essentially linguistic in nature. Even more so, Rosny follows Flaubert in summoning the world of the Xipéhuz from names and words, most of which are invented but *sound like* words left behind at the dawn of human civilization.

20. Pascal Ducommun, "Alien Aliens," in *Aliens: The Anthropology of Science Fiction,* edited by George Slusser and Eric S. Rabkin (Carbondale: Southern Illinois University Press, 1989), 36–42.

21. Guy de Maupassant, *Contes et nouvelles,* vol. 2, ed. Louis Forestier (Paris: Editions de la Pléiade, 1979), 918: "S'il existait sur la terre d'autres êtres que nous, comment ne les connaîtrions-nous point depuis longtemps; comment ne les auriez-vous pas vus, vous?" (If beings other than us were to exist on earth, how come, for a long time now, would you

not have known of their existence, why wouldn't you have seen them?") The narrator has this skeptical "scientific" approach to the fantastic figures carved on the church: they are figments of the primitive imagination, their existence cannot be verified by ocular evidence. The monk takes the argument one step farther: "Est-ce que nous voyons la cent millième partie de ce qui existe?" (Do we see even the hundred thousandth part of what exists? [918]) So these beings, like the wind we cannot see either, may indeed exist. And their existence is even more plausible in our scientific age.

22. See George Slusser, "The Frankenstein Barrier," in *Fiction 2000: Cyberpunk and the Future of Narrative*, edited by George Slusser and Tom Shippey (Athens: University of Georgia Press, 1992), 46–74.

23. See "Symposium on Posthuman Science Fiction," in *Foundation* 75 (spring 2000), 98–121. The mind-matter duality is still very much alive in this discussion, with a writer like Greg Egan being discussed in terms of a "radical materialism" that abdicates mind to *res extensa*. Other discussions look for the ghost in the machine of posthuman "information" constructs.

24. It could be argued that the existentialist act, in Pascal's sense, is an anthropocentric act, the only and final act human beings have in the face of the material infinite. In Pascal's gambit, mankind in the act of being crushed affirms its uniqueness in perpetual opposition to this *néant* (nothingness, the void): we know, but it, the material extended world, does not know. It is in this sense that Sartre can proclaim "l'existentialisme est un humanisme." The existential act, which Sartre also sees as an act of self-creation (*se faire*), can therefore be seen as something quite different from Targ's ecological altruism. For Sartre, this act, the freely giving of one's self, but as a form of self-creation, is not altruistic in Rosny's sense. It remains but another gambit that (as with Pascal) snatches something uniquely human from the indifferent process of evolution. As Sartre says, we are *condemned* to be free. In realizing this, once again we affirm our uniqueness as the rational consciousness of our situation, in the face of certain annihilation.

25. For a similar use of this term, see Wendy Wall, *The Imprint of Gender: Authorship and Publication in the English Renaissance* (Ithaca, N.Y.: Cornell University Press) 1993.

26. Mary Shelley's Last Man is anachronistic (speaking like an educated man of 1822) and thereby abstracted from any sense of evolutionary transformation. Recent avatars such as Nietzsche's *letzter Mensch (Also Sprach Zarathustra)* or Blanchot's *dernier homme* retain their abstract centrality in the face of historical process by associating finality with negativity, presenting mankind at its nadir, not its zenith. As is said of Blanchot's figure: "Le dernier homme est sans mémoire. Il se nourrit d'amnésie pour recouvrer une mémoire qu'il n'a jamais eue" (The last man is without memory. He feeds himself on amnesia in order to recover a memory he has never had.) Maurice Blanchot, *Le dernier homme* (Paris: Gallimard L'imaginaire, 1957), 26.

27. Darwin did not use the term "altruism" but discussed the evolutionary paradox of what he called "benevolence," especially in *The Descent of Man* (1871). Eric Strong sees scientists still actively debating "the causes and effects of altruistic behavior" a century after Darwin. Eric Strong, "The Evolution of Altruism," *New York Times*, Science sec., December 11, 1997.

28. Gregory Benford, *Timescape* (New York: Simon and Schuster, 1980). Citations are to this edition.

29. Gregory Benford, "Mozart on Morphine," in *Matter's End* ((New York: Bantam Spectra, 1995, 9–24.

The Xipéhuz

1. Rosny's title is full of implications for his later pluralistic vision. Mankind's God, declaring Itself the alpha and omega, offers an all-encompassing structure in terms of temporal order, with human destiny at its core. Rosny's other "race" is, with its *x* and *z*, still conceivable in terms of our alphabet. But as such, it turns the neat genesis scheme on its head. For it contends with mankind for mastery of the early Earth. Rosny carefully embeds in the name the Xipéhuz are given a set of contradictions. First, the spelling seems to imply they are an "omega" rather than an "alpha," a species that has already run its course. It also implies that, however radically different from humans they seem, they are somehow made of the same alphabetical building blocks. Or perhaps, they are a genuinely nonanthropomorphic rival to the story of human evolution on Earth, and the name given to them reveals the vanity of human attempts to seek to incorporate the truly alien within our systems of order.

2. Léon Hennique was a naturalist writer who was born in 1850 in Guadeloupe and died in 1935 in Paris. A close associate of Edmond de Goncourt, Hennique was executor of Goncourt's will. In compliance with the terms of that testament, he worked to establish the Académie Goncourt, and was its first president, in 1907–1912. In dedicating his first novel to Hennique, Rosny was certainly prescient, as if looking ahead to his own later relations with Goncourt and his own nomination as president of the Académie Goncourt in 1926.

3. Joseph-Henri Boëx, on his return to France from England in 1884, adopted the pseudonym "J.-H. Rosny," apparently to reaffirm francophone roots. In the year 1887, Joseph began a collaboration with his younger brother Justin that was to last officially until 1909. During that period, the name "J.-H. Rosny" covered the two writers, who began to be known, informally, as "Rosny aîné" (Rosny the Elder) and "Rosny jeune" ("Rosny the Younger"). *Les Xipéhuz*, in fact, was the first work published under the collaborative name. *Un autre monde* (1897) still bore the name "J.-H. Rosny." By the time of its publication, however, it had become clear that, of the two, the real talent was Joseph. His unique vision is especially notable in the scientific and prehistoric novels. Indeed, by 1906, with *La Mort de la Terre*, Joseph was already signing his novels "Rosny aîné." In 1936, a legal list was published whereby Joseph reclaimed possession of the "J.-H. Rosny" works that were his in conception and style. Both *Les Xipéhuz* and *Un autre monde* are on this list. For this translation and edition, we have chosen to designate the author "J.-H. Rosny aîné."

4. We notice the strangely precise yet vague nature of Rosny's "chronology" here. However long this "great gathering of peoples" took, we can give precise dates to the cities mentioned. Nineveh, located on the Tigris River in ancient Mesopotamia, was founded

around 5000 BCE. In 705 BCE it becomes prominent as the capital of Assyria. It was destroyed in 612 BCE. The city of Babylon, on the Euphrates River about 160 kilometers southeast of modern Baghdad, was founded by the Akkadians around 2800 BCE. Ecbatane, capital of the Medes, located in what is today northwest Iran, flourished 612–550 BCE. Chapter 1 of the apocryphal Book of Judith (written around the Maccabean period, 167–64 BCE), mentions these legendary cities: "In the twelfth year of the reign of Nabuchodonosor [who took Jerusalem in 587 BCE], who reigned in Nineve, the great city; in the days of Arphaxad, which reigned over the Medes in Ecbatane [approximate date 650 BCE] and built in Ecbatane walls round about of stones hewn three cubits broad and six cubits long, and made the height of the wall seventy cubits, and the breadth thereof fifty cubits." These were high walls for the time; one cubit is 45.72 centimeters.

5. Rosny has invented the names of these prehistoric tribes, as is fitting for something unwritten and unknown. There is, however, a Kzour area in modern Tunisia. The important thing was to invent ancient-sounding names. We are reminded of Flaubert's fascination, in *Salammbô*, with names that have come to us from the night of time, and to which we can no longer attach concrete meaning.

6. The French word is "strates," a technical term from geography that refers to sheets of rock or sediment layered on one another. Rosny's narrator describes mineral beings whose form seems to be sheets of sedimentary mass, which the narrator simply calls "strates." The narrator speaking here is the "first" seemingly "omniscient" narrator of this novella, who uses descriptive and technical terms like this that only a scientist of Rosny's time would know. Bakhoun, later, will not have this narrator's collective and cumulative scientific knowledge, and consequently should not be using a term like this in any technical sense. His early genius, however, could allow him to *describe* the phenomenon he sees as having the form of strata, layers.

7. Much has been made of Rosny's ability to model "real" aliens. We contend, however, that "alien" is the wrong word. These beings do not necessary come from "somewhere else," invaders from outer space or brought to prehistoric Earth by chariots of the gods. Humans share with them the same basic symmetry, the same geometric shapes (witness Renaissance drawings of human geometry). In the initial sighting, they are seen through the eyes of superstitious tribesmen. This vision, however, is "corrected" by Rosny's third-person narrator, who methodically describes their forms and actions, indeed personifies them as "The Forms."

8. Compared in fact to the barbaric slaughter of noncombatants in human wars down to modern times, Rosny's Forms show real "nobility" in sparing these. They are merciless warriors, with whom there is neither dialogue nor compromise. But they strictly follow their own ethical code. The eighteenth century used "savage" morals to make comparisons quite unflattering to "civilized" France or England; Rosny uses this prehistoric "alien" morality to like ends.

9. Sentences like this may seem awkward, but we have rendered Rosny's austere, almost hieratic style as faithfully as possible, except in cases where it ceases to be English. That style is typified by lists, or more commonly, parallel constructions of object nouns or adjectives of emotion. These are commonly set against each other, without transitional articles.

10. As of this point, in the French text, the names of these beings, first simply described as cones, cylinders, strata, etc., are capitalized. Apparently, for the narrator, they have become bona fide classes of being.

11. Rosny uses short clauses like this to track an action. We realize our literal translation here may seem awkward in English. But instead of altering the rhythm by making a sentence like "They decided, beyond the limit of Safety, to trace a wall of stakes," we have kept the flow of the sentence as Rosny wrote it.

12. We notice here that, despite their superstitious fanaticism, these nomads do possess "human" ingenuity, as they test the limits of the Xipéhuz's power, and stake out boundaries. Bakhoun does not represent a total break with these ancestors but a logical evolutionary advancement.

13. The reference here is to what medieval historians call "les terreurs de l'an mil," the apocalyptic expectations associated with the approach of the year 1000. There is little surviving evidence of any such widespread terror, and the importance of this date in medieval history is much debated today. If, as some claim, the year 1000 is a creation of Romantic historians, then Rosny may be contrasting irrational terror with rational, "scientific" enlightenment. Through such "topical" allusions as this, as with that to the "red man in the forest," Rosny's "objective" narrator betrays his nineteenth-century location.

14. The French has "des silhouettes d'inspirés, des hommes de silence." Because the word "silhouette" has a poetical vagueness about it, we have chosen "shades," which appears to be an analogous word in English. Rosny's images of this "cult of darkness" and concurrent medievalizing terrors are as vivid as the cinematic rendering of Ingmar Bergman in *The Seventh Seal*. The film likewise contrasts superstitious horrors of the theological imagination with the realities of practical, physical life in nature, milk and strawberries.

15. "Quarters of great stones" translates the French "des quartiers de rocs." Rosny refers here to the "cyclopean" architecture of the walls of ancient Mycenae as described by Pausanias in his *Description of Greece*, written in the second century CE. Pausanias recounts that the great stones that comprise the Lion Gate at Mycenae were said to be the work of the Cyclopes, the huge, one-eyed creatures of Greek legend, the only creatures deemed strong enough to move such stones. The "tent that does not move" (in French "la tente fixe") is what we today call a metonymy, where the shift from nomadic to sedentary culture is figured as the visible shift from mobile tent to fixed dwelling.

16. Bakhoun not only represents the shift, in human evolution, from nomadic to sedentary, agricultural existence. His views also place him squarely as a forerunner of Renaissance science, a prehistoric Galileo, and (more extraordinary yet), in his use of the quantitative method, a Descartes lost in the night of time. In addition, his natural theology and cult of reason position him even closer to our age of European intellectual history: as a postrevolutionary figure, indeed as a positivist. Bakhoun is in fact a resumé of the development of Western rational man.

17. Bakhoun's written record is in fact a perfect example of the modern scientific method: observation, hypothesis, testing, and verification.

18. A search of world libraries revealed no such author or title. M. Dessault and his work are fictitious (in fact a search on the web came back to Rosny's novel itself as exclusive reference, as does the search for any number of names and places in his texts). The

fiction of a fictitious scientist deciphering and mediating an ancient text to a contemporary audience is a common device in a nineteenth century fascinated with archeology and prehistory. Rosny's narrative has some interesting shifts in focus. In the first several chapters, pre-Bakhoun, the narrative voice affects an "ancient" tone and distance. Then we have the sudden shift to a narrator of Rosny's time, speaking in the first person, or in a form of "scientific 'we,'" the consensus voice of a body of specialists, speaking to the lay reader. This leads the way to the "Book of Bakhoun," the ancient text that the fictitious M. Dessault has translated.

19. Our translation generally follows Rosny's text to the letter. However, in the case of certain cryptic phrases—an example is "l'indépendence partielle," which we translate here as "the partial capacity for independence of mind"—we have taken a small interpretive liberty in order to make the text clearer to the reader. Generally, however, we seek neither to "second-guess" the author nor to interpret his words. Many times, we record them literally. His phrases are often as enigmatic in French as in English, and we imagine his design was to cultivate a certain imprecision or vagueness that obliges readers to work their way into the future world he presents—a thoroughly science-fictional process.

20. Bakhoun's preservation of this strange metallic "debris" is an act that will allow modern chemists to study this matter. Rosny's narrator presents him as a Lavoisier *avant la lettre,* for whom this debris is not rejected as an alien, unearthly substance but is accepted as one that does not fit in the known table of elements. As it is never a question of something not of earthly origin, it is implied that future science may find the means of breaking down and recombining this matter.

21. We are reminded here of the first impressions of Wells's Time Traveler among the Eloi, who also have no visible signs of industry. The nature, however, of these observed facts, and their role in determining the course of the narrative, is very different in Wells. An apparently innocent fact, the absence of industry first leads, in the imagination-driven investigations of the Traveler, to a utopian misinterpretation of the situation. This error becomes all the more horrific as further evidence points to the deeper mystery of the Morlocks and the nature and purpose of their "industry." Bakhoun, in contrast, presents the fact but does not conclude. His stress on the words "*tangible or visible* industry" suggests that some other kind might exist: telepathic or telekinetic industry for example. But Bakhoun remains the positivist—he restricts himself in Comtean manner to strict facts, and beyond that he says: "I don't know."

22. The French "barrières idéales" is as vague in the original as in the translation; Rosny could mean "virtual" boundaries, or "absolute" ones.

23. Bakhoun, in his supremely quantitative analysis of the Xipéhuz's mobility, speaks of physical "limits" that are in fact evolutionary limits. Rosny's creatures are in effect a collective entity. The field of action of any individual unit is directly proportionate to the number of individuals present, and to the energy field they generate. Robert A. Heinlein's later rejection of collective beings and "group minds" is relevant here. Heinlein's protagonist Kip in *Have Space Suit, Will Travel* shouts defiantly at the group entity that would judge humanity: "We have no limits." The idea here is that evolutionary development depends on the initiative of individuals, each one imperfect, but each with a desire to strive, to invent, to substitute dynamic actions for equilibrium: in short, to defy the

apparent "laws" that regulate the action of the Xipéhuz, that make them, effectively, an evolutionary dead end. In all of Bakhoun's descriptions of the Xipéhuz, nothing emerges that could be called "individual." Bakhoun, by contrast, is—like his god—a unique being, the individual who initiates evolutionary change.

24. In the light of evolution, the reproductive patterns of the Xipéhuz, described by Bakhoun, are of particular interest. They reproduce four times a year, by means of the fusion of three beings into a single group. From this, one might imagine rapid expansion of their energy field, by which they could essentially conquer all in their path. This potential for insect-like expansion, however, has compensating limits. For example, the Xipéhuz "newborn" are huge, vague, vaporous forms who begin to shrink at birth and within ten days transform into amber cones. Their period of "childhood" lasts two months, after which they become like others of their species. One thinks of Rabelais's Gargantua, born a sprawling giant, who must learn to conform, physically and socially, to human norms. In terms of the evolutionary category of neoteny, the Xipéhuz have a short developmental period, a disadvantage in relation to the long "childhood" gestation of humanity. Gargantua, we remember, after a few gigantic antics, rapidly shrinks to human proportions. His education, however, is a long and arduous process, during which he "matures" into a creative individual. Again the information Bakhoun gives, though not interpreted, details for the reader aware of evolutionary theory a species that cannot beat humanity in the survival of the fittest.

25. We have used other signs than in Rosny's text, as the latter could not be reproduced typographically. Our use of signs, however, is consistent with the original, and each Rosny sign is given an equivalent in our system.

26. The "literal" nature of the Xipéhuz language is curious, given the earlier suggestion that they might possess some kind of telekinetic faculty, whereby mind moves matter. But if all their signs are out in the open, so to speak, how can there be any hidden "inner" thoughts or motives that accompany the act of communication? Moreover, because this practice of "signing" one's interlocutor is so ponderous and slow, it is hard to see how (as Bakhoun suggests) they can engage in abstract discourse, as the process of building ideas would take an inordinate amount of time. Unless, of course, the observed long moments of inability are in fact moments of telepathic communication. Finally, because they inscribe signs or characters literally on each other's bodies in order to communicate, they have not reached the stage of writing as Bakhoun practices it, for he inscribes symbols on a tablet, or other external object, that can then be transported in space and time. Thus their language, like their system of energy distribution, reveals itself a closed system, which denies them the mobility of ideas necessary for rapid and complex evolution.

27. Again the word "individual" does not designate the upward-striving monad. Bakhoun refers rather to character traits, which allow certain beings among the Xipéhuz to be more or less taciturn, friendly, or reclusive. Bakhoun of course does not have much time to observe and classify. Nor can he do much more than remark that the Xipéhuz teach their young. But he is a bit hasty in crying inscrutable mystery, the inherent limitations of his "poor senses." Rosny's mutant observer in *Un autre monde* realizes that science is long, life short. Bakhoun, in his defense, has a more immediate and practical observational task: to discover points of vulnerability, and devise a plan accordingly to defeat the enemy.

28. The shifting tenses here are carefully calculated to illustrate Bakhoun's aptitude for scientific discourse. When Bakhoun says "They educate their young," he expresses a general observation, a "law" valid for all times. When he recounts individual adventures, or provisional conclusions of the observing scientist ("To me these lessons *were* marvelous"), he limits his field of observation to his own past, be it to a singular event or a plural observation ("How many times . . ."). Bakhoun after all is the first human to think "scientifically."

29. The superstitious tribesmen, faced with the strange appearance and great power of the Xipéhuz, have assumed them to be gods. Bakhoun, in contrast, patiently observes, allowing no metaphysical idea to prevail until it is tested, and either verified or rejected. He discovers that they can physically perish.

30. In solving this problem by the process of reason, Bakhoun proves a forerunner of the famous Asimov protagonist in stories like "Reason," where the key to the narrative is less an action than a reasoned solution to a crucial problem, often one on which the fate of humanity hinges. In extremis a solution is always reached, and it is always a solution based on principles of rational scientific investigation.

31. The word "solitude" has connotations of meditation for French Romantic literature (Lamartine's *Méditations poétiques*). Solitude, the condition of being alone and finding harmony with self and nature, is also associated with genius in English Romanticism (e.g. Newton sailing strange seas of thought, alone; or Keats's nightingale). Rosny presents Bakhoun as such a solitary genius, who by means of his meditations on the Xipéhuz is able to bridge the gap between humanity and the natural world, of which they are a menacing presence. If one wonders what happens to Bakhoun's many wives and children during such solitary moments, one must realize they are expendable in this thoroughly patriarchal prehistorical world. And Rosny, alas, did not benefit from today's political correctness: Bakhoun has license to shut out family problems around him; his wives serve to bear the children he needs to win humanity's battles, and no more.

32. Bakhoun is not only a keen observer and reasoner. He is also crafty, using ruse against superior force, a key survival trait for homo sapiens.

33. There is more here than a simple statement of so-called Darwinian "survival of the fittest." When the destruction of one species becomes "the terrible condition of life" for the other, we are reminded of the religious overtones that surround that other, modern, evolutionary tale Stanley Kubrick's *2001: A Space Odyssey*. In the famous scene in which prehistoric humankind discovers weapons, human advancement is inexorably linked to a vision of the Fall, whereby all subsequent Edenic or utopian constructions of humankind—machines waltzing to Strauss, moon colonies, spaceships controlled by a supposedly beneficent machine intelligence, the white room at the end of infinity— are somehow "wormed" with the original stigma of the Fall. Bakhoun's words imply that there may be more than just the necessary survival traits involved in mankind's survival. A teleological dimension, in fact an almost Calvinist election, is suggested by this "terrible condition of life" that says that of two comparable species, one survives, the other perishes.

34. The question of a linear calendar dating back (or forward) to the precise date 22,649 is interesting. The Sumerians may have used artificial time units as early as the

twenty-seventh century BCE in referring to such things as the tenure of public officials and agricultural cycles. If Rosny's dates do refer to a time before the Common Era, this calendar is much earlier than subsequent known calendars, Assyrian or Babylonian. "The sixth moon of the year 22,649" implies they counted months as well. The Sumerians of Babylon were probably the first people to devise a calendar that used phases of the moon, with twelve lunar months to a year.

35. All the names of these "tribes" are invented by Rosny, with the exception of one: the Khaldes. The Khaldes apparently came from the region of Kurdistan, in what today is Armenia or Georgia. Again, Rosny probably chose the name for its "ancient" sound, not for any particular characteristics of a given people. The invention of suggestive names for yet-unknown or nonexistent "peoples" has a long history in modern SF, and Rosny seems to be the first to pursue such invention. Just as Frank Herbert bases his names in the *Dune* series on "arabized" or arabic-seeming names, so here Rosny improvises on cradle-of-civilization-sounding names like "Khaldes," whose very orthography is highly suggestive.

36. The cubit is the first recorded measure of length. It is apparently based on the average length of a human forearm. The ancient Egyptians divided the cubit into "palms" and "digits," with six palms or twenty-four digits equaling one cubit. This is posited on the average length of the human finger, palm, or forearm, which is approximately eighteen inches. This helps us understand the military tactic being described. The Xipéhuz is on the average one and one-half cubits tall (twenty-two and one-half inches), much shorter than the average ancient human carrying the six-cubit frame. Because the frame is six cubits long, and the inclining crossbeams five cubits long, the latter can be inclined upon encounter with the Xipéhuz, allowing the men inside to use lances and arrows, while protected from their shorter adversaries. Rosny's technical descriptions, on the whole, are amazingly precise. They find their equal only in the technicallly specialized descriptions of a modern military SF writer like David Drake.

37. All we humans know is human history. Thus here, as in subsequent fictional future (or past) histories, the speculative writer is destined to adapt the known to the imagined unknown. One could say that Bakhoun here is *preadapting* Roman military tactics to this key battle with the Xipéhuz. The Romans used similar square formations to resist cavalry (*repellere equites*). Foot soldiers within tight squares advanced holding *pila* (javelins) in the spaces between their shields. Bakhoun adjusts these tactics in accordance with his battlefield analysis of the strengths and weaknesses of the enemy, very much as Caesar says he did in his narrative of his wars in Gaul. We should note that Bakhoun, like all good generals, is in fact modifying, turning to his advantage, tactics the enemy has used. For in the previous battle, the Xipéhuz routed their adversaries by forming similar battle squares, their vulnerable stars pointing inward in order to protect them from arrows. And note that Caesar admired and respected his enemy, the Gauls, just as Bakhoun respects the Xipéhuz.

38. The memory of Napoleon's usurpatory reign is still vivid for Rosny, who echoes Benjamin Constant's condemnation of absolute power. Bakhoun, that summation of French history, is acts as a prehistoric incarnation of the man of the French Enlightenment, invoking Wisdom as the sole ruler of mankind.

39. Rosny's term here is a strong one: "Meurtre," personified with a capital M. The

invocation of such a dark, murderous Fatality has Jansenist overtones that go beyond the simple statement of "nature red in tooth and claw." The term *fatalité* would not be used by a Darwinist, for whom evolution is a nonteleological process.

Another World

1. Gelderland is a rural province in the middle to eastern part of Holland, bordering on Germany. Its principal city is Arnhem. We must remember that Rosny is Belgian by birth. Although a Francophone, he is culturally linked to Flemish and Dutch speakers. What is more, a French-language readership would have a mixed reaction to the presentation of Gelderland as the place where what is ostensibly a mutant species of human being emerges. For such a reader, there are two Hollands: the homeland of Renaissance freethinkers and the freedom of expression that produced Erasmus and sheltered Descartes, and the Flemish provinces as depicted in, e.g., Balzac's *La Recherche de l'Absolu* (1834)—a stolid, unimaginative, bourgeois world that is hostile to science and all manner of change. Indeed, the Amsterdam Rosny's mutant finds is a world of genuine enlightenment. For this, we need only compare Rosny's Van den Heuvel and the way he treats the protagonist with how people with "special" powers are treated in the world of Rosny's contemporary Guy de Maupassant, where they are routinely institutionalized as madmen.

2. Rosny's mutant is aware of the long tradition of "monstrous" births that precedes him in Western culture. Physical deformities, at least since the Renaissance, were seen as signs of moral depravity. The line runs from Shakespeare's Richard III to Frankenstein's monster. Indeed, the treatment of the latter's physical abnormality by average humanity certainly lurks in the background of Rosny's work. But what is remarkable in Rosny, in fact, is the relative *lack* of revulsion his protagonist's family and peers have toward his oddities. They do not reject him; he decides of his own volition to find a scientist who will study his mutations. Moreover, while Frankenstein's creature possesses physical and intellectual powers that make people all the more fearful because these powers frighten them, Rosny's protagonist's new power, is a change in the organ of sight, which is the conventional instrument of knowledge in Western culture. This, along with the relatively unmenacing nature of his other differences, makes it easy for Rosny's scientist to accept him, indeed to *utilize* him as one would a microscope or telescope.

3. A strong aromatic schnapps from the city of Schiedam in southern Holland.

4. Readers and critics in Rosny's time commented (often pejoratively) on his use, often seemingly gratuitous, of highly specialized scientific terminology in his stories. This sentence is an example that seems strange coming from the mouth of a country boy in the early stages of formation (unless he possesses some extraordinary innate knowledge). "Corneous" means horn-like. "Elytra" are the anterior wings of beetles that serve to protect the posterior pair of functional wings. "Coleoptera" are beetles.

5. Rosny's mutant possesses powers not immediately visible to human observers, which prove to be much more significant than his physically observable deviations from the human norm (skin color, rapid speech). What surprises the SF reader is the equanimity with which these, once known, are accepted by human society. In A. E. Van Vogt's *Slan* (1940), for example, mutants are persecuted for having the same extrasensory perception

as Rosny's mutant, as well as thoughts so fast they cannot be recorded by normal human media. In comparison with Rosny's world of dignified science, Van Vogt's (like many others in SF) is a world of paranoia and power fantasy. Van Vogt's sacrificial mutant is even named Jommy Cross.

6. Violet represents the shortest wavelengths of light visible to the human eye. Ultraviolet [ultra: Latin "beyond"] light is electromagnetic radiation with wavelengths shorter than visible light, but longer than X-rays. Near ultraviolet light waves (closer to visible light) measure 400–320 nanometers, far to extreme ultraviolet light (toward X-rays) measure 200–210 nanometers. Near or long-wave ultraviolet light is sometimes called "black light." Some animals, birds, and insects (bees) can see into the near ultraviolet spectrum. Rosny's mutant apparently sees into the far ultraviolet end of the spectrum. One has to assume that the reason ordinary glass remains opaque to his eyes is because ordinary glass blocks far ultraviolet light. At the same time, his ability to see through objects that are ordinarily opaque to human eyes makes him literally a "man with X-ray eyes."

7. Green is midspectrum for the human eye (c. 565 nanometers). We remember that Rosny's protagonist sees primarily in the ultraviolet end of the spectrum (380 nanometers and fewer). Green is thus a zone where his faculty of sight overlaps the human, in the imprecise manner described.

8. This idea is astonishing for its time. The turn of the century was a period when writers in England and France were obsessed with tales of alien invasion, other worlds intruding on our own with the express purpose of destruction. Here to the contrary is a species that both is unperceived by us and does not perceive us. Even more troubling however, if you think about it, is the fact that its actions (however unintentionally) might have some negative effect on the environment, the physical realm, it shares with us. In turn, our actions might effect its environment. But has this species perceived us yet? Or our potential impact on their world? It appears from the story that they go blithely about their doings, while the advent of the mutant seems to give humans a subtle evolutionary edge, a window into their world.

9. One thinks of Edwin A. Abbott's popular *Flatland*, published in 1884, which Rosny may have read in England. In Abbott's book a two-dimensional being named Square discovers the marvels of the world of three dimensions. Abbott's work remains, despite its accurate geometry, a conventional imaginary voyage, in which a contemporary observer (Square is a typical late nineteenth-century Englishman) compares the strange place with his familiar world, in ways invariably unflattering to the latter. Rosny's narrator, in contrast, is a neutral observer, an *instrument* of pure scientific investigation.

10. "Why does Rosny capitalize the word *Kingdom*? The French word is "règne," and here it refers to the "kingdom" of life forms. Rosny, on the one hand, uses it as a technical world, part of the scientific classification system that includes "species," "kingdoms," etc. On the other hand, Rosny has an almost mystical reverence for Life as a vital force. His personification of the word signals this. The scientist would not capitalize the word; the mystic would. Rosny's application of scientific method may be more rigorous that that of Verne or Wells. But in these capitals, Rosny the mystic is ever present. In an interesting sidelight on this matter, Jacques Chabot and Normand David, in their article "La Majuscule dans la noménclature zoologique," published in the June 1988 issue of the *Bulletin de*

l'entomofaune, of the Centre de recherches écologiques de Montréal, see French-language science, as early as Rosny's time, normalizing a practice that capitalizes the generic names of species (as well as any attached adjectives), while using lowercase for such general categories as species, genus, kingdom. Rosny's use of the capital, then, is not standard scientific usage.

11. Rosny's protagonist seems to be a born scientist. From the earliest age, he is drawn to study the beings he perceives in this alternate dimension. He has an innate ability to observe and analyze unusual "alien" phenomena (like Bakhoun, also a stranger in a strange land). As in *Les Xipéhuz,* Rosny's other species consists of geometrical forms. These forms may in fact prove not truly alien. For what first seems unhuman may in fact be something common to human consciousness in general. Arthur C. Clarke plays ironically with this idea in *Childhood's End.* His Overlords have horns and tails. We learn, subsequently, that early unenlightened mankind perceived these beings as devils, but in fact they are benefactors. Those who have read *The Xipéhuz* know that Rosny has suggested that there were others, in the night of time, who perceived and described such Forms. Were Bakhoun's Xipéhuz somehow related to the Moedigen? And might not such ancient sightings have impressed these geometrical forms on the human psyche as a universal heritage? The fact that the narrator of *Un autre monde* cannot explain where he got the name Moedigen suggests deep racial memory.

12. We notice again that Rosny's Moedigen have the evolutionary disadvantage of being a closed system. Their existence obeys a principle of transfer of energy from weaker to stronger. While this transfer implies a form of perpetual motion, it excludes catastrophic losses or leaps—forces that lead either to annihilation or to advancement of a species.

13. This trait of rapid speech, which Heinlein calls "speedtalk," becomes a sign of human advancement, indeed a mark of election, in his novella *Gulf* (*Astounding Science Fiction,* November and December 1949; reprinted in *Assignment in Eternity* [New York: Signet Books, 1953], 7–68). Protagonist Kettle Belly Baldwin belongs to a secret society of advanced humans. In a literal application of Korzybskian semantics (that human thought is performed only in symbols, a theory developed by Alfred Korzybski), Baldwin's ability to master speedtalk denotes a kind of evolutionary superiority: "Any man capable of learning speedtalk had an association time at least three times as fast as an ordinary man . . . a New Man had an *effective* life time of at least *sixteen hundred* years, reckoned in flow of ideas" (56). Rosny's protagonist may have the same life-extending power, but he is totally unaware of it, as is Dr. Van den Heuvel. On the contrary, he realizes he must find ways to slow down his speech in order to communicate his knowledge to beings who do not speak fast. He does not seek to detach himself from normative humanity, but rather to reintegrate his vision with that of human science. Again, he is blithely unaware of what we might call "the Superman gambit": exploiting one's special abilities as the means of gaining great power in the human world.

14. This may refer to Bakhoun's desire to inscribe knowledge in order to pass it on to distant posterity. The mutant's problem is different. He is deprived of normal writing, as his thoughts outrun the medium. What is needed is shorthand, a rapid form of writing that will capture his vision, just as electronic playback at slower speed will translate his speedtalk. Interestingly, in radically different contexts, we have two observers in search

of a medium of expression. Bakhoun, at the "dawn" of humankind, uses a cumbersome medium the very opposite of "speed" writing. Yet his text has apparently come down to M. Dessault, its contemporary translator. The phonograph replaces the stylus, and is an advance in terms of rapid "pickup" of information. But what of its durability, a key factor in evolution of ideas and species? For continuity of thought, the end of *Un autre monde* suggests another "slow" medium: successive generations of mutants serving as investigators.

15. *Frankenstein* is surely on Rosny's mind here. Earlier Rosny's mutant, like Frankenstein's monster, has lamented his isolation from mankind, even asserted that his new faculties make him superior to those who reject him. Despite this, the mutant reveals a steadfastly anti-Frankensteinian purpose. He will not destroy those who reject him, but instead prove his ultimate usefulness to them. The tale of science must never swerve into one of gothic horror.

16. The Heerengracht ("Gentlemen's Street") is the main canal in Amsterdam.

17. At the time of this story, Borneo was part of the Dutch East Indies. Borneo became independent in 1945 and now comprises the modern nation of Indonesia.

18. A device called the "phonautograph" was patented March 25, 1857, by Edouard-Léon Scott. It could record sound, but not play it back. Charles Cros formulated the theory of the phonograph in 1877. Thomas Edison announced his invention of, and demonstrated, the first working phonograph November 29, 1877. The device was still somewhat of a novelty at the time Rosny wrote his story.

19. In essence, the narrator's visual faculties comprise what is called today extrasensory perception, a paranormal power. It is interesting that Van den Heuvel places them in the context of chemical and physical theories that, in the earlier nineteenth century, shaded toward the paranormal. The theory of "elective affinities" belongs to early nineteenth-century chemistry. It posited a force that caused chemical reactions between dissimilar elements, forming new (and unstable) compounds. Wolfgang von Goethe, in his novel *Die Wahlverwandtschaften* (Elective affinities; 1809), uses this term to describe moral unions, in accordance with the adage "Opposites attract." Modern chemistry redefines such "affinities" in a measurable manner as the tendency of atoms to combine by chemical reaction with atoms of unlike composition to form compounds. Likewise, the term "magnetism" looks back to earlier science. In physics, it refers to the phenomenon by which materials exert an attractive or repulsive force on each other. But in the early nineteenth century, "magnetism" was Mesmerism, unexplained action at a distance. Thus, despite Van den Heuvel's scientific objectivity, he still acknowledges the shadow of the paranormal that hovers over the mutant.

20. "Le monde du quatrième état." Again, the expression can refer to supernatural phenomena such as ghosts and spirits, but need not. The "fourth state" of matter (the first three are: solid, liquid, gas) is ionized gas, a substance identified by Sir William Crookes, the inventor of the cathode ray tube, as "radiant matter" in 1874. This substance was dubbed "plasma" by Irving Langmuir in 1928. "Ionization" describes the dissociation of one electron from a given body of atoms or molecules, creating a "free" electric charge. Rosny, well versed in scientific discoveries, surely knew of radiant matter.

21. The phrase "a world just as much prisoner of the earth" represents Rosny's central formulation of an ecological vision that was merely implicit in *Les Xipéhuz*. In this case,

the beings in question are as invisible to us as we to them, yet both enact "modifications of shared ground," and are assumed to obey the same physical laws of causality, mortality, and so on. The ferromagnetics in *La Mort de la Terre* are again beings of a shared environment, as well as a common evolutionary path.

22. Rosny no doubt means by *humus* organic compost. But the fact that he italicizes the word in his text may mean he is thinking of the more technical sense of the word. In terms of soil science, humus is organic matter that has broken down to a point of stability and uniformity at which it can remain for centuries. If the Moedigen can penetrate humus while remaining refractory to defined minerals and material objects (we humans are also thus refractory), could not this somewhat basic entity (indeed humans and all organic matter as we know it decompose into humus) mark a point of convergence between the two worlds?

23. The Moedigen are not specifically cannibals, as are Wells's Martians. Nor do they not kill their adversaries, they merely "take energy without exhausting the sources of life." Through the conservation of energy, they seem to have reached a form of homeostasis. Yet Rosny here seems to challenge such closed systems. For he introduces a wild card into the closed equation: the mutant who can see into their world while they cannot see into ours. This seems an element of evolutionary chance. Heinlein will later call such changes "serendipity," an unforeseen something that allows an otherwise weaker humanity to make fortunate "paradigm" leaps like the one we witness here.

24. "La Fable." Given the capitalization of the word in the French text, one can only imagine that this is the miraculous story of Christ, the Greatest Story Ever Told. The capital letter shows that the scientist has respect for this Story, but remains too much the believer in evolution. He has before him the product of this process, a "miracle" made flesh and blood in a very different manner, through what appears to be random selection.

25. The mutant's hymn to the random process of natural selection has also a religious ring to it, as if there were still some higher providence operating above human vanity and evolutionary theory alike.

26. One wonders whom the narrator is addressing here, who is "you"? He seems to turn away from the specified context of his narrative, and to address an audience who needs to be aware of the fact that, beyond his own limits, science will continue to be served by his progeny. Dr. Van den Heuvel seems very happy with a mutant progeny. The narrator however, perhaps aware of possible misgivings on the part of his audience as to what could be a potentially dangerous event for humankind, seems to address them directly, hoping to assuage their possible fears.

27. *Hyperesthésique*, a highly technical medical term: a sufferer from hyperaesthesia, a pathological sensitivity of the skin or other sense organ to a particular stimulus. This is an example of the scientific language that Rosny's contemporaries considered a barbarism in his texts.

28. Again we have what seems a Frankensteinian gloss. Frankenstein's creator refuses to give the creature a bride, fearing such a union would generate a new "race" of monstrous beings. This idea obsesses Dr. Frankenstein. What astounds here is that Dr. Van den Heuvel never seems to give this a thought, even though there appear to be other beings

similar in physical nature to the narrator, and that their mating produces effortless replicas. This would have been nemesis to Dr. Frankenstein.

The Death of the Earth

1. This epigraph is curious. The tone is one of warning, and implies that human hubris was the major factor in the death of the Earth. Yet this is qualified by the word *annonçait* ("heralded"), which does not attribute causality. In fact, we will learn later that this "death" is not the destruction of the physical Earth, but rather the destruction of humankind in a physical environment whose conditions have changed to the point that it no longer supports carbon-based life forms. Moreover, even if our working of iron engendered the rise of the ferromagnetics, we later learn that this activity was a natural by-product of human industry, thus the "natural" course of evolution for humans.

2. What exactly is this "Great Planetary," which Rosny presents on the first page of the novella without further details? The author invents here a literary device developed by later SF writers such as Heinlein, Van Vogt, and Dick, where peoples, things, and machines are given names but as objects are not explained, in terms of origin, function, or other properties. Any explanation, if there is one, must emerge from the text itself, readers familiarize themselves with its strange new world and learn to negotiate it. Readers thus becomes active participants in building a new world that is extrapolated from their own, but clearly different. Here, at first, we can only guess what it might mean to be the "watchman" of the "Great Planetary." We gain more of an idea as the narrative unfolds. But nowhere is this entity explained in full.

3. The French word is *veilleur*, literally "watchman." It is used in modern French principally in the expression "veilleur de nuit" (night watchman). In Rosny's context, its meaning is the more archaic one of "veiller sur" (to watch over), which carries quasi-religious connotations (as in the English word "wake").

4. Targ and Arva are in effect the "beautiful people" of this far future, where humankind has mastered all forces, except those that prove beyond its control. Theirs is a long lineage, from Wells's earlier Eloi to the late humans of Arthur C. Clarke's *Against the Fall of Night* (1952) and a myriad other SF futures. Typically in such scenarios (Rosny is no exception) one or several last humans remain who revolt against this gathering darkness.

5. In this narrative, Rosny invents a series of devices and materials proper to this distant future world and gives them names and descriptions, just as Hugo Gernsback and others known as pioneers of SF will later do. Like later SF neologisms, Rosny's coinages are often Janus faced, looking backward as they look forward. An example is the Great Planetary (Grand Planétaire). It performs great technical feats, sending and receiving messages across vast empty spaces. Yet its components are described as "conch" (*conque*) and "corolla," the ancient *shell* and *flower*. "Arcum," however, is a made-up substance; the word is found in no dictionary in French or English. But it sounds oddly familiar, as if it did exist.

6. Rosny's description of these sleek, overevolved birds looks forward to much later SF depiction of future skyscapes, from Frank R. Paul's *Amazing Stories* back covers of the

early 1940s, to the stylized visions of French artists such as Moebius and Philippe Druillet. Interestingly, these birds still augur, even though no gods remain to bring back signs from. While the superstitious prehistoric tribes in *Les Xipéhuz* practice haruspicy, the reading of entrails of sacrificial animals, Rosny's elegant future birds remain close to the *oscines* of Roman times, the divining of future events according to the direction from which birds call or fly. These birds are the last vestiges of once teeming animal life, and a world without them would be unbearable. This reminds the reader of the world of Anarres in Ursula Le Guin's novel *The Dispossessed* (1970), an austere desert inhabited by sophisticated people, but void of animal life. One thinks as well of Kate Wilhelm's 1976 novel *Where Late the Sweet Birds Sang,* in which Shakespeare's Sonnet 73 is literal reality. In that work, however, all the environmental disasters that bring about a world of monotonous sameness are manmade. The result is a die-off of all species, in a world where mankind can survive only in the form of exact clones.

7. The process of evolutionary checks and balances expressed here by Rosny is more pessimistic than that articulated by Wells's narrator at the end of *The War of the Worlds* (1898). There the all-powerful Martians are destroyed by microbes to which humans, over a long period of suffering and death, have become immune. In Rosny, immunity to one set of conditions brings about susceptibility to another set. "Progress" may have an ironic ring in the mouth of Wells's narrator, yet Wells offers no reason why humanity, within reasonable limits, cannot advance. In Rosny, progress is an illusion. In overcoming one set of problems, we invariably create others. Thus, by eradicating organic parasites, we create mineral ones.

8. *Motrice:* a neologism. The French noun *motricité* has the specialized, physiological meaning "motor functions"; the noun *automotrice* refers to an electric railcar. Rosny's neologism clearly refers to a motorized vehicle, a variation on the automobile. In order to suggest its future potentialities, we translate it "motocruiser."

9. *Appareils sismiques.* A mercury seismometer was invented by Luigi Palmieri in 1855, and an English seismologist invented a horizontal pendulum seismograph in 1880.

10. *Ondifère,* a neologism, with root in *onde* (wave), that expresses the idea of a conveyer of (sound) waves. As this seems here a two-way device, we have translated it "sender-receiver."

11. *Resonateurs,* a neologism. The *Online Etymology Dictionary* lists the first recorded use of the verb "to resonate" as 1873. In 1910 Rosny coins a noun that suggests a wireless device that receives and transmits sound waves.

12. *Les météores.* The *Dictionnaire Littré* defines this term in the "modern" sense (which would be that of Rosny here) as "phenomena like heat, light, wind, thunderstorms that occur on the Earth's surface in relation to atmospheric disturbances."

13. We have rendered the tense and voice changes as they occur in the text, in order to give the reader a sense of the shifts of narrative perspective. The reader notices the hiatus that occurs here in the text. The new section begins with a different speaking voice, that of five hundred centuries of postcatastrophe generations, with a sweep in time that goes from the "have occupied" of postcatastrophe memory all the way back to precatastrophe memory. In relation to convention, Rosny's narrator seems to lack consistent focus. We

can see this either as "bad writing" or as a means (either conscious or unconscious on Rosny's part) of making the reader think differently about narrative time and its conventions. Rosny's narrative begins from what seems conventional "omniscience," sub specie aeternitatis. At this moment in the text, the focus narrows, and the narrative is now that of human memory, restricted in time and space. Then, in the middle of this narrative, there is further restriction, marked by the appearance of a first person plural, and then (surprisingly) a first person singular speaking subject. The narrator seems to become an intimate part of Targ's world. From this point on, the narrator shows increasing familiarity with Targ's innermost thoughts. If one considers the possibility, suggested by the narrator speaking in the past tense *after* the death of Targ, that Targ has been the genetic and memetic vector of carbon life into a posthuman era, then it is tempting to see this refocusing narrator as "retracing" the evolutionary path that inscribes the rise and fall of humankind, the final compression of this experience in Targ's final "dream." As we caution in the introduction, what is important here is not the correctness of any given interpretation. It is the fact that we are urged by Rosny's narrative, because it seems to operate in a new perspective of evolutionary space-time, to seek explanations outside of conventional limits. In the very form of his narrative, Rosny seems to invent the literature of extrapolation we call "hard SF" today.

14. This passage has an eerie ring today, when very similar cries of alarm against global warming are being ignored in an apparent world of plentiful water, oil, and other commodities.

15. The French phrase here, *révolutions sidéreales,* means radical transformations or "upheavals" determined by the motion of the stars. Such a vision seems strangely "primitive" for this overevolved humanity.

16. Rosny seems here to have envisioned genetically modified organisms, as well as the controversy that surrounds this process.

17. The *Oxford English Dictionary* defines zoophytes as "various animals of low organization, formally classed as intermediate between animals and plants, being usually fixed, and often having a branched or radiating structure, thus resembling plants or flowers."

18. *Les spiraloïdes,* another marvelous neologism.

19. Though the Darwinian term *sélection* is used, the term *acquis* (acquired) points rather to the theory of the transmission of acquired characteristics, subsequently disproven, of Jean-Baptiste Pierre Antoine de Monet, Chevalier de Lamarck (1744–1829) the great French biologist and pioneer of evolutionary theory.

20. Here is another example of Rosny's complex evolutionary ecology. This is not the us-versus-them scenario that has proliferated in twentieth-century SF. At work here is a much more subtle interplay of oblique forces, such that a life form simply fills an evolutionary niche. If this is at the expense of humanity, it is not a *willed* or *purposeful action,* in the sense that humans understand these terms. It is, at the same time, perfectly "natural" for humans to think in terms of purpose.

21. Rosny's ferromagnetics are an early example of what today is called alternative biochemistry: speculation on possible alternate chemical compositions of life forms. Such forms make use of atoms other than carbon to construct a primary cellular struc-

ture, where atoms are bound using solvents other than water. Modern SF (and modern science) abounds in such extrapolations. The most common substitute for carbon is the silicon atom. Silicon has chemical properties similar to carbon, and is in the same periodic table group. There is also speculation on nitrogen compounds providing the basis for bio-chemical molecules, and on substances such as ammonia or methanol acting as solvents. Rosny proposes life forms based on iron compounds, with electromagnetic forces appar-ently acting as solvent. This is not as far-fetched as it seems. Among SF novels written by scientists, Fred Hoyle's *Black Cloud* offers a life form composed of interstellar "dust," whose particles interact by means of electromagnetic signals, as do cells in carbon-based life. Robert L. Forward goes farther in *Dragon's Egg*, conceiving a life form that builds on "nuclear chemistry" rather than electromagnetic forces. Günther Wächterhäuser, in his article "Origin of Life: Life As We Don't Know It," *Science* 289 (August 2000), 1307–1308, proposes an "iron-sulphur world theory" in which he conjectures that primitive life may have occurred as a metabolic cycle that takes place on iron mineral surfaces in the sea, from which more complex compounds of life are generated. This iron-based metabolic process is said to predate genetics in the creation of life in the seas.

22. Rosny uses the archaic term *corpuscule* (the same as the English "corpuscle"), a free-floating "little body," which today would be called a cell.

23. In this description, Érê seems offer a promise of union between the mineral and organic kingdoms, a union that, arrayed against the forces of nature, can only be a passing fancy.

24. Vega is the brightest star in the constellation Lyra (the Harp), and the fifth bright-est star in the sky. At twenty-three and a half light-years from Earth, it is a "close" star. It is a special star in that it holds the position of a jewel in the harp.

25. There are clear echoes of Pascal's Pensée 347, which sees man as a thinking reed, the feeblest thing in nature (ironically for Rosny's story, it is "a drop of water" that suffices to kill him). The compensating consolation is that this vast unthinking universe (Rosny's mineral kingdom does not—yet—have thought) may crush us, but does not *know* it does so, though we know we are being crushed. It would seem that Pascal's proportions, which restore some equity between infinite, unthinking nature and feeble, thinking mankind, are contradictory to Rosny's general evolutionary vision. It is easy for the voice of evolution to say that mankind, born of water, must disappear with it. But it is hard, as with Pascal's "misère de l'homme," to accept this.

26. From Sinop or Sinope (Latin: Sinopis), a city on the Black Sea in Turkey; the color of a red iron quartz that comes from this region.

27. One thinks of Harlan Ellison's comment on a passage in Robert A. Heinlein (cited in Samuel R. Delany, *The Jewel-hinged Jaw: Essays on Science Fiction* [New York: Berkley Books, 1977], 34): "Heinlein has always managed to indicate the greater strangeness of a culture with the most casually dropped reference: The first time, in a novel . . . that a char-acter came through a door that . . . dilated. And no discussion. Just: 'The door dilated.' I . . . was two lines down before I realized what the image had been. . . . A *dilating* door, it didn't open, it *irised!* Dear God, now I knew I was in a future world."

28. The narrator's use of the present tense fits with the shifting pattern of voice and

tense. How should we see this? As a "lapse" on the part of the author? Or as a new narrative dynamic suggested by the evolutionary context of the narrative? The lapses of Rosny's narrative, on the contrary, call on us to read it "backward" from our experience in reading subsequent SF texts. His lapses encourage us to play a game of speculation; we imagine a narrator that is one with the *process* of carbon life, speaking as a single individual as Targ is increasingly isolated, the sole survivor of what now becomes a shared process.

29. Canis Major (the Greater Dog) is one of eighty-eight modern constellations. It is said to represent one of Orion's hunting dogs. It contains Sirius, the brightest star in the night sky. Sirius means "scorching," as since ancient times it was noticed that summer heat followed its rising; hence the expression "dog days."

30. These are all constellations. Aquila is one of the forty-eight constellations listed by the ancient astronomer Ptolemy. Its alpha star is Altair, the vertex of the Summer Triangle. Pegasus, also one of Ptolemy's constellations, is a northern constellation configured as a square of four bright stars, notably Sirrah. Perseus, named after the Greek hero who slew the Medusa, contains the star Algol. It is the location of the annual Perseids meteor shower. Finally, Sagittarius, a constellation of the zodiac, has the form of a centaur drawing a bow. It is located to the east of Ophiuchus. Targ has certainly a long visual sweep to be able to embrace all these celestial locations at once.

31. We think here of the technical manuals the Time Traveler in George Pal's 1960 version of *The Time Machine* takes with him to the resurrected Eden in the Eloi future. Where original mankind fell for eating the apple of knowledge, now new mankind will resurrect itself by that same knowledge.

32. Alpha Centauri is the closest star beyond our solar system, 4.39 light-years away. It is the brightest star in the southern constellation Centaurus. The stars Targ sees along the way indicate that his machines let him sail from one end to the other of our known Earth.

33. Rosny does not overdramatize the cataclysmic event that forever dashes hope for the human species. More in line with modern chaos theory, it is a small variable, of insignificant size, that causes the collapse of a larger, apparently solid structure. We seem to have here an early example of the so-called butterfly effect. Targ, however, as one who believes in the possibility of a second Eden, cannot abandon his sense of a "cosmic" destiny.

34. Rosny's humanized machines are forerunners of Heinlein's famous waldoes, a name that has passed from fiction to real-world nanomachines that work as extensions of the human hand.

35. Calamites are fossil plants that, according to the *Oxford English Dictionary*, "are abundant in the Coal Measures." "Arrowhead" is the English name for the endogenous plant genus *Sagittaria*. It has floating leaves shaped like arrowheads. This is a prime example of Rosny's use of highly specialized scientific terminology. The narrative context and mood seem to call for use of simpler terms.

36. Targ's "dream" encompasses the evolutionary rise of carbon life and its fall. As befits the voice of human evolutionary science speaking inside his head, some of the terms are specialized: the "deinotherium" is a giant prehistoric ancestor of the elephant, reputed to have been the third largest land mammal known to have existed; "machaero-

dus" is the generic name for sabertooth cats; the "aurochs" and the "urus" are ancestors of today's domestic cattle; the "diplodocus" is a giant grass-eating dinosaur.

37. While Targ's statement here has provided the epigraph to the novella, it is now further qualified, in the perspective of his terminal experience and wisdom: the "death of the Earth," he adds, means the death only of *our reign* on this planet, which witnesses the birth of a new life form, of which he now accepts becoming a part.

Annotated Bibliography

Editions and English Translations

The first editions of the SF-related works of J.-H. Rosny aîné are as follows.

Les Xipéhuz (Paris: A[ndré] Savine, 1888).
Vamireh (Paris: Kolb, 1892).
Les Origines (Paris: Borel, 1895). Nonfiction.
Eyrimah (Paris: Chailley, 1896). With Rosny jeune.
Elem d'Asie (Paris: Collection Guillaume-Lotus Bleu, 1896).
Nomaï, amours lacustres (Paris: Collection Guillaume-Lotus Alba, 1897).
Un autre monde (Paris: E. Plon, Nourrit et Cie, 1898).
Le Pluralisme (Paris: Alcan, 1907). Nonfiction.
La Mort de la Terre (Paris: E. Plon, Nourrit et Cie, 1910).
La Guerre du feu (Paris: Fasquelle, 1911).
La Force mystérieuse (Paris: E. Plon, Nourrit et Cie, 1914).
L'Aube du future (Paris: Crès, 1917).
Dans les étoiles (Paris: Figuière, 1919). Nonfiction.
L'étonnant voyage d'Hareton Ironcastle (Paris: Ferenczi, 1919).
Le jeune vampire (Paris: Flammarion, 1920).
Le Félin géant (Paris: E. Plon, Nourrit et Cie, 1920).
Les Science et le Pluralisme (Paris: Alcan, 1922). Expanded version of *Le Pluralisme*.
L'Assassin surnaturel (Paris: Flammarion, 1924).
Les autres vies et les autres mondes (Paris: Crès, 1924). Nonfiction.
Les Navigateurs de l'infini (Paris: Nouvelle Révue Critique, 1927).
Les Hommes-Sangliers (Paris: Edition des Portiques, 1929).
Helgvor du fleuve bleu (Paris: Flammarion, 1931).
La sauvage adventure (Paris: Albin Michel, 1935).

Few editions of Rosny's SF works have been published in French since World War II. His speculative work barely survived in specialty SF series, including the Plon paperback edition of *L'étonnant voyage d'Hareton Ironcastle* (Paris, 1937), and *Les Navigateurs de l'infini*, vol. 69 (1960) in *Le Rayon fantastique* (Paris: Gallimard and Hachette, 1951–64), a pioneering series of paperback SF. Mostly translations of American and UK SF authors appeared initially; after vol. 60, works by French-language SF authors under their own names began to appear (several pseudonymous works by French authors had appeared earlier in the series). Rosny's work was the second such "open" publication of a French-language writer in the series. The *Rayon fantastique* publication was the first appearance in print of Rosny's sequel *Les astronautes*, which was never published in his lifetime. Other significant postwar editions and publications are *La Mort de la Terre, précedé de Les Xipéhuz* (Paris: Denoël, 1958); *Un autre monde*, in *Fiction* 80 (March 1960; Editions Opta, Paris); *La force mystérieuse, suivie de Les Xipéhuz* (Verviers, Belgium: Nouvelles Editions Marabout, 1972); *Récits de science-fiction* (Verviers, Belgium: Nouvelles Editions Marabout, 1975; contains *Les Xipéhuz, Un autre monde, La Mort de la Terre*, and other stories and novels); *La force mystérieuse, suivie de Les Xipéhuz* (Paris: Oswald, 1982); *Romans préhistoriques* (Paris: Robert Laffont, 1985; contains *La Guerre du feu, Les Xipéhuz*, and other novels); *La Mort de la Terre* (Paris: Flammarion, 1998).

English translations of Rosny's work are few and far between. All of the translations listed here are either abridged, are inaccurate, or otherwise show signs of haste.

The earliest translations were *The Giant Cat; Or The Quest of Aoun and Zouhr* [*Le Félin géant*], translated by The Honorable Lady Whitehead (New York: McBride, 1924), and *Helgvor of the Blue River* [*Helgvor du fleuve bleu*], translated by Georges Surdez, *Argosy* 230, 1–4 (May 28, June 4, 11, 18, 1932).

The success of Jean-Jacques Annaud's film *La Guerre du feu* (1981) led to a number of more recent paperback editions of *The Quest for Fire*, in a translation by Harold Talbott that was originally published in 1967 (New York: Pantheon Books).

Damon Knight's translation of *Les Xipéhuz*, titled *The Shapes*, appeared in the *Magazine of Fantasy and Science Fiction* 34, 3, whole no. 202 (March 1968), 91–112, and was reprinted in Damon Knight, ed., *One Hundred Years of Science Fiction* (New York: Simon and Schuster, 1968). *Ironcastle*, Philip José Farmer's version of *L'étonnant voyage d'Hareton Ironcastle* (New York: DAW Books, 1976), is not a translation but a rewrite.

The 1978 translations by George Edgar Slusser of *The Xipéhuz* and *The Death of the Earth* (New York: Arno Press), done for a limited edition reprint series, take liberties with the text.

Several recent anthologies of world SF have reprinted Damon Knight's translation of *Un autre monde*, including "Another World," in *The Science Fiction Century*, edited by David Hartwell (New York: Tor Books, 1997), 539–57, and "Another World," in *The Road to Science Fiction*, vol. 6, *Around the World*, edited by James Gunn (New York: Scarecrow Press, 1998), 25–99.

The UK online journal *Collapse*, in "Unknown Deleuze," a special issue devoted to the philosophy of Gilles Deleuze (who apparently had a fascination with the work of Rosny), vol. 3, September 18, 2007, claims to print the "first English translation" of *Un autre monde*. This is none other than the Knight translation.

Special mention must be made of the recent Black Coat Press set of translations, six volumes in all, under the general title of *The Scientific Romances of J.-H. Rosny Aîné*. The second volume in this series, *The Navigators of Space and Other Alien Encounters* (2010), contains translations of the works translated here (*Les Xipéhuz, Un autre monde, La Mort de la Terre*), as well as *La Légende sceptique* and *Les Navigateurs de l'Infini*, followed by its "sequel," *Les astronautes* (Rosny is said to have invented this term). The edition announces that the works are "adapted" by Brian Stapleford. This indicates that, in these translations, passages are abridged. What is more, the translations themselves are sometimes inaccurate, due to the prodigious speed with which they were done. There are general introductions and a few historical notes. The purpose of these Black Coat Press publications is to bring French-language science fiction, sadly neglected by major publishing houses, to a wider English-speaking audience.

Biography and Commentary

Of interest for Rosny's biography is Rosny's *Portraits et souvenirs: Notice bibliographique de Robert Borel-Rosny* (Paris: Compagnie Française des Arts Graphiques, 1945). Articles on Rosny appear in standard literary reference works, including Gustave Lanson, *Histoire de la littérature française* (Paris: Librairie Hachette, 1912), and Daniel Mornet, *Histoire de la littérature et de la pensée françaises contemporaines, 1870–1934* (Paris: Bibliothèque Larousse, 1927).

The most interesting contemporary commentary on Rosny is in Jules and Edmond de Goncourt, *Journal: Mémoires de la vie littéraire* (Paris: Robert Laffont, 1989), vols. 2 and 3, and in Anatole France, *La Vie littéraire*, vol. 3 (Paris: Calmann-Lévy, 1892).

After World War II, there was a revival of critical interest, in France, in SF and in Rosny. The first postwar commentaries on Rosny and SF were by Jean-Jacques Bridenne, in *La littérature française d'imagination scientifique* (Lausanne: Dassonville, 1950), 191–98, and "J. H. Rosny aîné, romancier des possibles cosmiques," *Fiction* 32 (February 1956; Editions Opta, Paris), 68–72.

Two significant dissertations have appeared, both dealing with the entire corpus of Rosny's work. Both tend to dismiss Rosny's "scientific" novels and to disparage SF. Amy Louise Downey, "The Life and Works of J. H. Rosny aîné, 1856–1940" (Ph.D. diss., University of Michigan, 1950), makes claims based on access to Rosny's letters and papers that are today in the hands of the Borel family. Some claims are documented; many others are not. The research in Lorrie Victor Fabbricante, "J. H. Rosny aîné and His Novels: Social, Analytical, and Prehistorical" (Ph.D. diss., Columbia University, 1980), is solid as far as it goes; interpretations are based essentially on primary sources. There are no dissertations in French devoted entirely to Rosny to date.

The following commentaries on Rosny have been published since 1975.

J.-P. Vernier, "The SF of J. H. Rosny the Elder," *Science Fiction Studies* 6 (2), July 1975, 156–165, is a valuable bibliography of articles in French journals and magazines of the 1920s–1940s that pertain to both Rosny's SF and his naturalistic novels.

Europe: Revue littéraire mensuelle 64, 681–82 (January–February 1986), special issue, features several articles comparing Rosny and Wells: Roger Bozzetto, "Wells et Rosny devant l'inconnu"; Daniel Compère, "La fin des hommes"; Daniel Congenas, "Préhistoire et récit préhistorique chez Rosny et Wells."

Pascal Ducommun discusses Rosny's alien-like beings in "Alien Aliens," in *Aliens: The Anthropology of Science Fiction*, edited by George Slusser and Eric S. Rabkin (Carbondale: Southern Illinois University Press, 1989), 37–42.

Arthur B. Evans has published several articles that discuss Rosny: "Science Fiction vs. Scientific Fiction in France: From Jules Verne to J.-H. Rosny Aîné," *Science-Fiction Studies* 15 (1), 44 (March 1988), 1–11; "Science Fiction in France: A Brief History," *Science-Fiction Studies* 16 (3), 49 (November 1989), 254–76; "Functions of Science in French Fiction," *Studies in the Literary Imagination* 22, 1 (spring 1989), 79–100; Evans's article "The Origins of Science-Fiction Criticism: From Kepler to Wells," *Science-Fiction Studies* 26 (2), 78 (July 1999), 16–38, discusses Rosny's pluralist vision.

A summary version of Eric Lysoe's 1999 article "*The War for Fire*: An Epic Vision of Evolution," translated by Stephen Trussel (available at the website Prehistoric Fiction: www.trussel.com/f_prehis.htm), served as afterword to a new edition of *La Guerre du feu* (Arles: Babel, 1994).

A review by Edward James of *Human Prehistory in Fiction*, by Charles De Paolo, *Science-Fiction Studies* 31.1 (March 2004), 321–30, has remarks on Rosny's prehistoric fiction.

"Jules Verne and J.-H. Rosny aîné: The Science in the Fiction," a paper by George Slusser, was presented at the annual meeting of the North American Jules Verne Society, Albuquerque, June 7–10, 2007.

The twenty-first century has seen signs of a strong reviving interest in Rosny's SF in the francophone world; these include the following two collections of significant essays.

Three-quarters of the essays in Arnaud Huftier, ed., *La Belgique: Un jeu de cartes? De Rosny à Jacques Brel* (Valenciennes, France: Presses universitaires de Valenciennes, 2003), by Gérard Klein, Arnaud Huftier, Roger Bozzetto, Daniel Compère and others, all in French), are devoted to establishing a "cartographie" of Rosny's work.

Otrante No. 19–20: Rosny aîné et autres formes (Paris: Editions Kimé, 2006), a collection of essays (again by Roger Bozzetto, Arnaud Huftier, and Daniel Compère, as well as Eric Lysoe and Daniel Fondanèche, all in French), was sponsored by the Groupe d'étude des esthétiques de l'étrange et du fantastique de Fontenay.

A conference on Rosny was held in Bayeux, France, November 16–17, 2006; presenters included Arnaud Huftier and Eric Lysoe, as well as a number of scholars from French and Italian universities. Paper sections were (1) "Fonder un monde"; (2) "Les Mondes romanesques"; (3) "Un Monde à part?" and (4) "Autres mondes." The papers, as yet unpublished, are all in French.

The Wesleyan Early Classics of Science Fiction Series

General Editor • Arthur B. Evans

ABOUT THE AUTHORS

J.-H. ROSNY AÎNÉ (pseudonym of Joseph Henri Honoré Boëx) was born in Brussels, Belgium, in 1856. An autodidact, Rosny spent eleven years in England (1873–1884), where he was exposed to evolutionary theory. Relocating to Paris in 1884, he published two novels in 1887—*Les Xipéhuz* and *Nell Horn de l'Armée du Salut*—which launched a successful literary career in two distinct genres: prehistoric and science fiction, and naturalism. Rosny adopted the designation "aîné" (senior) to distinguish himself from his younger brother and (until 1909) collaborator Justin, who signed "Rosny jeune" (junior). Edmond de Goncourt, the high priest of naturalism, befriended Rosny; after the former's death, Rosny served as president of the Académie Goncourt, a prestigious literary honor. Rosny was also highly respected by the French scientific establishment, and in 1925 published the acclaimed *Les sciences et le pluralisme*. He remained active in French literary and scientific circles until his death in 1940, on the eve of the German entry into Paris.

GEORGE SLUSSER is professor of comparative literature and curator of the Eaton Collection at the University of California, Riverside. He is the author, editor, and/or translator of thirty-six books and has published more than a hundred articles on comparative literature and science fiction topics. He is a recipient of the Pilgrim Award of the Science Fiction Research Association, for advancement of the field of SF studies.

DANIÈLE CHATELAIN is professor of French at the University of Redlands. She is the author of *Perceiving and Telling: A Study of Iterative Discourse* (1998); coeditor of *H. G. Wells's Perennial Time Machine* (2001); and coauthor and translator, with George Slusser, of the critical edition of Balzac's *The Centenarian* (2005).